About the au

Gill Sherry was born and raised in the English city of Coventry where she went on to enjoy a successful career in insurance. In 2014 she moved to the Middle East where, inspired by the exotic climate and culture, her long suppressed talent for writing began to emerge. As editor and columnist for a lifestyle magazine in Kuwait she gained a faithful following of readers across the Gulf region. Now living in Scotland, she continues to entertain her Middle Eastern followers as well as those closer to home in Ayrshire. *Serious Foul Play* is her first novel.

Photograph: Gerardo Jaconelli

SERIOUS FOUL PLAY

Gill Sherry

SERIOUS FOUL PLAY

Vanguard Press

VANGUARD PAPERBACK

© Copyright 2020
Gill Sherry

A CIP catalogue record for this title is
available from the British Library.

ISBN 978 1 784658 57 1

Vanguard Press is an imprint of
Pegasus Elliot MacKenzie Publishers Ltd.
www.pegasuspublishers.com

First Published in 2020

Vanguard Press
Sheraton House Castle Park
Cambridge England

Printed & Bound in Great Britain

Dedication

For Mum and Dad.
My welcome distractions.

Prologue

He checked his watch again. Twelve minutes late. He was a stickler for timekeeping and his own early arrival meant he had been waiting for almost half an hour. His palms were moist and his shirt collar, comfortable on his neck all day, was now cutting into his skin like a blunt knife. He stretched over the passenger seat and felt around for the hand gel in the glove compartment. The tiny light lit up the inside of his car like Wembley Stadium and he slammed the door shut, cursing under his breath. He squirted a dot of gel into his palm and rubbed his hands together, the sweet, acidic smell at odds with his seedy surroundings. He checked his watch once more and peered into the darkness, the isolated car park looking more sinister by the minute. He felt vulnerable. Nervous. Guilty.

A tap on the window startled him and he jumped before pressing a button to release the locks. A man climbed in, silent but for his laboured breathing. There was no eye contact, he just stared straight ahead. Quiet, but menacing.

The entire exchange took less than three minutes. Instructions were issued. Payment was made. The deal was done. His heartbeat sounded like an enthusiastic round of applause but he felt far from jubilant. Eager to remove himself from the scene of his deception, he drove across the car park towards the exit, more conscious than ever of his distinctive, personal plate. He held his breath, repulsed by the unmistakable scent of sin lingering in his car, then turned on the headlights and drove home.

Chapter 1

It took Thomas three attempts to get his key in the lock. Not that he was drunk, far from it. It was adrenaline running through his veins rather than alcohol. Once inside, he kicked off his shoes and made his way silently through to the kitchen, a trail of moist footprints evaporating behind him. He plucked an ice-cold beer from the fridge and, after wrestling with the bottle opener, transferred the contents from one neck to another. Unsteady on his legs, he perched uncomfortably on the edge of the Italian marble dining table and drained the bottle, swallowing the belch that threatened to erupt. A smile formed at his lips and he shivered involuntarily, emotions swinging wildly from elation to shame. Still shaking, he rubbed a hand across his soft facial hair. Images of an earlier, similar gesture mocked his tormented mind and he squeezed his eyes shut to dispel the erotic scene.

The day had begun as any other—he was a creature of habit after all—but had ended in a much more remarkable fashion. He'd enjoyed a pint in The Half Moon, an old-fashioned pub within spitting distance of his studio and a regular haven from family conflict. It was raining when he left resulting in the spontaneous decision to flag down a passing taxi, an act duplicated by the stranger who appeared beside him. Thomas conceded and gestured for the other man to continue.

'Where are you going?' the man asked, shoulders hunched against the rain, voice raised above the taxi's diesel engine.

'Chelsea,' he replied, already on the lookout for another yellow light. 'Don't worry, I'll get the next one.'

'Nonsense, I'm heading that way myself. Hop in.'

He hesitated only a second before joining the man in the back of the cab and shaking the rain from his hair. They introduced themselves with a brief handshake. 'Vince,' the man said, before confirming his address to the driver. They exchanged pleasantries and commented on the cabbie's choice of music, then fell silent, each watching London pass by through their respective, rain-spotted windows. Thomas was conscious of the other man's breathing, the sound of his leather jacket as he shifted in his seat, and the smell of cigars, smoky and sweet. As their first destination grew closer, Vince gave instructions to the driver, who finally brought the cab to an abrupt halt outside a traditional, terraced townhouse. He slid a note through the hole in the glass divider and hopped out. The stationary cab chugged like a tractor, filling the street with noise and visibly rattling at least one sash window.

'Would you like to come in? My taste in music is much better than his.' He nodded towards the driver, an arm draped across the top of the open cab door, an inviting smile playing on his face.

Thomas smiled back. 'Why not?'

Once inside he could barely breathe, aware of nothing but the hammering in his chest and the alien smell of someone else's life. Vince shrugged off his leather jacket and hung it over the newel post. Neither of them spoke, although Thomas was desperate to chastise him for the careless disregard of his coat. He kept his own denim jacket on and for a brief second considered running away. Vince, however, clearly had other ideas. He grabbed Thomas by the chin, a gesture both alarming and seductive, then kissed him greedily on the mouth. The invitation to follow him upstairs was unspoken but Thomas, shocked by his own recklessness, accepted nonetheless.

The pain was temporary, the pleasure more than making up for any initial discomfort. Thankfully, the need for awkward small talk was eliminated when Vince promptly fell asleep. Thomas, meanwhile, lay awake wrestling with every emotion from regret to relief. He was no stranger to sex; at twenty-four years of age and the son of celebrity parents he'd had his fair share of willing and able females. But there was always something lacking. Not on their part, but his. Regardless of how attractive they were, how experienced or, in some cases, how old (a very fit forty-five-year-old sprung to mind), it never felt quite right. Tonight, on the other hand, had felt pretty damn good. So good in fact, he was keen for a repeat performance.

He studied the sleeping form beside him and tried to guess his age. It was difficult to tell. It was dark in the bedroom and the triangle of light poking through from the landing did little to brighten the room. He carried too much weight, his hair was receding and slightly grey at the temples and his skin was creased with lines. His clothes, currently scattered across the floor, whilst good quality, didn't exactly scream youth. Late forties maybe? What did it matter anyway? Age was irrelevant. What was important was he'd finally made the leap. Given in to what his body had been telling him for the last five years. Since he'd borrowed one of his mother's albums, ignored the bikini-clad supermodels and masturbated over the naked male torsos. He felt himself stiffen and shifted position to release his erection, now pointing upwards like the arm of an eager school boy.

'Need a hand with that?' Vince had asked, waking from his slumber and eyeing the makeshift tent in the sheet. Thomas hadn't bothered to reply. Instead, he'd guided his lover's mouth downwards until he couldn't have answered even if he'd wanted to.

Back home, he placed his empty beer bottle in the recycling box, picked up his shoes and, still shaking, slowly climbed the stairs. He usually sprinted, two steps at a time, keen to avoid the gallery of photographs mocking his every step. For Thomas, the pictures were a constant reminder of his own failures. His father's disappointment in a son who couldn't play football and his mother's despair at his casual dismissal of fame. He kept his eyes down, refusing to look at their disapproving faces. He could still smell Vince's scent, the scent of a secret, as delicious as it was distressing. The familiar sound of his father's snoring assaulted his ears. He crept into his room, closed the door behind him and turned on the light.

'Where the fuck have you been?'

'Jesus, Abi, you frightened me to death!' he hissed at his sister, his shoes landing noisily on the polished oak floor. 'And what have I told you about swearing?'

'Don't make this about me, Thomas. You're the one sneaking in at one o'clock in the morning.'

As if he wasn't shaky enough, his heart now threatened to beat a hole through his chest.

'Where have you been?' she asked again.

'Out.' He disappeared into his en suite, keen to avoid eye contact.

Not to be put off she followed him and leant against the door frame, arms folded across her *Little Miss Naughty* nightdress. 'Out where?'

'Just out, okay? Now get to bed and keep the noise down, you'll wake Mum and Dad.'

'No chance of that, have you heard him snoring? And Mum took one of her pills, she'll be unconscious till lunchtime.'

'So will I if I don't get some sleep, now scoot.' He ushered her out of the bathroom and marched her to the door where she breathed a sigh of defeat.

'Don't think I don't know what you've been up to, lover boy. And I'll tell Mum and Dad unless you cover for me.'

'Out!'

He watched as she scurried across the landing and blew him a kiss before closing her bedroom door. *Cheeky minx.* He wondered what scrape she'd managed to get herself into now and frowned as he recalled her words. *Don't think I don't know what you've been up to.* She was bluffing he was sure of it. Nobody knew. Nobody but him. And Vince. As long as it stayed that way he was safe.

It was after ten when he woke the next morning and reluctantly washed the sex from his body. He stepped out of the shower and studied himself, naked, in the mirror. *I'm gay.* He repeated the words over and over in his head until he laughed out loud at his own revelation. He leant closer to the mirror. He looked different. His saddle-brown eyes, in his opinion, were still a tad too close together, his nose, still a fraction too long for his narrow face, and his immaculately trimmed beard, grown to hide the acne scars from his youth, still failed to disguise his long, slightly pointed chin. Realising the reason for the subtle shift in his features, he laughed once more. *I'm happy!*

Dressed in jeans and an old George Michael tour T-shirt he went downstairs to find Abi, still in her nightdress, slice of toast in one hand, smartphone in the other.

'Thought I could smell burning,' he joked. 'Where's mine?'

'What did your last slave die of?' she asked, without looking up. 'Make your own, I'm busy.'

He switched on the kettle and scanned the headlines on the numerous tabloids scattered on the counter. Thousands were homeless following floods in the North East and an ageing rock star had overdosed on heroin. He flipped one of the newspapers over, glancing at the pictures of various footballers before turning his attention back to his sister.

'Busy doing what, exactly?'

She took another bite of toast before answering. 'I'm trying to find something to wear tomorrow night.'

'I think you'll find your wardrobe is upstairs, little sister, not in the kitchen.'

'Very funny. I need something new. It has to be the perfect outfit.'

He peered over her shoulder at the bright green, skin-tight dress on the screen.

'Perfect for what? Are you going to a fancy dress party as a frog?' He jumped backwards as she swung her arm behind her, just missing his thigh.

'Don't be a prick, Thomas. You wouldn't understand.'

'Try me.' He perched on a stool and settled next to her at the breakfast bar, stealing the crumbs from her now empty plate.

'I'm going to a party tomorrow night. I need you to cover for me, say I'm going somewhere with you.'

'Oh no, Abi. Not again. You can't just go to a party and not expect them to find out. Someone will take a picture of you, they always do. It'll be all over social media before you even get home.'

'It's not that kind of party. It's a private party. At someone's house.'

Thomas didn't like the sound of it at all. 'Whose house?'

'Just some guy, you don't know him.'

'If you want me to cover for you, you'll have to do better than that.'

She chewed on a fingernail before answering. 'Cory Flemming.'

'Cory Flemming! You can't be serious, Abi. Dad will go nuts!'

'Not if you don't tell him. Come on, Thomas, this is important. He invited me. I'll look stupid if I don't go, like I'm not allowed out or something.'

The kettle switched itself off with a click and Thomas jumped off the stool to make a coffee and buy himself some time. Cory Flemming was the new hot signing for his dad's team, a promising young striker from America who turned heads off the pitch as well as on it. He didn't look like your typical footballer. His messy blond hair, usually held back with a head band, and his boy-next-door smile, were more suited to an episode of *Bay Watch* than they were to a Premiership football club. And regardless of his looks, what was he doing inviting a sixteen-year-old to his house?

'Why aren't you going with Sasha?' he asked, returning to his seat with his mug of instant coffee. 'You two are usually joined at the hip.'

'Because he didn't invite Sasha, he invited me. He asked me last week when I went to meet Dad at the club, said he was having a few friends round for a housewarming. Come on, Thomas, please. Pretty please.' She batted her eyelids at him, a gesture she'd used to her advantage on more than one occasion.

If Thomas was supposed to be out with his sister, he could hide out in Fulham with Vince. His thoughts drifted back to the previous evening and a smile crept to his lips.

'Anyway, you owe me,' she said. 'You were obviously out shagging last night and if you expect me to keep my mouth shut, you'd better return the favour.'

Thomas reluctantly agreed and together they concocted a story for the benefit of their parents, one that included Thomas collecting Abi in a taxi on his way home.

'On one condition though,' Thomas added as he rinsed out his cup. 'You don't wear that Kermit dress.'

Chapter 2

Florentina Kelly squinted at her daughter through a green mist of jealousy, an ever-present haze that clouded her vision at the very sight of her female offspring. Abi was everything Florentina used to be: young, slim and incredibly beautiful. She knew she should be proud, particularly when Abi looked as breathtaking as she did tonight, but she simply didn't have it in her. One glance at her daughter in her little black dress – a dress that hugged her blossoming curves, accentuating her long neck and smooth, tanned legs – was enough to stoke the bitterness and self-pity that burned inside her ageing body. Since her own modelling career had spectacularly crash-landed, she'd watched her daughter grow more exquisite by the day. Something she was finding increasingly difficult to handle. *She* was the beautiful one, the one who'd adorned the cover of *Vogue* and *FHM*, the one millions of men fantasised about, the one they'd called 'Flawless Florrie'. But the mirror doesn't lie and she was far from flawless now, despite the regular dose of Botox she pumped into her body. She still turned heads, but the accompanying comments were rarely complimentary. She'd come to accept the jibes about her sagging tits, scraggy neck and telltale wrinkled elbows, after all, she heard those from Crawford on a regular basis. No, it was the constant mention of Abi that really twisted the knife. *Where's Abi tonight? Is Abi modelling yet? Where's your daughter, Florrie?* Abi was the one grabbing everyone's attention, attention *she* was once the centre of, and she hated her for it.

Thomas strolled into the kitchen, breaking the silence with one long, appreciative whistle at the sight of his sister. Florentina tried to find something gracious to say but the words stuck in her throat.

'Where are you going all dressed up like a dog's dinner anyway?' was all she could muster.

'We're heading into town,' answered Abi, a little too quickly. 'Checking out that new bar in Hobbs Corner.'

She noticed a look pass between the siblings and wondered why they were lying.

'Come on, sis, let's go. I think I heard the taxi outside. Don't wait up, Mum.'

Florentina waited until she heard the taxi pull away then poured herself a large gin and tonic. She stared at the clear liquid, bubbles jostling for space between ice cubes. Gradually, the frigid ice began to melt and the sparkling effervescence emerged victorious.

Thomas was having second thoughts about leaving Abi at the party. She might look and act like a twenty-year-old but she was still only sixteen and it would be his fault if anything happened to her. Okay, she would be seventeen next week, but even so.

'Call me if you need me, okay?' he said as she clambered out of the taxi, her towering heels already tilting precariously. 'And keep a low profile. If Dad finds out you were here, he'll ground us both for months.'

'Stop worrying. Just stick to the plan and we'll both be fine. I'll see you at two.' She slammed the door of the taxi then teetered up the steps before being swallowed up by the giant double doors. The house was lit up like an airport runway and the circular drive looked like a Park Lane car showroom. The cabbie appeared in no hurry to leave, clearly impressed by the grandeur in front of him. He would doubtless expect a generous tip based on the size of the two properties he'd seen so far. Thomas slid open the privacy hatch, confirmed the Fulham address and sat back in his seat. He still felt uncomfortable leaving Abi on her own, particularly in a house full of footballers with egos as big as their salaries. She'd promised not to drink but who knew what she might get up to, especially if goaded by the latest object of her affection. He didn't know much about Cory Flemming but he'd met enough footballers to know they enjoyed breaking the rules, despite the clean-cut image they all liked to portray. Their father was evidence of that. Thomas continued to torment himself until the taxi came to a halt. Stepping out onto the pavement, he slammed the cab door behind him, all thoughts of Abi now well and truly forgotten.

Chapter 3

Crawford Kelly watched his players perform their regular post-training stretches. He usually participated as he put them through their paces on the training field but he'd been a spectator for most of today's activities. He had the new physio to thank for that. She may be slightly older than his usual conquests, but she certainly had stamina. She wasn't shy when it came to experimenting either. His muscles were still objecting to the hours of acrobatic ecstasy they'd been subjected to last night. Not that he was complaining, far from it. In fact, he was looking forward to their next encounter which, with a bit of luck, would involve a celebratory shag if the result went their way on Saturday. Mind you, the boys would have to pull their socks up if they wanted to beat United. The performance on the training field today was far from encouraging; the result of a certain housewarming party at the weekend if his sources were to be believed. Cory Flemming may be the new hero as far as the fans were concerned, but he was already ruffling a few feathers at the club, something that hadn't gone unnoticed by Crawford.

'Same time tomorrow then, lads. And I expect a big improvement from today's piss-poor performance.'

He watched as they made their way back to the dressing room, followed closely by Simone and her team of physios. Players didn't know they were born these days. When he started out there was one old boy with a bucket and sponge. You soon got up off your backside if you saw him trotting towards you. The Scottish weather was enough to freeze your nuts off without the shock of an ice-cold sponge. At least the winters weren't quite as fierce down south. He'd like to see some of this lot playing at Ross County in minus three degrees. These wimps won't even open the fridge without a pair of gloves on. Shorts down to their knees, socks pulled up to their gonads. Bunch of bloody wusses. Mind you, they can wear what they damn well like if they come up with the goods on match day. Even pink boots.

He switched his attention back to Simone and her chums, their progress hampered by bags full of health and fitness paraphernalia. Clubs have a whole team of medical staff nowadays. Doctors, physios, nutritionists, fitness coaches. Not to mention the tangible perks. The facilities at their training ground were better than a five-star hotel. Imagine winding down in a sauna, steam room or hydrotherapy pool. All he used to get was a cold shower. He had to admit it was worth it, though. Players were in a different league these days, literally. They were proper athletes, not just chancers who could run fast and kick a ball. And it was the likes of Simone that kept them on the team sheet and off the injury list. *Lucky bastards.* He pictured her hands working their magic on their young, muscular bodies. He wasn't the only one who found her attractive. He'd heard comments bouncing around the pitch on more than one occasion and had been quick to remind his players that sexual liaisons between staff would not be tolerated. A rule he had broken many times but which he expected others to observe.

Leaving his backroom staff to gather and store the training equipment, he changed into his suit, signed autographs for the handful of fans waiting at the gates then sped off in his Jaguar. It was Abi's seventeenth birthday today and he was taking her out for lunch.

It had taken Abi all morning to get ready, trying and rejecting so many outfits her bedroom looked like the Top Shop fitting rooms during sale week. She had deliberated for so long she hadn't even had time to take a selfie, the sound of her father's car horn finally forcing her away from the mirror, down the stairs and out of the door.

The valet greeted them with well-rehearsed efficiency, casting an admiring eye at Abi and her endless legs as he did so. An immaculately presented maître d' led them to their table, the only window seats in the restaurant, and left leather-bound menus for them to browse.

'How did training go this morning?' Abi asked. She wasn't usually interested in the day-to-day goings on at the club but was fishing for information about Cory and curious to learn if her dad knew about the party.

'Not as well as I'd hoped. Hopefully they're saving their best for Saturday. Now, what are you having?'

She glanced at the menu. 'Caesar salad, I think. Chicken, no anchovies.'

'You're just like your mother,' he laughed. 'She won't eat anchovies either. Where is she today anyway?'

She was used to her parents not communicating. In fact, she often wondered why they stayed together. They hardly saw each other and when they did they were barely civil.

'She was in bed with a migraine when I left.'

She didn't expect her father to offer any sympathy in relation to his wife's health so his nonchalance came as no surprise. The appearance of a waiter erased the need for any further conversation in relation to Florentina, her father confirming his order of pan-fried sea bass instead.

'No anchovies on the salad,' Abi added, handing the menu back to the waiter. 'And no dressing either.'

The waiter scrawled her request on his order pad, removed the excess cutlery from the table, and retreated.

'So, how does it feel to be seventeen?' her father asked. 'I must say, you look even more beautiful than you did when you were sixteen.'

Abi switched her smile to full beam. He always made up for her mother's indifference. 'It feels good. I'd had enough of being sweet sixteen. And I'm looking forward to my driving lesson tomorrow. I can't wait to be able to drive.'

'That reminds me. I have a little something for you.' He produced a slim, gift-wrapped box from his jacket pocket and handed it to her. Still beaming, she began to untie the neat, red bow. Sliding off the paper, she removed the lid and retrieved the key from inside. Her father, clearly expecting her confused frown, gestured for her to look outside. She gasped at the sight of the gleaming, white Mercedes parked just across the road, its lights winking as she pressed the button on the key.

'Oh my God!' she cried, jumping out of her seat. 'I don't believe it. Is that really mine? But I can't even drive yet!' She wrapped her arms around her father's neck and smothered him with kisses. 'Thanks, Dad, it's amazing, I love it!'

'You're more than welcome. Now how about you lock it up then I'll take you for a spin after lunch? We'll come back for my car later.'

Abi pressed the key to lock her new car and tried, unsuccessfully, to stop the grin from spreading even further across her face.

They chatted contentedly over their lunch, Abi's eyes batting from her father to her car and back again, as though watching a game of tennis. Whilst she was excited at the prospect of being driven around London in her brand-new Mercedes, she was just as thrilled when her father began talking about his new signing from LA Galaxy.

'He's certainly talented, but whether he's worth the seventy million we paid for him remains to be seen. The fans have soon taken to him that's for sure.'

'Thanks to the hat-trick he scored on his debut?'

His surprise was clearly evident. 'Since when have you kept track of what my players are up to?'

'Oh, come on, Dad, everyone's talking about him. I may not know much about football but I do know Cory Flemming's the new hero for the Blues. The newspapers are full of him. What's he like anyway?' She tossed her chicken around with her fork, keeping her eyes on her food.

'He's a nice enough kid, although, some of his off-the-pitch antics have already attracted the attention of the chairman, which is unfortunate. The less he knows about the players, the better, as far as I'm concerned.'

Abi bristled at his comments, not wanting to believe that Cory was anything other than perfect.

'He's got himself a pretty spectacular pad in The Boltons I know that much,' her father added.

'Yeah?'

'Aye. Went to his housewarming party on Saturday.'

Abi struggled to swallow the piece of chicken she'd just put in her mouth and stared at her father. Was he testing her? Had someone told him she was there? One thing she did know for sure was that *he* definitely wasn't there. He certainly didn't seem angry with her – he was tucking into his sea bass rather than watching her for a reaction – and he wouldn't have given her such an extravagant gift if he thought for one minute she'd been fraternising with the team playboy.

'You don't usually socialise with the players,' she said eventually.

'I know, but it was good of him to ask me and it meant I could keep an eye on the lads. Monitor their booze intake and so on.'

Abi didn't know why he was lying but she was pretty sure it had nothing to do with her and Cory. She knew he hadn't come home on Saturday night but that wasn't unusual after an away match, even it was only the other side of London. Not wishing to dwell on what was becoming an increasingly uncomfortable subject, she steered the conversation back to her new car and, impatient to try it out, insisted they skip dessert.

Chapter 4

Thomas had every reason to resent his little sister. Not only had she inherited his share of the family good looks as well as her own, she was also the apple of their father's eye. She could do no wrong as far as Crawford Kelly was concerned and that in itself was enough to make Thomas want to hate her. But their mother was way ahead of him in the hatred stakes and given the amount of venom she spat at Abi on a regular basis, Thomas couldn't quite bring himself to join the 'Let's be nasty to Abi' club. Besides, he loved his little sister and would do anything to protect her. That said, it was still difficult watching their father dote on his blue-eyed girl. And it hurt like hell that he'd bought her a brand-new Mercedes for her birthday. All he'd received when he'd turned seventeen was a one-way ticket to Thailand. Admittedly, that's what he had asked for but that was hardly the point. What happened to treating both children equally? It wasn't Abi's fault, but he had to admit to feeling more put out than usual at the sight of her shiny, white sports car. His churlish thoughts weren't even warranted. He'd always balked at the idea of owning a car, preferring instead to take taxis to and from his studio. It was impossible to park in London anyway (unless you were prepared to take out a small mortgage to pay for the privilege) and he liked to be able to enjoy a pint if he wanted one. He'd passed his test six years ago but rarely drove. Cars were unsociable things in his opinion. Abi was welcome to her new toy. Besides, if he had his own car, he would never have met Vince.

He thought back to their chance meeting and his subsequent surrender to the inevitable. As traumatised as he was by the experience, he could no sooner resist another than he could turn down a bag of pork scratchings in The Half Moon. Both were equally delicious, highly addictive and undeniably sinful. At least he could cite spontaneity as an excuse for the first encounter. Their second, pre-arranged union was a little trickier to justify.

Vince had responded instantly to his text message, agreeing to the suggested time and date. Again, there was no preamble. In fact, this time, they didn't even make it upstairs, such was the urgency of their carnal desires. Thomas was more than happy with the lack of conversation. The less he had to disclose about himself, the better. Admittedly, he was curious about Vince, but he was content to be drip-fed information for the time being and to gather clues from other sources. He couldn't help but notice that the Rolex Vince wore on his wrist was a cheap imitation. He'd also noted that the curtains didn't quite meet in the middle of the bay window, the mirror above the fireplace was mottled and smeared and the dark wooden coffee table was stained with rings. There were no photographs, no pictures or paintings on the walls, no ornaments or plants. In fact, it was devoid of any personal items at all. Perhaps it was because he'd always been surrounded by such things that their absence was all the more noticeable. He couldn't help thinking it needed a woman's touch but soon realised just how ridiculous that particular thought was.

'I haven't been here long,' Vince confessed, as though reading his thoughts. 'Still need to get the place straight.'

'Where did you live before?'

'Here and there. Moved around a lot.'

'I know the feeling.' Thomas instantly regretted his admission. 'My job's a mobile one,' he added, keen to disguise his blunder.

'What's that then?'

'I'm an artist. I travel where the work takes me.' Well, it wasn't exactly a lie.

'You any good?'

'I'd like to think so. A gallery in Islington displays my work. I've sold a few paintings that way. It's all about word of mouth with art. Impressing the right mouth is never easy.' He blushed at his choice of words but Vince's earnest expression remained unchanged. Thomas continued, happy to be talking about the subject he loved.

'I used to get up before daybreak to catch the sun rising over the Thames. Concentrated on landmarks for a while, St Paul's, Big Ben, the London Eye, then started getting commissions. Portraits and pets, that sort of stuff.'

'So you're not just a pretty face then, you're also good with your hands?'

This time the innuendo was deliberate and the suggestive compliment caused his confidence to soar. He was no longer a shy, confused boy full of nerves and naivety. Thanks to Vince, he was an assured adult, revelling in his newfound sexuality and loving every minute of it. He may be a disappointment to his parents, but from now on he was determined to ignore their jibes and putdowns. From now on, he would live his life exactly as he wanted. So long as they didn't find out, he'd be fine.

Chapter 5

Abi gazed longingly at her new car as she waited for Cory to arrive. She had agreed he could collect her from home knowing Thomas would be at his studio, her dad was playing golf and her mother had yet another hair appointment.

She heard him before she saw him, the throaty sound of his supercar charging up the lane and eventually, into the crescent drive. Her own Mercedes was soon forgotten as she watched the passenger door rise towards the sky revealing the plush red leather of the interior and, more importantly, Cory's seductive smile.

'Looking good,' he said, his eyes roaming over her long, bare legs. She caught his glance and wondered if he was remembering the party; her legs wrapped around his neck, his tongue exploring.

'Let's go,' she said, already aroused by his hand on her thigh and the prospect of more delicious sex with this American Adonis.

Going to his housewarming party had sealed the deal as far as Abi was concerned. She had recognised a hint of attraction when she'd first met him at the football club, but it had been a different ball game entirely when she'd arrived at his house. He had spent the entire evening either with her, or watching her. By the time they'd got to his bedroom she was dripping with anticipation. He'd slipped his fingers inside her as soon as he'd closed the door and she'd come almost immediately. But it didn't end there. Determined he wouldn't think of her as 'just a kid' she'd pulled out all the stops – tried out tricks she'd seen on the internet, read about in magazines and learned from previous, if less sophisticated, lovers – and enjoyed a delirious couple of hours of sexual exploration. She was well and truly smitten. Abi knew only too well that Premiership footballers were every girl's favourite prey. Sasha would've sold her precious French Bulldog, Eiffel, for the chance to be at the party. But Cory Flemming was hers, and she had no intention of letting him go. Which is precisely why she'd kept details of the party to herself.

If she thought the sex was good the first time, she was unprepared for the ecstasy of their second marathon encounter. Without a house full of people and the need to suppress joyous cries of delight, Abi really let herself go. Her previous fumbles with inexperienced college boys paled into insignificance at the hands of Cory's expertise. The things he could do with his tongue were beyond belief and she felt sure she'd never come down from this lust-induced high. It was hard enough disguising her obvious post-coital glow after the housewarming party, but trying to keep the smile from her face after this particular afternoon would be nigh on impossible. Okay, so he hadn't remembered her birthday but she'd only known him for a week, what did she expect?

She traced her finger along the outline of the tattoo that decorated his chest – an eagle, wings spread, talons poised – and marvelled at his lean, hard body.

'What d'ya think?' he asked. 'Cool, right?'

'Yeah. Did it hurt?'

'Why do chicks always ask that question?' he said, reminding Abi of his playboy reputation. 'Nah, it didn't hurt. Just felt kinda scratchy.'

Her finger continued its journey along the top of its wing, around the tips of its feathers and down towards its legs. 'Why an eagle?' she asked.

'It's America's national symbol. I'm pretty patriotic so it was an obvious choice. The talons are ready to catch its prey. Nothing will get in its way. That's how I feel. If I want something, I'll get it. Nothing's gonna stop me.'

'Does that include me?' she dared to ask, her silky blonde hair falling seductively over her shoulders.

'He grabbed her hand, bringing her tracing to an abrupt halt, and kissed her.

'What do you think?'

She was prevented from answering as his kisses got harder and he rolled on top of her, pushing himself into her and leaving her in no doubt of the answer.

The food he'd ordered from the deli remained mostly untouched. Abi couldn't deny it looked delicious, but she had learned to say no to such calorific delights at an early age. She had grown up watching her mother push away her plate after swallowing the smallest of mouthfuls and believing that any size bigger than an eight was obese. Cory had gorged on the pasta salad and beef sandwiches, but Abi had limited herself to the fruit cocktail and a handful of olives.

They swam in the pool and fooled around in the sauna. She had resisted the temptation of joining other party-goers in the pool at the housewarming, confident she would receive a more exclusive invitation from the host at a later date. The fact that none of them had brought swimsuits hadn't stopped them jumping in. Some swam in their underwear, others stripped off completely. One particular couple had no qualms about getting it on in the Jacuzzi (she was pretty sure it was the reserve goalkeeper) leaving her reluctant, even today, to step into it.

Despite her own lavish upbringing, even Abi was impressed by the opulence of Cory's home. Not that he could take any credit for it, it was rented after all, but even so, she was dazzled by the sheer grandiosity of it all. She hadn't paid much attention to it at the party, there were far too many beautiful bodies milling around to notice anything other than teeth, tits and testosterone. Today, however, she could really take it in. Wander through the rooms, admire the plush furnishings and generally play at being the lady of the house. She pictured her own clothes in the walk-in wardrobe upstairs, her photographs on the walls, her car on the drive.

'What are you thinking?' asked Cory, draining the last of the champagne into her glass.

Abi watched the bubbles dart excitedly to the surface, her own emotions almost following suit. As tempted as she was to share her wedding related thoughts, she kept them to herself.

'I was just thinking how very overdressed we both are.'

Knocking back the champagne, she licked her lips, removed her bikini bottoms and invited him in.

Florentina slid, rather ungainly, down from the driving seat of her Lexus. Despite her protestations, Crawford insisted she drove a robust 4x4 rather than the soft-top sporty model she would have preferred. 'It's safer,' was all he was prepared to say on the matter. Florentina suspected he didn't want her drawing attention to herself. Well she'd certainly managed to draw attention to herself today. Admittedly, she probably shouldn't have had that second glass of wine with lunch, but Lydia had insisted. Besides, it was one of the few pleasures she enjoyed these days. It wasn't as though she was drunk; she just hadn't seen the Mini parked behind her. She had reversed a tad too quickly and smashed into the little car, causing considerable damage to its front end. She had been sorely tempted to drive away but there were far too many witnesses and someone was bound to recognise her. Lydia had already disappeared, preferring to park in the Pay and Display rather than take her chances in the side streets. Florentina was beginning to wish she had done the same, but at least it meant Lydia had not witnessed her calamity. She searched her handbag for a piece of paper, finding only the receipt for their lunch, and scribbled her name and number on the back of it. Placing it under the windscreen wiper of the Mini she was aware of numerous pairs of eyes watching her. There was a time she would have relished such a feeling, but not today. Today she couldn't get out of there quick enough.

Back home she poured herself a large gin and tonic, not only to steady her nerves but also in case the police came knocking. She didn't know which was the worse prospect; Crawford coming home and seeing the damage, or the police wanting to speak to her about the accident. Reason told her the police wouldn't be interested, even if someone did report it. She had left her details, after all. It probably wasn't the best idea leaving them on an itemised till receipt showing two main courses and four large glasses of Chablis, but it was too late now. *They wouldn't ask in the restaurant, would they?* The receipt was bound to show the time as well as the date and it wouldn't take a genius to figure out that the accident had happened a mere ten minutes after she had paid the bill. And consumed the best part of a bottle of wine.

She took another large sip from her glass and wandered through to the lounge, kicking off her heels before stepping on to the thick, ivory carpet. Newspapers lay scattered on the glass coffee table. Florentina had long since given up scanning the tabloids for pictures of herself, but she occasionally flicked through them for other celebrity gossip. She knew better than anyone that you shouldn't believe everything you read – she was once reported to be having an affair with a rather fit, Swedish male model which was completely untrue (much to her regret) – but she was more than happy to indulge in the odd bit of scandal. There was little in the papers to distract her. A previous *X-Factor* winner was rumoured to have had a nose job, a former Conservative politician had been accused of sexual misconduct, and a radio DJ was divorcing his wife of thirteen years. Unlucky for some. The sports pages had never held much interest to Florentina. Despite being one of the original 'WAGs' and being married to a former player, now a successful manager, she had no interest in football whatsoever. She could probably only name two of the players in Crawford's team and had no idea what the off-side rule was. It usually took less than ten seconds of looking at the sports pages before boredom set in and she cast the newspaper aside. Today, however, the picture of a rather handsome footballer caught her attention. The sentence under the picture said: **The Blues' new hot shot, Cory Flemming.** But Florentina didn't care who he played for. Nor did she care that she was old enough to be his mother. She was completely transfixed by the face staring back at her and was enjoying a pleasant sensation between her legs that she hadn't experienced in a long time.

'Cory Flemming,' she purred. 'Oh, the things I could do with you.'

She awoke with a start to the sound of the front door slamming in its frame.

'Florentina! What the fuck happened to my car?'

She scrambled up from her position on the sofa and smoothed down her hair. A glance at the clock told her it was five thirty. How long had she been asleep? She just had time to hide her empty glass behind the sofa before Crawford stormed into the lounge.

'What've you done to the car?'

Typical Crawford. No preamble, just straight to the point with anger fuelled confrontation. She often wondered if all Scots were the same but didn't know enough of them to form judgment. Certainly, his accent was more pronounced when he was angry. As it was now.

'It was an accident. I didn't do it on purpose.'

'You shouldn't have done it at all. What the hell were you doing?'

She knew better than to make excuses. Even if someone had run into the back of her, which for all he knew, was what had happened, he would still blame her. She could do no right as far as Crawford was concerned. She looked at him now, his dark eyes almost black, his square jaw clenched, his forehead creased. It was a far too familiar sight.

'There was a Mini parked behind me. I didn't see it,' she said, by way of explanation. 'I've told you before that car's too big for me.'

'I might've known you'd blame the car. That's what mirrors are for. Where were you anyway?'

'I'd been to get my hair done. Then I met Lydia for lunch.'

'Oh, I get it. You'd been supping wine all afternoon and shouldn't have been driving anyway. For God's sake, will you ever learn?' He was referring to a previous incident when she had hit the gatepost outside the house after a liquid lunch with Lydia.

'I only had two glasses. You've driven after more than that so don't you dare preach to me.'

'This isn't about me. It's you that's put a bloody great dent in *my* Lexus'.

Florentina ignored the jibe, yet another reminder that it was his money that paid for her luxury lifestyle, and pushed past him through to the kitchen. The tiles were cold on her bare feet but she ignored the icy sensation and began a half-hearted attempt at making dinner in the hope it would bring their conversation to an end. She could feel his eyes piercing the back of her head as she tossed some salad into a bowl, drizzling it with fat-free French dressing.

'Don't bother making me any,' he said eventually. 'If you give me any more lettuce, I'll turn into a fucking rabbit.'

Crawford tried not to look at the Lexus when he left the house an hour later. He was feeling particularly good in his new Ralph Lauren chinos and Hugo Boss polo shirt – even though there was a good chance they'd be thrown on the floor in Simone's apartment within the hour – and he didn't want anything to dampen his mood. He wasn't expecting to see her again until after the match on Saturday, but she had made him an offer he couldn't refuse by inviting him round tonight. It certainly beat a night at home with the Ice Queen. He no longer felt guilty for his betrayals of Florentina. She had made it quite clear she was no longer interested in sex (not with him, anyway) and, if he was honest, he had no appetite for her scrawny body. He couldn't remember when they had last shared a bed, apparently his snoring kept her awake, and they hadn't had sex for months. The last time had not been an enjoyable experience for either of them. He may as well have been shagging a blow-up doll for all the effort she put in. She hadn't even bothered to fake it. Yes, she was fabulous in her day, the envy of women worldwide, but she was well past her sell-by date now and he no longer had the desire to dabble.

Conscious, but not entirely aware, of his own maturing body, he sucked in his stomach and lifted his chin, casting an eye in the rear-view mirror as he did so. It was a short drive to Simone's and he could hardly wait to get his hands on her pert little ass. It's a shame her tits weren't a bit bigger, but at least they were in the right place. Parking his Jaguar around the corner from her Hammersmith apartment, he checked his reflection one last time before grabbing the bottle of Rioja from the back seat and heading to an evening of promise.

The first thing that struck him when she opened the door was the noise. The second was her rather cool welcome.

'Evening, boss, come on in. We're about to sit down.'

'We?'

She relieved him of the Rioja and pushed the door closed with her hip, frowning as she did so.

The size of her apartment prevented any further clarification. Two steps forward and they entered the sitting room. A chorus of 'All right, boss?' followed as he took in the sea of faces that smiled up at him from various positions in the room.

What the fuck? Numerous bottles of Evian suggested an alcohol-free zone and the dining table, set for six, reinforced the point with tumblers in place of wine glasses. Crawford followed Simone into the kitchen although, in an open-plan apartment, a private conversation was impossible.

'What the fuck's going on?' he asked as quietly as he could manage. 'What's with the audience?'

Simone was still frowning. 'Did you not read my text?'

Obviously he had or he wouldn't be here, but something was definitely amiss.

'Of course I read your text,' he replied, a little louder than intended. 'But it didn't say anything about a children's tea party.' If looks could kill, he'd be zipped up in a body bag and slammed in a deepfreeze, but he had no intention of apologising. He had a horrible feeling he'd been set up and he didn't like it one little bit.

'Maybe not, but you'll fit right in, won't you?' she hissed.

They were beginning to attract attention from the sitting room. Simone picked up a dish of olives and glided past him, all smiles.

'Take your seats everyone, supper's almost ready.' She placed the olives in the centre of the dining table and encouraged everyone to sit down. Crawford, in the meantime, was hastily scrolling through his text messages to the invitation from Simone.

Are you free tomorrow evening? Come over at 7.

That was all he had read when he had opened the text. The prospect of another sexual liaison with his favourite physio had prevented him from reading the message properly. Had he done so, he wouldn't be feeling like the class-A prick he was now. The rest of the message read:

Dinner with the fitness crew. Lots to discuss. S x

Bollocks. Not only had he pissed off his new lover, he'd also put himself in a situation he would normally avoid at all costs. Social events with his backroom staff were not a good idea. Conversations about the team, *his* team, should be had at the club or at the training ground. 'Keep it professional' was his motto (unless it involved his sex life) which meant off-pitch discussions like this one were asking for trouble. He took his seat at the table and stabbed an olive with a cocktail stick. He would rather stab his own eyeballs than endure the next few hours with this lot, but what choice did he have? Eyeing the bottle of Rioja on the kitchen counter, he swallowed a mouthful of water. Just when he thought things couldn't get any worse, a slice of quiche appeared on his plate.

Chapter 6

Thomas stood back and studied his work in progress. He cocked his head, squinted a little, then let out a sigh of frustration. He'd been working on this piece for days and still couldn't get it right. He wouldn't mind but he wasn't even being paid for it. His mother had asked him to paint a portrait of Sasha's dog, Eiffel. It was her birthday soon and Lydia Templeton-Howe, Sasha's mother, had asked if Thomas would paint him. He could just hear his mother's reply: '*Of course he will, darling. He'll be delighted. Cost? Don't be silly, he wouldn't dream of charging, you're almost family.*'

He abandoned his brushes and leant against the window, the cold glass a shock against his bare arm. The view was usually all the inspiration he needed, but even that couldn't lift his spirits today. The ancient jumble of chimney pots appeared dwarfed by colossal clusters of satellite dishes. The pigeons, so often a soothing sight and sound, seemed disarmingly sinister. The weather wasn't helping either. The whole scene looked like a sepia tone print rather than the usual canvas of textures and shades. Not a splash of colour could be seen. Thomas thought his eyes were playing tricks on him until he spotted a red dot in the distance, a double-decker bus creeping through the city like the pulsing spot on Google Maps.

He pulled his phone from the back pocket of his jeans and checked it, yet again, for messages. Still nothing. He hadn't heard from Vince for over two weeks. His own messages and calls had gone unanswered and he was struggling to concentrate on anything besides the threat of apparent rejection. He'd had so few relationships he was unsure what his next move should be. The last thing he wanted was to appear needy, but he really thought the two of them had connected. He wasn't looking for commitment, just the opportunity to explore his newly discovered sexuality further and to extend his experience beyond two somewhat brief encounters. It's not as though they were teenagers with callow attitudes and uncontrollable hormones, but even the age-old cliché, *It's not you, it's me,* would be preferable to silence.

He turned his back to the window and stared at his unfinished painting. He was sick of the sight of Eiffel the French bloody Bulldog. Grabbing his keys, he barked 'Au revoir' at the black, scrunched-up face and ran down the stairs.

There was no answer at the house. He was both relieved and disappointed. It looked different in the daylight. It carried an air of neglect. Paint peeling from window frames, weeds escaping from paving slabs, cobwebs tucked under sills. The downstairs curtains were still closed. He took a few steps back and looked up to the bedroom window. No sign of life there either, just evidence of a pigeon on a recent diet of blackberries. A length of guttering hung diagonally across the small upstairs window, its muddy contents ready to spew over the path. For the first time, he took in the other houses in the street. Smart, well-maintained properties with small but immaculately manicured gardens and elaborate brass door knockers. Houses with names instead of numbers. Vince's house looked like a rotten tooth in an otherwise perfect smile. A feeling of unease stirred in the pit of his stomach. He hoped to God he was wrong, but he was beginning to think he never should have trusted Vince.

Crawford watched as Simone untangled herself from the sheets and walked, naked, to the bathroom. His dick usually stood to attention the minute he set eyes on her pert backside, but it hadn't yet recovered from having her lips wrapped around it. There was a time he could have performed all night but it took a little longer to re-charge these days. He'd still be up for another go, though. What was it his old fella used to say? *Never turn down a shag and treat every one as if it's your last.* Not bad advice. Although his mam would have had something to say if she'd known about it. His dad had been a player in every sense of the word. Pat Kelly's brief footballing career with Partick Thistle had been cut short thanks to a broken leg. He'd turned to drink and women to make himself feel better, but Crawford doubted either of the two could ever make up for the loss of a bright, footballing future. His mam had thrown his father out on more than one occasion but always took him back, full of the same old apologies and empty promises. That's what it was like in those days. You stood by your man, no matter what. Better to have a cheating bastard paying the bills than no one at all. He wondered if that was Florentina's thought process then laughed at the absurdity. He hadn't been able to figure out his wife's thought process in twenty-five years, so he wasn't about to start now.

'What's so funny?' Simone asked, returning to the bedroom in all her naked glory.

Crawford's dick rose, along with the corners of his mouth. 'Absolutely nothing, sweetheart,' he said pulling the duvet aside, his father's advice ringing loud and clear in his ears.

He could barely walk by the time they'd finished. His legs were shaking and his heart sounded like the last furlong of the Grand National. *That's all I need, a bloody heart attack.* He grabbed his clothes from the floor and tried to make himself look respectable. He'd have a shower when he got home. If he showered here, chances are Simone would follow him in and he really didn't think he could manage it again, despite his old man's advice. At least things were back on track now. Their relationship had cooled slightly after the incident at her flat with the welcoming committee but he had been forced to apologise after going without sex for eight days. Eight days! Any longer he might have knocked on Florentina's door. On second thoughts, a bit of DIY would have done the trick.

'Leaving already?' asked Simone. She was drinking Evian, straight from the bottle and offered it to him as he walked through to the kitchen. He shook his head and grabbed his car keys from the counter.

'Aye. I promised Abi I'd take her out driving. It's her test soon so she wants all the practice she can get.'

'Right. Well, I'll see you at training in the morning then.' She stood on tiptoes to kiss him, her oversized T-shirt riding up over her naked bottom reflected perfectly in the glass oven door. He turned to leave, his mind automatically switching to business at the mention of tomorrow's session.

'Give Delaney priority, will you? He needs work on his ankle. And make sure Flemming's A1. I need him firing on all cylinders this weekend.'

Chapter 7

Florentina was sipping an espresso, wondering how on earth she was going to fill her day. Her Lexus was at the garage being repaired and they had given her a courtesy car that she had absolutely no intention of being seen in. It didn't even have air-con for God's sake. As for the colour, it was enough to make you want to vomit.

She watched a blackbird splash around in the bird bath and adjusted her seat on the patio for a better view. At least the weather had improved. A faint breath of air stroked her forearms, but the sky was stonewashed blue. Just a single, lonely cloud loitered above.

Crawford had left early for the training ground as usual and Abi, as far as she was aware, was still in bed. As if she needed any more beauty sleep. She could hear Thomas clattering around in the kitchen. Maybe she could help him at the studio. Tidy up a bit, offer some constructive criticism. He must have finished his painting of Eiffel by now. Maybe she could go and collect it.

'Okay if I join you?' Thomas appeared at her side balancing a mug of coffee and a bowl of muesli.

'Of course it is, darling. Come and sit down.' She moved the newspapers from the seat beside her and pushed aside her empty cup.

'Anything interesting?' Thomas asked, nodding at the papers.

'Oh, the usual rubbish. Nothing of interest unless you're into politics. Or football.'

They shared a smile.

'Are you heading to the studio today? I was thinking I might join you.'

There was a moment of silence while Thomas chewed and swallowed a mouthful of cereal.

'I probably won't go until later. I need to buy more materials so I'll hop on the tube to Notting Hill.'

The mention of the tube was enough to put her off the idea. She'd never set foot on the tube in her life and didn't intend to start now.

'Oh. Okay. I might just pop over and see Lydia instead, see if she wants any help with the party.'

'Party?'

'Sasha's eighteenth. You can't have forgotten, Thomas. That's what the painting is for. You have finished it, haven't you?'

'Of course. When's the party again?'

'Saturday night. You will come won't you? It would mean so much to the Templeton-Howes.'

'Is Dad going?' he asked.

'We're all going, darling. Won't that be nice?'

Thomas failed to respond to her sarcasm.

'I wish you wouldn't drink that stuff,' she said, turning her nose up at the smell of his instant coffee. 'Why don't you use the machine?'

'There's nothing wrong with instant coffee, Mother. And you know why. I only drink decaff. That stuff you buy gives me a headache.'

'You should try herbal tea. They do all kinds of flavours these days.'

Thomas pulled a face. 'They always smell better than they taste. It's as though the teabags are second hand, like someone's already used them and left you with the weak dregs.'

She couldn't help but smile. He had a way of describing things. Even as a child he was articulate and expressive. He would see beauty that no one else would see. The iridescent feathers of a starling, the papery petals of a poppy, the ageing bark of an elm tree. And all without moving from their own back garden. He once described that tree trunk as 'the same as Nan's hall carpet'. Florentina had laughed for days. She did so now, just thinking about it.

'I'd like to see you drink herbal tea,' Thomas said, assuming she was laughing at his previous comment.

She shivered at the thought. 'No thank you very much,' she said. 'It's like drinking liquid compost.'

'Have you ever even tried it?' he asked.

'What? Liquid compost?'

He laughed. 'Herbal tea.'

40

'I have actually,' she said, thinking back to a holiday in Sri Lanka many years earlier. 'Your father and I stayed in a tea plantation hotel. They were so passionate about their tea I felt obliged to try it. Horrible stuff, tasted like cardboard. Insisted they made me an espresso.'

Thomas laughed again. 'Only you could go to a tea plantation and ask for a coffee.'

'Yes, well. We're all different, I guess.'

'Exactly. So leave me be and let me drink my instant coffee in peace.' He took another sip, eyeing her over the top of his mug and making her laugh with exaggerated grunts of approval.

Feeling uncharacteristically playful, she rolled up a newspaper and held it aloft like a policeman with a truncheon. Thomas leapt from his seat, spilling his coffee in the process and ran, yelping, into the kitchen.

Her cheerful mood was short-lived, her son's vacated seat a sign of the long, lonely day ahead. She reached for her phone and called Lydia, but her friend wasn't answering and Florentina tutted in frustration. She briefly considered changing into her bikini and stretching out on the lawn, but sun rays were the enemy, everyone knew that, and it was getting hotter by the minute. She glanced again at the newspapers on the table, the top one now curled up like a stubborn sheet of wallpaper. Boredom forced her to flatten it and flip it over. Spotting a familiar face, she lifted her Prada sunglasses from her eyes and smiled at the handsome footballer. 'I think it's about time you and I met, young man,' she purred. Abandoning the papers, she dashed upstairs to change.

Crawford could hardly believe his eyes when he saw his wife climb out of a taxi and stride towards the training ground. 'What the hell is she doing here?' he said, to no one in particular. On the field, heads began to turn. 'Keep your eyes on the ball, lads,' Crawford shouted. 'What's up, never seen a supermodel before?'

The sarcasm was designed to hide his own discomfort but with every step of her designer heels, his anxiety increased. The players were clearly doing their best to ignore the unexpected visitor, but curiosity was getting the better of them. Crawford could only imagine what they must be thinking. Florentina had never been seen at the training ground and looked more than a little out of place in her shrink-wrap dress and ankle-breaking heels.

'To what do I owe the pleasure?' he asked, without taking his eyes off the players.

'You're always telling me I should take an interest in your job. So here I am.'

'Pull the other one, Florentina. What do you really want?'

'I've told you. I've come to see what all the fuss is about. See what I'm missing.'

'You're missing the fucking dress code that's for sure. Have you any idea how ridiculous you look?'

'I'm not sure your team agrees with you,' she said, apparently enjoying the attention of more than one distracted footballer.

'What exactly do you want, Florentina? In case you haven't noticed, I'm busy.'

'Well, I'm not stopping you. Carry on. I'll just watch.'

For the first time since she arrived, Crawford turned to look at her. With sunglasses shielding her eyes, it was hard to read her expression. 'You're making a fool of yourself,' he hissed, 'as well as me. Why don't you totter off and get your nails done or something?'

He marched towards his players, inwardly seething. 'Come on, you bunch of slackers, move it!'

He did his best to focus on the session but was flustered by Florentina's presence. She was a constant blur in his peripheral vision, her bright pink dress like a discarded blob of bubble gum too sticky to wash off. At least Simone had had the good sense to make herself scarce. She'd bolted to the changing rooms as soon as Florentina had arrived and hadn't emerged since. He checked his watch, impatient for this agonising situation to end and cursed at the amount of time still remaining. He spotted Grayson Delaney sniggering, whispering behind his hand to Willis. Crawford felt his blood pressure rise and clenched his fists in an attempt to stave off his anger. A high-pitched wolf whistle turned heads towards the car park where a huddle of fans pointed and laughed behind the steel gates. Cameras and phones were poking through the bars, their owners, as ever, searching for that elusive money shot. But they weren't aimed at the training field and the high-profile players showcasing their skills. Today, Crawford noticed, they were aimed very much in the direction of his wife.

Abi was painting her toenails in the kitchen when Thomas returned from the studio. He had Sasha's painting under his arm and lay it flat on the centre island.

'What's that?' his sister asked, without looking up.

'Sasha's birthday present.'

She turned her head to look at him, placing the brush back in its bottle. 'What is it?'

'Eiffel.'

'Seriously? I didn't know you were painting her dog.'

'Mum asked me ages ago. I've been working on it for weeks. I'm sick of the sight of it if I'm honest.'

'How come? Let's have a look.' Abi unfolded herself from the chair and walked, barefoot, across the tiles, wedges of bright pink foam in between each toe.

'Wow! That's brilliant, Thomas. She'll love it! How come I didn't know you were doing that?'

'I guess Mum never told you. She promised Sasha's mum that I'd do it.'

'Mum doesn't tell me anything, as you well know. Seriously, Thomas, it's fab! The detail is amazing. Look at his paws… and his eyes… it's like a photograph. It's so much like him it's spooky.'

'What's spooky?' Their father appeared at the doorway. He looked even more formidable than usual, his bad mood almost tangible. Thomas felt himself shrink in his presence.

'Thomas's painting of Eiffel. It's so lifelike. Come and have a look, Dad. It's for Sasha's birthday.'

'Aye, great,' he said, without moving from the doorway. 'What's that smell?' He looked around the kitchen as though searching for a wet dog.

'Sorry, it's me. I was just painting my toenails.' Abi peered down at her feet to illustrate the point.

'Where's your mother?'

Acutely aware of his father's bad mood and unwilling to engage in conversation, Thomas shrugged his shoulders, despite the fact his father wasn't even looking in his direction.

'Not seen her,' answered Abi, clearly disinterested in their mother's whereabouts.

The sigh of frustration that followed felt like a tornado tearing through the kitchen. Thomas felt the force of it from his position behind the island and almost cowered under its strength. Even Abi looked startled. Thomas held his breath anticipating the next torrent, but let it out again when his father took his search elsewhere, his heavy footsteps a clear indication of his whereabouts.

'Gotta go,' said Abi. 'I promised Sasha I'd help her choose a dress for the party.'

Thomas marvelled at his sister's ability to carry on as though nothing had happened. He was still choking on the noxious clouds left behind by their father. Abi, on the other hand, was like a rainbow, oblivious to the storm and lighting up the sky with her smile. He watched her run, barefoot, out of the kitchen, a trail of pink foam littering the floor.

'Don't mention the painting!' he shouted, but she'd already gone.

Thomas looked down at the scrunched-up face he'd taken so long to perfect and allowed himself a small smile. It was almost as if the dog could smell the acrid scent of nail varnish that tainted the air, its nose objecting slightly to the intrusion. Or maybe it could sense the potent atmosphere in the Kelly kitchen. Either way, Abi was right. It was indeed lifelike.

Crawford was still searching for his wife. 'Florentina!' He had no idea if she was at home or not without her car to confirm her presence. The loan car was parked outside but that hadn't moved since it had been delivered. He could have asked Thomas but his obvious dismissal of his son's work had already soured that particular encounter. He didn't do it on purpose, he just couldn't get excited about a painting, especially one of a dog, and still found it difficult to accept that his only son had no interest in football. Football was in their genes. It was in the Kelly blood, part of their DNA. His father may not have given him much, but he had given him football, and for that he would always be grateful. Still, it could have been worse; it could have been Thomas who was painting his toenails.

'Florentina!' His search of the house continued. Such was its size, it would take all day to search every room. The lounge was empty, as was the dining room, the formal sitting room and the so-called snug. No sign of her in her bedroom either, or in Abi's or Thomas's room. He didn't bother to check the guest rooms. The doors were all closed and they weren't expecting visitors. What the hell was she playing at? He was still livid after the stunt she'd pulled at the training ground earlier and was determined to get to the bottom of it. She'd humiliated him in front of his players, stood there looking like a tart in an Amsterdam peep show. He'd never been so embarrassed in his life. One thing was for sure, she wouldn't do it a second time. He'd make damn sure of that.

Abi was sitting in the window seat in Sasha's bedroom, admiring her freshly painted toenails and stroking Eiffel's warm, smooth back. Sasha, in the meantime, was perfecting her walk in her brand-new Jimmy Choos.

'Will you stand still?' complained Abi. 'You're making my dizzy.'

'You're already dizzy,' grinned Sasha. 'It's a blonde thing.'

Abi grabbed a cushion and threw it at her friend, missing by some distance. 'Cheeky bitch. Anyway, you're only jealous. Everyone knows blondes have more fun.'

'That's what you think,' answered Sasha, finally sitting down and kicking off her shoes. 'I'll be the one having fun tomorrow night when Jock the Doc turns up.'

'No way! He's coming to your party? How did you manage that?'

Jock the Doc, or Justin McKenzie, was Max Templeton-Howe's new understudy at the clinic. Sasha had met him when he had called at the house to collect her father on the way to some fancy black-tie dinner last week. Abi could still recall her friend's breathless words when she had called: 'Not only does he have an accent that had me wetting my knickers at "Hello", he's got the brightest, greenest eyes I've ever seen!'

'Dad invited him,' Sasha said now. 'Said he didn't know many people in London and would I mind if he came along. Would I mind? Are you kidding me?' Sasha stretched out on the bed, a dreamy expression betraying her thoughts. Eiffel jumped down from the window seat and snuggled up next to her.

'Well, at least one of us has something to be excited about,' grumbled Abi. She still hadn't told Sasha about Cory. The two girls usually shared everything, including details of their sex lives, but Abi wasn't yet ready to share this particular, delicious secret. She was hoping to sneak away from the party early tomorrow night, but with her parents on guard, there was absolutely no chance.

'Remind me again why my parents are invited?'

'You know why,' said Sasha, sitting up and disturbing Eiffel in the process. 'Your mum is my mum's best friend. And your dad is practically A-list. They were the first names on the guest list.'

Abi sighed. Her parents rarely went anywhere together these days and when they did, they usually argued. Apparently her mother had turned up at the training ground earlier. Abi had no idea what possessed her to do so. Cory's text message didn't really say much, other than he saw where Abi got her looks from. At least Thomas would be at the party to share the humiliation if they kicked off. Although, for some reason, his presence was quite often the cause of it.

'Wait till you meet Jock the Doc, he's absolutely dreamy,' said Sasha. 'Keep your hands off though, I saw him first.'

'Yeah, yeah, whatever. Which dress did you decide on anyway? Black or red?'

'Blood-red, baby. It'll give the doc something to work on!'

They laughed so loud Eiffel hid under the bed.

Chapter 8

Florentina was thrilled to see herself in the papers, despite the unflattering comments that accompanied some of the pictures. She had felt more than a little foolish following Crawford's rebuff at the training ground but had been too proud to leave. She may have antagonised her husband but she had achieved what she had set out to do. That's if the flirtatious smile from a certain blonde striker had been anything to go by.

'The very least you could've done was stick a pair of jeans on,' said Crawford, cringing at the picture on the front page of the tabloids. 'What the hell were you thinking?'

They were both in the kitchen, waiting for Thomas and Abi to appear from upstairs. Florentina had just polished off her second glass of Chablis.

'Oh, chill out, Crawford. What are you getting so worked up about? Anyway, as you're so very fond of telling me, there's no such thing as bad publicity.'

Abi breezed into the kitchen then in a white, strapless mini dress, a cloud of Prada Infusion following close behind.

Florentina immediately turned to stare out of the window, although she could still see Abi's perfect reflection in the glass. She felt as though a spotlight had suddenly gone out overhead, only to light up stronger and brighter above her daughter, her entire persona extinguished by Abi's dazzling aura.

'Wow. You look absolutely sensational, princess,' she heard Crawford say. 'Guaranteed to outshine the bride.'

'It's not a wedding, Dad,' laughed Abi. 'It's Sasha's eighteenth.'

'Aye, I know that. But even so… Come on, give us a twirl.'

Abi indulged him by twirling around, first one way, and then the other. Florentina couldn't bear to watch.

Thankfully, Thomas emerged, wiping the smile off Crawford's adoring face.

'You look stunning, Abi,' he said, smiling at his sister. 'And you, Mum.'

Second best again, thought Florentina. 'Are we all ready then?' she asked, anxious to remove herself from this tortuous situation. 'I'll drive.'

'You fucking well will not,' said Crawford, snatching his car keys from her hand. 'You smell like a Glasgow bottle bank.'

The four of them filed out in silence.

Lydia had really gone to town with the decorations. Aside from the usual balloons and embarrassing photos of Sasha – from giggling baby to sultry teenager – there were fairy lights, banners (professionally done, obviously) and more flowers than Chelsea Flower Show. The scent of lilies filled the reception hall where a giant vase of the beautiful white blooms took centre stage on the circular table at the foot of the winding staircase, illuminated by the crystal chandelier overhead. The house wasn't quite as grand as the Kelly's, in Abi's opinion, but a plastic surgeon could demand a pretty hefty salary so consequently, coupled with Lydia Templeton-Howe's flair for interior design, it was an impressive pad. Desperate to thaw the icy mood that had settled at well below zero in the car, Abi went off in search of Sasha, and a large glass of something bubbly.

'You look amazing, Sash!' said Abi, greeting her friend with exaggerated air-kisses, sound effects and all. Sasha's glossy, black hair was piled at the back of her head in an elaborate up-do that defied gravity, her dark eye makeup emphasised her slate-grey eyes, already shining with excitement (and, knowing Sasha, a shot or two of tequila) and her long, red dress, slit to the thigh but high necked, drew attention to her smooth, bare shoulders. She oozed glamour and sophistication, qualities Abi would usually resent in anyone but herself. Tonight, however, she was thrilled at her friend's transformation.

'Wait till Jock the Doc clocks you in that,' she said. 'His blood pressure will shoot through the roof!'

'Speaking of which,' said Sasha, taking Abi's hand and leading her through to the sitting room.

'Where are we going?'

'He's here!' whispered Sasha, her inner child belying the mature image she'd taken hours to perfect.

'Who? The doctor?'

'Of course, the doctor! Although, technically speaking he's not actually a doctor. But who cares? He's here and he looks divine!'

They'd barely moved when Sasha's mother appeared in front of them.

'Sasha! There you are, darling. Spare me a moment would you, your father and I have something for you. Hello, Abi, you look wonderful, as always.'

'Thanks, Mrs Templeton-Howe.'

'Oh, do call me Lydia, Abi. I've told you before. It's such a mouthful otherwise.'

Abi smiled and admired the older woman's lilac creation, its long, lace sleeves and modest hemline befitting of a fifty-something mother. She wished her own mother would dress more appropriately. Cover those puckered knees and developing bingo wings.

'Max!' Lydia shouted. 'Turn the music down, would you? I think you should say a few words.'

Max Templeton-Howe swiftly obliged, tapping his glass with a fancy fountain pen, plucked from his jacket like a magician's wand.

'Looks like Jock the Doc will have to wait,' whispered Abi.

The house fell silent and Max cleared his throat. Despite his bald head, currently shining like a polished cue ball thanks to the glare of the ceiling lights, he looked at least five years younger than his actual fifty-one. Abi briefly wondered if he'd indulged in a spot of cosmetic surgery himself.

'Ladies and gentlemen,' he began. 'I'd like to thank you all for coming and joining us for the celebration of our daughter's eighteenth birthday. It only seems like yesterday we were bringing her home from the hospital, wondering what on earth we were going to do with this bundle of noise, mess and smell. Eighteen years later and we're still wondering.'

The chuckles were followed by expressions of mock horror and a predictable 'Dad!' from Sasha.

'Seriously, we couldn't have wished for a better daughter and I'm sure you'll all agree, she looks absolutely stunning tonight.'

Nods of agreement and cries of 'Here, here!' followed.

All eyes were now on Sasha, whose false eyelashes were batting frantically at unwelcome tears. Abi took her hand and squeezed it.

'I'd also like to wish her the very best of luck at university in her chosen subject of sports therapy. Watch out, Crawford, she'll be knocking on your door for a job before you know it!'

More laughter ensued, along with a smile of acknowledgement from Crawford.

'Just one more thing before we really get this party started. Lydia and I have a little something for Sasha…'

Lydia stepped forward, holding a large, flat package wrapped in red metallic paper with a shiny gold bow. She handed the package to her daughter, who frowned in curiosity and began tearing at the paper. Sasha's eyes lit up as the painting was revealed. She sought out Thomas in the throng, immediately recognising his work, and bolted in his direction, throwing her arms around him, almost dropping the gift. He blushed at the unexpected attention.

'What is it, Sasha?' everyone wanted to know, stretching their necks like a mob of meerkats.

She held it aloft for all to see. 'It's Eiffel,' she beamed.

More applause followed along with Kylie's 'Spinning Around'. Meanwhile, Florentina grabbed another glass of wine, Crawford went to chat to Max Templeton-Howe, Thomas fielded questions like 'Will you paint my Tilly?' and, with Sasha now distracted, Abi scanned the faces for the elusive Jock the Doc.

By the time Thomas had extracted himself from the hordes of adoring fans – well, two old-aged pensioners, a student artist and an architect who wanted an abstract for his office – he was absolutely ravenous. He'd consumed two glasses of wine on an empty stomach and was in serious need of sustenance. He made his way to the kitchen where a burly chef, in full whites, was making light work of carving a hog roast. The unfortunate animal was prostrate over the central island, held up by an elaborate hoist, a metal rod disappearing into its mouth. Thomas had no desire to see where the rod emerged, nor to join the line of over-enthusiastic spectators all waiting to feast on the pale, fatty flesh. Not for the first time, he seriously considered becoming vegetarian. Despite the nausea rapidly developing in his throat, he smiled at the thought. That would really tip his father over the edge. He could just hear the protestations: 'Not only does my son not play football (or even *like* it, for that matter), he also draws pictures and doesn't eat meat!' No, his dad had enough ammunition without Thomas handing him the gun. Besides, he had no intention of giving up pork scratchings.

Retreating from the kitchen he made his way back to the lounge where the party was now in full swing. A gaggle of girls, having abandoned their shoes, was dancing in a circle to Olly Murs. Most of the younger lads were watching from a safe distance, preferring to drink the free booze than embarrass themselves on the makeshift dance floor. He noticed Abi chatting to a suave looking guy with a bright green bow-tie, eyes to match, and wondered who he might be.

'There you are, Thomas,' said his mother, appearing at his side. 'I've been looking everywhere for you. Lydia is delighted with the painting. And Sasha, obviously. And Lydia was so grateful you'd thought to gift-wrap it. You're such a darling.'

Thomas nodded before dodging his mother's incoming kiss. He felt self-conscious enough as it was without having a pair of red lips smudged across his cheek.

'Who's that with Abi?' he asked.

Florentina turned towards her daughter. 'I have no idea,' she said, dismissively. 'Shall we get another drink?'

'Actually, I'm thinking of heading home.'

'Oh, don't be such a party pooper, Thomas. Why would you want to go home when all those lovely girls are making eyes at you?'

'Don't start, Mother,' he said. He was easily riled by her matchmaking efforts and was in no mood for her clumsy meddling. Besides, contrary to his mother's suggestion, Abi's mystery companion was apparently the sole object of attention tonight. Almost every female pair of eyes was aimed in his direction.

'Suit yourself,' she said. 'I'm off to find Max. I've heard he does a marvellous job with buttock lifts.'

He watched her saunter towards Sasha's unsuspecting father, a pang of pity adding to the cocktail of emotions already stirring in his heart. He wasn't in the mood for a party. He wanted to leave, but where would he go? He still hadn't heard from Vince and it was too late to go his studio. Working without natural light was like walking in the desert without water. A tray of drinks appeared in front of him and he accepted a glass of red wine, oblivious to the French Bulldog sniffing at his shoes.

Crawford was beginning to tire of adolescent company. The same group of lads had monopolised him all evening and if another smartphone camera was thrust in front of his face, he'd shove it down the owner's throat. In the end, Sasha unknowingly came to his rescue, insisting the lads join her and her pals for a group photograph in the lounge. Crawford immediately headed for the kitchen, where he tucked into a hot pork bap the size of a party balloon. The luminous red digits above the built-in oven told him it was eleven thirty. He briefly wondered what Simone was up to, but he was in a bad enough mood already. Torturing himself with images of her naked body wouldn't help at all.

He caught sight of Thomas nursing a glass of red wine. He actually looked half-decent tonight in his charcoal grey suit and pale pink tie. He wasn't a bad looking lad, just had no social prowess. Maybe if they'd stayed in Glasgow, things would have been different. It was tougher up there; hard. If you told your mates you wanted to be an artist, they'd likely beat the crap out of you. Unless it involved an aerosol and a railway bridge. He thought back to his own schoolmates. Last he heard, Billy MacArthur was locked up for GBH and Jimmy McDuff was dribbling from all orifices in a wheelchair, one too many bare-knuckle boxing matches having sent him doolally. What a waste. Jimmy was set to become the next big thing in the boxing ring when Crawford signed up with Partick. Both were young, fit and ambitious. Four years later Crawford was the top goal scorer in the Scottish Premier League and Jimmy was burying his younger brother in the local cemetery. Angus McDuff had been beaten to death in Glasgow city centre after a night out with his mates. He was nineteen years old. Jimmy never got over it. He hit the bottle, took his boxing underground and ended up brain dead. Tragic.

No, they'd done the right thing moving south. Not that the streets of London, or any city for that matter, were any safer than Glasgow, but the opportunities were greater. For all of them. His own career, as a player and manager, had certainly benefited from the move. Florentina too, had doubled her income in just a few short months, until she'd fucked-up spectacularly. As for Abi, she was set to become the next Kate Moss without even trying. Which just left Thomas. He watched him for a while, effeminacy coming off him in waves. He tried to imagine him with a football, playing keepie-uppies, practising penalties. It was no good. It was like trying to imagine Florentina in a pair of wellington boots.

By midnight, the party was beginning to draw to a natural end. Bodies were slumped across sofas in a state of drunken exhaustion. Hair escaped from grips, clips and bands. Ties draped over chair backs like tongues with nothing to say. Crawford had been standing at the front door for over ten minutes waiting for his family to join him and was getting more agitated by the second. The Templeton-Howes were hugging, kissing and waving as guests began to depart. Sasha was sitting on the bottom stair stroking a bewildered looking Eiffel, the red folds of her dress forming a pool at her feet. Florentina eventually appeared clutching a full glass of wine. He sighed at the inevitable confrontation. Abi followed, still a vision of loveliness in a room full of overindulgence.

'Where's Thomas?' Abi asked.

'Christ knows,' answered Crawford, impatiently fingering the keys in his trouser pocket. 'Tell your mother to get a move on, will you? I'll wait in the car.'

Ever the gentleman, in the public eye at least, Crawford thanked his hosts before letting himself out.

'Dad's waiting outside,' Abi said to her mother. 'Are you ready?'

'Does it look like I'm ready?' she answered, taking another sip of wine.

Abi sighed. 'Have you seen Thomas?'

'Last I saw, he was heading upstairs to use the bathroom.'

Abi left her mother in the hallway, side-stepped Sasha on the bottom step and made her way upstairs. Presumably the downstairs cloakroom had been engaged. 'Thomas!' Familiar with the house, she knew exactly where the bathroom was and softly knocked on the door. 'Thomas! Are you in there? We're ready to go.'

'Just coming!' he shouted from inside, more literally than Abi would ever realise.

'Hurry up. Dad's waiting in the car.'

Reluctant to return downstairs to her mother, she leant against the wall opposite the bathroom door, enjoying the cold sensation on her back. She was hot, a combination of the warm August temperatures, dancing to Jess Glynne and slightly too much champagne. She closed her eyes, enjoying the quiet after the raucous atmosphere of the party. She thought she heard voices in the bathroom but assumed it was someone downstairs or perhaps in one of the bedrooms. She wished Thomas would hurry up, their father would be livid if they kept him waiting much longer.

Thomas was startled when he opened the door and realised Abi was still there. He quickly closed the door behind him, but not before his sister had noticed the green bow-tie, lying abandoned on the bright white floor tiles. Thomas ignored her frown and guided her downstairs.

Florentina was laughing at something Lydia had said when the two of them joined her in the hall. 'Are you ready then, Mum?' Thomas asked, anxious to remove himself from the scene of his misdemeanour.

'In a minute, darling, I haven't finished my wine. Lydia was just telling me that Eiffel's been under the weather. Poor little thing, probably picked up something he shouldn't.'

He's not the only one, thought Thomas.

'He's not used to crowds,' said Sasha, now leaning against the centre table, Eiffel snoring loudly in her arms. 'Are you, baby?'

'I think we should go now, Mum' said Abi. 'Dad'll be wondering where we are.'

Florentina ignored her daughter and took another sip from her glass, an ugly red lipstick stain stamped on the rim. Thomas thought back to the near miss earlier, thankful his cheek had remained stain-free.

Clearly annoyed by her mother's obtuse behaviour, Abi tried to take the glass from her hand. This was, Thomas reflected afterwards, the catalyst for a series of disasters. Florentina snatched her hand away, spilling wine all over the polished oak floor. Thomas, seeing his mother wavering, lurched forward to stop her from losing her balance. In doing so, he knocked against the table, upending the vase of flowers and, unable to prevent it from falling, watched in horror as the lilies left a trail of orange pollen all over Abi's white dress. As the vase crashed to the floor, a startled Eiffel jumped from Sasha's arms cutting his paws on the broken glass. In her haste to rescue her dog, Sasha slipped on the spilled water, slid across the floor and knocked herself out on the table leg.

Chapter 9

For days after the party, the atmosphere in the Kelly household was even more frosty than usual. Thomas, uncomfortable with conflict at the best of times, had spent almost every waking hour at his studio. In fact, he'd seriously considered putting a bed in there; anything to avoid the cold front that had moved into Hollywood Road, bringing with it, atmospheric pressure and violent, unpredictable storms.

His father, despite not having witnessed the carnage, was convinced Florentina was responsible for the whole sorry episode, including deliberately ruining Abi's white dress, and was threatening to do the same to her favourite Versace gown. She, meanwhile, appeared oblivious to his contempt but had developed a new and unhealthy obsession in the form of her Twitter account. Abi, clearly embarrassed and not wishing to be reminded of the disastrous events, was dividing her time between Cory and Sasha and was, like Thomas, spending as little time as possible at home.

At least Abi hadn't mentioned the bathroom incident. He'd been as surprised as anyone when the man with the green eyes had followed him in. They hadn't even spoken before Thomas had his trousers round his ankles and his dick in the stranger's mouth. Not that he was complaining. He'd introduced himself afterwards. Justin. An unfortunate name but hopefully no reflection of his sexual capabilities. If he'd been a betting man, he would have put his house (if he had one) on Abi being more Justin's type. His gaydar technique clearly needed some work. Justin's, on the other hand, was spot-on and Thomas could only hope that his own homosexuality was not as obvious to everyone else, as it was to Justin.

Arriving at his studio, Thomas gathered the mail from his mail box then bounded up the stairs. As usual, the industrious smell instantly lifted his spirits, a heady combination of the painting materials from his own studio and the waxy smell of scented candles from the ground floor. He rarely saw the two Polish girls who seemed to work all hours, day and night, making novelty candles, but they were pleasant enough when he did. Upstairs, he threw open the windows in the hope of circulating some air. Temperatures were unusually high for September and although the bare walls and high ceilings of the converted nineteenth-century warehouse offered some relief from the heat, it was still uncomfortably hot. He stood for a while taking in the view and enjoying the slightest breath of wind, like a whisper, on his face. Rooftop terraces bore evidence of impromptu barbecues. Empty bottles and cans lay discarded on balconies. Beach towels lay abandoned on patios. Some were playing host to morning coffee and croissants, hungry pigeons waiting for a wayward crumb. Mindful of his workload, Thomas reluctantly left his lookout and removed the sheets from his works in progress. The architect he'd met at Sasha's party had actually come good and commissioned four paintings for his offices, all of which he wanted delivered by the end of October. Thomas had managed to convince him that cityscapes would be more fitting for his newly refurbished Mayfair offices, rather than the abstracts he originally favoured, and was now working against the clock to produce the promised paintings. He hadn't heard anything from Justin since the party but, if he was honest, he hadn't really expected to. He had learned from Abi that Justin had recently moved from Glasgow and was working with Max Templeton-Howe at his clinic. Other than that, he knew very little about the audacious surgeon. He hadn't heard from Vince either and had resigned himself to the fact that he'd been well and truly dumped.

He sifted through the mail as he waited for the kettle to boil. A menu from the local Indian takeaway, a free newspaper and a plain brown envelope. The envelope had been hand delivered. There was no address or stamp, just his name, Mr Thomas Kelly. Intrigued, he opened the envelope. Then promptly threw up over his shoes.

There were twelve photographs in total, all black and white. His hands were shaking as he went through them, one by one. Some, showing him arriving at Vince's house, had obviously been taken from across the street, from a car, maybe? Innocuous enough on their own, but different entirely when viewed with the rest. The others all showed himself and

Vince in various states of undress and in a variety of positions on the sofa. He swallowed down a ball of bile and sat with his head in his hands, rocking back and forth. He shuffled the pictures once more, searching for a note, but found nothing. He thought back to the gap in the curtains and realisation began to sink in. Someone had been watching them from outside. He had to speak to Vince. Whatever game he was playing, he had to stop him. He reached for his phone in the back pocket of his jeans and scrolled to Vince's number. His hands were still shaking as he listened for the ring tone. No answer. The smell of vomit engulfed him as a pool of different scenarios spilled in front of him, all of them disastrous. Shame, once again, poured over him but this time it was fear that threatened to drown him.

Abi was back at Sasha's house. They rarely met at the Kelly's, both girls preferring the laid-back atmosphere and warmth at the Templeton-Howe's. It was cosier somehow, probably thanks to Lydia's interior design skills. She had a knack of combining textures and shades that seemed to embrace you as soon as you walked in. The Kelly house was much colder in comparison, both in terms of décor and occupants.

She had finally confided in Sasha about her relationship with Cory. Sasha was heading off to university soon anyway, so Abi figured her friend wouldn't keep pestering her for a double-date with one of his teammates. As it was, Sasha still had her sights firmly set on her father's understudy. Abi had spoken to him at the party and thought him rather dull but Sasha insisted he was worth the chase.

'That accent though… isn't it just dreamy?'

'It's the same as my dad's,' said Abi, pulling a face. 'And isn't he a bit old?'

'He's only twenty-nine. And who cares how old he is when he's got eyes like that? Did you see how they matched his bow-tie?'

Abi frowned at the mention of the bow-tie and tried to recall a morsel of information. She felt sure she had something to say. It was like having a pip on the tip of your tongue and not being able to spit it out.

'They were the colour of a Quality Street triangle,' continued Sasha. 'My mouth's watering just thinking about them!' She lay back on the bed and let out a dreamy sigh.

'Put your tongue back in, Sash, you're so unattractive when you dribble!'

Sasha grabbed a slipper from the floor beside the bed and threw it playfully at her friend.

'Ouch!' said Abi, rubbing her elbow. 'That hurt!'

'Serves you right for not telling me about your hot-shot boyfriend! Talking of which, when are you seeing him again?'

'Not sure. I'm waiting for him to text me. Hopefully I won't have to wait too long. He can do the most amazing things with his tongue! Honestly, Sash, he makes all those college boys look like the Teletubbies!'

The two girls giggled conspiratorially. Eiffel trotted in from the landing.

'Come here, baby,' said Sasha, gathering him in her arms before lying back down on the bed.

'How is he?' asked Abi.

'All better now. Aren't you, baby? What an absolute nightmare! I'm still getting headaches from that damn table leg!'

Abi laughed but she felt awful about what happened and had not spoken to her mother since. 'I'm so sorry, Sash.'

'Will you stop apologising? It was an accident. I'm just glad no one else was there to see it. Thank God most people had gone home. And at least my dress is okay, yours was ruined!'

'I probably wouldn't have worn it again anyway,' she admitted. 'You know how it is, can't possibly be seen in the same dress twice!'

'Yeah, you're right. And you'll have more dresses than you know what to do with when you start modelling. Don't they let you keep all the clothes from fashion shows and stuff?'

'Too right! I can't wait to get started. I can understand why Dad wanted me to finish my exams but I could've made a fortune by now. Millennium Models wanted to sign me when I was fourteen! Can you believe it?'

'You couldn't have actually started at that age though, could you? Wouldn't that be child exploitation?'

'No. There are plenty of child models. You've only got to look in the Next catalogue. Not that I've got a Next catalogue, but you know what I mean.'

'I guess. So why did you have to wait then?'

'I told you. Dad wanted me to finish school. I suspect Mum had something to do with it as well.'

'It's probably for the best though, Abs. You'd be a right diva by now if you'd started that young.'

'How dare you?' she said with her nose in the air. 'Now run along and get me a large Malibu and Coke, not too much ice, and don't forget the lemon.'

'Dream on,' said Sasha, laughing at her friend's poor attempt at role play. 'Your blog's taken off big time though, hasn't it? And how many Instagram followers have you got now? Twenty thousand? Thirty?'

'Something like that.'

Abi knew exactly how many followers she had. She posted pictures and updates on all of her social media accounts on a daily basis and received gifts from sponsors almost as often. Free makeup, perfume, clothes, shoes. Not forgetting the free tickets to premieres and events. She was already living the high-life and, thanks to the allowance she received from her father, had a hefty balance in her bank account. And to top it all, she now had the celebrity boyfriend to go with it. Not that she was allowed to tell anyone. Cory had made it perfectly clear no one was to know, but even so, as far as Abi Kelly was concerned, life was pretty much perfect.

Florentina and Lydia were sharing a bottle of wine in a trendy new wine bar in Chelsea. It was brimming with suits and clearly only open to those of a certain stature, certainly if the price of their chosen tipple was anything to go by.

'So, remind me who told you about this place?' said Lydia.

'Oh, I can't remember off-hand. Crawford must have mentioned it I think.'

Actually, she knew exactly who had told her about it. Indirectly, the recommendation had come from Cory Flemming. He had referred to it on more than one occasion via Twitter and that was enough for Florentina to drag her best friend down here on a Wednesday evening in the vain hope of bumping into him. She was dressed to impress in a white mesh crystal studded top paired with black leather-look leggings and her ever-present stilettos.

'Well, it's certainly dragging them in,' said Lydia. 'Have you seen the queue at the bar? On a Wednesday!'

'Yes, it's obviously the place to be seen. Is that Abi Clancy over there?' It pained Florentina to even look in the direction of the gorgeous, leggy blonde but, along with the rest of the room, she couldn't tear her eyes away.

'It is indeed,' said Lydia. 'She certainly knows how to play the room. There are more eyes on her than in an Apple product catalogue!' Lydia laughed at her own wit and joined the party of admirers transfixed by the model's beauty. 'Grayson Delaney's here too,' she added.

'Who?'

'Grayson Delaney. He plays football for your husband's team. Really, Florentina, how could you not know that?'

Florentina shrugged to confirm her disinterest. There was only one footballer she was interested in and his name wasn't Jason or Grayson, or whatever Lydia had said.

'Actually, I think a few of the team are in here,' Lydia added. 'That's the goalkeeper over there, the one with the ponytail. And that's Aran Hennessy with the Danish guy, what's his name? Oscar Christianson.'

Florentina waited for Lydia to continue her roll call but no further names were forthcoming. Even so, she was still hopeful. It was barely eight o'clock so all was not lost.

'I thought they didn't drink, these footballers. I wonder what Crawford would say if he knew they were all out drinking on a school night.' Lydia looked affronted on Crawford's behalf.

'They're not playing until Monday evening so maybe it's allowed,' answered Florentina, surprised by her own knowledge.

'See. You do know something about football!' teased Lydia.

'Only because I heard Crawford mention it this morning. He was talking to the chairman on the phone.'

'Don't disillusion me, darling, I was almost impressed!'

The two women laughed and Florentina topped up their glasses, draining the bottle.

'I suppose table service is too much to ask for in this establishment,' she said, glancing around in the hope of attracting the attention of a passing waiter.

'I'll see if I can spot someone on my way back from the Ladies,' said Lydia. 'Same again?'

Florentina nodded and watched her friend disappear through the throng of drinkers, her jet-black hair, styled in a short, neat bob, as shiny as her patent stilettoes.

She twirled a finger around her own shoulder-length locks, the coarse texture yet another reminder of the cruel mockery of time. She drained the last of the wine from her glass, only to watch it being refilled by an unfamiliar hand.

'I hope you don't mind. I asked the barman what you were drinking.'

She tried to hide her disappointment as she stared up at the smiling face of Grayson Delaney. Irrational as it was, she thought the hand may have belonged to Cory Flemming and was more than a little deflated to realise it didn't.

'Not at all,' she answered, as pleasantly as she could manage. 'That's very kind of you, thank you.'

'My pleasure. Need to keep the boss's wife sweet. Mind if I join you?'

'Well, I'm here with my friend, but...'

Ignoring her apparent reluctance, he sat at Lydia's vacated seat and smiled a sickly smile.

Florentina had already decided she didn't like him. He was far too presumptuous and arrogant for her liking. Or maybe it was just because his name wasn't Cory. She wished Lydia would hurry back from the Ladies.

'Will you be gracing us with your presence at the training ground again any time soon?' he asked, idly turning the chunky, glass tea-light holder at the centre of the table. 'It's always a treat to see a pair of legs that aren't hairy.'

She smiled at his attempt at humour but decided not to comment. Besides, the fumes from his aftershave were clogging up her throat.

'It might not be a bad idea if you made it a regular thing,' he continued. 'Might stop that husband of yours banging his balls against the physio's back door. If you know what I mean.'

Forentina stared at his smug face, sorely tempted to smash the tea-light holder into it.

'Unless of course you fancy some off-pitch fun of your own. In which case, I'd be more than happy to help out.'

She was just about to tell him to piss off when Lydia arrived at the table with another bottle of wine. 'Oh, you've already got one,' she said, apparently more surprised by the full bottle than the intruder sitting in her seat.

'My treat,' said Grayson, getting to his feet. 'I'll leave you ladies to it. You know where to find me, Mrs Kelly.'

She still couldn't bring herself to speak. Most forty-nine-year-olds would be flattered to be propositioned by a young, fit (not forgetting, rich) footballer but she was indignant. She was also sickened to learn that Crawford was up to his old tricks. She knew he was no saint, she wouldn't trust him with a hole in a fur coat, but messing around with someone at the club was a step too far. She could cope with his one-night stands – he had to get his kicks somewhere and he certainly wasn't getting them from her – but if he'd hooked up with the team physio, that was a different matter entirely.

'Are you going to drink that or just look at it?' asked Lydia. 'Come on, we've got two bottles to get through now.'

Florentina produced a model smile. Hiding behind a mendacious face was one thing she could still do well. Very well, if Lydia's oblivious chatter was anything to go by.

'I wonder who did the interior design for this place?' Lydia said. 'I'm not sure about the Roman blinds, Venetian would've been so much better. And the chandeliers are a little OTT, don't you think?'

Florentina nodded in all the right places but was preoccupied by the thoughts spinning round in her head. If Crawford was shagging his new physio, he'd be less concerned about what *she* was up to. And if *he* was getting down and dirty with a younger, fitter model, then why shouldn't she?

Chapter 10

Crawford's mood had failed to improve since the party. Florentina had been hitting the bottle at an increasingly alarming rate, Simone was demanding more of his time and his energy, and his team was playing like a bunch of Sunday league amateurs. Abi, the one person in his life guaranteed to raise his spirits, had been notably absent of late. Thomas, on the other hand, seemed to have taken root in his bedroom and was behaving like a love-sick schoolgirl. All he needed now was a call from the chairman. That would really finish him off. It was bound to come sooner or later, though. His tally of eight points from a possible eighteen was far from acceptable and if he didn't turn it round soon he'd be out of a job. Again. The last thing he needed was another ride on the management merry-go-round.

He pondered his team selection from the squad list on his desk and seriously considered dropping the lot of them, giving some of the youth team a chance instead. That would soon put a rocket up their backsides. But, tempted as he was, he was neither that brave nor that stupid. Flemming had got off to a great start with a hat-trick at Selhurst Park but had failed to get on the score sheet since. In fact, their last two games had been goalless with barely a shot on target. Delaney had missed a sitter that even his granny would have buried and Christianson had selfishly blasted the ball into Row G instead of passing it to Willis for a tap in. It must be the only job in the world where you fail to hit targets and still get paid a fortune.

He thought back to his own measly salary when he was their age and laughed at the injustice of it. Not that management didn't have its perks, of course it did. He had received an eye-watering pay-off from his last club when they had failed to finish in the top six. It wasn't just about the money, though. It was pride. No one wanted to get sacked from their job and he was no different.

'Can I come in?'

Simone poked her head around the door, knocking as she did so.

Her clingy behaviour was becoming a concern; her regular visits to his office were at best unnecessary and at worst, contrived.

'Aye, come in. What's up?' He kept his irritation in check but the novelty of this particular illicit affair was beginning to wear off.

'We have a problem with Willis. Hamstring. I don't think he'll be fit for Monday.'

'Bollocks!' Crawford banged his fist on the desk. 'That's all I fucking need.'

He leant back in his chair, sighed, and linked his hands behind his head. Simone was still standing by the door. She looked sexy, even in a tracksuit. A quick blow job would be just what he needed to take his mind off the injury list, for a few minutes, at least.

'Shut the door, would you?'

He loosened his tie, undid his fly and pushed his chair away from the desk. She was quick to catch on, her eyes instantly reflecting his own lust-induced thoughts. It would be risky but undeniably worth it. Besides he had a bulge in his trousers the size of the football.

Simone was just about to kneel in front of him when a voice in the corridor rendered them both motionless, as though someone had pointed a remote control and pressed 'pause'. Recognising the chairman's deep, accented tone, Crawford pushed Simone aside, fastened his fly and slid his chair back towards the desk. Simone picked up a sheet of paper and pretended to study its contents.

'Crawford. My office. Now.'

The chairman hadn't bothered to knock. Neither did he wait for a reply. And those four simple words, along with the fact that someone had let the air out of his football, were enough to put Crawford in an even worse mood than he was before.

Thomas hadn't dared return to his studio since receiving the photographs two days ago. Scared of what might be waiting for him, he had locked himself in his bedroom and tormented himself with worry. Eventually, he had realised that if Vince knew where he worked, he probably knew where he lived as well. Which meant, of course, that he also knew who he was. Or rather, who his parents were. He dragged himself to the bathroom to pee, appalled by his reflection in the mirror. Usually fastidious when it came to personal hygiene, his standards had well and truly slipped. His short, neat beard was now grubby and unkempt, his face pale and spotty, his eyes ringed with shadows. *It's just a few photographs,* he told himself for the hundredth time. *It's not the end of the world.* But he knew if his father found out, it would be. This particular thought finally spurred him into action so after a shower and a shave, he called a taxi and made his way to Fulham.

Once again, there was no answer at the house. In fact, it looked exactly as it had the last time he'd called, but with slightly more pigeon shit than before. This time, however, he had told the cabbie to wait so he jumped straight back in and, on impulse, asked for Hyde Park. He'd fully intended to go straight to his studio but felt the sudden need for open space. He needed time to think, ponder the situation he found himself in and try to figure out what to do about it. The stop-start journey kept jolting him back to reality. The V&A Museum loomed large as the taxi inched its way past. He considered jumping out. It had been an age since he'd been inside and an hour or two wandering the halls would certainly distract him from his current torturous predicament. A sudden burst of speed thwarted his plan. Instead, he watched Japanese tourists taking photographs, harried office workers rolling up their shirt sleeves, and smiling couples laden with shopping. At that moment, he had never felt so lonely. The sun may be shining over London, but a cloud had settled over Thomas and he had a horrible feeling it was there to stay.

He'd never been good at making friends. Thanks to his father's footballing career, the family had never stayed in one place long enough for Thomas to bond with anyone. He was always the new boy trying to infiltrate long-established boyhood relationships. Always on the peripheral, never accepted or embraced.

Not for the first time, he wished his nan was still alive. He had fond memories of his childhood holidays in Scotland. Trips to the seaside at Ayr with a bucket and spade, followed by an ice-cream with a chocolate Flake. He could still picture the melting ice-cream running through his fingers, his nan catching the drips with a hankie moistened on her tongue. They would sometimes take the bus to Dunure where he would explore the castle ruins, play in the park and watch the boats sailing in and out of the harbour. Quite often it was just the two of them, his parents having better things to do than enjoy themselves. And then, when Abi was small, his mum and dad stayed in whichever city they were living in at the time, sending him to Scotland on his own, escorted on the train by a paid chaperone or driven up the motorway in a taxi. He didn't mind. He was excited by the journey and felt grown up being allowed to travel without his mum and dad. And his nan was always so pleased to see him. She would bake dozens of scones in advance and buy Irn-Bru as a treat. Her house always smelt delicious, like an old-fashioned sweet shop. He could talk to his nan about anything. She'd once told him that nothing was more important than following your dreams, so long as they were *your* dreams and not someone else's. He hadn't taken much notice at the time, but thinking back, he was sure she was talking about his dad. Crawford made no secret of the fact that he expected his son to follow in his footsteps, the same as he had his own father. Thomas had never met Grandpa Kelly; he'd died before he was born. Thomas had heard all about him though, and his cup winner's medal was still in the house somewhere. But football had never interested Thomas. Probably because he was no good at it. He suspected his nan had sensed his discomfort and was encouraging him to go his own way. He wondered if she was up there somewhere, looking down on him, proud of what he had achieved. More likely, she was shaking her head in disgust at the lifestyle choices he had made.

It was a mistake coming to the park. Surrounded by laughter, it simply made him feel even more miserable and alone. He wasn't naive enough to believe he was the only one with problems – the guy struggling to walk with crutches was clearly not having it easy – but he was unable to see beyond the dilemma that was currently plaguing his mind.

Right on cue, two young men strolled by holding hands. Clearly, they had no issues with their sexuality. They looked as happy and carefree as any other couple in the park. Thomas knew there was less of a stigma attached to gay men (and women) these days, but he just wasn't ready to share his secret with the world. And certainly not with his dad.

A stray Frisbee landed beside him on the grass and a panting Jack Russell dashed over to retrieve it. Thomas watched it return to its owner, then repeat the chase as the Frisbee once again sliced through the air. *Life would be so much simpler as a dog*, he thought.

The taxi pulled up outside his studio and he paid the driver, not waiting for his change. Inside, everything was exactly as he had left it. His unfinished paintings surrounded him like a pack of starving puppies, neglected and reproachful. Dried vomit stained the floor and decorated the sink in which he had hastily rinsed his shoes, the sour smell a further reminder of his wretched predicament. The envelope lay discarded on the table, ripped open in curious haste. How he wished he could turn back time and leave it unopened in his mailbox. Or better still, to decline Vince's offer of sharing a taxi all those weeks ago and wait for another, one that would have taken him straight home. He had replayed the events in his mind so many times it was like watching a penalty appeal on Sky Sports. Not that he made a habit of watching Sky Sports but sometimes, particularly in the Kelly house, it was unavoidable.

He had come to the conclusion it was a set-up from the start. Vince had appeared from nowhere. He must have been waiting for him. Let's face it, he wasn't difficult to find. Any day from Monday to Friday, chances are he'd be in The Half Moon. Only for an hour, admittedly, but it was a safe bet nonetheless. What Thomas wanted to know was why?

A text alert interrupted his thoughts. Vince. His heart betrayed him with a brief acceleration – clearly it hadn't caught up with his brain – but it skidded to an abrupt halt when he read the message.

50 grand or it goes viral. You've got 7 days.

His heart was back up to Formula 1 speed, panic fuelling its progress. Fifty grand! Where was he going to get that sort of money? He had a pretty healthy bank balance, thanks to recent commissions and the allowance from his father, but he didn't have that amount of cash lying around. What the hell was he going to do? He had no car to sell. No house to re-mortgage. His studio was rented. His mother was broke. As for his father, it just didn't bear thinking about.

Chapter 11

Crawford wasn't a fan of Monday night games. Football matches should be played at three o'clock on a Saturday afternoon, none of this Monday or Friday night lark. Or Sundays, come to that. He had never played on a Monday night in his life. Mondays were for reflecting on the weekend's results, analysing mistakes and talking tactics for the next match, not getting backache on the visiting team's bench. Not that you could call them benches any more. Most were designed and manufactured by Audi or BMW or some other major sponsor. Although, he was convinced there was less padding in the visiting bench at this particular ground than there was in the host's.

Tonight's game hadn't got off to a good start. They were one-nil down after twelve minutes, thanks to a howler by the goalkeeper, Krause. That's what you get for trusting a German in your last line of defence. Still, at least they had time to turn things around. The crowd was already getting on his back, chanting obscenities to wind him up. Fickle, the lot of them. Not that he'd been any different as a fan.

'Referee!' he shouted, jumping out of his seat as if he'd sat on a spring. 'Penalty!'

Waving 'play on' the referee clearly saw nothing wrong with the two-footed foul by the home team's number five. Neither, it seemed, did the Video Assistant Referee.

'For fuck's sake!' yelled Crawford.

Having gone to ground faster than Shergar, Flemming was now rolling around on the floor like an over-excited Cockapoo. Simone stood on the line waiting impatiently for the referee's nod. As did the St John's Ambulance crew, clearly thrilled at the prospect of blowing the dust from their stretcher. Eventually, Delaney kicked the ball out of play and Simone ran to Flemming's aid. Crawford watched and waited for news but there was none forthcoming, verbal or otherwise. He looked expectantly at his assistant coach, clearly in conversation with Simone, two fingers placed on his earpiece, a crease of concentration between his eyes. 'Come on, give me a clue,' he muttered, gritting his teeth and pacing his technical area. Eventually Simone rolled two fingers around each other. Substitution. 'Bollocks!'

Crawford ordered Josh Franklin off the bench. The seventeen-year-old was so surprised he looked like he'd just been caught masturbating by his mother. He tugged off his tracksuit and, with no time to warm up, performed a couple of hasty stretches on the sideline. Meanwhile, Flemming limped gingerly off the pitch, along with the disappointed stretcher crew.

'Make a difference kid!' Crawford shouted as Franklin jogged into position.

That was another thing about evening matches, Crawford mused the following morning, you had to wait two days to read about them in the papers. This morning's papers were, quite literally, full of yesterday's news and, in his post-victory jubilance, held absolutely no interest for him whatsoever. He picked up his iPad instead, scrolling through the headlines with a smug grin.

Franklin hits two to rescue the Blues!
New boy Josh shows how it's done!

There was little mention of his inspired substitution – probably because it had been forced on him – but Crawford was happy for Franklin to take the glory. He deserved it. He'd *earned* it. He'd gone out there and played an absolute blinder, scoring two goals and creating the third. Unsurprisingly, he was man of the match. Not bad considering he'd only played thirty-five minutes of the game. Shame he was too young to drink the champagne.

His phone rang beside the bed and he picked it up, still smiling at his iPad. 'Yep?'

'Bus leaves in ten minutes, boss. You ready?' Simone had joined the players for the buffet breakfast in the hotel restaurant while he enjoyed room service upstairs. He could never manage much more than a coffee anyway so there was little point enduring the circus that always followed them round in these places. And the less he was seen with Simone the better. They'd spent the night together (she might be getting clingy but she did have her uses), but she had returned to her own room at first light and was now clearly ready to go.

'Aye, on my way.'

He paused at the mirror before leaving and straightened his blue tie. 'Look smart, think smart,' he said to himself, liking what he saw. A navy suit and tie were his go-to staples for match days – he had more blue suits than Christiano Ronaldo had trophies – and his standards didn't drop for away fixtures. He could no sooner wear a sloppy tracksuit than he could wear a see-through negligee.

Whistling his way to the lobby, he braced himself for the bustle of fans that always gathered around the team bus. Some days it was an absolute chore but others, like today, he was happy to sign autographs, pose for photographs and partake in a bit of harmless banter. The only thing casting a cloud over his otherwise sunny disposition this morning was Cory Flemming. The extent of his injury had yet to be confirmed, although Simone was hopeful it was nothing more than a badly bruised ankle. In the meantime, he would bask in the glory of another three points.

Florentina had a lot to thank Lydia for. She was the first – only – genuine friend she'd had since arriving in Britain. Her family had left Italy when was she was just a child, twelve to be exact, and had moved to Glasgow to open a new restaurant. She hadn't known at the time, but they had fled to escape the Mafia, the financial and emotional stress finally proving too much. She could still remember the hurried packing, whispered instructions and long, dark drive to the airport. They had promised her a new life full of adventure; warm, cosy nights by the fire and lots of friends. She was sad to be leaving Pia, her best-friend-forever with her big, rabbit-like eyes and curly-wurly hair, and was devastated when they wouldn't even let her say goodbye. 'It's for the best,' was all they would say.

There were certainly plenty of nights by the fire, Florentina had never been so cold, but they were far from cosy. Her parents worked day and night in the restaurant downstairs, leaving her to entertain herself with books she couldn't read and a TV she couldn't understand. At school, no one wanted to be friends with the scruffy-looking girl who barely spoke. She withdrew into herself, rejecting offers of help from well-meaning teachers and concerned neighbours, and began experimenting with her hair. She borrowed what little makeup her mother had in her dressing table and daubed it on her eyes, cheeks and lips. She spent hours in front of the mirror, her confidence growing every day. Her English improved too. It was as though, by the age of sixteen, everything suddenly made sense. She gave up writing to Pia, she never replied anyway, and decided she didn't need any friends. She'd do just fine on her own.

It wasn't until she met Lydia she realised how much she'd missed having a girlfriend. She'd met plenty of girls in the modelling world but none were genuine friends. Most would stab you in the back as soon as look at you and, if she was honest, she was no different. Everyone was out for themselves and there was no room for sentiment. You certainly wouldn't share a secret; it would be headline news the next morning without as much as a shred of guilt for the betrayal. Lydia had been the first person to see Florentina as a woman rather than a model. They'd met at the health club soon after Crawford had moved the family to Chelsea. Florentina had spent a little too long in the steam room and Lydia had come to her aid, sitting her down and bringing her water until she was able to stand. Her genuine concern had taken Florentina by surprise and she was equally stunned the following morning when Lydia had called to ask how she was. There appeared to be no ulterior motive, just an honest enquiry about her wellbeing. Florentina accepted the hand of friendship and never looked back. It helped that they had daughters of a similar age and that Crawford got on reasonably well with Lydia's husband, Max. Not that the two men saw much of each other. Max, it seemed, spent just as much time at work as Crawford did. Perhaps that was another reason why the two women got on so well.

Lydia was pretty shrewd when it came to business too. Her interior design company was in its infancy when Florentina had first met her but she'd since added some pretty big names to her client list. She didn't take on too many contracts, but those she did take on, she charged a premium for. Her latest project involved the re-design of a private clinic in Harley Street.

'There's only so much you can get away with in a clinic,' she told Florentina now as they walked, arms linked, along a bustling Oxford Street. 'They don't want fussy florals or psychedelic art, just something clean and simple. It doesn't give me much scope for experimentation or flair but the money's ridiculously good.'

Florentina also admired her ability to put things into perspective. To realise what's important and what's not. They had talked about Crawford's indiscretions many times in the past and Lydia had simply said it as it was. 'He's never going to change, Florentina. Turn a blind eye. They're just dumb girls who mean absolutely nothing to him. At the end of the day he comes home to you and that's all that matters.'

She still hadn't told her about his latest dalliance with the club physio. Florentina wasn't sure how she felt about it herself, assuming it was true, so wasn't yet ready to share the information with her friend. They did talk about Abi though. Lydia was no fool and knew exactly how Florentina felt about her daughter. Lydia's latest idea, though, rendered Florentina almost speechless.

They'd left Oxford Street empty handed, aside from Florentina's impulsive purchase from Victoria's Secrets, and were now enjoying a cool bottle of Chablis in a discreet backstreet bistro.

'You know the modelling industry inside out, Florentina. You may as well keep it in the family. Why watch someone else get rich off the back of your name? It's the perfect solution.'

'You're not serious? Me? Abi's agent? Why on earth would I want to do that?'

'Listen to me. I know you wish it was you, but that ship has sailed, darling. You may as well accept it. Haven't you had enough of people dictating how you should look? How you should stand? How you should dress? All that prodding and poking, pushing and shoving? Isn't it about time you did the pushing? Not only do you get to tell Abi what to do, she'd have to listen to you. And you'd get paid for it.'

Florentina twisted the stem of her wine glass between her fingers. She didn't have to answer Lydia. Her friend knew her well enough to know she'd taken everything in but that she'd need time to think about it. Florentina wasn't one for spontaneity. She preferred to mull things over, wrestle with the pros and cons and, eventually, come to an informed decision. Having said that, she was currently struggling to think of one good reason why she shouldn't do exactly what Lydia had suggested. Other than Abi. Quite what her daughter would make of the idea was anyone's guess.

'You have to be joking!'

'Oh, come on, Abi, it makes perfect sense. The modelling world is full of perverts masquerading as agents and photographers. I should know. I know we don't always get along, but I'd only have your best interests at heart. Which is more than can be said for most of the greedy, double-crossing conmen out there.'

Abi could hardly believe her ears. Her mother, the woman who would leave a room if Abi walked in, wanted to be her agent. She couldn't have been more surprised if she'd told her she'd signed for Arsenal.

'But why? You don't need to work. And what do you know about running a business anyway?'

'Lydia will help me. She'll divide her time between the agency and her interior design business. And I'm bored, Abi. This is exactly what I need. It could be the start of something really big. Please say you'll think about it.'

This was unchartered territory. Her mother was practically pleading with her. Abi chewed on a fingernail, not trusting herself to answer. Could she really work with her mother on a daily basis? She struggled with authority at the best of times, but taking orders from her mother? Maybe she should stick to the plan and sign with Millennium Models.

'What makes you think clients will trust you? Your reputation was shot to pieces, remember?'

Abi didn't mean to say it quite so vindictively, but still, she felt a flutter of triumph at her mother's obvious discomfort.

'That was a long time ago, as you well know. I was in a bad place. And the press exaggerated things. I didn't hit her.'

'You punched her in the face! I've seen the pictures!'

'It looked worse than it was. I barely touched her.'

Abi had heard the full story regarding her mother's downfall. Her father had entertained her with it on more than one occasion, the two of them laughing like hyenas at the well-told tale. Apparently, thirty-year-old Florrie had been booked to do a shoot with Per Jorgensen, a Danish male model, and was a little too brazen with her poses. Having already been rejected by a number of clients for being too old, Florrie was feeling more than a little insecure and wanted to show off her body to its best advantage. But 'sexy' wasn't in the client's remit and Per wasn't too impressed either, which just made her all the more determined to seduce the camera.

Abi wasn't sure exactly what was said, but it was something like, "You look like an old tart looking for a trick. Get off my set and back to your brothel!" That's when her mother had launched herself at the client like a screaming banshee. Not the best idea, especially with a photographer in the room. Needless to say, Florrie's bookings had dried up quicker than a nun's fanny (to use Crawford's expression) and that was the last shoot she ever did. Such was the client's influence, Flawless Florrie never worked again.

'I need to speak to Dad,' Abi said, unable to stop herself from smirking at the images their conversation had evoked.

Florentina sighed. 'Speak to Thomas first,' she said. 'You've always valued his opinion.'

'Okay. But I'm not promising anything.'

Thomas was at the bar when Abi arrived at The Half Moon.

'Perfect timing,' he said, kissing her on the cheek. 'What are you having?'

'A Malibu and Coke, please,' she said. 'May as well make the most of it before I pass my test.'

The barman nodded to acknowledge her request then busied himself with the ice and lemon.

'How did you get here, taxi?'

'No. Mum dropped me off.'

Thomas raised his eyebrows in surprise.

'The garage returned her car this morning. I think she was just looking for an excuse to drive it.'

He nodded, as though agreeing with her assumption.

'Grab a table,' he said. 'I'll bring them over.'

The pub was quiet so she hesitated, spoilt for choice, before sitting at a round table in the corner. Thomas put the drinks down, spilling his pint as he did so.

'Mucky pup,' she said, finding a tissue in her handbag and mopping up the spillage.

'So, what did you want to talk to me about?' he asked.

Abi was still reeling from their mother's proposal and was unsure whether it was a good idea or not. She relayed the details to Thomas and waited for his response. They were all the same, Abi, Thomas and their mother. All needed time to digest information, dissect details and surmise the verdict. Unlike their father who just ploughed in, no room for reason or consequence. She watched her brother intently. He began picking at his beer mat, stripping off the layers and littering the table with tiny balls of paper. Abi knew better than to push him. He was deep in thought and wouldn't appreciate the interruption. Besides, she had told him everything already, her own concerns, their mother's determination and Lydia Templeton-Howe's involvement.

'I think it's a great idea,' he said, at last. 'I can understand your reluctance, Abi, but it can only be a good thing as far as your relationship's concerned. And she's right. She knows the industry better than anyone. She may've been out of it for a while, but she still knows who's kosher and who's not. And with Sasha's mum on board I think it could really work. In fact, I can see them going on to have a really successful agency.'

'But she hates me,' said Abi, playing with the plastic stirrer in her Malibu and Coke.

'She doesn't hate you, Abi. She's jealous of you. There's a difference. Put yourself in her shoes. How would you feel if the one thing you always relied on let you down?'

'You mean Dad?'

'Dad? No, not Dad. I mean her looks. She relied on her beauty for so long, it must be difficult knowing you're getting old and there's not a damn thing you can do about it.' He took a sip from his beer, licking the froth from his top lip. 'Why did you say Dad?'

'Oh, it's nothing really. He lied to me about something. You know that night I went to Cory's party? Dad said he was there too but, obviously, he wasn't.'

Thomas frowned. 'Why would he do that?'

'Fuck knows. Sorry,' she said, before he could reprimand her for swearing. 'Do you think he's having an affair?' she asked.

'Probably,' answered Thomas.

Abi looked at him sharply. 'Don't say that!'

'Well, you asked. It's the most logical explanation. And we know it wouldn't be the first time.'

'I know, but…'

'Don't worry about it, sis. Since when could we influence anything Dad did? Or Mum for that matter?'

'I guess…'

Thomas finished his beer and stood to get another. 'Same again?'

Abi nodded. She took advantage of his absence to check her social media accounts. She hadn't posted a picture yet today. She looked around her and wrinkled her nose. The backdrop wasn't ideal for a selfie, too dingy. Abi liked glass, chrome and sparkling chandeliers, not dark wood panels and tarnished brass light fittings.

Thomas returned with the drinks and she pocketed her phone. He stretched to reach another beer mat from a neighbouring table before retrieving a packet of pork scratchings from his back pocket.

'Thanks, Thomas,' she said. 'For your advice, I mean. I think I might give it a try.'

'With Mum? That's great! She'll be thrilled.'

Although he sounded happy, Abi couldn't help but notice a hint of sadness in his eyes.

'How are things with you anyway?' she asked. 'We haven't spoken properly for ages. Have you finished those paintings for the architect yet?'

'Not yet,' he said, sucking on a pork scratching.

'I thought they were urgent.'

'They are. I just can't seem to concentrate on anything at the moment.'

'That's not like you. Is anything the matter?'

'No, not really. I think I just need a holiday. I've been thinking of going to Scotland actually.'

'Scotland? Back to Ayr you mean?'

'Yeah. I've been feeling a bit nostalgic of late. Thought I might go back and revisit the old haunts.'

'Rather you than me. Isn't it always raining up there?'

Thomas laughed. 'Not always. Scotland's beautiful. The west coast in particular. I've been to some fabulous places around the world but I've never seen a sunset as spectacular as those in Ayrshire.'

'Really? I don't remember it at all. Maybe I should come too.'

'One day,' he said. 'But you need to concentrate on your career first, young lady.'

'Yes, sir!' She raised her hand to her head in a mock salute and then shook her head at the offer of a pork scratching.

'What's she going to call this modelling agency of hers anyway?' he asked.

'That's up for debate. I vetoed her first suggestion.'

'Which was?'

Abi cringed. 'The Body Bureau.'

Thomas almost spat out his beer, then choked at the effort of keeping it in.

'The Body Bureau? It sounds like a mortuary!'

'Tell me about it. I suggested The Kelly Corporation.'

'Not bad,' he said.

'She wasn't impressed. Said she didn't want Dad's name on it.'

'It's her name as well! I take it he doesn't know yet?'

'Not yet. I wanted to talk to you about it first.'

'Well, I don't envy you that conversation.'

Thomas sat for a while after Abi had left. The pub was starting to fill up and the noise was strangely therapeutic. He was glad Abi had agreed to the agency. From his position at the bar, he had seen the appreciative glances being cast in his sister's direction. Abi, as usual, was more interested in her smartphone than the goings on around her and was oblivious to the attention. Most were genuine looks of admiration but some, Thomas had noticed, were downright lecherous. Their mother was certainly right about one thing; the world was full of dodgy conmen just waiting to rip you off. But he knew that already. In fact, he knew that better than most.

At least things would be more bearable at home if their mother had something to occupy her time. Of course, there was nothing to say the two women would get on any better, but time would tell. Besides, if things went to plan, Abi would rarely be around anyway. She'd be jetting off to exotic photoshoots, pouting on red carpets and posing on catwalks. Thomas felt a pang of sorrow. He'd miss her, he realised.

His heart had dropped when she'd asked about his latest commissions. He hadn't touched the paintings for days, not since the photos had turned up, and desperately needed to get them finished. He'd briefly considered telling her about the mess he'd got himself into. He'd even contemplated asking her for the money. But how could he? She was on the verge of the most exciting time in her life. Her balloon of adventure was about to take off and he had no intention of bursting it.

Chapter 12

The two women tottered through the kitchen and out onto the patio, their stiletto heels tapping a tune on the tiled floor. The morning sun, weak as it was, justified their designer shades, but whilst Lydia had opted for a casual, long-sleeved trouser suit, Florentina's arms and legs were, as usual, bare.

'I see Crawford managed to keep his job for another week then?' Lydia was never one to beat about the bush, often using humour to lighten a serious subject.

'You wouldn't think so to look at him,' said Florentina. 'He has a face like Razor Ruddock's dietician.'

Lydia snorted with laughter. 'I'm surprised you even know who Razor Ruddock is,' she said, once she'd regained her composure. 'Are you taking more interest in our national sport or am I imagining things?'

'You're imagining things. I met him once, that's all. At a charity dinner at The Grosvenor.'

'And was he with his dietician?'

'Of course not, you fool! He was with this wife.'

'You really are a blast, Florentina. When you're not sulking, that is. Talking of which, how is Abi?'

Florentina sighed in resignation. There was no point denying her jealously of Abi, not to Lydia anyway. But equally, she couldn't deny she was excited about the agency.

'As beautiful as ever,' she answered begrudgingly. 'And happy for me to represent her.'

'Really?' Lydia's delight was evident. 'That's fabulous, darling! Simply the best news.'

'I think it was your involvement that swung it, actually,' she admitted. 'The prospect of having a mediator on hand finally sealed the deal.'

Florentina rose from her seat on the patio and plucked a bottle of champagne from the fridge. She placed it on the table between them, along with two chilled flutes, and deftly popped the cork. With as little spillage as possible she filled both glasses and immediately proposed a toast.

'To KTH. The newest – soon to be biggest – agency in the business.'

'KTH? Kelly Templeton-Howe? I like it,' said Lydia. 'But shouldn't Abi be here for this?'

'Let's not spoil the party,' said Florentina, clinking her glass against her friend's. 'Cheers. Anyway, she can't be drinking alcohol now. It plays havoc with your weight. And your skin. By the way, were you serious about using Max's old consultation suite?'

'Of course. I told you before, he hasn't used it since they moved to new premises last year so it's just sitting idle. Why fork out for expensive office space when there's a ready-made solution at the bottom of our garden? And I can transform it in the blink of an eye. It may look sterile and stark now but you won't recognise it when I've finished. And there's plenty of room, it's quite the Tardis inside.'

Florentina was more than happy with the idea. As far as she was concerned, the further away from Crawford, the better, and, with its own separate entrance, there was no need to disturb anyone in the house if she wanted to interview a client early morning. Or entertain a guest late at night. Florentina had learned from Cory's Twitter account that he'd be out of action – in footballing terms only, she hoped – for at least four weeks. That explained Crawford's formidable mood. It was also the reason for her own secret smile. Yes, she was cheered by the prospect of the agency and potential for earning her own money, but she was also delighted with her idea of asking Cory to be their first client. Well, second if you included Abi, but she didn't really count since she was part of the set-up negotiations and would be used as bait to lure new talent onto their books. With a month off from training and travelling to away games, Florentina felt sure she could persuade Cory to partake in a little extra-curricular activity. And if signing him for a photoshoot or two would result in a private tête-à-tête, she was more than happy with that.

Chapter 13

His initial reaction to his wife's agency had been one of predictable incredulity, but the more Crawford thought about it, the more he thought it was actually a good idea. Not that he'd tell her that. She couldn't even be bothered to tell him about it herself, so why should he go out of his way to congratulate her. Although, from what Abi had told him it wasn't even Florentina's idea and if anyone deserved congratulations, it was Lydia.

'You can't seriously want to work for your mother?' he'd said, when Abi finally broke the news.

'I won't be working *for* her, I'll be working *with* her. In fact, technically speaking, as my agent, *she'll* actually be working for *me*.'

'Either way, it's a risky move. You never do anything with your mother. What makes you think working with her is a good idea?'

They were sitting at the dining table, the weak September sun shining in through the window, highlighting Abi's golden hair.

'I didn't at first. But at least I already know her flaws. If I sign with another agency, I won't know who I can trust and who I can't. Besides, Mrs Templeton-Howe will be around to stop us scratching each other's eyes out.' She was smiling as she said it, but Crawford knew his daughter was only half joking.

In the end, both he and Abi had agreed that having something to occupy Florentina's time – and her mind – would hopefully make her easier to live with. And with Lydia Templeton-Howe casting an expert eye over the business side of things, there was no reason why it couldn't make them all a lot of money. Max was forever blowing Lydia's trumpet when it came to her business acumen and he knew for a fact she wouldn't accept any nonsense from Florentina. Or Abi for that matter. As much as he loved his daughter, she could be a right little prima donna at times. Maybe he only had himself to blame for that particular trait – she'd certainly never wanted for anything in her short, privileged life – but what father wouldn't want the best for his daughter? Thanks to an intensive driving course and a lenient examiner, she was certainly enjoying her new Mercedes, though he hoped to God she was careful with it; the insurance premium alone was more than the cost of his first car. He may be wealthy beyond his wildest dreams, but he would never forget where he came from and he would certainly never squander money like some of his players seemed to.

The sound of a key in the front door disturbed his thoughts. He was enjoying the rare treat of being home alone and was far from ecstatic at the intrusion, particularly when he realised it was Thomas. He turned his attention to the golf on the television, seemingly engrossed at Rory McIlroy's putt for a birdie at the seventeenth. He needn't have worried, though. Thomas shot straight upstairs without as much as a glance, slamming his bedroom door behind him. Something was definitely eating his son. They may not communicate much, but Thomas was a creature of habit and, despite their tetchy relationship, he could tell when something wasn't right. Abi had hinted at some kind of problem as well, but if Thomas had said nothing to his sister, he certainly wouldn't say anything to him. He'd like to think he didn't care, but of course, he did. He did love Thomas; he just didn't *like* him very much. They were a footballing family. He had stepped into his father's boots and had expected Thomas to do the same. To say he was disappointed was an understatement. Admittedly, it didn't seem to bother David Beckham that none of his sons appeared to carry the footballing gene – Harper was apparently the only Beckham child likely to take up the sport – but that didn't mean he had to follow suit. When it came to women in football, he was definitely in the Richard Keys and Andy Gray camp. Not that he would admit it, obviously (he didn't want to be banished to Qatar), but women playing football was like men playing at synchronised swimming. Ridiculous. They were even taking over the *Match of the Day* studio. Who gives a shit what some dumb chic thinks about Sergio Agüero's new haircut? The Blues had a women's team, as did most Premiership clubs, but there was no room for makeup and ponytails in football in his opinion. Not since David Seaman retired, anyway. His old man wouldn't just turn in his grave, he'd do somersaults! He thought back to a match at Goodison Park, pre-VAR, when a female assistant referee had waved her flag for off-side, wiping out a perfectly good goal that would have earned them three points. He felt his blood pressure rise at the very thought. And since when did they become 'assistant referees'? They'd always be linesmen in Crawford's eyes, regardless of their gender.

His mobile phone beeped to indicate a message and Max's name filled his screen.

You need to talk to Thomas.

What the hell? Never a fan of text messages (unless they were confirming an illicit rendezvous), he scrolled to his friend's number and waited for him to pick up.

'Crawford.'

'Max. What's with the message?

'You need to talk to Thomas, Crawford. And soon.'

'What are you talking about? If there's something going on, just tell me.' He heard Max sigh on the other end of the phone.

'I can't, Crawford, I promised. But trust me, he needs your help. And your support.'

'Is this some kind of joke? I thought you were a plastic surgeon not a counsellor.' Crawford was pacing around the sitting room, the clandestine phone call as welcome as a swarm of bees.

'I didn't ask to be involved, mate. He came to me for advice. I promised I wouldn't say anything, but I'm worried he might do something stupid.'

'What?! Is this for real? If he needed advice, why didn't he come to me?' Crawford already knew the answer to that question but the conversation was making him nervous. He stood at the window, his attention momentarily caught by a Labrador peeing against the gatepost.

'At least give me a clue.'

'I can't, Crawford. Just talk to him.'

Crawford threw the phone on the sofa and rubbed his hands over his face. As if he didn't have enough to worry about. He could hear Thomas moving around upstairs. Drawers opening and closing, taps running, floorboards shifting. *Well, he's not dead yet.* He immediately cursed himself for his atrocious thoughts and pondered whether to go up and knock on his bedroom door. He wouldn't be welcome, he was sure. And where would he start, anyway? *'Hi son, Max tells me you might be thinking of topping yourself. Anything I can do to help?'* No, such was their relationship, his interference would only make things worse. Besides, he had a horrible feeling he was responsible for the drama unfolding above him. The best thing he could do was make himself scarce.

After drawing a blank with Max Templeton-Howe, Thomas had returned home to pack. There was no way he was going to sit around waiting for Vince to throw his grenade. And he'd rather walk out of the house than give his father the pleasure of throwing him out. Thomas hadn't banked on his father being at home, but he probably wouldn't hang around. Crawford Kelly behaved like a fly trapped in a conservatory if he stayed in one place for too long.

Thomas recalled his conversation with Max and, not the first time, wished his own father was more like Sasha's.

'It's not exactly unusual, is it?' he'd said, when Thomas had opened up about his sexuality. 'Why are you so adamant your father will disapprove?'

'Because he's judgmental, chauvinistic and openly homophobic, that's why.' He'd almost spat out the words, ashamed of his father's outdated attitude and palpable disapproval.

'I think you're doing him a disservice, Thomas, I really do. You're his son. He'll still love you regardless of your sexual orientation.'

'Then you don't know him as well as you think you do. He'll disown me, cut me off financially and probably throw me into the Thames.'

Max had laughed. 'That's absurd. You can't live a lie your entire life, Thomas. And you'll need to stand up to your father eventually. Why not now?'

Max obviously had no idea how his father operated. Thomas was surprised the two of them got along so well. Max was as gentlemanly and respectful as his father was coarse. He couldn't imagine Max ever raising his voice at Sasha, or Lydia come to that, and he certainly could never imagine him balking at his daughter's choice of career, whatever that choice may be. Thomas envied the Templeton-Howes their tight-knit family unit. He remembered the framed photograph on Max's desk. The stereotypical family holiday shot, all sunshine and smiles. He didn't think such a photograph had ever been taken of the Kellys, let alone lovingly printed, framed and displayed. The only pictures in his father's office were of himself.

'I take it this means you won't lend me the money?' Thomas had asked, impatient to remove himself from the scene of Max's perfectly balanced life.

'Of course I won't lend you the money, but not because I don't want to help you, because I don't believe in blackmail. Never have, never will. If you pay this scumbag what he wants, he'll just come back for more. Let him print the pictures, or upload them, or stream them, or whatever it is he's threatening to do. The world has seen much worse and by this time next week it'll all be forgotten.' Max had hesitated before adding, 'He's likely to circulate the pictures whether you pay him or not. You know that don't you? It'll be all over social media in a heartbeat.'

Thomas, already walking the plank, pictured himself balanced precariously on the end of it.

'But on the plus side,' Max continued, 'imagine the publicity you'll get. Sales of your paintings will soar! It didn't do George Michael any harm, did it?'

'George Michael's dead.'

Max sighed. 'Elton John, then. Will Young. The list is endless. Which just highlights my point.'

Thomas wasn't at all convinced. He'd be sent to Coventry by his father and would probably never sell another painting again.

'It's all about confidence, Thomas. And you've done the hardest part by telling me. Besides, you've nothing to be ashamed of. We are what we are. They didn't legalise same sex marriage for nothing. Get out there and live your life. You can't bend over for toe-rags like Vince – pardon the expression – and you certainly can't keep pandering to your father's ideal.'

He knew Max was right, but thinking it and doing it were two entirely different things. He'd never been the most confident of individuals and he valued his privacy higher than anything else. But if Max wouldn't lend him the money, what choice did he have? There was no one else to ask.

He'd tried calling Vince's number again but knew he was wasting his time. The second text message had made it clear what he had to do and, more to the point, what would happen if he didn't. He felt sick just thinking about it. Just when he thought he'd finally discovered his sexual identity, when he'd accepted who and what he was and how he wanted to live, his whole axis had shifted. He felt like a butterfly, newly released from its chrysalis tomb, free at last to extend its wings and fly away to freedom, only to be stamped on by a pair of size nines. He knew Max was right. The only way to deal with shysters like Vince was to stand up to them. Easy for him to say, he wasn't the one about to have his reputation cut to shreds. What was it his mother always said? *Better to have a reputation than to have no reputation at all.* That was one way of looking at it he supposed, although he doubted his father would see it that way. Still, by this time tomorrow he would be half way to Scotland and, more importantly, four hundred miles away from his father.

Chapter 14

KTH was officially open for business. Florentina and Lydia had pulled out all the stops and were now making plans for their launch party. Lydia had done a fabulous job transforming the office suites. Out went the clinical desk, cabinets and hardback chairs and in came contemporary leather sofas and sleek white furniture. The walls were painted a French grey and a luxurious dark grey carpet softened the look. Narrow Venetian blinds controlled the light at each of the windows and a giant portrait of Abi hung behind the reception desk. Florentina was far from enamoured with that particular wall decoration, but Lydia had insisted. In response, Florentina had hung some of her own most iconic photographs along the opposite wall. The 1990 Givenchy campaign in Nice, the face of Estee Lauder in '92, astride a ranch horse in Dallas for Ralph Lauren in '93. She was slightly mollified as a result.

Artificial lilies decorated the two desks (Lydia would never buy fresh ones again after the disaster at Sasha's party) and the old kitchen now included a separate changing area, shower and lounge. Stationery had been delivered, office equipment had been installed and social media accounts had been set up. Florentina hadn't been this excited for years. She practically jumped out of bed each morning, eager to get to the office and continue where she had left off the night before. Thank heavens for the espresso machine. She forgot to eat at the best of times, but with her mind so pre-occupied with everything 'business', food was the last thing on her mind. Even alcohol had taken a back seat. In fact, if it wasn't for the coffee she'd be running on empty.

'Should we invite the whole team, do you think?' Lydia asked, pen poised over a list of invitees already threatening to blow their modest party budget. 'Most of them are dating wannabe models, aren't they? One of them might just be the next big thing.'

Florentina didn't want to invite any of Crawford's team if she was honest (with one notable exception). Inviting the team meant inviting

Crawford and she really didn't want his patronizing face spoiling the otherwise perfect setting. Although, she had to admit, he wasn't as opposed to the agency as she had expected him to be. She had prepared herself for a string of derogatory comments but instead, was met with a nonchalant shrug. His couldn't-care-less response was both a relief and a concern.

'And the more Premiership footballers we have, the more publicity we'll get.' Lydia was still scribbling down names at an alarming rate until she abruptly stopped, as though a life shattering thought had occurred to her.

'They're not playing away that day, are they? That's all we need, an away match at Newcastle or some other Godforsaken place. They wouldn't be back till midnight.'

'No. They're at home to Fulham. I checked the fixture list this morning.'

'Oh, thank goodness for that. Although, I'm starting to wonder where on earth we're going to put everyone. It might be a Tardis, but it does have its limits.'

Florentina looked around her and tried to imagine the room wall-to-wall with guests. They could manage fifty at a push. Their current list of eighty was ambitious to say the least. If only there was somewhere else they could host it. Having already rejected either of their homes as a potential venue (this was a professional event and was to be kept strictly business) their options were somewhat limited. Catching sight of the gallery of photographs behind Lydia's desk, Florentina had an idea.

'Why don't we use Thomas's studio?' She rose from her chair, animated by the prospect of finding a solution. 'It's easily big enough and the location is perfect.'

'Wouldn't he mind?'

'Thomas? Of course not. He might even sell some paintings. You know what these footballers are like, more money than sense.'

'I think it's a great idea,' Lydia said, 'if Thomas agrees. And we could invite more guests if we hold it there.'

Florentina sat back down and picked up her phone. 'Let me ask him before you start inviting the entire football league.'

Contrary to everyone else's opinion regarding Cory's disastrous injury, Abi was quite delighted at his incapacitated state. It meant he spent less time at the club and more time at home, giving her the perfect excuse to indulge in her footballer's wife fantasy. She'd called him earlier to invite herself over and, after letting herself in with the spare key, was now rummaging in the fridge for something to eat. Not that she was particularly hungry, but Cory needed to keep his strength up. Finding an unopened packet of smoked salmon and a bag of pre-washed rocket, she cut open a bagel and smothered it with cream cheese, adding a sliver of salmon and a few leaves. She filled a glass with water from the fridge dispenser then set off upstairs with her freshly made snack.

The bedroom was empty, the sheets tussled, as though thrown back in a hurry. Still carrying the bagel and water she checked the en suite. Also empty.

'Cory?'

Re-tracing her steps she returned downstairs and poked her head around the lounge door. Nothing. 'Cory?'

Deciding he was probably relaxing by the pool she headed in that direction, her heels echoing in the tiled passageway. Seeing his floating form face down in the middle of the pool, the glass and plate slipped from her hands, smashing into dagger-like fragments on the floor.

'Oh my God! Cory!' Kicking off her shoes she jumped into the water, her tight skinny jeans clamped to her legs like forceps. She took clumsy strokes towards him, arms circling like a fast bowler. 'Cory!'

Before she knew what was happening, he'd grabbed her around the waist and pulled her under the water. She kicked out, but her water-laden jeans weighed her down. She thrashed her arms in a state of panic unable to comprehend what was happening. Resurfacing, she gasped for air only to swallow a mouthful of water. Strands of wet hair obscured her vision and she floundered blindly, a choking cough now stealing her breath.

'Abi! Stop it! Abi!'

She felt him grab one of her wrists but this only heightened her fear. The next thing she knew, she felt a stinging blow to the side of her face.

'What the fuck? You hit me?'

'Sorry. I couldn't calm you down. It was only a slap.' He held a hand up in front of him as though to apologise, but she wasn't about to be appeased.

Still treading water, Abi could only stare at him in disbelief.

'It was a joke, Abi. I was fooling around, that's all. What? Did you honestly think I was dead or something? The pool's not deep enough to drown in. Look.'

She continued to stare at him as he stood in the water, his head and shoulders clearly visible.

'A joke? Do you see me fucking laughing?!'

She swam to the edge of the pool and, with difficulty, hauled herself out of the water. Her cheek was stinging where he'd slapped her and she could taste, as well as feel, the makeup running down her face. Makeup she'd so carefully applied only an hour before.

'Come on, Abi, don't be like that. It's just my sick sense of humour, that's all. And you do look kinda cute all wet like that.'

In no mood to be placated, she grabbed her shoes and, being careful to avoid the shards of glass, headed for the door. Cory, she noticed, was still standing in the centre of the pool. As a parting gesture she retrieved the bagel from beneath a lounger and hurled it at his pitiful face.

Chapter 15

The speed of the train came as a surprise to Thomas. He was no stranger to the tracks, particularly the tube and the DLR, but this was something else entirely. His childhood trips to Scotland appeared, at the time, to take forever, particularly those with only himself for company. But today's journey north was mercifully fast. And with every acceleration of speed, his heart became a little steadier. The ugly industrial warehouses and duplicated residential towers were soon replaced by sprawling farms, majestic church spires and winding streams. The scene alone calmed him. The lush greens of grazing pastures. Two-tone cows, pink udders full to bursting. Glass-like lakes, ducks diving for their dinner. He was a regular visitor to London's parks, but although they provided some relief from the oppressive, grey, city streets, they failed to lift the heart quite like this. He was mesmerised by the tiny houses with matchbox gardens. Some boasted conservatories where the garden once was, the train offering a perfect, if fleeting view into their ordinary world. He envied them the normality of their lives. The monotony. The mundane. They probably complained about their jobs – if they had one – and their neighbours. Maybe even the trains rattling their windows and disturbing their sleep. But Thomas would do anything to swap places with them now. To substitute his dysfunctional family, mediocre artistic talent and plush room in his parents' mansion – not forgetting the small matter of blackmail – to live in a terraced house smaller than his studio with weeds in the garden, graffiti on the walls and a view of the train track. He'd often wondered what it would have been like to be born into an ordinary family. A family where dad took a packed lunch to work, mum made casseroles and watched *Coronation Street*, a sister with pigtails, freckles and scabby knees. Okay, Abi was once like that, but it was so brief, she seemed to go from seven to seventeen in a few short weeks. Summers with his nan were the closest he ever came to normality. She served the softest, yellowest poached eggs, on doorstop toast with proper butter the colour of buttercups. Tea was made in a brown, crock teapot with real tea leaves, and lunch was called dinner. Evening meals were six p.m. prompt and always home cooked. Steak and kidney pudding with suet as thick as his mattress. Toad in the hole, perfectly crisp with fat, meaty sausages. Her own special hotpot (or stovies, as she called it) with every imaginable vegetable, served with a scoop of mashed potato and a genuine smile. He didn't think his mother had ever cooked a proper meal in her life. Surprising when her parents had owned an Italian restaurant. She was well acquainted with the salad bowl and the microwave but the oven and hob were well beyond her limits. He and Abi had learned to fend for themselves at an early age with pasta becoming their staple diet.

For once, he was thankful his travel companions were happy to disengage. The elderly woman directly opposite him had also embarked at Euston. She had greeted him with a matron-like 'Good morning', and after stowing her small suitcase in the overhead rack, had surprised him by plugging in a laptop. He would've expected a hardback crime thriller, or maybe *The Times*, and was reminded how wrong first impressions can be.

The young man to the side of him had boarded at Coventry. He had avoided eye contact completely and immediately covered his ears with giant headphones. A more predictable character maybe, if his Manchester United T-shirt, ill-fitting jeans and gum-chewing jaw were anything to go by. He briefly wondered if any football fans actually lived in the same city as their chosen team these days, then chastised himself for thinking about football at all. Hadn't he come on this trip to forget everything about London? To focus on the positive and leave the negative behind?

He turned his attention back to the passing scenery. The fells and mountains of Cumbria, the castle at Carlisle, the distant scattering of wind turbines rendered lifeless by the sun. He'd never actually seen a wind farm, only on the TV. They looked quite menacing lined up on the horizon; like an army of space monsters in a sci-fi movie.

At the sound of raucous laughter, he looked towards the end of the carriage. A giant candy floss was floating down the aisle. Actually, it was a slightly overweight girl – but pretty, nonetheless – dressed in pink from head to toe, with L-plates around her neck, a lace veil pinned to her hair and eyelashes longer than her perfectly manicured fingernails. 'Don't mind us,' she announced in a broad Scouse accent, 'we're just passing through.'

Along with the other passengers, Thomas could only stare at the parade of girls making its way through the carriage. They were clearly competing with each other when it came to the length of their skirts (short) and the height of their heels (high), but every single one of them wore a smile as wide as the bride-to-be's backside.

You wouldn't get that in first class, thought Thomas, who, for the first time in his life, was travelling cattle class. Realising he may soon have to wave goodbye to the monthly allowance from his father, he had rejected the three-figure first-class ticket in favour of the cheaper economy option. Now, tempted as he was to disapprove of their noisy, brash behaviour, he found himself in envy of the fun and frivolity on display. He had never enjoyed such camaraderie and could only wonder at the devilish activities about to unfold. He caught the eye of the back-marker and smiled at her 'Chief Bridesmaid' sash. Then all too soon, silence resumed.

Eventually, the train manager announced their imminent arrival at Glasgow. The skyline looked unfamiliar – less congested than London – and the River Clyde reflected colours he'd never once seen in the murky waters of the Thames. The train crawled into the open jaws of the station, but he was in no hurry to disembark, the train to Ayr was not due to leave for another twenty minutes. Instead, he watched the jumble of passengers stretching for luggage, searching pockets for tickets and grabbing seatbacks as the train lurched to a stop. The lad with the headphones had long gone. The old lady, laptop back in its bag, navy slacks and beige cardigan crease free, was upright and alert, like a racehorse waiting for the off. *Perhaps she writes crime novels,* he thought to himself, *rather than reads them.* He was tempted to ask but was spared the dilemma by the hiss of opening doors and the hurried exodus of impatient bodies.

He lifted his hold-all from the luggage rack and stepped off the train. His pace was slow compared to those around him. Usually, he was in just as much a hurry as everyone else. But not today. The change was a refreshing one.

Weekends in the Kelly household were nothing if not predictable. Crawford was up and out before daybreak each Saturday, pristine in his blue suit and tie, but as tense as Harry Redknapp's accountant. Abi, usually hungover following a night out with Sasha, would surface mid-morning, dehydrated and dishevelled. Thomas would take advantage of his father's absence by relaxing at home and doing absolutely nothing. And Florentina, for the want of anything better to do, would spend the entire day at the leisure club enjoying a yoga class, body massage, liquid lunch and token gesture swim, in no particular order.

Today, however, Florentina observed that only Crawford was sticking to routine. Abi, without Sasha to party with, had stayed at home last night and was busy making herself a usually forbidden bacon sandwich at nine a.m. As for Thomas, his whereabouts was anybody's guess. She tried to recall the last time she'd seen her son, but the pressing need to find her car keys took precedence.

Dressed in a chic, grey Elie Tahari skirt suit and black Kurt Geiger heels, she rummaged around in her handbag, impatient to leave for the office.

'Have you seen Thomas?' she asked Abi, her eyes scanning the kitchen counter for her missing keys.

Abi shook her head, her attention divided between her iPhone and her bacon sandwich.

'His bed hasn't been slept in and he's not answering my calls. I've been ringing him since yesterday afternoon.'

'He mentioned going away for a few days. Maybe he's gone already.'

Florentina abandoned the search for her keys and stared at her daughter. 'Away? Away where?'

'Scotland, I think.'

'Scotland?' Receiving no response, she asked again. 'Scotland?'

'Will you stop repeating yourself?' said Abi, finally looking up from her phone. 'Yes, Scotland. He wanted to go back to Ayr.'

'Ayr? Whatever for?'

'How should I know?'

'Did he leave the keys to his studio?'

'How should I know?'

'Now who's repeating herself? You're not being very helpful, Abi.'

'What? I don't know where he is and I don't know if he left his keys. I'm not his keeper.'

She returned her attention to her phone, her disinterest in the conversation clearly apparent.

'Well, if he calls, tell him I need to speak to him. It's urgent.'

'Yes, Mother.'

Florentina sighed at her daughter's petulance before recovering her keys from the bottom of her Gucci handbag.

'I'm off to the office,' she said. 'Make sure that's your last bacon sandwich, Abi. I won't have KTH's top model looking like Miss Piggy.'

The Blues won by four goals to one. Florentina and Lydia were still in the office when Max came to update them with the final score. Not that either of them was particularly interested. Florentina assumed he was using the score up-date as an excuse to find out what time his wife was likely to return to the house.

'At least Crawford will be in a buoyant mood tonight, Florrie.'

She tensed at the mention of her pet name but let it go. Some people still referred to her by her model name, although it was rare coming from Max.

'I doubt he'll be home tonight. He rarely comes home after an away match.'

'I wouldn't have thought West Ham counted as an away match,' said Max. 'It's only down the road.'

'Yes, well. That's Crawford for you.' She pretended to search for something in her office drawer, trying not to think of the reason why Crawford was unlikely to come home. Thankfully, Lydia came to the rescue with a change of subject.

'We're up to six now, Max. Sadie Torch signed with us this afternoon. Well, she didn't sign exactly, but as good as. And Jenna Constance agreed to come in next week and talk to us.'

Lydia was beaming, clearly proud of their early progress.

'That's great news. Well done both of you. You'll hit double figures before you know it.'

Florentina knew Lydia was already thinking of the commissions London Fashion Week could earn them next year. She, on the other hand, was thinking that the more models they signed, the more names she could recommend before having to suggest her own daughter. It was this motivation, and this alone, that kept her on the phone all hours of the day and night searching for new talent.

'Thanks, honey,' said Lydia, rising from her chair and kissing Max on the cheek. 'Give me ten minutes to finish up here then I'll come and get supper. Did you want to join us, Florentina?'

'Oh, no. You guys carry on. Thanks anyway. I might just give Thomas another try. He still hasn't replied to my messages and we can't send the invites out till we know we can use his studio.'

'It's not like Thomas to be AWOL is it?' asked Max.

'No, it isn't. Abi thinks he may have gone to Scotland.'

'Scotland? Really? Well, I guess we all deserve a holiday,' said Max. 'And he has been under some pressure of late.'

'What do you mean?' asked Florentina. 'What sort of pressure?'

'Oh, you know. Pressure to finish his paintings. He had a few on the go from what I understand. Pretty tight deadlines too.'

'Oh, right. Well, even so. He should still have the decency to call me back.'

'Would the landlord have a spare key?' asked Lydia. 'To his studio?'

'Lydia, you're a genius!' Florentina began a new search on her laptop. 'Of course. Why didn't I think of that?'

Whilst his wife was burying her head in business, Crawford was burying his head between Simone's legs. Their four-one thrashing of West Ham had heightened both his appetite and his energy and, thanks to a hat-trick from young Josh Franklin, all was well in his world. The fans were no longer chanting obscenities, the chairman was no longer baying for his blood, and Simone, for the time being at least, was no longer behaving like a love-sick limpet. Her orgasmic cries of pleasure were increasing in volume so Crawford inserted two fingers to accelerate the process. Besides, if she didn't go down on him soon, he'd be spunking on the sheets like a spotty adolescent.

'How long till Flemming's back training?' he asked afterwards, unable to forget about football for any longer than a few lust-filled minutes.

'Two weeks. Maybe three,' she replied, retrieving the duvet from its heap on the floor and folding herself underneath it. 'He won't be match fit for at least a month, maybe in time for the Liverpool game.'

'You'd better keep Franklin fit then. Keep an eye on him. Make sure he winds down properly. If he gets injured, we're bollocked.'

'Sure. What about you? Have you wound down properly?' Her seductive smile, coupled with her fingers curling around his dick, sparked an instant response.

Franklin won't be the only one celebrating a hat-trick tonight, he thought.

Seconds later the duvet was back on the floor.

Abi could hear her mother clattering around in the kitchen. She was famished herself but the thought of making polite conversation over a beetroot salad didn't exactly fill her with joy, even if she did throw some pine nuts on it. But two consecutive nights at home had left her starved of company and, deciding even her mother's company was better than none at all, she dragged herself downstairs.

'What are you making?' she asked, amazed to see a frying pan on the stove.

Her mother glanced up, clearly surprised at Abi's unexpected appearance. 'Smoked salmon omelette with rocket. Want some?'

Abi inwardly cringed at the mentioned ingredients, images of a pool-drenched bagel flooding her mind. 'Erm, yeah, okay. Thanks.'

She perched on a stool and watched as her mother whisked the eggs in a bowl.

'How come you're not out partying?'

'Didn't feel like it,' she lied. 'Did you get hold of Thomas?'

'No. But I called his landlord. I'm meeting him at the studio first thing Monday morning. He's giving me a key.'

'Is he allowed to do that? Without Thomas's permission, I mean?'

'Probably not. But I promised him a signed photo.'

Abi shared a rare smile with her mother. They both knew how easy it was to manipulate men.

'So the party's going ahead then?'

She watched her mother divide a bag of pre-washed rocket onto two plates, adding a handful of cherry tomatoes and diced cucumber.

'It is indeed. Next Saturday. Most of the invites have already been sent by email. Lydia's organising the catering.'

'Do you need help getting the studio ready?' she asked.

'I think I can manage.' The clipped response made her wish she hadn't offered but, for once, she didn't bother to bite back. With her mother now concentrating on the frying pan, Abi turned the conversation to her brother.

'I hope Thomas is okay,' she said, genuinely concerned about his wellbeing.

'Thomas can take care of himself,' her mother replied. 'Although, quite why he'd want to go to Scotland I don't know. Cold, miserable place.'

'I'm not saying that's where he's gone. I'm just guessing, that's all. He mentioned it in passing when I talked to him about the agency.'

A misshapen omelette appeared in front of Abi, slightly too runny for her liking. She gingerly forked a sliver of egg.

'Talking of the agency, we have six girls on the books already, including you, obviously. I'll make a start on the men on Monday.'

'How come you've signed up so many already?' Abi was both intrigued and impressed.

'Calling on a Saturday was an inspired idea, though I say so myself. Very few of them were working and once one had signed, word soon got around. Most have jumped from Platinum. They were unhappy with their current deal and were only on short-term contracts.'

Abi spiked a cherry tomato, but it escaped and rolled across the counter. Florentina caught it and popped it in her mouth.

'Are you excited? About the agency, I mean?' Abi asked.

Still chewing the tomato, her mother nodded her response, finally saying, 'Of course. I can't remember the last time I was so enthusiastic about something. I don't know why I didn't think of it myself.'

Abi finally gave up on her omelette and pushed her plate away. Her mother, she noticed, hadn't eaten anything, other than a single cherry tomato.

'Are you not eating?' Abi asked.

'Lost my appetite,' she said, topping up her wine glass. 'I'll get something later.'

Abi knew she wouldn't. Her mother lived on wine, espresso and bitterness, and very little else.

'If you change your mind about the studio,' Abi said, sliding off her stool, 'let me know. If you're serious about selling his paintings I know which are for sale and which are commissioned. You'll be in serious shit if you get them the wrong way round.'

She could tell from her mother's expression, she hadn't even thought of that.

Chapter 16

Standing outside the studio in a burgundy Reiss skirt suit and matching patent heels, Florentina began to wish she'd opted for trousers. There was a biting wind snapping at her bare legs and she was beginning to lose all feeling in her toes. She'd be grateful of the skirt this afternoon, though. Having finally plucked up the courage to call Cory, he had agreed to meet her at the office later that day to discuss 'a little proposition'. She hadn't divulged too much information, just enough to pique his interest and entice him into her lair.

At last, a black Audi TT pulled up alongside her Lexus and she watched as a gangly, bespectacled man unwound himself from the seat. Upright, he was at least six-foot-two. With wild, grey hair and eyebrows to match, he looked more like a mad professor than a property developer.

'Mrs Kelly?' he asked, with an outstretched hand. 'Keith Forrester. Pleased to meet you. I'm a big fan.' His handshake was unpleasantly damp and limp. She extracted her hand and smiled her thanks.

'It's good of you to help me out like this,' she said, as he opened the door and led her inside. 'Thomas was beginning to panic. If his client doesn't get his painting on time, there'll be hell to pay.'

'Well, we wouldn't want that would we? Where did you say he'd gone again?'

'Scotland. Visiting family. I can manage from here, Mr Forrester. If you just let me have the key, you can be on your way. I'm sure you're very busy.'

'Nonsense, it's no trouble.' She followed him up the stairs, conscious of her vulnerability, especially as she had left her phone behind in her haste to get here on time. She knew nothing about this man, other than the fact he was Thomas's landlord, and she was alone with him in a deserted warehouse.

'I would've thought he'd have gone further than Scotland, in the circumstances.'

Florentina stared up at his ascending form, trying to remember exactly what she had said when she had called and asked for a spare key.

'This door has been known to stick on occasions,' he told her, inserting the key and pushing it exaggeratedly with his hip. 'Here we are. Gosh, he's quite a talent, isn't he?' he said, striding towards a colourful painting of Big Ben at sunset. He wrinkled his nose then and looked around the room. 'What's that smell?'

Unwilling to make herself any more vulnerable, Florentina remained at the doorway. 'I'll check the fridge before I leave,' she said. 'Maybe he's left something in there.'

'Rather you than me,' he said, his contorted face resembling that of a pug.

'I don't mean to be rude, Mr Forrester, but I have another meeting in...' she checked her watch for effect, 'thirty minutes. And you know what the traffic is like this time of the morning.'

'Oh, yes, of course. I'll leave you to it then.' He walked back to the doorway and handed her the keys. 'You won't forget the photograph, will you, Florrie?' he said, all formalities now abandoned. 'Although, I have to say, you look so much better in the flesh.'

She inched backwards, keen to remove him from her personal space. 'Of course, Mr Forrester. I'll make sure it's mailed to you. And I'll ask Thomas to return the spare keys when he gets back.'

'*If* he gets back,' he said. 'And there's no need. I have plenty more.'

Once he'd gone, Florentina locked the door behind him, leaving the key in the lock, then promptly washed her hands. He was right about the smell, it was rancid. She threw open the windows, inviting more goose bumps to her arms and legs, before searching for air freshener. Finding only an old can of Lynx, she sprayed it liberally and then rooted around for the source of the smell. Suspicious stains marked the sink and the floor and she doused both with bleach, wrinkling her nose in distaste. Cleaning task complete, she took time to admire her son's work. He really was very good. She rarely got to see his paintings these days. In fact, she rarely got to see Thomas. She lifted the cover from the nearest easel, taking a step back to appraise his work in progress. She recognised the outline of the Shard and the unmistakable shape of Tower Bridge. She briefly wondered who the painting was for before moving on to the next one. She threw the cover aside and gasped at the face staring back at her. He had captured his sister beautifully; the defiant gleam in her eye, the pout of her raspberry-soft lips, the spirited slant of her chin. It was exquisite. She wanted nothing more than to smash her fist through it. Feeling nauseous, she slumped on to the sofa and closed her eyes, unwilling to look at her daughter's perfect face. Conscious of the time and her impending meeting with Cory, she sat upright, rubbing her legs in an attempt to dispel the cold. At the same time, her attention was caught by something under the table. A photograph. She slid it out with her finger and lifted it from the floor.

'Oh, Thomas,' she said aloud. 'What have you done?'

Back in her car she cursed herself for forgetting her phone. Wherever Thomas was, he shouldn't be on his own and she needed to call Abi to find out what else she knew about his whereabouts. She was pretty sure Keith Forrester knew more than he was letting on as well. What was it he'd said? *In the circumstances*. What did that mean?

Letting herself into the house she strode straight through to the kitchen where she had left her phone plugged into its charger. Sixteen missed calls. *What the hell?* It rang again before she could even unplug it.

'Where the hell have you been? Have you seen the papers? This is all I fucking need, Florentina! Who does he think he is, bringing shame on the family? Where the hell is he anyway?'

Having already seen a photograph of her son in what can only be described as a compromising position, Florentina could easily guess what Crawford was talking about, or rather, shouting about. She retraced her steps to the hallway where she'd idly discarded the daily papers on her way out that morning and began to leaf through them one-handed. It didn't take long to find the offending page. *Shit.*

'Florentina! Are you there? What the hell are you doing? He can't get away with this you know. As if I haven't got enough to worry about.'

It didn't go unnoticed that Crawford's only thoughts were for himself rather than his son. Florentina was tempted to ask him exactly what it was he had to worry about in his blessed life but decided not to antagonise him further.

'I'll try calling him,' she said, knowing already that he wouldn't pick up.

'You do that. And tell him not to show his face round here for a while or I'm likely to ram those pictures down his scrawny little throat!'

Florentina winced as Crawford cut the call. Checking her phone she saw that Abi and Lydia had also tried to call her. Presumably they had seen the pictures too. Continuing her scan of the papers, she found the story in all but one of the tabloids. She sighed and sunk down onto the bottom stair, resting her head in her hands. She thought back to all the times she had asked herself if her son was gay. The way he always sat with his legs crossed at the thigh, how he chased his hair off his face with a gentle flick of the wrist, his lack of interest in Abi's beautiful friends. She'd certainly suspected, she just never wanted to believe. Not because she was ashamed, but because it wasn't the life she wanted for her son. She knew better than anyone how judgmental people were and she would hate to think Thomas was the victim of abuse, verbal or otherwise. Her phone rang again and, seeing it was Lydia, she answered the call.

'Before you ask, yes I've seen it. I'm on my way.'

Arriving at the office, Lydia greeted her with a warm hug. 'I'm so sorry, darling. Did you have any idea?'

'That my son was gay or that his face, and Lord knows what else, was going to be plastered all over the papers?'

Lydia withdrew from the hug and looked at her friend. 'Both, I suppose. And it's not just the papers, I'm afraid. It's all over social media too.'

Florentina let out a sigh of despair then reached for the espresso machine. 'I don't know. Maybe. I mean, I've often wondered. It's not normal to have so few girlfriends at his age, is it? I suppose I just didn't want to ask. I didn't want to know. So long as he was happy, it didn't really matter.'

'And was he? Happy, I mean?'

'I'm not sure. I never really took the time to find out.' Florentina surprised herself by crying genuine tears. She was ashamed, she realised. Not of Thomas, but of herself. She was so wrapped up in her own life, wallowing in self-pity, resenting her own daughter, that she'd failed to notice if Thomas was happy or not. Failed to even care. She carried her coffee to her desk with shaky hands.

'Don't cry, darling. It's not the end of the world. What is it they say? No publicity is bad publicity?'

'I'm not sure Thomas would agree with that at the moment,' she said, sniffing away more tears. 'Where is he, Lydia? I hate to think of him all on his own.'

'He'll be back when he's good and ready. Seems to me like he knew what was coming and made himself scarce. I can't imagine Crawford will be delighted at the news.'

'You're not wrong. He's already been on the phone, ranting and raving.' She sat down and blew her nose, then blotted her tears with a clean tissue.

'Did you know, Lydia? You and Max. Did you know he was gay?'

Lydia perched on the edge of Florentina's desk and stroked the petal of an artificial lily. 'Sasha asked me last year if I thought he was gay. She'd suspected for a while. I suppose I'd never really thought about it. Thomas is just Thomas, you know? I think Max knew. Men can generally tell, can't they?'

'He must have known what Crawford would say. I bet he's been tormenting himself with worry!' A fresh bout of tears erupted and she blew her nose once more.

Just then, there was a knock on the door.

'Sorry. Am I interrupting something?' The unmistakable American accent stopped Florentina mid-blow.

'Cory! No, no, of course not, come in, come in.' How could she have forgotten he was coming in this morning? She must look frightful. He, on the other hand, looked absolutely delicious. Without his trademark headband, his hair was long and loose. His jeans hugged in all the right places and a glimpse of soft, tanned skin teased her from beneath his V-neck T-shirt.

'Erm, this is Lydia Templeton-Howe, my business partner,' she managed. 'Lydia, this is Cory Flemming, he plays for Crawford's team.'

The two of them shook hands.

'Yes, I know. Good to meet you, Cory.'

'You too, Lydia. Is it okay to call you Lydia?'

'Please do. What brings you to KTH?'

'I've no idea, actually,' he said, treating them both to a knockout smile. 'Mrs Kelly invited me over. May I?' he asked, nodding towards the leather sofa.

'Of course, please take a seat. How is the ankle?' asked Lydia, leaning his single crutch against her desk.

'Getting there, thanks for asking. So, what is it you wanted to talk to me about?'

Florentina was frantically trying to repair the damage to her face. She'd banked on Lydia being out – she was sure she had said she had a meeting with an interior design client this morning – and was hoping for some time alone with Cory. Time to work her magic.

Both Cory and Lydia were now looking expectantly in her direction.

'We were hoping we could persuade you to partake in a photoshoot or two.'

'We were?' said Lydia.

'We were,' confirmed Florentina. 'Your cheekbones are just what we're looking for.'

Lydia was clearly amused by the exchange, but thankfully, made her apologies and left. She rose an eyebrow at Florentina on her way out.

'Erm, I'm not sure what to say. What kind of photoshoot? It's not anything dodgy, is it?'

Florentina laughed out loud at the question. 'Dodgy? You mean pornographic? Certainly not. We're a high-end modelling agency, not some seedy, backstreet joint.'

'Yeah, sorry. Just checking. So, what kind of photoshoot?' he repeated.

'We're a relatively new agency. We need some big names to get us started. I was hoping I could persuade you to do a few test shots. See if the camera likes you. You'd be doing me a huge favour. And I'd be sure to tell my husband how helpful you've been.' That bit wasn't necessarily true, but it wouldn't hurt to convince him that Crawford was on board with the idea.

'I'm not too sure the club would approve, Mrs Kelly. I'm paid to play soccer. And win games. Not to prance about on some catwalk.'

She was finding it hard not to react to his condescending comments but forced another smile to her face.

'Just a few pictures, Cory. That's all I ask. You're big news in London. People can't get enough of you. If you're associated with KTH, it could be just the start we're looking for. Come to our launch party, at least.'

'Launch party?'

'Yes, next Saturday. My son's an artist, we're holding it in his studio in Fulham. My daughter, Abi, will be there. And Crawford, of course. Perhaps some of your teammates too. It's not to be missed.'

At the mention of Abi, she saw him look up at her daughter's photograph on the wall. Keen to distract him, Florentina moved from her position behind the desk and helped herself to another espresso. 'Would you like one?'

'No thanks, I try to avoid caffeine.'

'Of course. So, will you think about it?' she asked, leaning against Lydia's desk and crossing her ankles. She'd been right to wear a skirt. Her legs really were her best asset.

'Sure, I'll think about it. If I get to meet chicks like that,' he said, nodding at Abi's photo, 'it can't be a bad thing.'

Florentina swallowed the familiar knot of jealousy. 'I think you'll find experience is so much better than youth,' she said.

They stared at each other for slightly longer than was comfortable. Or necessary.

Abi was waiting for Cory when he got home. She'd forgiven him for his pool antics (even though it had taken an age for her car seat to dry out) and was sitting astride a kitchen chair wearing nothing but a smile. 'I've missed you,' she said, running a tongue over her lips.

'Likewise,' he said, laying his crutch on the table and taking her tongue in her mouth. 'I'm sorry for being an arse.'

'I'm sorry for over reacting.'

She undid the zip of his jeans and tugged them down to his ankles. Lifting herself up onto the table she lay backwards and guided him in, happy to be back where she belonged.

They weren't even dressed before she told him about Thomas.

'I don't know what to do. He won't answer my calls. I'm really worried about him.'

'Did you know he was gay?'

'No. Well, not really.'

'What d'ya mean, not really?'

'I thought he might be but I never asked. He's had girlfriends.'

Cory took a bottle of Evian from the fridge and twisted off the cap. 'Want some?'

Abi shook her head.

'Maybe he plays for both teams,' he said.

'Maybe. It doesn't matter though, right? We're all different. Unique. You can be whatever you wanna be, right?'

'Sure. No one gives a shit these days. Each to their own.'

'I'm not sure my dad would agree.'

'Yeah, he's old school, for sure. A spade's a spade. A gay's a pansy.'

'Don't say that.'

'Hey, I'm just saying. Some people still have old-fashioned attitudes. When your dad was born, homosexuality was considered a crime. Men got locked up for being gay.'

'Seriously? I didn't know that.' Abi nibbled the end of a sharp fingernail.

'It's true. And folks like your dad still think that way. He's not exactly discreet when it comes to his opinions, is he?'

Not used to people disrespecting her father, Abi was unsure what to say. She wanted to spring to his defence, but she suspected what Cory was saying was true. Her father was very much a man's man.

'I guess not,' she said, eventually.

'He's chauvinistic too,' he went on, 'as well as homophobic. I wouldn't wanna be in your brother's shoes, that's for sure.'

Abi checked her phone for the hundredth time, but there was still no response from Thomas. She hoped he was in a bar in Scotland somewhere, enjoying a pint and a packet of pork scratchings, maybe chatting to the locals about castles and kilts. More likely, he was hiding out in a hotel room, making himself ill at the thought of what their father would say or do when he found out. *Poor Thomas.*

'I saw your mother today,' Cory said, later. They were lying of the sofa, half dressed, scanning the TV schedule for something to watch.

'My mother? When?'

'She invited me to the office. Wants me to do a photoshoot.'

'What?' Abi sat bolt upright, staring at the side of his face. 'Why didn't you tell me?'

'I'm telling you now.'

'What did you say?'

'I said I'd think about it. She invited me to the launch party too.'

'What?' Abi was stunned. They'd been apart less than three days and suddenly he was best friends with her mother!

'Why would she do that?'

'To attract more clients, I guess. You should know, you're in the business. I suppose the more top names she can attract, the more business she can attract. It's a cycle, right?'

'But why you?'

'Why d'ya think? Look at this face.' He turned his attention from the TV and looked towards her, a smug grin showing perfect white teeth. 'Who wouldn't wanna look at this face?'

'Arrogance doesn't suit you, Cory.' That wasn't strictly true. One of the reasons she fell for him was his assured confidence and self-belief. 'Besides, you're a footballer, not a model.'

'Who says I can't do both?' His attention was back on the TV, his fingers poised on the remote control.

Abi didn't answer. She wasn't sure she liked the idea of Cory mixing with other models. She knew how they operated and didn't trust them one little bit when it came to her man. Particularly if they didn't even know he *was* her man.

'Did she mention me?' she asked.

'Not really. Only to say you'd be at the party.'

'Did you tell her we'd already met?'

'Course not. I'm not stupid. It should be fun though, right? Us in the same room as your parents.'

'Fun? Sounds more like hell to me.'

Chapter 17

The studio looked amazing. In a rare fit of domesticity, Florentina had pulled on the overalls and rubber gloves she had found under the sink and transformed it from a sparse, dusty loft into a swanky, cutting-edge gallery. Thomas's works in progress (including the portrait of Abi) had been stowed carefully away in a locked cupboard, the photographs of both Abi and herself had been removed from the office and now stared down from the walls, and the paintings to be sold were displayed (with inflated price tags) on numerous easels around the room. A long trestle table covered with a starched white cloth stood at the door bearing rows of champagne flutes, and a huge arrangement of lilies stood in the far corner. Lydia, still traumatised by the previous 'lily incident', would have preferred artificial ones, but Florentina wanted the scent to flood the space. Besides, neither of them was wearing white and the arrangement was far enough away to be safe. The only lighting came from strings of fairy lights, artistically arranged around the windows, and spotlights pointing purposefully at each easel. She'd briefly considered asking the girls downstairs to provide candles but soon vetoed the idea. Naked flames sparked memories she would much rather forget.

Florentina checked her watch, yet again, as she prowled around the studio.

'Relax, darling,' Lydia urged. 'We've another half an hour, at least.'

The handful of staff employed for the evening stood at their posts like penguins, upright and expectant. Florentina recognised one of them, a rather dashing young man with a slick of black hair, from Sasha's eighteenth.

'What if it's a disaster? What if nobody turns up?' she asked.

'It won't be. And they will. For heaven's sake, Florentina, sit down. You're wearing out the floorboards.'

She ignored Lydia's advice and stood at the window, trying extremely hard to resist the temptation of starting on the champagne. 'Abi and Sasha should be here by now.'

'They'll be here soon enough. Along with everyone else.'

Max arrived then, struggling with a large cardboard box. 'More vodka,' he announced. 'Just in case.' He placed it next to the other boxes, full of various different spirits, before stealing an hors d'oeuvre from a nearby tray.

'Max!' the women exclaimed in unison.

'Sorry! Just the one. I'm starving! Florentina, you look beautiful, as always.'

He kissed her on both cheeks then winked at his wife.

Florentina was wearing a charcoal grey, Stella McCartney gown, slit to the thigh. Her bleached blonde hair, highlighted and trimmed that morning, was stroking her bare shoulders. Colour was provided courtesy of shocking pink toenails peeking out from black Gianvito Rossi heels, and a slash of pink lipstick. She did, indeed, look beautiful, albeit in an obvious, overstated way.

'Thank you, Max' she said. 'You've brushed up quite well yourself.'

Max was looking particularly dapper in an olive-green three-piece suit and white shirt, open at the neck. Next to Lydia, in a navy-blue pant suit from Phase Eight, they made quite a pair. Although, Florentina thought wearing anything from Phase Eight was risky. You never knew who else might turn up in the same outfit.

'Well, look at you two!' Max said, as Abi and Sasha entered the room, a vision of scarlet and black elegance, respectively. The girls beamed, their perfect skin glowing with youth.

'Hello. Sorry we're a bit late,' said Abi. 'The taxi was late and then I pulled a ladder in my tights. Wow! It looks amazing in here.'

'Doesn't it?' said Lydia. 'Your mother's done a fantastic job.'

Florentina was still cringing at the mention of tights. Why would anyone dress their muff to look like a deformed bank robber? The fact that it was her own daughter was both amusing and disturbing.

Abi made a beeline for the paintings, stopping at the first easel. She gasped at the price tag. 'This is too much! It won't sell for that! And this one. And this one.'

Florentina ignored her.

'Mum? You've added an extra zero to all of these prices!'

'Yes, I have,' she said, finally turning around. 'Your brother's selling himself short, the prices were far too low. No one wants a cheap painting in their home. Besides, he's famous in his own right now. People will be desperate to get hold of his paintings. It's just a shame there aren't more of them.'

'He's not famous, Mum. He's just been outed. There's a difference. And he won't thank you for inflating the price of his work. He'd rather sell five at five hundred pounds than none at five thousand.'

'We'll see.'

The conversation was brought to an abrupt halt as guests began to arrive.

Abi had been tempted to remove the price tags from the paintings, but the last thing she wanted was a public altercation with her mother. She would just have to tell Thomas people weren't buying. They were here for the launch after all, not to buy paintings.

Thomas had finally replied to a text message from Abi a few days earlier. He confirmed he was in Scotland and that he was happy for them to use his studio (which was a good job because the invitations had already been sent out). He apologised for embarrassing them and said he'd be back soon. '*Once Dad has calmed down.*' Abi had no idea when that would be – she still wasn't allowed to mention his name in her father's company – but at least she knew Thomas was okay.

As the room began to fill, Sasha became slightly star-struck by the famous faces. 'Oh. My. God. Is that Sadie Torch? She looks amazing! And Grayson Delaney. He looks good enough to eat!'

'Calm down,' Abi laughed. 'I thought you were saving yourself for Jock the Doc.'

'I am. I'm just looking. Like shopping without my purse. Is Cory coming?'

'He will be later, with a bit of luck.' She pushed her cheek out with her tongue, to illustrate her thoughts.

'Don't be disgusting! Oh. My. God. Is that Jamie Redknapp? It is! You didn't tell me he was coming!'

'I didn't know! Honest! Anyway, tell me more about Jock the Doc. Have you seen him since your party?'

'No. I've had no time to do anything other than study. Uni is harder than I thought. I don't get a minute to myself. Life is sooo dull.'

'Well, now's your chance to liven it up a bit.' She nodded towards the door where the handsome Justin McKenzie was just shaking hands with Max. As he turned around, Abi caught a glimpse of his striking, green eyes and was instantly reminded of his green bow-tie at Sasha's party.

'Of course! The bow-tie!' she said, not quite quietly enough.

'What? What bow-tie?' Sasha was looking at her, confusion spread across an otherwise perfect face.

'Oh, nothing. I've just remembered something, that's all. Shall I get us another drink?' Abi lost herself in the crowd, anxious to avoid any further conversation about Jock the Doc. She didn't want to break it to her friend that the guy she'd been salivating over for the last few weeks was actually gay.

'Poor Sasha,' she muttered.

Florentina was holding court among a troop of young models. She hadn't enjoyed this much attention in years. They weren't interested in her fall from grace. They just wanted to know who she'd worked with, where she'd travelled to and how much money she'd earned. The adoration was addictive and she was more than a little disappointed when their attention was diverted towards an approaching footballer, even if it was Cory Flemming.

'Evening ladies,' he drawled. 'How you doin', Mrs K?'

Florentina greeted him with her best smile, her knickers fizzing like shaken champagne.

'Very well thank you, Cory. 'Would you excuse us, ladies? I need a quick word with this gentleman.'

The girls slowly moved away, giggling behind their hands.

'Glad you could make it,' she said, helping herself to a glass of champagne from a passing tray. 'I hope you didn't struggle too much with the stairs. I don't think lifts were invented when this place was built.'

'I managed okay. That's the great thing about us soccer players, we can use both feet.'

She watched his lips as he spoke, imagining them kissing her neck, his messy blond hair tickling her shoulders, his hands stroking her...

'I've been thinking about your proposal,' he said, bringing her fantasising to a temporary halt.

'And?'

'So long as it doesn't interfere with my soccer, I'm happy to give it a go.'

'That's wonderful news. Thank you, Cory. You won't regret it, I promise.' She ran her tongue over her top lip, a gesture designed to entice. 'Let's schedule something for next week.'

They were interrupted by Grayson Delaney, somewhat rudely, it had to be said, when he patted Cory on the back.

'Hey, Blondie! How's it going, man? How's the ankle?'

All three of them looked down at the object of discussion.

'Yeah, getting there, thanks, mate. Another couple of weeks should do it.'

'You'll be lucky to get your place back at this rate. Young Franklin's netting more than Captain Birdseye. Could be the sub's bench for you, my friend.'

He let his poisonous words sink in before turning to Florentina. 'Good to see you again, Mrs Kelly.'

'Sadly, the feeling's not mutual,' she said, before heading off to find Lydia.

By the end of the evening, all of Thomas's paintings had sold. Florentina was feeling particularly smug as she placed the final 'SOLD' ticket on a blue and white image of Chelsea Harbour, although she was still seething at one particular comment suggesting the paintings would triple in value if the artist's suicide rumours were true. The person responsible for these despicable words was still reeling from Florentina's subsequent wrath.

'You were right. Well done,' Abi conceded. The words were music to Florentina's ears, although she was still putting on a brave face following her husband's obvious snub of the event. Most of his players had come along with their respective model, actress or wannabe girlfriends, but Crawford had failed to show. On one hand, she was immensely disappointed. On the other, she was glad to avoid the strained atmosphere and derogatory comments that usually accompanied his presence. At least Cory had turned up, although she hadn't been able to orchestrate much time alone with the object of her desire. No thanks to Grayson Delaney. Or Abi, for that matter. Florentina had seen the two of them together shortly after Cory had arrived and had felt her blood pressure rise instantly. He did agree to a test photoshoot, though, so her plan was beginning to take shape. She was looking forward to getting back behind the lens. She'd dabbled in photography for a short while after the modelling work had dried up, but, as with most things, she'd bored of it quickly. She was happy to give it another go, though, particularly if Cory Flemming was her willing subject.

'Well, as they say in the modelling world, that's a wrap!' Lydia slid onto one of the tall, leather bar chairs hired in for the occasion, and kicked off her shoes. 'Any champagne left, Max?'

A full glass appeared on the table beside her and she took a long, appreciative sip.

'I think you deserve that,' he said. 'Are you joining us, Florentina?' He pulled up another stool and sat next to his wife, filling two more flutes. The staff were busy collecting empty plates and glasses and generally tidying up.

'Don't mind if I do,' she said, joining them at the table. 'The influencers were an inspired idea, Lydia,' she said. 'We're all over social media.' She held up the screen of her smartphone to demonstrate the point.

'Cheers to that!' Lydia replied, as the three of them clinked glasses.

'Shame Crawford didn't make it,' said Max. 'It's not like him to miss the opportunity of a party after a big win. Three-nil is a great result against Fulham.'

'Yes, well. He's still refusing to have anything to do with Thomas. Which, presumably, includes setting foot in his studio.'

'He's a fool,' said Max. 'He should be proud of Thomas, not ashamed of him. Those paintings were snapped up quicker than the hors d'oeuvres.'

'Who bought them?' asked Lydia.

'Your next-door neighbours bought one of them.'

'Liz and Graham? Really? I barely got to speak to them tonight. I do hope they enjoyed themselves. Although, if they went home with a painting, I'm sure they must be delighted!'

'One of the players bought one,' Florentina continued. 'He was Swedish, I think, or Danish.'

Max and Lydia laughed.

'Oscar Christianson?' Max suggested.

'Yes, that's the one. And one of the new models, Sophie Kruse.'

'Well, Thomas will be thrilled,' said Lydia. 'Have you heard from him?'

Florentina shook her head. 'He's been in touch with Abi, but he still won't answer my calls.'

'At least you know he's okay. Maybe he'll speak to you when he knows how much money you made him tonight. He's twenty-five grand richer thanks to you!'

'Did you know he was gay?' Sasha asked Abi the following day. For once, they were sitting in Abi's bedroom, her red dress hanging on the outside of her wardrobe door, as though a third, mute person was in the room.

'Who? Thomas or Justin?'

'I dunno. Both, I suppose'

'I didn't know Thomas was gay, not for sure. Not until those pictures flashed up on social media. I told you that already.'

'What about Justin?'

'I realised last night. They were together at your party, but I didn't remember until I saw him last night.'

'So, while I was wetting my knickers at the thought of getting inside his, he was dipping his wick into your brother's—'

'Don't say it!' Abi put her hands over her ears in protest. 'I don't want to hear it. He's my brother and I love him, but I don't want to hear the gory details of his sex life, thank you very much.'

Sasha eased her friend's hands away from her head. 'Sorry. What a waste though. How can somebody as drop dead gorgeous as Jock the Doc waste himself on some gay bloke?'

'That gay bloke you're referring to is my brother.'

'Sorry. I didn't mean it like that. I love Thomas as well; you know I do. It's just, how can I get it so wrong? How did I not know he was gay?'

'Who? Thomas or Justin?'

'Jeez, this is confusing! Justin. I mean, how many weeks have I wasted drooling over someone who'd rather have Sacha Distel then Sasha Templeton-Howe?'

'Who?'

'Sacha Distell, he's… Oh, it doesn't matter. It's a good job I heard him chatting up that waiter, that's all I can say. Imagine if I'd brazenly thrown myself at him. How embarrassing would that have been? I wonder if my dad knows he's gay?'

'Who? Thomas or Justin?'

The two girls laughed at their continued confusion and the question remained unanswered.

'Anyway, how did it go with Cory last night?'

'Good. Great, actually. When he finally got home. I waited for him for over an hour before he finally got back. Struggled getting a taxi, apparently.'

'I can't believe he gave you a key to his house!'

'I know,' said Abi, smiling with mischief. 'Although he took some persuading. Anyway, he was on fine form. It just keeps getting better!'

'And is he doing the photoshoot you mentioned?'

'Yeah. Can't say I'm thrilled at the prospect. Did you see those girls eyeing him up last night?'

'Yeah. He wouldn't give you a key to his house though, would he? Not if he had something to hide, or if he wanted to get off with someone else.'

'Guess not. Anyway, talking of photoshoots, I've got my first official job next week. Max Factor hired me for a shoot in Oxfordshire in some stately home or other.'

'Not Blenheim Palace?'

'Yeah, that's it.' Abi couldn't have sounded more laid-back if she'd tried. Sasha, on the other hand, was brimming with excitement on Abi's behalf.

'Wow! That's fantastic, Abi! I'm sooo jealous. Think of me slaving away at uni.'

'I might. If you're lucky. Just for a minute.'

'Bitch!' said Sasha, pushing her off the end of the bed.

Crawford was riding high on the Josh Franklin wave. The atmosphere in the dressing room was buoyant, they were climbing the Premier League table at a rapid pace and, as a result, the chairman was leaving him well alone. And it was all thanks to their seventeen-year-old wonderkid. The papers were already linking him with a move to Manchester United, but he had no intention of letting them get their grubby little hands on his star player. 'Over my dead body,' he muttered to himself as he leafed through the newspapers on his desk.

The only thing sullying his otherwise perfect life was Thomas. Abi had told him about the paintings at the launch party (Florentina still wasn't talking to him after his no-show), and he'd been begrudgingly impressed. Thomas must be better at this painting lark than Crawford had thought. But that still didn't detract from the shame of having his son's arse spread across every newspaper. As if the fans didn't have enough to goad him with. He could live with the comments about his wife's sagging tits, even the ones about his daughter's ample ones. What he couldn't live with was the latest chant to hit the terraces of every football stadium in the country. 'Your son's a fucking poofter' was not what he wanted to hear when he emerged from the tunnel every weekend. The flame of shame ignited by those noxious words didn't just affirm his burning humiliation, it also fuelled his guilt. Because, the more he thought about it, the more he believed he was somehow responsible for this disastrous turn of events. And he had no idea what to do about it.

Chapter 18

The day of the photoshoot had finally arrived. Florentina was beyond excited as she waited for Cory to arrive. Lydia was in Surrey measuring up for the re-design of a private dental practice, and Florentina had diverted the office phone to her mobile, which was now switched off. They wouldn't be disturbed. She busied herself plumping cushions, spraying room fragrance and straightening photographs which had dared to slip from a perfect, horizontal line. She caught sight of herself in the mirror and admired her reflection once more. Business-like but sexy. She'd nailed it in her Donna Koran skirt suit. Its caramel tones matched her eyes perfectly and her nude stockings lived up to their 'barely there' description. She rarely covered her legs, but today the October temperatures justified it. Plus, she wanted to give him a little surprise when she dropped her skirt to the floor.

A knock on the door signalled his arrival and she let him in with a predatory smile.

'Walking unaided?' she enquired, noticing the lack of a crutch.

'Yeah. Glad to see the back of the damn thing if I'm honest.'

She stepped aside to let him in, locking the door behind them. He still bore a slight limp, she noticed.

'So, what do I need to do, exactly?' he asked, glancing at the equipment in the corner. Florentina had spent most of the previous evening erecting tripods, lighting and a brilliant white backdrop, ready for today's session.

'Have a seat first,' she told him. 'There's no rush. I'll show you some pictures to give you some idea what to expect. Coffee?'

'No thanks, I try to avoid caffeine.'

'Of course, you said. Water?'

'Sure.'

She handed him a bottle of Evian from the fridge, then sat down beside him. His scent was making her giddy, Tom Ford's Fabulous, if she wasn't mistaken.

'I'll just take a few test shots to start with,' she told him. 'You don't need to do anything special, just be natural. Be yourself.'

'You're taking the pictures yourself?' he asked, clearly surprised at the news.

'Of course. It's a hobby of mine,' she lied. Although, she was happy to take it up again if it meant more time with this delectable subject.

He picked up an album from the coffee table and began to leaf through the pages. Florentina had deliberately chosen those with pictures of herself, even if they were over twenty years old.

'You were quite something,' he said, pausing at one of her particular favourites, taken on a yacht in St Tropez, wearing the teeniest bikini, grains of sand highlighting the curve of her breasts.

She blanched at the 'were' but quickly recovered.

'The best,' she said, simply.

Having made a show of adjusting the umbrella, tripod height and camera lens, she finally began clicking away behind the camera. The window blinds were now closed and Cory looked more than a little uncomfortable on the hard, metal stool.

'That's great. Perfect. Keep looking at me. That's it. Good. A little to the left. Yes. Chin up a little. Try tilting your head to the side. Yes. Good. Move your hair away from your eyes. That's it. Good.'

He was actually beginning to enjoy himself. Florentina could tell from the glint in his eye. The more pictures she took, the more relaxed he became. This is exactly what she'd intended. It was also a huge turn on. And, if she wasn't mistaken, he'd been eyeing her tits for most of the session. These push-up bras were a godsend; there was more cleavage in here than there was in *Downton Abbey*. She was so intent on executing her plan of enticement that her heart literally stopped when someone knocked at the door.

'Mum? Mum, are you in there?' The knocking continued. 'Cory?'

Furious at the interruption, Florentina unlocked the door and pulled it open, almost yanking it off its hinges.

'Why was the door locked?' Abi asked. 'I tried calling but your phone was switched off. Dad's been arrested. He needs you at the police station.'

'What?' was all Florentina could manage. 'What do you mean, arrested?'

'Drink-driving. He's at Hammersmith. Can you go and collect him?'

Florentina struggled to absorb the information. 'Drink-driving? What are you talking about?'

In the mayhem that followed, a seething Florentina barked instructions at Abi to dismantle the photographic equipment and revert the office back to its original formality. She also muttered an abrupt apology to Cory, who, bad ankle or not, swiftly made himself scarce. Then, still wet between the legs from her attempted seduction, she drove at full speed to Hammersmith police station. Only when she pulled up in the car park did she realise what Abi had said.

'Cory?' How did she know he was there?

At least Crawford had the good grace to look abashed. He also looked pasty, his usual healthy complexion now ghastly grey, as though the decay from the police cell had clung to him and hitched a ride. He smelt alien too, like an old people's home. A mixture of urine and boiled vegetables. The little green pine tree swinging from the rear-view mirror did little to camouflage the unwelcome invasion.

The journey home was a silent one. Crawford was clearly traumatised by the whole sorry episode and Florentina was too distracted by the day's other events to engage in conversation. Consequently, she kept her hands firmly on the steering wheel and her eyes on the road. Of course, she was inwardly smug at his misfortune. *That's the last time you lecture me on drink-driving,* she thought. At the same time, she was furious at his irresponsible behaviour and the negative impact it could have on her business. Thomas's little indiscretion was bad enough, but this juicy piece of gossip was likely to attract much more attention. And, what Florentina wanted to know more than anything was what was he doing in Hammersmith in the first place?

To fill the increasingly uncomfortable silence she turned on the radio, just in time to hear the news of Crawford's unfortunate misdemeanour. She turned it off again and connected to her Spotify account. 'Things Can Only Get Better' filled the car. She turned to hide a wry smile.

'What on earth were you thinking?' she asked, when they finally arrived home. 'Why didn't you get a taxi?'

Crawford was sitting on the edge of his bed, waiting for his wife to leave him in peace so he could undress and take a shower. He daren't undress in front of her, suspecting his back still bore the scars of a vigorous post-training session in Simone's apartment. She'd produced a bottle of wine, intending to use it in some kind of sex game, but they'd ended up opening it and drinking it. The drink-driving scenario never even occurred to him.

'Just leave it, Florentina, I'm not in the mood. I fucked up, okay? Is that what you want to hear?'

'Where had you been?'

'What?'

'I said, where had you been? Why were you drinking in the first place?'

Crawford rubbed his hands across his face. He'd spent the last three hours thinking what to say and still hadn't come up with anything convincing.

'I had a few whiskies with the chairman. He was in high spirits and wanted to celebrate our recent form. I couldn't really say no.'

'Bullshit,' she spat. 'You were stopped in Hammersmith. Is that where *she* lives?'

'What? Who?' Crawford didn't like where this conversation was going.

'Your physio friend.'

'What physio friend? What are you talking about?' He tried to appear casual but his heart felt like it had been invaded by an overzealous woodpecker. *How the hell did she know about Simone?*

Florentina just stared at him, increasing his inner panic. He desperately needed to change the subject. Spotting an opportunity, he allowed himself a small smile.

122

'Are you wearing tights?' he asked.

'Fuck you, Crawford,' she said, slamming the door behind her.

Result.

Chapter 19

Who said you could run but you couldn't hide? Thomas was proving that wasn't necessarily the case. He had never advertised the fact that his parents were famous, never used their names to gain favours or score points. If anything, he had done all he could to avoid divulging their identity, if only to prevent the resulting, predictable questions that would surely follow: 'How come you don't play?' or 'Fashion not your thing?' And he'd never been more thankful for his lack of bragging than he was now. No one in Scotland either knew, or cared, who he was. The story had appeared in the tabloids, but it was far from headline news. Besides, from what he could gather, in Scotland you supported Rangers or Celtic and didn't give a toss about anyone or anything else. He had bought a baseball cap in anticipation of needing some kind of disguise, even shaved off his neatly trimmed beard, but as it happened, he needn't have bothered. The ink was barely dry on the paper before it was dumped in recycle bins the length and breadth of the country. He laughed now at his misguided belief that people actually gave a shit about his personal life. The pictures could still be viewed on the internet, but he suspected the viewing figures had, by now, dwindled to nothing.

His anonymity in Ayrshire was proving rather therapeutic. After a brief stay in a dreary town centre hotel, he had rented a 'wee cottage' in the grounds of Culzean Castle, a decision initially based on nostalgia, but which was proving an absolute gem. He was using the dining room as a studio, the natural light flooding in through the sea-facing window and recently added skylight, the surrounding countryside providing inspiration by the bucket load. He had even been able to sell a couple of his paintings in the castle gift shop, as well as re-starting, finishing and couriering his outstanding commissions to the City architect.

It was a lonely existence at times but no more so than in London. His lack of friends allowed him to roam at his leisure, reflect on his past and ponder his predicament without judgment or interference. He had spoken to Abi (she had even tried to convince him she had known he was gay all along), but he had yet to pluck up the courage to call his mother; partly from shame, but also from embarrassment at his cowardly running away. Her last text message, however (albeit three weeks ago), telling him she had sold five of his paintings for five thousand pounds each, must surely deserve an acknowledgment of thanks. How ironic to learn that if he'd had more faith in his own ability, he could have sold many more paintings and avoided his whole sorry mess altogether.

Predictably, he had heard nothing from his father. He had yet to check if his monthly allowance had been paid into his account, but his own lack of concern cheered him. He had enough money to keep him going for a few months, at least. Not giving in to Vince's demands had been the right thing to do. He hadn't heard from Vince since the final text message demanding more money and he doubted he would hear from him again. Scumbag.

The castle itself was magnificent, more so than he remembered. He recalled sitting astride the canons, legs wider than was comfortable, a gappy smile at the camera. The smell of wild garlic, strong but strangely pleasant. And the giant hands of the clock tower, always moving faster than he'd hoped. He had been spooked by the Gas House as a child, refusing to return after his first visit, convinced it was haunted by ghosts. He smiled to himself as he retraced his childhood steps, breathing in the salty, sea air and marvelling at the view. He didn't just come here to escape, he realised, he came here to reconnect to nature, to appreciate life and – although he hated the expression – to find himself. This was as good a place as any for all of those things, he concluded.

He had bought a second-hand bicycle from a charity shop in Ayr, buying the necessary bits to spruce it up, then lugging it all home on the bus. He looked at it now, propped up outside the tea shop, and felt proud of his efforts. Someone had left a newspaper on the adjacent table and he stretched across to reach it. It wasn't a paper he would usually choose to read, but it would pass the time while he waited for his coffee. He surprised himself by starting at the back, genuinely interested in the Premier League reports; although he had to turn a few pages before he found any mention of an English team. Funny how he was keen to follow football now it wasn't rammed down his throat every day of the week.

A young waitress arrived with his coffee and he returned the newspaper to the neighbouring table. He turned his attention to the scenery instead. Ailsa Craig stood proud in the distance. He had read somewhere that granite from the island was used to make curling stones. From his point of view, it was the perfect subject for a painting, the ever-changing light of the west coast ensuring he never saw the same view twice. Unlike London. He leant back in his chair and breathed a contented sigh. Whoever said 'home is where the heart is' had got it just about right.

Chapter 20

Things couldn't have got off to a better start for KTH. Florentina and Lydia had been flat out since the launch party, receiving calls on a daily basis from models wanting to sign up. The so-called scandals involving Thomas's sexuality and Crawford's drink-driving had done nothing to damage their reputation. If anything, it had heightened interest in the Kelly family and propelled all of them, with the exception of Thomas, to the top of the A-list. Florentina was no stranger to hard work, but it had been a good few years since she had grafted to this extent, working twelve-hour days for six, sometimes seven, days a week. To her surprise, she loved every minute of it. She no longer had the time to worry about what Crawford was up to, or how Abi was stealing her limelight. Her concern for Thomas had also lessened now he had taken to sending regular updates by text. In fact, the only thing currently causing her concern was her unfinished business with Cory Flemming.

The pictures she had taken before being summoned to Hammersmith were, she had to admit, rather good. They had used the best ones for their website and their social media accounts and a rather sultry black and white close-up now stared down at Florentina from the office wall. Whilst it was a pleasure to see his handsome face on a daily basis, it was also immensely frustrating. Particularly today. She didn't need anyone to tell her it was November fifth, fireworks had been going off in her knickers all day. She thought of the vibrator in her bedroom drawer and let out a sigh. Regular bursts of relief certainly helped, but a pink, battery operated toy was not exactly ideal.

Her initial suspicions of Abi appeared unfounded. Apparently, Abi had heard a male voice from inside the office and presumed, from the American accent, it must be Cory Flemming. 'He's the only American I know,' she'd told her mother. Not wanting to dwell on the alternative, Florentina had accepted Abi's explanation. She was less convinced, however, by Crawford's story, although even he seemed to be towing the line since his altercation with the law.

'Remember that girl I saw at Marylebone?' Lydia asked now, a smile spreading across her face.

'I think so. Ula something or other?'

'Ursla,' Lydia corrected. 'She's just sent me an email. Her mum's agreed she can come in for a test shoot.'

Not having seen the girl concerned, Florentina was struggling to get excited. Lydia, on the other hand, was clapping her hands with joy. 'She's the next big thing, Florentina, you mark my words. You should've seen her. Her cheekbones are sharper than Max's scalpel.'

'Show me her picture again,' Florentina said, rising from her chair and striding across to Lydia's desk.

Lydia scrolled through the pictures on her smartphone until she found the one she was looking for.

Florentina looked at the screen and frowned. 'Seriously? She looks just like any other sulky teenager.'

'It doesn't do her justice,' Lydia said. 'Trust me, she's amazing.'

'When's she coming in?'

'When shall I suggest? You need to be here to take the pictures.'

Florentina returned to her own desk and checked her diary. 'How about Friday? Where's she coming from?'

'Milton Keynes.'

'Milton Keynes? I only ever went there once. Came home with a parking ticket and blisters the size of golf balls.'

'That's what you get for shopping in a pair of Louboutins. I'll suggest Friday afternoon then. Reserve it in your diary.'

Lydia began tapping on her keyboard, oblivious to her friend's wry smile.

'The blisters weren't on my feet, darling. They were on my knees. Carpet burns were a bugger in those days.'

Things were also looking good for Crawford. His team was unbeaten in the last six games, Cory Flemming was back to full fitness, and his sex life was back on track. Florentina's accusations had forced him to cut down his visits to Simone's apartment, but now she was preoccupied with the agency, he was free to come and go as he pleased. Although, he had to admit, his wife was a lot easier to live with since she had found something to occupy her time. She was also surprisingly good at it, if Max's reports were anything to go by. Apparently KTH was the name on everyone's lips and Florentina and Lydia were revelling in their early success. He wasn't particularly impressed when he saw Cory Flemming's face splashed all over the KTH website – he'll be signing up for *Strictly* next! – but there was no harm done. He was back on the pitch and that was all Crawford was bothered about.

'Hi, Dad.'

'Abi! What are you doing here? Why didn't you tell me you were coming?'

Crawford wasn't usually a lover of surprises but his daughter was the obvious exception. He stood to kiss her on the cheek as she sat on the edge of his desk.

'I was just passing, literally. I had to run an errand for Lydia so I thought I'd drop by and say hi.'

'Well, I'm glad you did. How's it all going? Any new pictures to show me?'

She opened her Instagram page on her phone and handed it to her dad.

'Wow! You look amazing, sweetheart. As always. Where were these taken?'

'In Birmingham, by the canal. It was a contract for Max Mara. And,' she said, standing up and twirling around, 'I got to keep the coat.'

Crawford smiled. 'It suits you, my angel. So, it's working out all right then? With your mother, I mean.'

'I guess so,' she answered, removing the coat and draping it over the back of a chair. 'As silly as it sounds, we don't actually see that much of each other.' She picked up a trophy from the desk and examined the plaque. 'Manager of the Month,' she read aloud. 'When did you win this?'

'October. We're up to sixth in the league, in case you hadn't noticed.'

'Sorry,' she said with a guilty smile. 'Well done.'

Crawford laughed at her less than enthusiastic response.

'What did I do to deserve a family with absolutely no interest in football?'

His thoughts immediately turned to Thomas. He hadn't spoken to him since news of his homosexuality became public. He was no longer angry. How could he be after his own idiotic behaviour? He was disappointed though. Disappointed by the way Thomas had handled it; ran away like a frightened boy instead of standing up for himself like a man.

'It wouldn't do for us all to like the same things,' Abi said, matter of factly. 'How boring would the world be if that was the case? Talking of which, I spoke to Thomas last night.'

Crawford bristled at the mention of his son's name. It was a habit he was finding increasingly difficult to shake. 'And?'

'And, what?'

'And,' he wasn't sure exactly what he wanted to know. 'How is he?'

'He's good. Very good, in fact. His paintings are selling really well. Are you still mad at him, Dad?'

He leaned forward in his chair and studied his daughter, resting his forearms on the desk as he did so and linking his hands. 'I'm not mad at him, Abi. I'm disappointed, that's all.'

'Disappointed he's gay? Disappointed he's not a footballer? Disappointed how, exactly?'

'Both, I suppose. No father wants his son to be gay. The very thought of it makes me want to throw up. And yes, of course I'm disappointed he doesn't play football. I just took it for granted that's what he'd do. His refusal to even consider it was like a kick in the teeth.'

Abi sat down in the chair opposite her father. 'He's no good at it, Dad. He tried. He practised like mad whenever you weren't there. He so desperately wanted to make you proud.'

This was news to Crawford. 'I had no idea,' he admitted. 'Why didn't he tell me?'

'He tried. You wouldn't listen.'

This, he could believe. He very rarely listened to anyone in his family, so obsessed was he with himself and his career. He wasn't about to admit that to Abi, though.

'Well, he didn't try very hard this time, did he? Why didn't he tell me he was gay? Why did I have to read about it in the fucking papers? Sorry.' He instantly regretted his outburst. The last thing he wanted to do was fall out with his daughter.

'It's not me you need to apologise to, Dad. Thomas may have made choices you disapprove of, but he's a talented artist and, more importantly, he's a decent human being. So what if he's gay? It's not like he woke up one day and decided he liked men. He was born that way. He's probably been in denial for years worrying about what you would say.'

Crawford pushed back his chair and stood to put on his jacket. 'I tried to make it easy for him. Served it on a plate, in fact.' He was talking to himself rather than to Abi.

'What do you mean?'

He stood in front of the mirror and adjusted his tie. 'Never mind,' he said. 'Can you see yourself out? I need to be somewhere.'

Chapter 21

'I'm so glad you suggested this, darling. I can't remember the last time we both enjoyed a drink.'

They were back at the wine bar in Chelsea, cashmere scarves draped over the backs of their chairs, leather gloves stuffed in their handbags, a bottle of Merlot rapidly receding on the table.

'It was the launch party,' said Florentina. 'We haven't been out since then.'

'Good God. That was a month ago. We really are becoming rather dull.'

'Which is why we're here. Cheers.'

The two women clinked glasses then took long sips of wine whilst eyeing the clientele. Florentina had no idea if Cory still frequented this particular establishment, or indeed, if he ever did, but with nothing else to go on she could only hope.

'I'm not keen on the lighting in here,' said Lydia. 'It's too harsh, don't you think?'

Florentina smiled. 'Are you missing the interior design already? It's only been a few weeks.'

'Not at all!' she protested. 'Well, maybe just a little. I'm finding it hard to strike a balance between the two, if I'm honest, but it's early days. I'll figure it out. Well done for signing our first male model, by the way. Excellent work.'

Florentina allowed herself a smug smile. She'd heard that Danny Venus was looking for an agent and wasted no time in tracking him down. Patrick, an old photographer contact (the only contact she still had from her modelling days), had tipped her off after taking pictures for his portfolio. 'He'll go far, Florrie,' he had said. 'Sign him up, before someone else does.'

For a novice, he was pretty good and she had no reason to doubt he would be a huge success. His startling blue eyes and shoulder length copper hair were a striking combination and, at only nineteen, he was definitely worth investing in. But it wasn't Danny Venus she was interested in tonight.

'Strictly speaking,' she said, 'he wasn't our first male client. That honour went to Cory Flemming.'

'Oh, yes. The blond bombshell. I do believe you have a bit of a soft spot for your husband's number seven.'

Florentina swallowed her wine and brushed away the suggestion with the flick of her hand.

'He's easy on the eye, I'll admit. But I've had my fill of footballers, thank you very much. They're so boring. They don't drink, they're not allowed out after ten o'clock and they're up and out before the milkman's even been.'

'Milkman? When did you last see a milkman? I hate to say it but you're showing your age now, darling.'

Both women laughed, but Florentina's smile was forced. She was sensitive about her age at the best of times without being reminded of it.

'As for not drinking,' Lydia continued, nodding towards the bar, 'I'm not sure that's strictly true.'

Florentina's smile slid from her face at the sight of Grayson Delaney. The object of his attention, a twenty-something brunette with legs as long as a football pitch and eyelashes to match, was clearly taken in by whichever career highlight he was describing. No doubt the free drinks were helping. He was ordering cocktails faster than she could drink them.

'He's a law unto himself, that one,' she said, unable to disguise the edge of bitterness that accompanied her words.

'Oh? Something you want to tell me?'

Florentina took another sip of wine before answering. 'Mr Delaney was kind enough to inform me that Crawford is shagging the club physio.'

'What? Really? When was this?' Lydia managed to look shocked and sympathetic at the same time.

'The last time we were in here, actually. He took great pleasure in sharing the news and offered his services should I wish to have a little fun of my own.'

'The scoundrel!'

Florentina couldn't help but laugh. 'Scoundrel? Now who's showing her age? I haven't heard that word in years. Anyway, I told him where to go, obviously. As for Crawford, I'm not sure I care if he's playing away or not.'

'Of course you do, darling. But why didn't you tell me? I can't believe you kept this bottled up for so long.'

'I wasn't sure if it was true at first. Then I thought it had ended. Now I really don't care.'

'I doubt that's true.' She placed a hand on Florentina's arm and squeezed it. 'You should tell me these things. A problem shared and all that. Oh, don't look now, but your boyfriend's just walked in.'

Florentina followed her friend's gaze just in time to see Cory Flemming stride to the bar. Her heartbeat accelerated and she tried, unsuccessfully, to appear disinterested.

'He's not my boyfriend,' she said. 'Although, given a choice between him and that prick Delaney, Cory Flemming would win hands down.'

'Don't you mean pants down?'

Their laughter attracted the attention of numerous other drinkers, including the group of footballers at the bar. At least five of Crawford's team were now looking in their direction. Cory, Florentina noticed, was the only one drinking water. She nodded a greeting and Lydia waved a hand. She was rewarded with a wink from Cory, but the treat was soured by Grayson's sneer.

'He's certainly a looker, I'll give you that,' Lydia said, still smiling in Cory's direction. 'And he sure did us a favour agreeing to that shoot. Those pictures were amazing. Thanks to your photography, obviously.'

In the little spare time that Florentina now had, she messed around with lenses, lighting and props, studied photographs by other, well known photographers and read tips and advice on the internet. Not only was she enjoying it, she was also pretty good at it. She was also more than happy to take the credit for Cory's lucrative photoshoot.

'Why, thank you, my dear. I'm enjoying being behind the lens as a matter of fact. I should have taken it up years ago. And it's keeping my mind off Crawford and his latest squeeze.'

'It'll fizzle out,' said Lydia. 'They always do. He knows where his bread is buttered, darling.'

Florentina wasn't convinced that was actually true, but with Cory Flemming's presence lighting up the room like a disco ball, she didn't really care. Spotting him walking towards them, she ran her tongue over her lips and sat a little straighter. She had teamed her Versace leopard print jeans with a black halter-neck from Guess, her bare arms and shoulders dusted with Dior bronzing powder.

'Ladies,' he said, 'this is a pleasant surprise.'

Having his crotch in her eye-line was more than a little distracting, but Florentina diverted her gaze and treated him to her best smile.

'Likewise.'

'Good to see someone's setting a good example,' Lydia said, gesturing towards the glass of water in his hand.

'Alcohol's the enemy, Lydia. And soccer's a short career. Those lot would do well to remember that.' He nodded towards his teammates, currently entertaining Miss Long Legs and her friends.

'Not that it's done you two any harm, obviously.'

'Flattery will get you everywhere, Cory,' Florentina said. 'Would you like to join us?'

As much as she was enjoying the view, she was getting more than a little hot under the collar. Or, between the legs, in her case.

'Sure, just for a while. I'm not staying long. Just came to show my face. It's Frankie's birthday so I promised I'd come along.' He sat between the two of them, his hands splayed on the arms of the leather bucket chair.

'Frankie?' queried Florentina.

'Josh Franklin. My competition.'

'He plays up front,' Lydia explained. 'The young lad over there, in the black shirt.'

'He looks just like our paperboy,' said Florentina. 'Only younger.'

'Eighteen today,' said Cory. 'No doubt Grayson will give him a birthday to remember. Or not, as the case may be.'

'I take it your boss doesn't know they're all out drinking?'

'I guess not. Although he's hardly in a position to criticise at the moment, is he? No offence.'

Florentina waved away his apology with the flick of her hand.

'Besides,' he continued, 'there's no game this weekend. It's international week. None of this lot were selected.' This morsel of information clearly amused him.

'And you? No call up for you either?' asked Lydia.

'Declared myself unfit. Didn't want to risk my ankle.'

'Of course. How is it?'

'Between you and me, it's fine. Young Frankie will be getting splinters on the bench again before long.'

Florentina was desperate to change the subject but found herself unusually tongue-tied. She was both amused and irritated by her teenage-like behaviour.

'Well, I should be going,' he said, rising from his seat. 'Good to see you again, ladies.'

'You too,' they said in unison.

They watched him shake the hands of his teammates, patting the birthday boy on the back as he left. Lydia began talking about her schedule for the following day. Florentina, although seemingly paying attention, was actually hatching a plan.

Having first dropped Lydia off at home, Florentina gave further directions to the taxi driver. Except, it wasn't her own address she had given him, it was Cory Flemming's. Convinced she had detected a spark of interest in those denim-blue eyes, she had decided a home visit was the perfect solution. Not usually one for spontaneity she felt emboldened by her actions. She couldn't wait a moment longer to see, and feel, his naked perfection. Besides, she must be keeping Duracell in business the number of batteries she was getting through of late. She was wet with longing and convinced Cory Flemming would, for once, enjoy an early bath.

'Here you go, love,' announced the cabbie. 'Twenty-six pounds fifty. Nice gaff.'

Florentina counted three ten-pound notes from her purse and slid them through the hatch.

'Keep the change.'

She was just about to climb out of the taxi when she noticed the cars in the drive. She knew Cory drove a red Ferrari – Crawford believed the whole squad should only drive blue cars and had been furious when Cory had arrived in a red one – but she was stunned at the sight of the white Mercedes. She'd recognise that car anywhere. It was Abi's.

She slammed the cab door shut and re-fastened her seatbelt. 'Take me back to Chelsea,' she barked. 'Hollywood Road.'

Chapter 22

The knock on the door caused Thomas to jump, sending a line of black paint across a brilliant blue sky.

'Shit!' he said to himself. Then louder, 'Just a minute!'

He balanced his brush on the palette, wiped his hands across his once-white apron and snatched open the door. A pair of bright green eyes stared back at him.

'Justin?'

'Hi. Sorry to call unannounced. Can I come in?'

'Sure. Yes. Sorry. Come in, come in.' Thomas stepped aside, confused by the sudden appearance of Justin McKenzie and more than a little embarrassed at the thought of their first meeting.

'This is a surprise,' he said, closing the door and gesturing towards the sitting area. 'Have a seat. Can I get you anything? Tea? Coffee?'

'Aye, whatever you're having. Thanks.'

Thomas busied himself at the sink, his back to his unexpected guest, now seated next to the idle wood burner. He couldn't have been more surprised if Superman had flown in. 'What brings you to Scotland?'

'Visiting my folks. I've been in Glasgow since the weekend. Thought I'd drop in and say hi.'

Thomas switched on the kettle and spooned coffee into two mugs. 'Milk and sugar?'

'Both. One sugar, thanks.'

'I take it you're still working with Max?'

'Aye. It was Max who gave me your address, actually.'

Thomas turned around to face him. 'Really?'

'Can I be totally honest?' He was shrugging off his khaki jeep jacket as he spoke.

Thomas frowned, apprehensive about what was about to be said, then nodded.

'It was Max who sent me. He asked me to check on you, make sure you were okay.'

Thomas smiled. Now it made sense. Max had texted him regularly since he'd left London. He should have known he'd check up on him somehow. Although, he couldn't help but feel a little disappointed that Justin hadn't come of his own accord.

'Does he know about us?' Thomas asked.

'Us? I wasn't aware there was an *us*.'

'You know what I mean.' He handed a mug of coffee to Justin and sat in the opposite chair.

'No. He knows I'm gay though. I told him in my interview. Didn't want it coming back to bite me at a later date.'

Thomas thought back to the conversation he'd had with Max in his office, when he'd asked him to loan him the money. 'He never said.'

'Why would he? Soul of discretion, our Max.'

Thomas took a sip of coffee and then, for the first time, looked properly at his visitor. He would never forget those eyes. He found it difficult to hold his gaze.

'What about your parents? Do they know?'

'I think they knew before I did. They certainly weren't surprised when I told them. They're cool. Supportive, you know?'

Thomas couldn't help but envy Justin. He was comfortable in his own skin, totally at ease and relaxed. Even the way he sipped his coffee, perched on a second-hand chair in a tiny, unfamiliar cottage, suggested a confidence that Thomas had never felt.

'So, how long are you here for?' he asked.

'I'm due back at work on Monday. Guess I'll stick around for a day or two. See the sights.'

Thomas wondered briefly if Max was playing some kind of matchmaking game but quickly quashed the idea. Max didn't play games. He sometimes forgot that other people's families had no hidden agenda. No egos to feed, no ulterior motives.

'I can show you around if you like? Be good to have some company. It's usually just me and my paintings.'

Justin looked through the open door into the dining room, where numerous paintings were propped up against the walls. 'May I?'

'Sure, go ahead.' He'd been making rapid progress with his paintings and was delighted with the results. There was something about the light up in Scotland. The sky in London was either dirty grey or watery blue, no in-between. Up here it could be as lavender as the fields in Provence, as red as a Christmas candle, or as purple as freshly bruised skin. He often watched the sun setting over the sea, trying to capture its ever-changing hues, torn between transferring it onto canvas and just gazing at its beauty.

'Wow, these are amazing!'

Still finding it hard to accept praise for his work, he muttered a bashful, 'Thanks.'

'Seriously, Thomas. I saw your paintings at your mum's launch party but these are something else.'

'I seem to have found my forte up here. It doesn't matter how many times I look out of the window, it's always different. Looking at the sky is like watching a drama unfold. The clouds can be beautiful. They can be fearsome. They can be downright evil. And the sunsets are incredible.'

'Well, your passion is reflecting in your work, that's for sure,' Justin observed. 'Where are you selling them?'

'The castle has a gift shop-cum-gallery. I sell most of them in there. I thought about selling some online, but I can only produce so many. I'd rather not paint under pressure. The results are always better when I don't have a deadline.' He thought of the cityscapes he'd painted for the architect and his mood instantly darkened as he recalled those days and weeks of anguish.

Justin had stopped in front of his latest work in progress.

'Accident?' he asked, his thumb aimed at the ugly black streak across the otherwise perfect sea view.

'I was just touching up the granite on Ailsa Craig when you knocked the door.'

'Oh! Sorry.' His look was sheepish, those green eyes ever mischievous.

'No worries. I can fix it. Another coffee?'

'No, thanks. I'd better get off.' He checked his watch. A classic, leather strapped Gucci, Thomas noticed. A sign of good taste. 'Need to check in to my digs.'

'Where are you staying?'

'I booked a B&B by the golf course. Nothing fancy.'

'Do you play?' Thomas had never been interested in golf, but he knew his father and Max Templeton-Howe liked a game.

'Aye. Badly. Didn't bring my clubs though. Besides, I'm not sure I could afford Turnberry's prices.'

'You might be right.' The golf resort along the coast had a reputation for both its quality and its green fees.

Thomas followed his guest towards the door. He'd enjoyed his company, brief as it was, and was sorry to see him leave.

'Give me a shout if you need a tour guide. A bit of fresh air will do me good. Do you want my number?'

'I already have it. I'll call you.'

Thomas didn't doubt that he would. He smiled for the rest of the day.

Florentina was suffering. Her self-loathing was second only to the private humiliation that burned inside her like a furnace. She'd sought solace in a gin bottle and a few too many pills and had woken this morning still clutching the empty bottle. Her hands were shaking and the stabbing pains in her stomach were almost as bad as those in her head. She'd dragged herself to the office but had barely looked up from her desk all morning and was now sitting with her head in her hands in an attempt to stop it from throbbing. Lydia was clearly struggling to understand why Florentina was in such a bad way when the two of them had consumed exactly the same amount of wine.

'You look dreadful, darling. You didn't drive here, did you?'

Through her fog of despair, Florentina had recognised the need to call a taxi and had struggled to contain the liquid contents in her stomach for the entire painful journey.

'Are you sure you're not coming down with something?' Lydia asked. 'It can't be the wine, we weren't exactly excessive, were we?'

Florentina couldn't answer. She felt sure if she opened her mouth, the whole sorry tale would emerge and she would die from shame. She felt tears sting her eyes and squeezed them shut.

'What is it, Florentina? Is it Crawford? Tell me, darling. Is it about that physio, is that it?'

Florentina remained mute. She felt a warm hand on her arm and flinched at the physical contact. She didn't deserve sympathy. She should be punished not comforted. She was a despicable human being.

'I can't help you if you don't talk to me. Whatever it is can't be that bad. Let me help you. That's what friends are for.'

In the end, Florentina stood up, plucked her jacket from the coat stand, and walked out.

At home, she opened a new bottle of gin and poured herself a large glass. She carried both glass and bottle upstairs to her bedroom. With Thomas still in Scotland, Abi on a shoot for Max Factor and Crawford at the club, she could drink, and cry, as much as she wanted. She felt bad for the way she'd treated Lydia, but she just couldn't tell her the truth; couldn't tell her anything, in fact. Where would she start? *'Oh, I threw myself at someone young enough to be my son, only to discover he's shagging my daughter. Never mind, it could've been worse!'* Admittedly, it *could* have been worse. At least her humiliation was private. Her attempted seduction of Cory hadn't progressed beyond harmless flirtation so no one was laughing at her behind her back. No one was talking about her, telling stories about the old hag who thought she could pull a twenty-year-old sex symbol, or the evil woman who tried to snare her daughter's boyfriend, or the has-been who thought she was still beautiful. She caught sight of her reflection. Her face looked like something from a child's face painting competition. She swung her arm back, about to throw her glass at the mirror. Instead, her face crumpled and she slid to the floor, the spilled gin quickly soaking into the plush carpet.

It was purely the need for alcohol that roused her, the bottle of gin an imaginary arm, pulling her from the floor. She poured herself a large measure and slumped on the bed, staring at her discarded Carvela snakeskin courts. Her vision blurred and the shoes merged together to form a python, sliding up onto the bed, over her lifeless body, before circling her neck and squeezing tight.

She coughed involuntarily and rose from her daze, her hand instantly stroking her neck. She reached for her glass, drinking the gin like water, both seeking and fearing oblivion. It was a feeling she'd experienced before. Losing both parents, so tragically, at the age of eighteen, was something she would never forget. The police, to this day, hadn't charged anyone with starting the fire; had no clue as to the culprit. Florentina had argued with her mother that morning. She was desperate to go to the Clothes Show the following day at London's Olympia. Obsessed with anything 'fashion', she had planned her outfit to perfection, even had her hair highlighted at the local salon where she worked part-time as a trainee. Her mother had forbidden her from going, said it was a waste of money and unsafe for her to travel alone. Florentina was beyond distraught. She was convinced the new live show, based on her favourite TV programme, would be the key to her success. It would be full of model scouts and famous faces, fashion shows and makeup demonstrations. There was no way she was missing it. Her father, as usual, had sided with her mother, agreeing she couldn't go. Unused to disobeying her parents, she felt particularly wretched when she left the house that night, sneaking down the stairs after they'd closed the restaurant and waiting for the sound of her father's exhausted slumber. She had walked to the bus station, constantly looking over her shoulder and jumping at the slightest noise. Once on the bus she had relaxed a little, safe once more in numbers, but still plagued with guilt at her betrayal. She had left a note on the kitchen table. They'd know where she was, at least.

She slept most of the way, unwilling to make polite conversation with strangers and unable to fight the weight of her eyelids. Arriving in London after the long, nine-hour journey, she bought coffee and a croissant in a scruffy, dimly lit café, slowly sipping the sour coffee until it was cold. She asked a policeman for directions, counted out coins for a bus driver, stared in wonder at Big Ben, and sheltered in doorways when it rained. Finally arriving at Olympia, she swapped her Nike trainers for her highest, peep toe stilettos, stuffed her denim jacket in her canvas shoulder bag and undid the top three buttons of her white blouse. Her acid-washed jeans, purchased in Top Shop just a week before, were high-waisted but tight. Long, feathered earrings swung from her ears and shimmering turquoise powder decorated her eyes. Being one of the first through the doors, the toilets were almost empty. She took advantage of the space and studied herself in the mirror, turning one way, and then the other. Pouting, winking, smiling. Eventually, satisfied with what she saw, she went in search of her future.

Returning home from London she had expected a verbal thrashing from her father. A lecture on disrespect, a reminder of how lucky she was, how disappointed they were, how worried they'd been. She had prepared herself for a scalding from her mother; expected to be grounded for a week, maybe two.

'But I was spotted!' she'd say. 'I told you, didn't I? Look.'

She would show them the business card from Melody Models, win them over with her excitement, calm them down with her apologies. But she didn't get to do any of that. She wasn't greeted with a ticking off from her father. She was greeted by a policeman and a burnt-out building.

There was a fire… There was nothing we could do… We were too late… Too fierce… Too strong… Too dangerous… So sorry…

She could hear the words as though it were yesterday, feel the heat on her face, smell the smoke in the air, see the tears in his eyes as he told her her parents were dead. And now, over thirty years later, she was still choking on the guilt.

Crawford couldn't remember the last time he and Max had enjoyed a pint together. The invitation to join him in All Bar One couldn't have come at a better time. He was anxious about his impending appearance at the magistrates' court on Monday and, with no Premier League games this weekend, was struggling to adjust to the shift in his routine. The two men were attracting a fair bit of attention, from staff and customers alike. Max found it amusing, but Crawford was more than a little irritated, particularly as he had overheard the words 'drink-driving' more than once already.

'Just ignore them,' Max urged, as they settled at a high table near the window. 'None of us are perfect. What's the prediction anyway? Has your brief told you what to expect?'

'Difficult to say. Depends who's presiding. Six months, maybe more. They'll no doubt make an example of me and add a zero to the fine.'

He took a sip of his Hiver Blonde and tried to get comfortable on the hard, wooden bar stool.

'The chairman's none too pleased, needless to say. Anything in the front pages gives him a hernia. It's the back pages or nothing as far as he's concerned.'

He watched as Max unwound the black, wool scarf from around his neck, sitting it on a neighbouring stool.

'Well, let's hope the court hearing is the end of it. You've had more than your fair share of front-page news of late.'

'Tell me about it.' He took another sip of beer and shook off his own heavy coat. 'Have you heard from Thomas?'

'Shouldn't I be asking you that? He's your son, Crawford.'

'I don't need a lecture, Max. Have you heard from him or not?'

Both men sighed. Crawford averted his eyes and watched a restaurant cruiser cut through the Thames.

'I text him from time to time, make sure he's okay.'

'And is he?' His eyes were back on Max.

'Obviously, yes. I'd tell you if he wasn't.'

'Would you?'

'Of course I would.' His indignation was clear. 'I tried to tell you before when something was wrong. Not that you listened.' This time it was Max who looked away.

'I tried to talk to him,' Crawford lied. 'But he buggered off to Scotland before I got the chance. What did he say anyway? I mean, I know he told you he was… you know…'

'Gay?'

'Aye, that.' He looked around uncomfortably. 'But what else?'

'What do you mean, "what else"?'

'Well, what made him come to you in the first place?'

'He was being blackmailed,' Max said, after a moment of hesitation.

Crawford stared at him, a knot of nausea forming in his throat.

'He asked me to lend him the money, but I refused. I tried to encourage him to tell the truth. Tell *you* the truth.'

Crawford still couldn't speak.

'He was scared, Crawford. Scared of what you'd say, what you'd think. The low-life wanted fifty grand.'

'Who was he?' he finally managed to ask.

'Some guy called Vince. It was a set-up, apparently, or so Thomas seemed to think. Appeared from nowhere outside The Half Moon.'

Crawford closed his eyes. Let out an audible sigh. The knot of nausea tightened.

'You can probably guess the rest. Thomas wouldn't, or rather, couldn't, pay the money. The pictures were printed and streamed and Thomas, terrified of what you'd say, made himself scarce.'

'Bollocks!' Crawford's fist hit the table, attracting even more unwanted attention.

Max grabbed his pint as it tilted on the table then mopped up the spillage with a tissue from his pocket. 'Crawford! What the hell?'

Crawford finished his own pint in one swallow and banged the empty glass on a beer mat.

'He should've come to me! I could've fixed it!'

'Calm down, mate,' Max said, moving Crawford's glass from arm's reach. 'It's done now. It's out in the open. I was really worried about him at first, but he's okay now, honestly. You just need to talk to him.'

'And what about that bastard Vince?' He almost spat the name at Max.

'What about him? Gone to ground I suppose. Or targeting some other rich kid. You couldn't see his face in any of the pictures so he knew what he was doing.'

'Didn't he just?' Crawford couldn't bear to hear any more. 'Same again?'

Chapter 23

He pulled up outside the terraced house and switched off the engine. A light smir settled on the windscreen. The street was only just waking up. Bedroom curtains were being opened, lights were switched on, and the postman was whistling a merry tune. *He must be fucking freezing*, he thought, noticing the postman's shorts. He rubbed his hands together to generate some warmth and wiggled his toes in his shoes. There was no movement in the house. The curtains were still drawn upstairs and down. His top lip curled at the apparent neglect on display. Crawford was not judgmental. He never looked down on the working class, he was from a working-class family himself, but there was no excuse for laziness. Lack of money didn't stop you from sweeping the leaves from your front step, or cleaning your windows. It didn't stop you pulling the weeds from between the paving slabs, or wiping the cobwebs from above your front door. The other houses in the street looked smart and well-kept and he wondered what the neighbours thought of the rotten apple that was number nine. He thought of his childhood home in Ayr. The terraced house in Barns Street shone like the North Star. His mam was forever polishing the brass door knocker and sweeping the step. He remembered her cleaning the windows with vinegar and old newspapers and pouring bleach down the outside drain. It was a solicitor's office now, more's the pity, the once cosy front room no doubt a waiting room for cheated wives seeking a divorce or drunk drivers trying to buy themselves a shorter ban. He smiled at the irony and forced himself from the past.

The postman was getting closer so Crawford climbed out of his Jaguar and made his way up the front path. He dug his keys from his pocket and pretended to open the door.

'Morning!' the postman said from behind him.

'Morning,' said Crawford, holding out his hand. 'Shall I take those?'

'Sure, there you go. Have a good day now.'

Crawford leafed through the envelopes waiting for the postman to disappear from view. Once he could no longer hear the whistled tune of 'Don't Worry, Be Happy', he returned to his car, the bundle of envelopes beside him on the passenger seat.

It had been surprisingly mild over the last few days. The bright morning sun chased away the usual November chill and the autumnal shades of the surrounding woods added their own spurious warmth. Thomas had taken to sitting on an old fallen tree trunk in the castle grounds, capturing the seasonal tones. Leaves the colour of custard spilled through the woods, dotted with strawberry reds and chocolate browns; a feast for the eyes. He was looking forward to sharing its extraordinary beauty with Justin. He couldn't have visited at a better time.

He arrived in his car at ten thirty prompt, parking in the allocated space and retrieving his coat from the back seat. Thomas locked up the cottage and led the way along the path towards the castle, eager to witness Justin's reaction. Although he saw the castle almost every day, he was still awestruck by its magnificence and felt sure Justin would be equally impressed.

'Wow!'

Thomas smiled at the look on Justin's face. The green eyes were sparkling even more than usual.

'Impressive, isn't it?'

'It sure is. I can't believe I haven't been here before. Glasgow isn't exactly far, is it? How come I've never been to Culzean?'

Thomas laughed at his pronunciation. 'It's pronounced Cul-ain. The z is silent. Don't worry, everyone gets it wrong. Anyway, Scotland's full of castles, as I'm sure you know. Maybe you just never got around to this one.'

'Shame on me,' he said, gazing up at the clock tower. 'Or, shame on my parents for not bringing me here.'

'Better late than never,' Thomas said. 'Come on, if we head this way we can walk around the duck pond. Well, it's more of a lake than a pond. And from there we can get to the beach.'

Thomas was enjoying the company immensely. He wasn't starved of company, exactly. There was Rupert, the guy in the cottage next door, and Heather in the gift shop. But quality time with someone his own age was a rare treat. The fact that it was Justin was an added bonus.

'So, do you want to talk about it?' Justin asked, as they watched a toddler throw chunks of bread to a raft of hungry ducks. 'The pictures, I mean?'

Thomas looked at him, unsure what to say. He didn't know if he wanted to talk about it or not.

'You don't have to,' said Justin. 'I just thought it might help to, you know, lighten the load.'

'There's not much to say,' he said, continuing along the path, hands shoved deep into his trouser pockets. 'I trusted someone I shouldn't have and paid the price. Well, I didn't pay the price, that's the whole point.'

'Max says your father is homophobic. Is he?'

The path widened and Justin fell in step alongside him.

'You could say that. He's old-fashioned. Things are black and white. Grey doesn't exist.'

'He's not exactly perfect himself though, is he? I take it you heard about his drink-drive charge?'

'Yeah, Abi told me. Stupid idiot.'

The path climbed to a hill and Thomas took his hands out of his pockets to aid the ascent.

'It's not just that, though. It's the whole football thing. He can't stand the fact that I don't play. I'm just one big disappointment.'

He stood for a moment to catch his breath. Justin appeared to do the same, waiting a while before responding.

'It happens to the best of us, mate. My dad still hasn't forgiven me for not working in insurance. Insurance! Can you imagine how dull that must be? Wanted me to take over the business when he retired. I couldn't think of anything worse.'

They continued through the woods. Daggers of sunlight pierced the earth.

'Why plastic surgery?' Thomas wanted to know.

'Used to watch this show on TV, *Nip Tuck*. Did you watch it? It's the usual American trash but the surgeons made a mint. And I was fascinated by the changes, you know? Not just nose jobs and tummy tucks but real, life changing stuff. Burns, birth marks, that sort of thing.

I wanted to help people, make a difference, not just flog them a car insurance policy.'

'And what does your dad think now? He must be proud of you.'

'Aye, I think he is. Besides, my sister's just started at the family firm so the pressure's off.'

His laugh startled a grey squirrel and they both watched as it raced up a birch tree.

'So, will you go back? To London, I mean?' Justin asked.

'I'm not sure. I love it up here and my paintings are selling really well. I'm finally standing on my own two feet and it feels really good. I'm not sure I could go back to the suffocating atmosphere at home.'

'You'll have to face him sooner or later, you know.'

Thomas stopped walking and let out a heavy sigh. Was he really so easy to read? He could feel Justin watching him, waiting for a response. He averted his gaze and stared instead at a cluster of fungi clinging to a Scots elm. He fiddled around with his phone, taking pictures from different angles, kneeling on a cushion of leaves to get closer to the gills. Justin remained silent.

'I'm in no hurry,' he said at last, brushing a stray leaf from the knee of his jeans. 'Come on, it's this way.'

They continued in silence for a while, Thomas stopping to take pictures of ancient, gnarled branches, a surprisingly tame grey squirrel and a glimpse of a sea view. They paused at a scenic spot overlooking the crescent beach at Maidens and smiled for a selfie, Thomas, as ever, seduced by the green eyes smiling back at him from the screen.

They descended the steps down on to the beach, both surprised by the strength of the wind. Justin pulled up the zip of his coat and lifted the collar around his neck. Rolls of surf unwound themselves onto the sand, releasing shells, reclaiming seaweed. It reminded Thomas of the two pence pusher machines in the old arcade at Girvan. He used to spend hours in there with his nan, feeding coppers into the slot, waiting for the wall to slide forward and push the coins off the edge. If he was lucky, he'd win enough to buy an ice cream with a chocolate Flake.

'I don't blame you for wanting to stay,' Justin said, his voiced raised over the wind. 'It's beautiful here.'

Thomas drank in the scene in front of them. The sun's rays were like spotlights through the clouds, dotting circles of light onto the sea. Boats danced in the harbour, their masts winking like frisky sailors. Ailsa Craig looked on elegantly from afar, an iconic, timeless beauty. The Isle of Arran stretched out across the horizon, its sleeping warrior moniker well earned.

'It already feels like home,' Thomas admitted. 'I feel more relaxed here than I've felt in years. And it's so much more stimulating than London. The light's different, the air's different,' he stopped to breathe in the air, as though to reinforce his point. 'Everything's different.'

They bought bottles of water in the village shop and Mars Bars for energy. They'd walked for over two hours but still had to walk back, rejecting the option of the bus. Thomas had offered to cook dinner for the two of them and he added a bottle of wine to his purchases, sliding it into his ever-present rucksack. He would often collect leaves from the forest or stones from the sea, recreating their texture and shade on canvas. More often than not, he would return with a bag full of plastic, retrieved from the beach. Bottles, crisp packets, straws and plastic bags would pour from his bag into the blue recycling bin and Thomas would slam the lid shut in disgust at people's disregard of their planet.

Justin was easy company, Thomas concluded later. He was making spaghetti Bolognese and Justin had helped to chop the onion and peel the mushrooms, whilst chatting about his childhood and, ironically, his love of football. He and his father were lifelong fans of Glasgow Celtic, the one thing the two of them still had in common.

Opening the wine and pouring it into two cheap, supermarket glasses, he handed one to Justin. 'Cheers,' he said, 'to friendship.'

Their glasses met but their eyes did not. Thomas had to look away. Those green eyes represented temptation and he knew, if he looked into them, it was a temptation he wouldn't be able to resist. He sipped his wine and stirred the bubbling contents on the stove. The delicious aroma of tomato, onion and garlic fought for space in the tiny cottage kitchen and Thomas's stomach growled with hunger. Justin was now seated, leafing through a leaflet he'd picked up at the castle. Thomas stole a look at him. Justin's eyes, to Thomas, were like a bottle of wine to an alcoholic. They taunted him, lured him, promised him utopia. But, like intoxication, it was a temporary bliss. It would be followed by guilt, shame and self-contempt. Or would it? He wasn't that person any more. He no longer had to hide a secret for fear of judgment or scorn. He didn't have a dangerous addiction that was damaging to himself or anyone else. Perhaps the relationship between himself and the object of his desire could be one of permanent euphoria, a blissful elation without the hangover. He looked again at Justin, resistance disappearing with the sunset.

Chapter 24

'Cheers, mate. You're a star. I owe you one.' Crawford was pumping the hand of his solicitor outside the magistrates' court. Having been told to expect at least a six-month ban, the six weeks actually imposed had been a welcome surprise. The fifty grand fine wasn't quite as easy to swallow, but he could live with that, although, he suspected the chairman would be issuing him with a fine of his own.

'Well, a couple of tickets to the Spurs game wouldn't go amiss.' The solicitor was still smiling, his pinstripe, three-piece suit announcing his profession to the stream of passers-by, as well as the posse of press pointing cameras and microphones in their direction.

'No problem,' said Crawford, 'it's the least I can do. I'll have them sent to your office.'

He was used to people asking him for tickets, it came with the job. More often than not he was irritated by such requests, hangers-on wanting something for nothing, but in this particular case, he didn't mind one bit.

After making a brief statement, his face a picture of remorse, he flagged down a taxi and headed home. He wasn't expected at the club this morning and he still had things he needed to do. With a bit of luck he'd have the house to himself, although Florentina was proving more than a little unpredictable of late. Her initial enthusiasm for the agency seemed to have plunged as quickly as it had peaked and, from what he could gather, she had barely left the house all weekend. He briefly wondered if she was ill but didn't dwell on the thought. He had much more important things to worry about.

His study, although not exactly spacious, was large enough to boast a selection of trophies along with a host of other football paraphernalia. Various autobiographies lined the bookshelves (Harry Redknapp and Peter Crouch yet to be read), signed photographs decorated the walls and his treasured collection of Scottish International caps formed a proud pillar beside the window. He poured himself two fingers of Scotch and sat heavily in his executive leather chair. He picked up the framed photograph of his father, taken when he'd won the Scottish Cup with Aberdeen, a red and white striped scarf draped over his shoulders, his lopsided smile as wide as the pitch. It pained him to see the photograph, to remember the man he became, a shadow of the victorious sportsman that smiled back at him.

He heard the front door slam and placed the photograph back in its place. Whoever it was wouldn't bother him. He swallowed a mouthful of whisky, enjoying the lingering burn at the back of his throat and down into his chest. The burn he could feel in the pit of his stomach was already there, had been for a while. Since someone had taken advantage of his only son. Since an action designed to help had backfired spectacularly. Since someone had dared to double-cross him. He pulled the wad of letters from his office drawer and scanned them once more.

'I'll find you, you bastard.'

Florentina could sense, rather than hear, Crawford in his study. A hint of his heavy aftershave lingered in the hallway and a menacing mood seeped through the walls. She kicked off her shoes at the kitchen door and trod a silent path to the fridge. He was no doubt seething after his court hearing this morning and the last thing she wanted was to interrupt his predictable fury. She dropped two ice cubes into a glass and poured herself a large measure of gin from the bottle in her tote bag. The convenience store two streets away really was just that. It certainly beat the intrusive eyes that usually followed her around the supermarket. The Indian cashier had barely looked at her when she'd paid for the gin. Well, she'd assumed he was Indian, she couldn't be sure.

Sliding the bottle back into her bag, she tiptoed upstairs, glass in hand. She wasn't in the habit of listening at doors but something in Crawford's voice made her pause mid-step.

'I don't care how you do it, or how long it takes, just find him! He's not that fucking clever, he's bound to leave clues… No one makes a fool of me. Do you hear me…? Just sort it!'

Florentina jumped at the sound of the phone being slammed down and ran the last few steps to her bedroom. She took a sip of gin and tried to make sense of what she'd just heard. The conversation had taken her by surprise, expecting only to hear words relating to whatever ban the magistrate had seen fit to impose and how many weeks wages were eaten up by his fine. She sat on the edge of the bed and replayed the words in her mind. *Thomas! He must have been talking about Thomas!* She topped up her glass with shaking hands, jumbled thoughts bouncing around her brain like a pinball. For the first time in years she thought about Pia. Pia always knew what to do. Pia was always there when she needed her. She would know what to do about Crawford. And Thomas. And Abi. And Cory… Where was Pia? She needed Pia…

The girl reminded Abi of a baby monkey she had once seen in Battersea Park Zoo. Eyes as wide as dinner plates and fists clenched tight white, she was visibly trembling with fear. Lydia had tried to put her at ease, offered her a coffee, laughed a little at the erratic London climate, even complimented her on her faux-fur zebra print coat. Ursla, however, still looked like a frightened infant abandoned by her mother.

'Shall I take your coat?' Abi said, anxious to relieve the tension that was sucking the air out of the room. Ursla didn't speak, simply tugged at the sleeves of her coat and shrugged it off her bony shoulders.

'Sorry we had to re-arrange your appointment. I hope it didn't inconvenience you too much.'

There was a hint of resentment in Lydia's tone. Abi knew her mother hadn't been to the office since last Thursday. Lydia had been covering for her ever since and, Abi suspected, was fast running out of patience.

'Problems with our photographer,' Lydia explained. 'We'll get started shortly.'

Ursla managed a slight nod of the head.

Thankfully, Abi knew the name of the one photographer her mother kept in touch with – the one who tipped her off about Danny Venus – and he'd agreed to come in and do the shots for Ursla. Although, if the girl stayed as stiff as she was now, it would be a waste of everyone's time. She'd be more use as a corner flag than a model.

155

'She could do with a shot of vodka,' Abi whispered to Lydia. They looked up at the wall clock synchronously and shared a sly smile.

'Do you want to follow me, Ursla? We have some props you may want to look at, jazz up your pictures a bit.'

Ursla obediently followed Abi, who pulled a floppy white sun hat from the shelf and a floral silk hand fan.

'Just because it's cold outside, doesn't mean we can't warm things up in here. Talking of which...' She grabbed the vodka from behind a pile of photo albums and looked questioningly at Ursla. 'Want one?'

The girl looked behind her, obviously wondering what Lydia would think. 'Oh, don't worry about Lydia,' Abi said. 'She's cool.'

Abi poured them both a generous measure and added tonic and ice from the fridge. She was astonished to see Ursla knock hers back in one go.

'Wow! Did you need that?'

Ursla responded by holding out her glass for a top up, a hint of a smile forming at her lips. Abi dutifully poured her another and continued looking for props.

'How about this?' she asked, winding a red feather boa around the girl's neck.

The photoshoot was turning out much better than either of them had hoped. Surprisingly, and with a little help from the vodka, Ursla was a natural in front of the camera. Her pale blue eyes were flecked with white, like bluebells dusted with frost. Her hair, mousy brown to the natural eye, was streaked with gold like a Tiger's Eye gemstone. And her cheekbones cast shadows Cliff Richard would be proud of.

Abi could tell Lydia was impressed; she couldn't keep the smile from her face.

'I knew it!' Lydia said, 'I knew as soon as I saw her she'd be a star. She's just right for Berry Cosmetics, don't you think?'

Berry Cosmetics were looking for a fresh face to launch their new makeup campaign. According to Lydia, they'd already rejected each of the models recommended by KTH, including Abi, much to her disgust. Abi waited for Patrick to leave before voicing her opinion.

'I think she's amazing.' She surprised even herself by her genuine like of the girl.

'She's not classically beautiful, but she's certainly got something. And the camera loved her. I feel as though I should be jealous, but I'm not. I really liked her.'

Abi was so used to brash, vain, vindictive women. It made a refreshing change to meet a likeable girl. Someone she could be friends with, perhaps.

'What do you think your mother would say?' Lydia asked.

Abi snapped open the window blinds and looked out at the dank, grey sky. One mention of her mother and her mood matched the weather. She turned her attention to Ursla's pictures on the screen. Bright, cherry-red lips framed perfect sugar cube teeth. Blood-red feathers stroked powder-white skin.

'I don't think it matters. Sign her up, Lydia. She's perfect.'

Chapter 25

It had been over a week since Justin had returned to London. Thomas's emotions swayed like the branches outside his window. One minute he was happy, laughing at memories of their time together, the next he was sad, missing him with an ache he had never experienced before. Justin had stayed the night, returning to his B&B the following morning to collect his things before heading home. They had slept together, obviously, but they had also talked, mainly about the Kellys and the fractious dynamic within the family home. It felt good to open up. Thomas had never talked about his family before, certainly not so openly. He had briefly wondered if he should consult a counsellor or a life coach, or whatever they call themselves these days. Max had suggested the same when he had visited him at his office.

'You have a lot of issues, Thomas,' he had said. 'Not just your sexuality.'

He was certainly right about that. Once he'd started talking to Justin, he couldn't stop. The root of the problem was definitely his father, or so he believed, but the animosity between Abi and their mother also saddened him. As did the loss of his nan in Scotland, the violent death of the grandparents he'd never met, the constant struggle with his sexual identity, and the lack of the footballing gene.

'I even began to wonder if Dad wasn't my dad, if you know what I mean.'

Justin had propped himself up on one elbow and looked at Thomas. 'Seriously? You think he may not be your real father?'

'Yeah. No. I don't know. I'm just being stupid. There's no reason to think so. I suppose I was just looking for an excuse, something to explain why I was no good at it.'

'Not all kids follow in their parents' footsteps. We've had this conversation before. No wonder you're mixed up. You're worrying about things that might not even be true.'

Thomas had been lying on his back. He turned his head towards Justin, grateful it was too dark to see into his eyes. 'Do you think I look like him?'

Justin fell back onto his pillow and let out a sigh of frustration. 'Stop it, Thomas. You're being ridiculous. You need to talk to him. You can hide up here as long as you like but you're never going to be happy if you don't sort things out.'

He knew he was right. He'd have to go back to London at some point, anyway. He needed to empty his studio – assuming he really was staying in Scotland – and he was curious to see how Abi and their mother were getting along. Both had suggested a companionable working relationship, but he wasn't totally convinced.

He realised he was squinting as he added a sherbet streak to his Isle of Arran sunset. Machine gun bullets of hail began to crash against the window and he stood to watch the storm blow the few remaining leaves from the trees. With the last of the natural light now hidden behind creosote clouds, he stretched like a contented cat and poured himself a glass of wine. The bottle he'd shared with Justin was long gone. This was a gift from Rupert next door to say thank you for sweeping up the leaves. He'd have to do it again tomorrow, he realised. Or maybe he'd leave it until he got back from London.

It was the look on Abi's face that did it. The sneer. The pity. Florentina knew she had let herself go. She hadn't bothered turning up for her last hair appointment and the dark roots, roots she was usually so careful to hide, looked like a toxic oil slick on a golden beach. She hadn't realised anyone was home. She'd heard Crawford leave at eight o'clock, two short beeps of the taxi's horn waking her from her stupor, and was desperate for a hit of caffeine. She was just leaving the kitchen, steaming espresso in hand, when Abi appeared in front of her. She looked immaculate in a Marella silk shirt dress, the colour of hazelnuts. Her hair, unusually, was tied back in a casual ponytail and her face bore only the slightest trace of makeup. Even through the ever-present mist of jealousy, Florentina could see she was more beautiful than ever.

Her daughter didn't actually say anything. Her eyes said everything she needed to say. They slid from her two-tone hair, across her sallow skin, over her braless chest, down her unshaven legs and back up to her dull, lifeless eyes. Shaking her head, she had swept past her mother, swung her chocolate faux fur coat around her shoulders, and left. Florentina thought she might choke on the cloud of contempt left behind. She turned around in her bare feet and, still holding her coffee, stared at her reflection in the hall mirror. One word spoke back to her. *Enough.*

If Lydia was surprised to see her, she kept it to herself. It was business as usual in the KTH office and, after more than a week of manning the phones singlehandedly, she simply continued to do so. Florentina had spent the entire morning transforming the haggard, pitiful eyesore she'd seen in the mirror, into something resembling her old glamorous self. She'd plucked, shaved and shaped even the most stubborn bodily hairs. She'd washed and blow dried her hair, the roots now cleverly covered with a jaunty, black beret. She'd cleansed, toned and moisturized her face and neck, then expertly applied her favourite makeup. And she'd dressed in sharp mauve Tahari trousers, a crisp white, ruffled shirt and a short, fitted black jacket. She'd made appointments with the hair stylist and manicurist for later that day and was now sitting at her desk as though she'd never been away.

'Who's this?' she asked, turning her computer screen in Lydia's direction.

'Ursla. The girl from Milton Keynes. She came in yesterday. I've just sent her pictures to Berry Cosmetics. I'm hoping they'll sign her for their new ad campaign.'

'Impressive.' She took in the milky-white skin, innocent eyes and oblique cheekbones.

'You were right. She looks amazing. Who took the pictures?' She had the sense to look abashed but Lydia was writing something in her diary, so missed her unspoken apology.

'Your friend, Patrick. He was asking after you, by the way.'

She felt more than a little put out that they'd approached Patrick without her say so, but what could she say? She knew they'd tried to contact her, they'd left messages on her phone. She had no one to blame but herself. And so what if they'd called him anyway? She'd rather he took the pictures than anyone else. And she owed him a favour for Danny Venus.

'What's the latest on Danny?' she asked now.

'BooHoo are interested. He's doing a go-see tomorrow.'

Florentina was well familiar with the age-old modelling term but it still sounded strange coming from Lydia's lips.

'What about Abi?'

Lydia looked up from her diary. 'What about her?'

'Where is she today? I saw her earlier, was she on her way to a shoot?'

'No, she was meeting Sasha. Sasha had no classes today, apparently, so they booked a spa day at the Lanesborough. I think they were having lunch there too.'

'Did you know she was seeing Cory Flemming?' Florentina asked.

'Who? Sasha?' Lydia was wide-eyed with surprise.

'No. Abi.'

'Really? No, I didn't know that.'

'I don't suppose Crawford knows either. I wonder what he'll say when he knows his star striker is shagging his little girl.'

'Stay out of it, Florentina,' Lydia urged. 'Shouldn't you be worrying about Thomas rather than stirring up trouble for Abi?'

At the mention of Thomas, she was reminded of the one-sided conversation she'd heard in Crawford's study.

'I was thinking of going to see him, actually. I might head up there at the weekend.'

'Really? That's a great idea.'

Florentina had half-expected Lydia to object. After all, she'd only just returned from one leave of absence and was already asking for another. Contrarily, Lydia seemed cheered by the prospect. So used was she to ulterior motives, Florentina could only hope it was a genuine reaction to her plans to reunite with her son, rather than a desire to get her out of the way.

Chapter 26

As Florentina drove north in her Lexus, Thomas travelled south on the Avanti West Coast main line. Communication between the Kelly family had never been good, but this particular farcical escapade trumped any previous cock-up. Thomas had timed his arrival to perfection, knowing the Blues were playing Spurs and that his father wouldn't be home until very late, if at all. This particular London derby always resulted in an extended drinking session, win, lose or draw. He paid the cab driver, noting with a jolt that his father's Jaguar was in the drive. It took him a moment to remember his drink-driving ban. His mother's Lexus was absent, but Abi's Mercedes was parked outside the garage. Like most families, their garage was so full of other stuff there was no room for the cars, despite it being larger than the average semi-detached.

'Hello! Anyone home?' He dropped his hold-all in the hallway and listened for signs of life.

'Thomas? Is that you?'

He looked up to see Abi leaning over the staircase balustrades, her long blonde hair covering her face like a pair of silk curtains.

'What are you doing here?' she asked, running down the stairs in bare feet.

'What sort of a welcome is that? I still live here... I think.'

They shared an awkward, sibling hug before she peeled herself from his embrace and shivered.

'You're freezing,' she said, rubbing her arms. 'Come on, I'll put the kettle on.'

'Hold on,' he said, following her into the kitchen. 'What did you do with the real Abi?'

'What do you mean?' she asked, a touch of indignation creeping into her voice.

'The real Abi wouldn't offer to make me a drink. I'd have to make my own.'

'Piss off! Cheeky sod!'

'That's more like it. That's the Abi I know and love. Actually, I'd sooner have a beer if there's one going.'

'Sure.' She plucked two bottles of Budweiser from the fridge, removed the caps and handed one to her brother.

'Thanks.' He tugged off his jacket and hung it on the back of a dining chair.

'So, seriously, Thomas. What *are* you doing here?' She leant against the breakfast bar, arms folded across her chest. 'You do know Mum's on her way to see you, right?'

'What?' The Budweiser hovered, inches from his lips.

'She left this morning. She's driven to Scotland.'

'You're kidding me. Are you serious?'

Abi laughed out loud at the ridiculous scenario. Thomas, on the other hand, simply looked aghast. 'Why didn't she tell me?'

'Why didn't *you* tell *her*?'

He held his head in his hands and groaned. 'What a nightmare. It's an eight-hour drive, at least. What time did she leave?'

Abi, clearly, was finding it quite amusing. 'About eight, I think.'

He checked his watch. *Three thirty*. 'Shit. I should call her.'

'Drink your beer first,' she said, sliding onto one of the chrome and leather stools. 'It's too late now, anyway. She'll be almost there.' She swallowed a mouthful of beer before continuing. 'I think she had some kind of breakdown.'

'Who? Mum? What kind of breakdown?' Thomas's words were laced with genuine concern and Abi appeared instantly contrite.

'I'm not sure. She was acting weird. And she looked dreadful. Like those refugees you see on the TV, all skin and bones and haunted eyes.'

'Why didn't you tell me?'

'I thought you probably had enough to worry about. Anyway, she's better now. According to Lydia, anyway.'

Thomas picked at the label on his beer bottle and pictured his mother knocking on the cottage door. A fresh knot of despair formed in his stomach.

'You didn't have to run away, you know. We still love you, gay or straight.'

He looked up at his sister and smiled, grateful for the reassurance. He wondered who she meant by 'we' but decided not to ask.

'I can't believe you didn't tell me. I mean, I suspected, but you should've told me.'

'I know. I wish I had. But it's done now. I can't change it. I just need to move on.'

'Does Dad know you're here?'

'No.' The mention of their father tightened the knot in his stomach. 'Not yet.'

'You do know they're playing Spurs today, right? It's probably not the best day for the prodigal son to return.'

Thomas couldn't help but laugh. 'True. I'll keep a low profile until tomorrow.'

'Shall we watch it?' she asked, instantly animated. 'The match, I mean. Kick-off's five thirty.'

'What? You want to watch the football?' Thomas couldn't remember Abi ever watching a game of football in her life. Her smile gave her away. 'Oh, I get it. You don't want to watch the football, you want to watch Cory Flemming.'

'Another beer?' she asked, jumping from her stool, her back shielding her from further questions.

'No thanks. I need to call Mum. Then take a shower. I'll be back down for kick-off.'

'It's a date,' said Abi, a wide grin lighting up her face.

He'd forgotten to pack his charger. He was about to call his mother when he noticed the red light in the top corner of his phone indicating only one percent battery life.

'Shit.'

Stripping off his clothes, he showered instead, standing under the hot jets of water until his skin was pink and the steam dense. He rubbed his hair dry then wrapped himself in the towel. He was actually looking forward to spending the evening with Abi. It had been months since the two of them had shared any quality time; although he wasn't entirely sure that watching football was time well spent, particularly if he was competing for her attention with a certain number seven. Pulling on a clean pair of jeans and a blue Nike sweatshirt, he blew the dust from an old pair of slippers and made his way downstairs. Phone in hand, he searched the usual plug sockets for a forgotten charger. Finding none, he decided he may as well use the landline. The cradle in the hallway was empty, the wayward handset nowhere to be seen. He knocked on the door of his father's study – a gesture born from habit rather than expectation – and stepped inside. The smell was unnerving, bringing back memories from his childhood that he'd rather forget; a combination of polished wood, aged leather, and masculine pride. He sat in his father's chair and took a moment to look around. Conversations from the past drifted from the walls; words barked at him from the photographs. *Disgrace... ungrateful.... lazy... embarrassment.* He closed his eyes to stop the barrage, impatient now to leave the room. He picked up the phone but was distracted by an envelope, the address partly obscured by the desk lamp. He slid it towards him, nausea gathering in his throat. *What the...?* Why did his father have a letter addressed to Vince? He looked inside but the envelope was empty. He stared at it, his hands shaking. *Vincent Savage, 9 Breer Road, Fulham.* He didn't know Vince's last name, but he recognised the address and could only draw one conclusion. His father had set him up.

The final whistle couldn't come soon enough for Crawford. He'd shaken the hand of the Spurs boss and was halfway down the tunnel before the whistle had even left the referee's mouth. Losing four-one to Spurs was not a good day at the office. The dressing room door almost fell from its hinges when he yanked it open and stormed inside. Most of the players sat with their heads bowed, forearms on thighs, hands clenched. It was the look of defeat and he hated it.

'What the hell was that? I've never seen such a piss-poor performance in my life! We were one-nil up for fuck's sake! What the hell happened?'

A chorus of 'Sorry, boss' floated up from the benches.

'Sorry, boss? Is that the best you can do? They're queuing up to interview me outside. What exactly do you want me to say? I don't think the fans will be too impressed with *sorry.*'

Simone was rubbing Oscar Christianson's thighs on the massage table in the centre of the room. The sight did nothing to dampen his fury.

'Hennessy. Where were you for the last twenty minutes? You may as well have been in fucking Disney Land. And Franklin, what was that free kick? The poor bloke in Row Z lost his pie thanks to you.'

He noticed Cory Flemming stifle a laugh, clearly delighted at the criticism aimed at his striking competitor.

'And you can wipe that smile off your face, Flemming. If you'd have passed the ball to Delaney instead of firing it at the corner flag, we'd have been two-nil up. An absolute shambles, that's what it was. A fucking disgrace!'

'He was trying to impress your daughter, boss.'

'What?' He looked at the line of players, steam rising from their sweaty bodies. 'What was that about my daughter?' He wasn't sure who'd said it, or exactly what they'd said, but mention of Abi sent his blood pressure skyward. His eyes darted from one player to the next, settling on none.

'Leave my daughter out of his. If you mention her again, I'll ram your boots down your fucking throat, do you hear me?' Unsurprisingly, the dressing room remained silent. Crawford took one last look at their pathetic faces and left. The chairman was waiting for him upstairs.

Thomas had barely said a word during the match. In fact, his thoughts were so far away from what was happening on the TV, he didn't even know who had scored. Not that his sister had noticed, such was her obsession with the front man for the Blues. Now the match was over, she'd presume he was disappointed at the result; the four-one score line was the one thing that hadn't escaped his attention.

'Dad will be livid,' she said now. 'Poor Cory.'

Thomas found it difficult to sympathise with any of the over-paid footballers in the Premiership. If a bollocking from their manager was all they had to worry about, they should count themselves lucky.

'I wouldn't expect any sympathy from Dad this weekend if I were you, Thomas. He'll be seething for days after that result.'

Abi was right. Not only that, he needed to find out the connection between his father and Vince before he orchestrated a cosy father and son reunion.

'You're probably right. I should've stayed in Scotland with Mum.'

Unable to stay in his father's office for a moment longer, he'd borrowed Abi's mobile phone to call their mother. Still shaken by his discovery, he'd struggled to concentrate on their conversation, but did manage an apology for his absence.

'You're welcome to stay at the cottage,' he'd told her. 'Rupert next door has a key.'

Surprisingly, she'd seen the funny side of their path-crossing journeys, but he still felt bad at the thought of her in Scotland all by herself, particularly after what Abi had said about her breakdown.

'Don't worry about me, I'll be fine.'

After getting no answer at the cottage, she'd driven to the Turnberry Resort along the coast and was enjoying an immaculately served espresso when he'd called to confess his whereabouts. He could picture her sitting in the Grand Tea Lounge, sipping her coffee from a china cup, elegantly seated with a view of the coast; legs crossed, back straight.

'I'll be back in a couple of days,' he'd said. 'Make yourself at home.'

He'd tried to remember what sort of state he'd left the cottage in, although he'd taken so few possessions to Scotland, it was virtually impossible for it to be untidy. The dining room-cum-studio was predictably chaotic, but he'd make no apology for that. He remembered straightening the red fleecy throw on the sofa and the matching cushions on the chairs, purchased to brighten up the faded, slightly worn furniture. The oak floorboards needed little attention, other than an occasional sweep with a broom, and there were plenty of logs stacked either side of the wood burner; although, he realised his mother was unlikely to light the fire. He knew the fridge was virtually empty – just eggs and cheese remained if his memory served him correctly – but there were biscuits and soup in the cupboard and plenty of pork scratchings. Not that his mother would eat those.

'You can get breakfast in the café at the castle,' he'd told her, 'and fresh milk at the shop in the village. Sorry, there's only instant coffee in the cottage.'

'Stop fussing, Thomas, you sound like an old woman.'

He'd heard the buzz of conversation in the background, American accents floating down the line. Golfers, he'd presumed.

'Be careful around your father, darling. He's… There's something going on.'

'What do you mean?'

'I'm not sure, exactly. He's behaving a little strange, that's all. You might not have picked the best time to visit.'

She was the second person to say that, although he suspected his mother wasn't referring to the Spurs match. He'd tried to extract more details, but she rang off, saying she had a few calls to make.

He helped himself to another beer from the fridge and leant against the French doors, watching as the light began to fade on their vast but vapid garden. The sky went from grey to black without ceremony. No sunset. No fanfare. He'd only been back a few hours and already his mood was deteriorating. It was as though the air was too thick. It stole your breath, squeezed your heart, and polluted your soul. He was missing Scotland already.

Chapter 27

It was the silence that woke her. So used was she to the rumble of buses, the sound of car horns, even the repetitive thud of helicopters, she was disturbed by the nothingness of her surroundings. She stretched to awaken her limbs and reached for her phone, surprised at the numbers on the screen: 09:35. She couldn't remember the last time she'd slept so well, not without assistance anyway, alcohol or otherwise. A smile crept to her lips as she recalled the previous evening. She'd been startled by a knock on the door, but a reassuring voice calmed her initial alarm.

'It's Rupert, from next door.'

She'd opened the door to the delicious aroma of garlic and basil. She may not be a cook, but she'd learned to recognise herbs and spices at a very early age.

'I made lasagne,' he'd told her, holding a large foil-covered dish in front of him. 'I thought you might like some. If you haven't already eaten, that is.'

Back in London she would have been annoyed at the intrusion; uninvited guests were, in her opinion, the epitome of rudeness. But up here, in a cold, isolated cottage with only a tiny TV for company, she welcomed the incursion. Besides, he'd been more than gracious when she'd knocked on his door earlier asking for Thomas's spare key.

'I'd love some,' she said. 'Come in.' She couldn't remember the last time she'd eaten lasagne – such calorie laden indulgence was sinful in her world – but her stomach was growling with hunger and the smell was making her mouth water.

He was easy company. It made a refreshing change to meet someone, particularly a man, who was happy to talk about himself rather than bombard her with questions about her career or, worse still, Crawford's. He was a widower, he told her, having lost his wife to motor neurone disease three years earlier.

'I moved to Dubai after Nancy died. I can't lie, it was a relief when she finally passed, but it was as though the disease was still there. I could feel it in the house, as though it had seeped into the walls. Far from being a home full of happy memories it felt more like a tomb.'

'So you sold up?'

'Yes. I'd been approached by an architectural practice in Dubai six months previously. Of course, there was no way I could even consider it back then, but when I looked them up afterwards, the job was still there. The house in Warwick sold as soon as it hit the market.'

'So, what happened? How come you ended up here?'

'I couldn't stand the heat!' He'd laughed. 'The job was okay, and it was just what I needed at the time, but seriously, it was *so* hot. And I missed the seasons. We'd always holidayed in Scotland and planned to retire here eventually. I wanted wildlife and mountains not skyscrapers and camels. Although, having said that, they're actually building a mountain in Dubai as we speak.'

She'd studied him as he spoke. He wasn't classically handsome but his obvious intelligence and gentle honesty gave him a kind, charming face. His short, black hair was woven with grey, his eyes were a dark, muddy brown and creased at the sides and his chin, despite the late hour, was clean shaven. She'd been glad she hadn't had to guess his age (she'd never been good at that particular game), spared the dilemma by the early disclosure of his fifty-six years.

The sound of a dog barking disturbed her thoughts and she stretched once more before forcing herself out of bed. The bedroom was cold and she reached for the blue fleece dressing gown she'd found in Thomas's room the night before. It was far too big for her slim frame, but at least it was warm. Her feet were still icy though. Used to plush carpets and under floor heating she'd never had to worry about slippers – hideous things – but the shaggy, green rug in the bedroom did nothing to disguise the cold wooden floor beneath. She slid her feet into her Moschino ankle boots then laughed out loud when she saw her reflection. Free of makeup, hair like Bonnie Tyler's on a windy day, stiletto boots poking out below a giant, belted robe, she looked like something from a bad 1970s porn movie. It was less than a week since she'd shocked herself into action at the sight of her own reflection. Looking at herself now, a smile playing at her lips, she was amazed at the transformation. But the change, she realised, was nothing to do with the material things she had relied on in the past. It wasn't thanks to a hundred-pound beauty treatment at the salon or the contents of a stiff, cardboard shopping bag from Chanel. This time, the change had come from the heart.

After a long, hot shower she changed into jeans and a rust-coloured cashmere jumper, her boots substituted for a thick pair of socks found in the laundry cupboard. Downstairs, the smell of lasagne still lingered in the air and she smiled once again. This time it was memories of her childhood that filled her mind. Her mother slicing onions on an ancient, wooden chopping board, a tissue stuffed under her watchstrap to wipe away the tears. Her father returning from the market laden with shiny, plump tomatoes, garlic bulbs shedding their papery skin, round, white mushrooms dusted with dirt, and giant eggplants as purple as the veins in his strong, bulging arms. An image of Pia appeared too, the two of them taking turns to play on the swing in the yard, mouthwatering wafts of oregano teasing their hungry tummies, ears straining for those magic words, *La cena è pront.* Dinner is ready. She was still smiling at the memories, but a sadness had settled in her heart. During the long drive up from London yesterday, she'd thought about visiting her parents' grave. Believing she was too emotionally fragile for such a visit, she'd talked herself out of it. Now though, after a relaxed evening with a man she hoped would become her friend followed by a long, dreamless night's sleep, she felt much better equipped for the task. Besides, she told herself, a thirty-year absence was long enough.

Predictably, their father hadn't come home last night. Thomas had slept badly, his restless mind both alert to the sound of a taxi that never arrived, and tormented with theories to explain the connection between his father and Vince, none of which were convincing.

'You look terrible,' said Abi as she joined him in the kitchen.

'Thanks a bunch.' He feigned offence but knew she was right. 'I didn't sleep well. Too much on my mind.'

Abi helped herself to a yogurt from the fridge and scrutinised the label before peeling off the lid. She was dressed to go out, her Carvela purple suede ankle boots the perfect match to her chunky, cowl neck jumper and her dark, perfectly manicured nails. Black leggings completed the outfit.

'Where are you off to?' Thomas asked, pushing his empty cereal bowl away and reaching for his mug of coffee.

'I'm picking Sasha up. We're going shopping and then to the cinema.'

'Would you mind dropping me at the studio on your way?'

She still hadn't eaten any yogurt, Thomas noticed. She was stirring it idly with a teaspoon.

'Sure.' She glanced at the chrome clock on the wall. 'I'll be leaving in ten minutes.'

He watched as she rinsed the teaspoon under the tap, threw the yogurt into the bin and sauntered from the kitchen.

It was the first time Thomas had been in Abi's car. It still had that showroom smell, a combination of cleaning fluid, leather and rubber. It was smart, he had to admit, but he preferred to travel in vehicles with a little more space between him and the road. He felt as though his backside was just inches from the tarmac.

'So you're really going for it then? Giving up the studio?' asked Abi, both hands gripping the steering wheel.

'I'm not sure. The rental agreement expires in March so I've got a little while to think about it. I just want to collect some stuff today. And make sure you and Mum didn't trash the place with your little party.' He smiled at her, but she was concentrating on the road. He turned his attention to the passing scenery instead. Progress was slow, as always in London, and the affluence was soon replaced by hardship and neglect. The diversity and geography of the capital's housing always fascinated Thomas. You could spend millions on an exclusive, luxury home with every conceivable extravagance and still be next door to the ugliest of tower blocks. The high-pitched bleep of a pelican crossing pulled his eyes forwards and he watched as an army of pedestrians marched across the road. Most were dressed for the cold, woolly hats pulled over their ears, hands shoved deep inside their pockets. Some wore earplugs, the wires disappearing inside coats and beneath scarves. Others were tapping away at their phones, eyes down, thumbs busy.

'Look at the state of that,' said Abi, a note of disdain in her voice.

She was referring to a young girl, maybe seventeen or eighteen, crossing the road in front of them. Her legs were bare, despite the cold, and a cheap black skirt rode up over her ample thighs as she walked. Tatty, flat ballet shoes were struggling to contain her swollen feet and a tight white T-shirt stretched across her chest. The denim jacket she wore over the top was futile, doing nothing to disguise the ill-fitting clothes beneath or to stave off the winter temperatures. Unlike his sister, Thomas found it hard to criticise.

'Don't be mean, Abi. You don't know what her situation is or what her personal struggles are. Not everyone was born with good looks and wealthy parents.'

'What?' She turned to looked at him. 'Are you for real? Since when did you turn into Mother Theresa?'

Thomas sighed. 'I'm just saying, that's all. You shouldn't be so quick to judge. She clearly didn't dress like that by choice, not in these temperatures.'

Abi was still staring at him when the driver behind blasted the horn of his white Transit van.

'All right!' she said, scowling at him in her rear-view mirror. Clearly flustered, she stalled the car and jerked forwards to a standstill. The driver behind, narrowly avoiding a collision, sounded his horn once more, adding an abusive hand gesture for good measure. Thomas remained silent, not wanting to antagonise Abi, who was still trying to restart the engine. Thankfully, it revved into life and she pulled off at speed.

'Sorry,' she said, eventually.

He dragged his eyes from the parade of fast food shops and looked at Abi. 'For the girl or the car?'

'Both,' she said, with an apologetic smile. 'Although, it doesn't cost much to wash your hair.'

'Abi!'

'I know, I know. But seriously, did you see the state of her hair?'

He had, of course, noticed her unwashed, badly dyed hair, but he wouldn't indulge Abi by admitting as much.

'Stop it, Abi' he said, not unkindly. 'Just remember how lucky you are and have a bit of compassion for those less fortunate than yourself.'

She chose not to reply. She did let out a heavy sigh though. Whether it was a sigh of frustration or acceptance, Thomas couldn't be sure.

They were silent for the rest of the journey, Abi steadfastly concentrating on the drive, eyes darting from the road, to the mirrors and back again, and Thomas distracted by their ever-changing surroundings. It was a depressing city, he concluded. Wherever you looked, you saw misery. It was etched on faces, young and old. It clung to buildings, littered the streets and polluted the air. And it bred. It bred so fast it was frightening.

'Are you getting out, or what?'

So lost was he in his thoughts he hadn't even realised they'd stopped. 'Sorry, I was miles away,' he answered, opening the car door. 'Thanks for the lift,' he said, struggling to haul himself up and out of the car. 'Have a nice day with Sasha. Tell her I said hi.'

'Will do. See you later.'

He watched until she was out of sight then let himself into the studio.

It looked bare without his paintings decorating the space. Cold too. He turned the knobs on the old column radiators then gazed out of the window at the familiar, grey scene. Not so long ago, the view would have cheered him. Not today. Today he found it depressing. He rubbed his hands up and down his arms to try and generate some warmth then filled the kettle, spooning some instant coffee into a mug. There was no sign of a party having taken place. Whoever had cleaned up had made a pretty decent job of it. Sipping his black coffee, he thought back to the last time he'd been here. Things had changed a bit since then. Was it really only ten weeks ago? With hindsight, he was ashamed of how he'd reacted; how he'd dealt with the whole sorry mess. So determined was he to keep his sexuality a secret from his father, he'd failed to see that he already knew. How else could the link between Vince and his father be explained? He'd fully intended to talk to his father today, assuming he could actually find him after the humiliating defeat yesterday, but the discovery of the envelope in his study had stopped him.

Swallowing the last of his coffee, he rinsed his cup and began gathering the bits and pieces he wanted to take back to Scotland. Most of it he could fit in a suitcase – brushes, paper pads, paint sets, etc. – other bits he would have to send by courier. He retrieved the paintings his mother had stashed in the cupboard and lined them up against the wall. The cityscapes he'd started for the architect remained unfinished, a reminder of the turmoil that had enveloped him. He wouldn't finish them, he decided. London landmarks no longer appealed to him. His painting of Abi stared back at him. It was his intention to gift it to her on her eighteenth birthday. He'd started early, expecting to paint it several times before getting it right, but he'd perfected it with his first attempt. Not usually one for blowing his own trumpet, he was embarrassed at his own admiration, but he couldn't deny that he'd captured her personality perfectly. He was surprised his mother hadn't mentioned it; she must have seen it. Then again, any conversation about Abi was a conversation worth avoiding as far as their mother was concerned. He wondered how she was getting on in Scotland and, once again, felt guilty at the thought of her up there by herself. 'Sorry, Mum,' he said aloud.

At that very moment, Florentina was on her way to St Peter's Cemetery in Glasgow. Her satnav had guided her expertly along the A77, onto the motorway, over the River Clyde and finally, into the city. She was surprised how unfamiliar everything looked, but whether it was the city that had changed or she herself, she couldn't be sure. Perhaps she was just seeing everything differently.

Unprepared for the biting northern temperatures, she'd been forced to borrow a woolly hat and scarf from Thomas's wardrobe, along with the Trespass hiking jacket she was now pulling on over her own inadequate jacket. No one would recognise her, of that she was certain. She parked her car, gathered the flowers from the passenger seat, took a deep breath, and walked slowly in the direction of her parents' grave. She may not have been here for thirty years but she knew exactly where she was going. Her Moschino boots did nothing to protect her feet from the chill and she must look quite ridiculous, she mused. Still, it would give her parents something to smile about. She slowed her pace as she approached, confused by the sight that greeted here. She thought, at first, she was in the wrong place, but the names on the headstone told her different: *Nicolo and Viola Vanzetti.* Tears spilled from her eyes at the very sight of their names but the confusion remained. Who had left flowers at her parents' grave?

Chapter 28

Crawford was nursing the hangover of all hangovers. He knew he'd regret the monster measures of whisky he'd helped himself to after the match, not to mention the countless glasses of red wine he and Simone had consumed in her apartment, but regret wasn't much use to him now. The urgent need to vomit had forced him from her bed in the early hours of the morning, but he hadn't moved very far since. And it was the first time he'd stayed overnight without the sexual benefits that usually accompanied his visits. He could hear her in the kitchen now, singing along to whatever crap she was listening to on the radio. Clearly she wasn't suffering to the extent he was, although she probably hadn't drank the quantity of alcohol that he had. He could vaguely remember her trying to pour him a glass of water when he'd opened the third bottle of wine, but he knew for a fact he hadn't drank it. She, on the other hand, Simone 'Sensible' Satchwell, would have drunk a glass of water for every glass of wine. He buried his head under the pillow as the singing volume increased, but all that served to do was stop him breathing. He wedged the pillow behind his head and inched up the bed until he was sitting up. His hands were shaking and the room was, most definitely, spinning.

'Welcome to the land of the living,' said Simone, poking her head around the bedroom door. She was fully dressed in black jeans and a white GAP sweatshirt, her hair tied back in a messy ponytail. He could only grunt in response.

'Do you want something to eat? Can't really call it breakfast, it's almost twelve o'clock.'

'Shit.' He pulled the covers back and swung his legs out of bed. He didn't have time to laze around in bed all day. The room spun violently and it felt like Anthony Joshua was using his head as a punch bag.

'Think I'll pass, thanks all the same.' He forced himself upright and slowly made his way to the bathroom. Simone retreated without comment.

'Can you call me a cab?' he shouted, wincing as he did so. 'I need to be somewhere.' He cringed at the sight of his reflection in the mirror and resisted the urge to throw up. *Old enough to know better,* he thought to himself. *Fucking Spurs.* He splashed his face with cold water and studied the image in front of him. But it wasn't the usual arrogant, self-assured face that glared back. It wasn't even a jaded version of his own familiar features. This time, it was his father who stared back at him. The realisation shocked him. Red-rimmed eyes, dry, cracked lips, sallow complexion. He tried to refocus, blinking rapidly to clear his bloodshot eyes, but the image was the same. He'd always been proud to be compared to his father. Proud to follow in his footsteps and live up to the Kelly 'big man' reputation. Now, naked in his lover's bathroom, his skin as green as the liquid soap, his mouth as furry as the towels, he realised what a fool he'd been. This wasn't the 1960s. Men didn't behave like chauvinistic arseholes these days. They were to be respected and admired. They treated women as equals, embraced diversity and encouraged freedom of choice. After years of idolising his father, he suddenly saw him for the loser that he was. Pat Kelly was selfish, lazy and disrespectful and Crawford had unwittingly followed in his footsteps. He didn't want to be like his father. He didn't want to be remembered for his drinking and his womanising. He didn't want to be compared to George Best or Paul Gasgoine, no matter how talented they were. He wanted to be pictured alongside his beautiful wife, not falling out of a taxi and throwing up in a gutter.

'I'm not like you,' he said to the man in the mirror. 'I'm better than that.' Turning on the shower, he watched the steam slowly erase his reflection and then stepped under the hot, powerful jets, his attitude disappearing down the plug hole with his ego.

The taxi dropped him at home, pulling up next to his redundant, blue Jaguar. Before today, he'd considered his driving ban a minor inconvenience, even feeling smug at his meagre six-week ban. Today, however, the first pangs of shame prodded his conscience. He did manage a small smile though; his solicitor wouldn't be happy with the result yesterday. *That's justice for you,* he thought.

The first thing he did was make himself a coffee, desperate to stave off the ball of nausea that had lodged itself in his throat. He deliberately avoided the papers that were spread over the kitchen counter; he knew what the match reports would say and had no desire to read them. One thing was for sure, his players were in for a shock at training tomorrow morning. No way were they going to suffer another humiliating defeat like that one.

Upstairs, he changed out of his suit, pulling on a pair of jeans and a clean, white T-shirt. He briefly wondered where his wife and daughter were, the lack of cars in the drive confirming their absence, but didn't delve any deeper into their whereabouts. In truth, he was thankful for the time alone. He had calls to make. He didn't care if people were tucking into a Sunday roast. He didn't even care that Arsenal were playing Burnley at that very minute. Someone knew where that toe rag Vince Savage was, and he intended to find out.

'The only way you're going to find out is to ask him.'

Thomas had confided in Justin about the envelope. They were enjoying a pint in The Half Moon, a bag of pork scratchings torn open in front of them. He'd come to the same conclusion himself but the thought of confronting his father made him feel quite sick.

'What choice do you have?' Justin asked. 'You're not going to find this Vince guy yourself, so short of hiring a private detective, you don't really have a choice.'

Thomas sat upright as though considering the idea.

'Don't even think about it!' said Justin, 'I was only joking. Just ask your father. The more you try and figure it out yourself, the more you'll tie yourself in knots.'

'You're right,' he said, slumping his shoulders in resignation and helping himself to another pork scratching. 'I'll talk to him.'

'When?'

'Soon.'

'How soon?'

'I don't know!' His raised voice attracted the attention of numerous other drinkers and he swung around on his stool to avoid their curious stares. 'Soon. I'll talk to him soon.'

Seemingly satisfied, Justin took a sip of his pint and changed the subject. 'When do you intend going back to Scotland? Is your mother still there?'

'Yes. As far as I know. She had dinner with Rupert last night.' He smiled at the image of the two of them in his tiny cottage.

'Your neighbour?' Justin had met him briefly but their conversation hadn't stretched beyond 'hello'.

Thomas nodded, a tough pork scratching preventing a verbal response.

'Well, at least she's not on her own. It's pretty isolated up there. I can't imagine your mother's used to spending time alone.'

Thomas's laugh was one of irony rather than humour. 'You'd be surprised,' he said. 'My mother and father are rarely in the same room together. Lydia Templeton-Howe is her only friend. In fact, before they set up the agency, I've no idea how she spent her time. It certainly wasn't with me or Abi.'

'Sounds a lonely existence.'

Said aloud, it made him realise how lonely his mother must have been. He'd always considered her to be self-absorbed. Her jealously of Abi was obvious, but maybe, under the egotistical façade, she was just lonely and sad. She must miss her parents too.

'It probably was,' he conceded. 'But the agency's done her the world of good.'

His words were unconvincing, even to his own ears. In truth, he had no idea how his mother was feeling. He hadn't seen her since September and their few telephone conversations had been brief to say the least. Abi's mention of a breakdown had concerned him, but he'd done nothing to follow it up. *Self-indulgence must run in the family*, he thought.

'I'll give her a call later,' he said. 'And I'll talk to Dad in the morning.'

Justin raised an eyebrow, his green eyes ever playful.

'I will!' he protested, his hands held up in front of him. 'I promise.'

'You don't need to promise me, Thomas. You're not doing it for me.'

Oh, but I am, he thought, looking into those green eyes. *I am.*

It was after midnight when Thomas finally let himself into the house. They'd stayed in The Half Moon until closing time, then shared a bag of chips from the Chinese on the way to the tube. After a salty kiss, they'd said their goodbyes before going their separate ways, Thomas to Chelsea, and Justin to Shepherd's Bush. After emerging from Parsons Green Station, Thomas had walked the rest of the way home, deliberately delaying his arrival. He'd promised Justin he'd talk to his father, but he had no intention of doing so tonight.

Despite the cold, the walk had been a pleasant one. Without the chaos that always accompanied daylight, the city was at rest. It was almost silent, just the distant buzz of a moped disturbed the night air. *Probably delivering a pizza,* he thought. A giant, flat screen TV lit up a house to his left, a cluster of heads seemingly enthralled by the tale being told. A cat prowled along a garden wall and, to his right, a Christmas tree stood proud in a bay window. Thomas laughed, but the sound was muffled beneath his giant, wool scarf. *It's not even December yet.* The sight of it made him wonder what his own Christmas would involve. Would he be in London or Scotland? Would he be alone? It was only a month away but until tonight, he hadn't even thought about Christmas.

At home, he took off his coat and shoes and carried them upstairs, choosing to find his way in the dark rather than risk waking his father by switching on a light. In his room, he relaxed a little, undressing quickly before brushing his teeth and finally, folding himself in the warmth of his bed. Sleep wouldn't come easy, he knew. The looming conversation with his father would not let him rest. Neither would the realisation that he was falling in love with Justin.

Chapter 29

After a restless sleep, Florentina showered and dressed, then warmed the croissant she'd bought on the way back from Glasgow yesterday. She took her breakfast into the sitting room and curled her feet up underneath her, savouring the taste of the buttery, flaky pastry. She licked her fingers and dabbed the remaining flakes on her plate, smiling to herself when she'd finished. *The sea air must be giving me an appetite.* It was cosy in the cottage. She'd finally mastered the central heating system, unwilling to light the log burner, and it was now toasty warm. She stretched her legs out in front of her and admired her new slippers, an impulsive purchase during her stroll around Glasgow city centre. She hadn't intended to go shopping, but it was a hard habit to break, so after a brisk walk around George Square, followed by a late lunch in the Malmaison in West George Street, she'd headed to the shops. She'd bought the slippers on impulse, their furry red and black pompoms impossible to resist. The four-hundred-and-sixty-pound price tag was perhaps a little excessive, but Joshua Sanders footwear didn't come cheap. Besides, they were her first adult pair of slippers so a little extravagance was allowed.

She rotated her ankles, left and then right, smiling at the alien fur balls on her feet. *Scotland is having a very strange effect on me,* she thought. She carried her empty plate back to the kitchen and made herself another cup of tea. She could just about tolerate teabags but had no intention of poisoning her bloodstream with instant coffee. She stood at the window as she sipped it, the restless sea just visible through the bare branches of the trees. She thought again of the flowers on her parents' grave and the uneasy feeling she'd experienced at the cemetery returned. It didn't make sense. They had no family in Britain. The three of them had moved from Italy in 1983 and, although they'd made Glasgow their home, they'd remained very much alone. A sudden movement caught her eye and she watched in horror as a sparrowhawk reduced an innocent blackbird to just a few scattered feathers. She wasn't sure if her tears were for the blackbird or her parents.

The knock on the door came at ten o'clock prompt. Rupert was driving them to Portpatrick, a seaside town about an hour down the coast. Along with the slippers, she'd also had the foresight to buy comfortable (but stylish) boots and a padded coat, both from Zara. She wouldn't normally shop in High Street stores but she'd actually enjoyed browsing the rails in Zara and was surprised at the quality of their clothes. Together with the cashmere turtle neck sweater she'd bought with her from London, and her favourite Guess jeans, she should be adequately dressed for the weather.

Florentina enjoyed the drive. It was a treat to be driven by someone else and be able to admire the spectacular Ayrshire coast. It was cold but clear and the watery sun followed them all the way down to Portpatrick. The giant ferry terminals at Cairnryan, considered an eyesore by many, simply added to the scenery as far as Florentina was concerned; she even took photographs of a huge, open-mouthed vessel on her smartphone. She felt comfortable in Rupert's company and enjoyed hearing about his home town of Warwick and his adventures in Dubai. His daughter, Izzie, was getting married next year and she could sense both excitement and sadness when he talked about the wedding.

'I'm thrilled for her,' he said, as they bypassed Stranraer and headed across country. 'Will's a great guy and I'm looking forward to welcoming him into the family. And I'll be so proud to give Izzie away.'

'But?' She could sense there was more he wanted to say.

'But… it just won't be the same without Nancy. I know it's been three years, but I just can't imagine the wedding without her. And I know Izzie will feel her absence on the day.'

'That's to be expected. But she *will* be there, you know that, don't you? She'll be there every step of the way.'

Rupert turned and smiled then squeezed her hand in gratitude. 'Thank you,' he said.

He rested his hand back on the gearstick, and Florentina studied the wedding ring that remained on his finger, a simple gold band, nothing fancy. It suited his slim hands which were clean and smooth, the fingernails short. An intellect's hands, she concluded. She wondered if

Thomas would ever get married and squeezed her eyes shut to dispel the image conjured by the thought. As for Abi, that was definitely a prospect she had no desire to contemplate.

'Are you okay?'

She snapped her eyes open, embarrassed. 'Oh, yes. Sorry. It's these hills. I was feeling a little queasy.' It wasn't a lie, at least. The winding road was proving quite a challenge for her delicate stomach. Maybe she just wasn't used to being a passenger.

'We're almost there,' he assured her.

Arriving in Portpatrick he parked the car near the harbour and guided her to a nearby café. 'Let's have a coffee first, then we can explore.'

The delicious smell of homemade scones greeted them as they opened the door of the cosy café, but they resisted the temptation, ordering only coffee. They settled at a table in the window with views of the harbour and the lighthouse. The sun was weak but strong enough for them to squint as they looked across the water at the bevy of boats.

'It's lovely,' she said, gazing through the window and winding her fingers around her espresso. 'Thanks for bringing me.'

'My pleasure. I've been meaning to come for ages, but it's never the same on your own, is it? I should be thanking you for coming with me.'

He added a spoon of sugar to his cappuccino and stirred it vigorously. 'And it's always nice to have a day off, particularly when the weather's like this.'

'True. I guess we're both playing hooky today.'

He smiled at her school yard terminology then took a sip of his coffee. 'At least I don't have anyone else to answer to,' he said, replacing the cup on its saucer. 'Doesn't your business partner mind you having time off?'

'Lydia? No. Sometimes I think she prefers it when I'm not there. I can be difficult to work with at times. It's the Italian in me.'

'I'm sure that's not true,' he protested.

'I'm afraid it is,' she laughed. 'But Lydia's my friend. She understands. In fact, sometimes I think she understands me better than I do.'

'You're lucky to have a friend like that.'

'You don't?'

He sighed before answering. 'Not anymore. Our so-called friends disappeared when Nancy became ill. First they stopped visiting, then they stopped calling. They came to the funeral, but by then, I had nothing to say to them. They let us down when we needed them the most. It's hard to forgive something like that.'

'So it was left to you and Izzie to look after her?'

'We had help from the MNDA, the Motor Neurone Disease Association. They were brilliant. I don't think we would have coped without them.'

'Well, at least you and Izzie have each other. And Will. You must miss her.'

'I do. But Warwick is their home. Their jobs are down there, and their friends. And they visit often, that's all I can ask.'

'Was moving back to Warwick not an option?'

He paused before answering, staring deep into his coffee as though the answer may lie in the bottom on his cup.

'Not really. I'm a firm believer in looking forwards not backwards. Warwick felt… still feels… like part of my past. We were happy there but it also represents the most difficult time of my life. I needed a change, a fresh start.' He drained the last of his coffee and turned his attention back to Florentina. 'And the best thing about my job is that I can do it anywhere. As long as I've got access to a computer and the internet, I'm pretty much sorted.'

'Do you not get lonely in the cottage?' She pictured the tiny rooms, the isolated spot among the tress, the eerie silence.

'Not at all. The opposite in fact. I love it there. I'm surrounded by nature, I can work without interruption and the beach is a ten-minute walk away.'

'You sound like Thomas. He loves it too.'

They both shivered as an elderly lady entered the café, bringing with her a blast of cold air. She trailed a shopping trolley behind her and parked it next to a corner table before scraping a chair across the tiled floor. They cringed at the sound and then stifled a laugh as she barked her order to the young girl behind the counter.

'Weak tea and a fruit scone please, love. And don't be shy with the jam.'

'I'm glad Thomas is happy,' Rupert continued. 'I was worried about him when he first arrived. He seemed to have the weight of the world on his shoulders.'

Florentina wasn't quite sure what to say. She didn't know how much Thomas had told him, if anything, and didn't want to divulge any family secrets. She wondered if Thomas had spoken to his father yet and thought back to the overheard conversation in his study.

'Anyway,' said Rupert. 'Have you finished your coffee? Shall we go and have a look around?'

She pushed her thoughts of Thomas to one side. 'Lead the way,' she said, raring to go in her new fur-lined boots.

The plan to talk to his father had backfired. Crawford was up and out of the house before Thomas had even stirred. *He doesn't even know I'm home,* he thought, unsure whether to feel smug or disappointed. He'd deliberately removed all evidence of his presence, ensuring all of his belongings were stashed in his room, but it was still hard to believe his return had gone unnoticed. Of course, the size of the house played its part.

He'd slept better than he thought, although an alcohol-induced sleep was never the most satisfying. There was no sign of Abi this morning so he presumed she hadn't come home last night. Whether she'd stayed at Sasha's or Cory's was anybody's guess.

With the house to himself, he returned to his father's study. The more information he could gather before confronting his father, the better, he decided. The offensive smell greeted him once more and he recoiled before forcing himself to sit down. He deliberately ignored the judgmental faces that stared at him from the photographs and concentrated on the contents of the desk. Other than the picture of his grandfather, only a desk lamp, telephone and paperweight stood on the surface. He picked up the paperweight, shaped like a football, and studied it. It was smooth and solid, like a black and white stone, with the slightest flat edge to prevent it from rolling. Like an almost-full moon. He juggled it from one hand to the other before returning it to its position on the desk. The desk drawers were unlocked and he pulled each one open in turn. The top drawer contained the usual scattering of writing equipment:

pens, pencils, rulers, a stapler and a pair of scissors. The second was full of paper and envelopes, varying in size, and an old Oxford English Dictionary. His heart stopped when he opened the third. Along with a box of tissues and a stash of old newspapers, there was a list of names. Each name had a telephone number beside it. The last name on the list was Vince Savage. He folded the paper in half and slid it in his back pocket.

The heavy breathing coming from the training field brought a sadistic smile to Crawford's face. He'd promised them a tough session today and that's exactly what they'd got. Their loss to Spurs had been disastrous, but Burnley's two-nil win over Arsenal meant they'd kept their position in the league. Sixth wasn't ideal, but they were still on target for a place in the Champion's League and that, he conceded, was something.

'All right, lads, let's call it a day,' he shouted. 'Same again tomorrow.' Their sighs of relief were audible and he chuckled at their obvious displeasure. 'Simone, spare me a minute afterwards, would you?'

He noticed her curious glance but turned his back, striding towards the changing rooms. He'd had second thoughts about his decision to end it with Simone, particularly when she'd bent down in front of him earlier, but until he'd resolved this thing with Thomas, he wanted to focus on his family. An ironic snort escaped from his lips. *I'll be wearing a fucking halo next!*

'What's up?' Simone asked, once the players had roared away in their supercars and the two of them were alone. He was in the changing room, looking more than a little out of place having changed into his suit and tie. He looked at her tracksuit-clad body, aware of the treasure underneath, and hesitated before he spoke.

'I need to call things off,' he said, looking into her beautiful, but startled eyes. 'I've got some stuff going on that I need to sort out.'

She stared at him, incredulous, the surprise turning to anger. 'And that's it? You're just walking away? Thanks, Simone, but no thanks?'

'What else do you want me to say?' He sat on the bench, the smell of body odour and sweaty socks combining with the potent dregs of aftershave and deodorant to clog up his throat. 'It's not like it was ever serious. We both knew it was a casual thing. No strings.'

'Oh, did we?' She put heavy emphasis on the 'we' and folded her arms across her chest like a child who couldn't get her own way. Crawford sighed in frustration.

'Come on, Simone. Don't be like that. We still need to work together. Let's at least try and be civil.'

'Civil? You bastard, Crawford! Who is she?' Her body language was comical, but he knew better than to laugh. Her hands were now resting on her hips, her chin jutting towards him, her eyes blazing. She'd be issuing him with a red card next. Serious foul play. It wouldn't be the first time. His disciplinary record was about as clean as his driving licence.

'I said, who is she?'

'What? What do you mean?'

'You can't go five minutes without lightening your load. Who is she?'

Simone had a point. He had wondered how he was going to manage without a regular outlet for his frustration, but now wasn't the time to admit it.

'There's no one else, Simone. As I said, I've just got some stuff going on. It's important, I need to sort it.'

She didn't believe a word of it, he could tell. Ironic really; the one time he was telling the truth, he was accused of lying.

'Well, don't expect me to be waiting for you when you've sorted your so-called stuff,' she spat. 'You only get one chance with me, Crawford, and you just blew it!'

He stayed seated after she'd left trying not to breathe in the thick, pungent air. Eventually, the smell forced him outside, where he buttoned up his coat against the cold. The temperature had dropped in the last hour, and not just because of Simone's icy response. At least he'd had the foresight to book a taxi.

'Dad?'

'Jesus Christ, Thomas, what the fuck are you doing? You scared me to death.'

'Sorry. Can we talk?'

Crawford was still trying to calm his rapid heartbeat, not to mention come to terms with the fact that his son was standing in front of him. He'd neither seen nor spoken to Thomas since his homosexuality became public knowledge back in September. He was torn between wanting to pull him into a hug and punch him for his cowardice. He did neither.

'I thought you were in Scotland.'

'I was. I came back to talk to you. Shall we?' He gestured towards the taxi and Crawford nodded a response. They both climbed in and banged the doors shut.

They sat in silence, the only sound coming from the grinding gears and growling engine of the taxi. For once, Crawford was grateful for the stop-start journey. He needed time to think. He'd already ruined one relationship today and he knew if he wasn't careful, he'd destroy a second. As much as he tried to convince himself that his treatment of Simone was virtuous, he knew he could have handled it differently. She deserved better than an unceremonious dumping in a grungy changing room. He hoped she wouldn't make things difficult at work. The last thing he needed was a mardy physio throwing temper tantrums every five minutes. He cast a sideways glance at Thomas, but his son was staring blankly out of the window. Crawford had no idea what he was thinking, and it was that, he realised, that was making him nervous. Crawford liked to be in control or, at the very least, know what he was walking into. Even Saturday's meeting with the chairman had been preferable to this. He'd known he was in for a bollocking and was able, therefore, to prepare his response. In that particular case, he'd blamed his players (obviously) and the fact that certain injuries had prevented him from picking his first eleven. He'd even managed to deflect the accusations of bad management by pointing the finger of blame firmly in the opposite direction. He needed a bigger squad and to build a bigger squad he needed a bigger budget. He'd ended the conversation by naming at least three players he wanted to buy in the January transfer window. The fact that he still had a job suggested he may have won that particular battle. The looming encounter with Thomas was another thing entirely.

Arriving at his father's office, Thomas hung his coat and scarf on the old-fashioned oak hat stand and sat on the leather sofa. He knew a little about office politics and had no intention of giving his father the advantage by sitting opposite him at his desk. Everyone knew the visitor's chair was always lower than the host's and with the desk acting as a physical barrier, it was hardly the environment for a fair and frank exchange of views. He watched his father slowly remove his own coat and realised, with a hint of satisfaction, he was nervous. His father never did anything slowly so seeing him now was like watching a slow-motion version of the real Crawford Kelly.

'Drink?'

'Coffee, thanks.' He didn't particularly want a drink but was interested to see whether he would make it himself or ask one of his minions to do it. He couldn't see a kettle or a coffee machine, just crystal glasses and a decanter full of what he presumed was whisky. He was still taking in the splendour of the office – an office he'd never set foot in before – when he heard his father pick up the phone.

'Two coffees please, Ivy. My usual and erm…'

'Black decaf,' said Thomas, filling in the blank. His father didn't even know how he liked his coffee. That just about summed up their relationship. At least he had the grace to look embarrassed, he noticed, although the fact that he'd chosen to sit at his desk rather than in the lounge area with Thomas was less gratifying.

His office was a larger version of the study at home. The same dark furniture, busy bookshelves and framed photographs. There was a picture of his father with the late, great Bobby Robson, and another with his hero, Sir Alex Ferguson. An impressive selection of trophies stood proud inside a glass cabinet, their collective glare a stark contrast to the gloom of the masculine décor.

Thomas looked at his father and tried to picture a female sitting in his place. It had to happen sooner or later. More and more women were securing the top jobs and sport was no different. Even with his own limited football knowledge, he knew of at least one female chairperson. Before long the Premiership would employ female referees, female coaching staff and eventually, female managers. And not just for the women's game. For all Thomas knew, they might already do so. He allowed himself a small smile and tried to imagine how different the office would look with a woman in charge.

'What's funny?' his father asked, regarding him from behind his desk.

'Nothing.' Thomas had no desire to hear a tirade of chauvinistic abuse so kept his thoughts to himself.

They both turned at the sound of a faint knock and watched as a pretty, dark-haired girl entered with a tray. Ivy, Thomas presumed. She was probably around eighteen or nineteen, wearing plain black trousers and a royal-blue blouse. Her hair was tied back in a neat plait and she visibly shook as she placed the tray on the desk, the teaspoons playing tunes on the saucers. Thomas wondered if she was terrified of her boss or could sense the strained atmosphere in the office. Probably both.

'Thanks, Ivy.'

She retreated swiftly, closing the door behind her. Thomas rose from his seat and collected his coffee from the tray, sparing his father the embarrassment of asking if he wanted sugar. He returned to the sofa, unwilling to play whatever power game usually took place over the desk. A series of unwelcome images flashed through his mind at the thought. He blinked them away, sipping his coffee as he did so.

'For someone who wanted to talk, you're not saying very much.'

'I'm not sure where to start.' He watched his father stand up and walk to the window, his breath casting clouds on the glass.

'Tell me about Scotland.'

'What do you want to know? It's cold.' He laughed, but his father didn't join in. 'I've rented a cottage at Culzean. It's small but cosy. I'm selling my paintings locally. I'm doing okay.'

'Do you intend to stay there?'

Thomas had asked himself the same question but still didn't know the answer. 'I'm not sure. Maybe.'

His father continued to stare out of the window. The elephant in the room seemed to be growing bigger and less surmountable by the minute. Thomas needed to tackle it before it crushed them completely.

'I'm sorry if I embarrassed you,' he said, a hint of bitterness creeping into his voice. 'It was never my intention.'

His father remained silent but moved away from the window and leant against the edge of his desk. 'I know.' His arms were folded and his legs crossed at the ankles. Thomas wished he would sit down.

'I've only ever wanted to make you proud, Dad.' He hated himself for sounding like a ten-year-old desperate for his father's approval but realised that was exactly what he was. He'd spent his entire life trying to live up to his father's expectations and had failed miserably.

'I know,' he said again.

'But you can't turn me into something I'm not.' He was referring to both his sexuality and his inability to play football and wondered which of the two his father would heed.

'I know.'

'Are you going to say anything else?' Thomas asked, his frustration finally getting the better of him.

'Thought I'd go for the hat-trick.'

His father had a smart answer for everything, but even Thomas had to smile at that one.

'I'm sorry, son. I know I put pressure on you and I should've realised from the start that football wasn't your thing, but it's all I've ever known. I just took it for granted that you'd play and couldn't get it into my thick head that you didn't want to.'

'It's not that I didn't want to, Dad. I was no good at it. I've seen dogs in the park with better ball control than me!'

Now it was Crawford's turn to smile. He unfolded his limbs and finally, sat next to Thomas. 'It's a nice life, son. An easy life if you play your cards right. I've earned more money than I ever thought possible. I just wanted the same for you. I didn't want you to struggle in some dead-end job lining someone else's pockets. I wanted you to have the best things in life, like I have.'

'But the best things in life aren't fancy cars and big houses,' he argued. 'There's more to life than designer clothes and exotic holidays.'

'I know that. And I'll never forget where I came from. But money doesn't just buy you material things, it buys you respect.'

'It doesn't buy you happiness though, does it?' His question remained unanswered, his father surprisingly lost for words. 'And you earn respect, Dad, you don't buy it.'

His father sighed. 'You're right,' he said. 'And I'm sorry.'

Their conversation was halted by the telephone, its warbling tone an unwelcome disturbance.

Crawford stood and snatched it from its cradle. 'Hold my calls,' he barked, without a please or a thank you.

'You won't earn respect talking to people like that.'

'Don't lecture me, Thomas. I'm not in the mood.' He sat back down, lifting one ankle on to the opposite knee and playing with his shoelace. 'I did my best you know, for you and Abi. I know it wasn't easy changing schools all the time, but they were always the best schools.'

'And I repaid you by taking up art?'

A defeated smile was all the confirmation Thomas needed. 'I'm creative, Dad. Football was your way of expressing yourself. Art is mine. We're not so different at the end of the day. You talk with your feet, I talk with my hands.'

'It's hardly the same, is it?'

'But it is! It's exactly the same. We both get paid for doing something we enjoy, something we're good at. I might not get paid as much as you but I get just as much satisfaction from it, if not more.'

Crawford shifted on the sofa, both feet now back on the floor. 'It's hardly going to make you rich though, is it?'

'I don't care! I don't want to be rich, Dad. I just want to be happy! You've got more money than you know what to do with and you're still miserable. You've got a house you rarely sleep in, a car you can't drive and a wife you don't even speak to. That doesn't look very happy to me.'

The outburst took him by surprise, but it needed to be said. Although, by the look on his father's face, he suspected he may have gone a little too far. His response, when it came, was an unexpected one.

'I could've done without the driving ban reminder, but you're right, life's not completely rosy. I'm trying to change that, though. I'm trying to be a better person.'

'You could start by apologising to Ivy.'

His smile was one of acceptance. 'There are a few people I need to apologise to, starting a little closer to home.'

'Mum?'

'Yes, your mother is certainly one of them. I haven't been the best husband recently, although she does push me to my limit at times.'

Thomas nodded. That much was true, he knew. 'I take it you know she's in Scotland?'

'Aye, I heard about your little crossover. Unfortunate but entertaining.'

Thomas noticed his wry smile.

'How long's she staying for?' his father asked.

'I don't know. Sasha's mum can't hold the fort forever, so I don't suppose she'll stay up there for too long.'

'It's a wonder she's not back already. It's not exactly brimming with activity up there, is it?'

'No,' he admitted, picturing his mother all dressed up with nowhere to go. 'But the change should do her good. Abi said she'd not been herself just lately.'

'I'm surprised Abi's had the time to notice. She's hardly been at home, what with all the assignments she's been doing.'

Thomas noticed the switch in conversation from his mother to Abi and had no desire to indulge his father by discussing his blue-eyed girl. Besides, the elephant, he noticed, was still very much in the room.

'Yeah. Seems I'm not the only one with his picture in the papers.' He saw his father clench his fists before turning to Thomas with sullen eyes. *It's now or never,* Thomas realised. 'Although I suspect you knew more about that than I did.'

'What? What do you mean by that?'

He watched him for a moment, waiting for a telltale sign of guilt or acknowledgement. His face gave nothing away.

'How do you know Vince Savage?'

The flinch was barely noticeable, but it was there nonetheless.

'Who?'

'Don't lie to me, Dad. I found his details in your study. Did you set me up?'

'What were you doing in my study? How dare you go through my stuff?' His father leapt to his feet, his face a picture of indignation. Thomas noticed that he hadn't answered the question.

'I didn't go through your stuff. I found them by accident. And that's not really important, is it? What's important is why you would do that. Why you would deliberately set out to humiliate me.'

His father was back at the window, angry clouds of breath obscuring his view. Thomas remained seated, waiting for a response. None came.

193

'Are you going to answer me?' he asked.

His father turned to look at him, his jaw clenched, his hands in his trouser pockets. 'I wasn't trying to humiliate you. I was trying to help you.'

'Help me?' Thomas could hardly believe his ears. 'You thought a dose of blackmail would help me? What the hell were you trying to achieve?' He leant forward and held his head in his hands.

'I knew you were gay, Thomas. I probably knew before you did. You were unhappy. Struggling. I thought if I gave you a little nudge, it would help you on your way. Stop you from fighting the obvious.'

He looked up at his father, aghast. 'Most fathers would take their son to one side and have a quiet word. Reassure him that it was okay to be gay, nothing to be ashamed of. Not arrange a blackmail campaign with the local villain!'

'That wasn't meant to happen.' He looked down at his shoes, unable to meet his son's eye.

Thomas was regretting ever starting this conversation, but there was no going back now. 'I think you'd better start from the beginning.' He leant back in his seat and waited for his father to sit down.

'I know I don't show it very often, but I do love you, Thomas. The same as I love your mother, and Abi. You're all really important to me. And it was heartbreaking to watch you struggle with your emotions, seeing you wrestle your own identity.' He paused, as if seeking permission to continue. 'I thought, if it was laid out on a plate for you, you'd finally accept it and come out. Tell everyone the truth instead of hiding behind a façade.'

'So you paid Vince to seduce me?'

He nodded, eyes downcast. 'But that was it. That's all it was. I paid him to seduce you, end of story. I told myself I was no different to those dads who took their sons to a prostitute. I just wanted to give you a push in the right direction. A push in *your* direction. I knew nothing about the blackmail until the pictures went viral.'

The information was rolling around in his head like socks in a tumble dryer. It was an unbelievable story yet it made perfect sense. The two of them rarely communicated, so the last thing his father would do was pull him to one side and say '*I know you're gay, son. Do you want to talk about it?'* As absurd and appalling as his actions were, it was just the kind of thing his father would do. As far as Crawford Kelly was concerned, money was the answer to pretty much everything, including, it seemed, encouraging his son to accept his sexual orientation.

'So the blackmail was down to Vince?'

'I assume so. I haven't been able to find him since.'

'You and me both. Who put you in contact with him?'

'Oh, you know how it is. Just someone who knows someone, who knows someone, who knows someone else.'

'No, Dad, I don't. We don't all play by your rules. Some of us have morals.'

His father looked as though he'd aged ten years in the last ten minutes. He stared up at the ceiling and let out a heavy sigh. 'I contacted Billy MacArthur in Glasgow, an old school pal of mine. He's recently done time. He gave me the name of someone down here, a fixer. He then referred me to someone else and so on.'

Thomas thought of the list of names in his back pocket, each one preceded by an arrow. Billy MacArthur at the top, Vince Savage at the bottom.

'And you told each one of them that your son needed a good seeing-to by the local rent boy?' He was starting to feel sick, the memory of vomit splattered shoes heightening the sensation.

'No. It wasn't like that. I didn't mention you. Not until I met Vince.'

'Where did you meet him?'

'In a car park in Ealing.'

Thomas laughed at the ridiculousness of it. 'Have you listened to yourself? This isn't some dodgy cop drama off the TV, this is my life you're talking about! Anything could've happened. He could have killed me! Or you!'

'I know. And I'm sorry, I really am. I know it was stupid and if I could turn the clock back I would. But I can't. Let's just forget about it shall we and move on?'

'Move on? You turn my life upside down and you just want to move on? How much did you pay him?'

'What? Who?'

'Vince. How much did you pay him?'

He loosened his tie and undid the top button of his shirt. 'It doesn't matter.'

'It *does* matter. It matters to me. How much, Dad?'

'Two grand.'

Thomas let the figure sink in before responding. 'Two grand? You're unbelievable. You're not fit to call yourself a father.'

A moment of silence followed. Thomas waited for his father to look at him, but he kept his eyes on the floor. He'd never considered his father a coward but that's exactly what he was. A loathsome, cowardly human being. He stood up and grabbed his coat and scarf, draping them both over his arm.

'Where are you going?'

'As far away from you as possible.'

'Don't be like that, Thomas. I said I was sorry. Thomas!'

With the little dignity he had left, Thomas turned his back on his father and walked out, closing the door softly behind him.

Chapter 30

Abi looked at her watch. She was due to meet Cory this afternoon and was desperate to leave. Thanks to her mother's disappearing act, she'd been forced to help Lydia in the office and was not at all impressed to learn that her mother intended to stay in Scotland until the weekend.

'She's taking a bit of a liberty, isn't she? Leaving you in the lurch like that?'

Lydia didn't seem at all perturbed. 'It meant rescheduling a couple of interior design appointments, but it's no big deal. A few days in Scotland should do your mother the world of good. She hasn't been herself of late. And Thomas will be glad of the company, I'm sure, when he finally gets there!'

Abi felt a stab of guilt. She hadn't even considered her brother's feelings. She really must learn to be less selfish. Besides, while her mother was up in Scotland, she wasn't making Abi's life a misery down here.

'Patrick did a wonderful job with Ursla's pictures, didn't he?' said Lydia, looking up at the stunning photograph on the wall.

Abi was glad of the change of subject, but as much as she had to agree with Lydia, she was still slightly mystified by the disappearance of Cory's picture. She'd noticed its absence as soon as she'd opened the door this morning, his moody stare replaced by Ursla's provocative pose.

'Can't be seen to show favouritism,' was all Lydia had said when Abi had queried the switch. Abi had wanted to object but realised she had to be careful what she said. She'd found Cory's picture stashed behind the props cupboard and desperately wanted to retrieve it and hang it back up. She'd resisted the urge and consoled herself with a sneaky peak each time she left her seat.

'Yeah. They're stunning,' she said now. 'She's a lucky girl. She'd probably be stacking shelves in some supermarket or other if you hadn't spotted her.'

'Maybe. Danny's portfolio is equally impressive,' Lydia said with a hint of pride. 'Did I tell you, BooHoo booked him without a moment's hesitation? I have a feeling Danny Venus will soon be a household name. And, let's be honest, a name like that deserves to be up in lights, don't you think?'

'I guess so. But not as bright as Abi Kelly's!' She treated Lydia to a cheeky wink and stood to leave.

'You're incorrigible, Abi,' Lydia replied, laughing. 'Get out of here before your head can longer fit through the door!'

She heard Cory's car pull up on the drive and felt the familiar pang of excitement as her heart danced the rumba. She'd made herself completely at home during his absence, swimming in the pool, relaxing in the sauna, then stretching out on a recliner before washing and drying her hair. She was still makeup free when she greeted him at the front door, naked but for a simple oversized sweater.

'Hello,' she beamed. 'How did it go?'

'The same as yesterday. I don't know what your father's problem is, but whatever it is, I wish he'd sort it out.'

She closed the door behind him, the sound of the latch muted by his kitbag dropping heavily on the solid oak floor. She followed him through to the kitchen, disappointed by the lack of a kiss. 'You know exactly what his problem is,' she said, 'you lost four-one to Spurs.'

'There's more to it than that,' he said, taking a bottle of Evian from the fridge and drinking straight from the bottle. 'If he carries on like this, we won't be match fit on Saturday, we'll all be fucking knackered.' He put the water back in the fridge and helped himself to a bowl of grapes. Abi watched him throw them into this mouth, one after the other, like basketballs into a hoop.

'He laid into Grayson earlier,' he said, between grapes. 'All he did was ask Simone if she could look at his shoulder.'

'Who's Simone?'

'Physio. I mean, I know Grayson can be a dick, but that was genuinely all he said. Your dad all but jumped down his throat.'

Abi frowned. 'I wonder if he's spoken to Thomas'

'Your brother?'

198

'Yeah. Thomas said he was going to speak to him, but I don't know if he has. I haven't seen him since Sunday.' She looked around for her handbag. 'I should call him.'

'Yeah, you should.' He threw the empty dish into the sink and grabbed an apple from the fruit bowl on the centre island, biting into it noisily. 'And tell him to apologise for fuck's sake. If your father carries on like this, he'll give himself a coronary. And the rest of us, for that matter.' The apple was demolished in a matter of seconds, core and all. 'I'm gonna sit by the pool for a while.'

Abi watched him disappear through the glass door at the rear of the kitchen. She sighed and dug around in her bag until she found her phone. The call went straight to voicemail and she wondered if Thomas still hadn't charged his phone. She left a message anyway then sauntered through to the pool. Cory was horizontal on a lounger, his clothes in a messy heap on the adjacent chair. His chest was bare, a pair of stars and stripes surf shorts embraced his hips. His hair was loose, his eyes closed. *He looks more like a surfer than a footballer,* she thought. She stood over him for a moment, her eyes scanning his rippled abdomen, his solid thighs and his smooth, hairless chest. The eagle tattoo was watching her, its evil eye strangely disturbing. The music she put on earlier was still playing in the background: Rita Ora's 'Hot Right Now' summing it up for Abi. Cory still hadn't moved. In fact, if she wasn't mistaken, he was actually asleep. She watched him a moment longer, his chest rising and falling with each restful breath. Her own breathing wasn't quite so steady. She'd anticipated a much friendlier welcome when he returned from training. His casual response had both surprised and irked her in equal measure. A wicked smile stretched across her face and, deciding she knew exactly how to grab his attention, she positioned herself behind his lounger. In one swift movement, she upended the lounger, then watched in delight as he slid into the water. Abi was helpless with laughter. Cory, on the other hand, was absolutely furious. Still splattering in the water, he looked up at Abi, his eyes filled with rage.

'What the fuck are you doing?'

Between giggles she managed to reply, 'I wanted to wake you up.'

His raging stare silenced her and she began to chew on a fingernail. She backed away slightly as he clambered out of the water, his eyes now matching those of the eagle. She thought back to the slap she'd received and was suddenly nervous.

'It was meant to be funny,' she muttered. 'It's no different to what you did to me.'

'It's not a fucking competition, you stupid bitch!' He grabbed a towel from a neighbouring lounger and rubbed his hair vigorously. Her heart was no longer dancing the sensuous steps of the rumba, it was dancing a fast-paced cha-cha-cha, complete with extra beats. She felt her chin quiver and, determined not to cry, marched towards the door.

'Abi!'

She heard him call her name but didn't look back. Instead, she pulled on her boots at the front door, left her door key on the hall table and let herself out.

Thomas had indeed recharged his phone; he'd bought a new charger in the shop around the corner from his studio on Sunday. His phone, however, had been switched off since yesterday, the continuous calls from his father finally proving too much. He was playing with the offending item now, turning it round and round on the table like spin the bottle. Tiring of the game, he slid it back into his jacket pocket and turned his attention to the commuters outside. He was sitting in a bar in Marylebone, waiting for Justin to finish his shift at the clinic. His coat and scarf were hanging on the stag's head coat hook behind him and an empty pint glass stood forlornly on the table, ladders of froth clinging to the inside. It was raining outside. Dots of drizzle were dropping on the window; umbrellas appeared like magic, creating a giant nylon canopy above bent, bobbing heads.

'Another drink, sir?' The accent was Eastern European, Polish perhaps. Thomas nodded.

'Two please,' he said. 'One for my friend.'

Right on cue, Justin pushed open the heavy glass door and dropped his umbrella in the cylindrical stand. Raindrops decorated the shoulders of his coat and a tartan scarf was knotted at his neck. He raised a hand at Thomas and walked towards him, sliding his coat from his shoulders and hanging it on the antlers.

'I've ordered,' Thomas said. 'How was your day?'

Justin sat in the opposite chair and unwound his scarf. He'd removed his tie and the top two buttons of his shirt were open. Thomas swallowed, unsure which was most alluring; the glimpse of chest chair at his neck or those now so familiar green eyes.

'Good. Plenty of happy customers. How about you?' The Scottish accent wasn't quite so alluring, but that was hardly Justin's fault. 'Have you spoken to your father yet?'

'Yes. Yesterday.'

Justin's eyebrows shot up in surprise. 'And? How did it go?'

The arrival of their drinks delayed his response and they both watched as two pints were placed in front of them. The waitress offered them a polite smile. Her chipped red nail polish matched her lipstick and the tip of a tattoo escaped under the sleeve of her blouse. Thomas wondered briefly what it could be. A flower perhaps, or a boy's name?

'Enjoy.'

'Thank you,' they said in unison.

'So?' Justin urged. 'What did he say?'

He took a long sip of his beer. 'He admitted to setting me up.'

'What? Seriously?'

The look on Justin's face was comical. He was obviously struggling to accept that any father could, or would, do something so malicious. Thomas filled him in on the details. How his father had known he was gay, how and why he'd found Vince, how much he'd paid him, what he'd hoped to achieve.

'If it wasn't so hideous it would be funny,' Thomas admitted.

'But the blackmail was nothing to do with your father?'

'Apparently not.'

'Do you believe him?'

Thomas thought about it for a second. 'Yes, I do. He had no reason to lie. And his story makes sense, as ridiculous as it is.'

'So what now?' Justin asked. 'Will you go the police?'

'The police? What for?'

'You were blackmailed, Thomas,' he said, as though he'd asked the most stupid question in the world. 'It's a criminal offence.'

Thomas sat back in his chair and looked at Justin. 'It hadn't even occurred to me.'

'Don't you think he should be punished, this Vince guy?'

'I didn't actually pay the money.'

'So what?' Justin was raising his voice in frustration and Thomas looked around the bar, embarrassed. 'He still tried to blackmail you, whether you paid the money or not. And he posted the pictures online, that has to be a cyber offence of some kind. Not to mention the profit he made from the papers.'

'I doubt the papers paid him anything. They're not allowed to do that anymore, are they? I think I'd rather just forget about it,' Thomas conceded. 'If I tell the police, the whole sorry mess will start all over again. People have forgotten about it now. They're more interested in that bent politician and who's going to win *Strictly*.'

'So you're just going to let him get away with it?' His accent became stronger when he was angry, Thomas noticed, just like his father.

'I can't tell the police without explaining my father's involvement, and I really don't want to do that. He's already been slated for drink-driving. If this story gets out, he'll probably get the sack, and I don't want that on my conscience.' He could feel Justin's eyes bore into him, but he daren't look into them. He had a feeling he'd disappointed him and didn't want to see that disappointment reflected in his eyes.

'I just hate the thought of someone taking advantage of you, that's all.'

The change in tone was a welcome one. It was the sound of genuine concern and to Thomas, after a lifetime of loneliness, it was music to his ears.

'Unless it's me, of course.' Justin's eyes were back to their mischievous best and they shared a conspiratorial grin. 'Max tells me your mother's still in Scotland.'

Thomas felt his shoulders relax with the change of subject. He hadn't realised how tense he'd become when regaling the tale of the meeting with his father.

'Yeah. She's staying until the weekend, apparently. I should probably try and head back before then, otherwise we'll be passing each other again at Carlisle.' He smiled at the memory of their respective, reverse journeys.

'Have you decided what you're doing yet? Long term, I mean. Will you stay up there?'

'I'm not sure. What about you? Are you happy here in London? Will you stay on with Max?' He'd aimed for a casual tone but wasn't sure he'd achieved it. In truth, he wanted to know what Justin's intentions were before he made any decisions of his own. He loved it in Scotland, but if it meant sacrificing his relationship with Justin, he wasn't sure he could do it. He suspected Justin had seen right through his enquiry.

'Max is brilliant. I'm learning so much from him, and there's still so much more to learn. I'd be a fool to leave.'

He was right, of course. Why should he leave? Thomas was being selfish, and more than a little presumptuous. For all he knew, Justin might be happy with a casual, no strings relationship. Thomas was the one falling in love. As if his life wasn't complicated enough already.

The whole world was ignoring him, or so Crawford thought. All of his calls had gone unanswered. Thomas, Abi, Florentina and Max were all clearly, otherwise engaged. He tortured himself with images of them all together, laughing and joking at his expense. He knew he was being ridiculous, Florentina was four hundred miles away, after all, but he was struggling with the isolation that had surrounded him since his confession to Thomas. And without Simone to stoke his fire, he felt utterly bereft.

A flash of lightning lit up the lounge and he walked to the window to watch the approaching storm. His Jaguar stared back at him from the driveway, its headlights like two accusing eyes, raindrops dripping like tears. He looked up to the sky, waiting for the rumbling clap of thunder that was sure to follow. It came but was too far away to be forceful. He was reminded of a date with Florentina many years ago. They hadn't known each other long; she was still only nineteen. He'd taken her to the pictures to see *Pretty Woman* and they'd fooled around in the back row. When they'd emerged from the cinema it was pouring with rain and they'd ran, hand in hand, to a nearby telephone box. Lightning flashed in the sky around them and thunder shook the glass in their temporary shelter. They'd clung to each other, hair stuck to their foreheads, raindrops dripping from their noses. Crawford remembered thinking that he'd never been happier. They'd stayed in the phone box for almost an hour waiting for the rain to stop. The acrid smell of urine and cigarette smoke clung to their clothes, they drew pictures in the steam on the windows, and kissed until their lips were sore.

Another flash of lightning brought him back to the present but the image remained. He'd been a good person then; caring, generous, kind. He caught sight of his reflection in the window and wondered exactly when he'd turned into the obnoxious, selfish bastard that stared back at him. One thing was for sure, unless he did something about it, he'd soon be a very lonely, very sad, old man.

Chapter 31

'Need help with those?'

Florentina turned at the sound of Rupert's voice. She was lifting supermarket shopping from the boot of her car, a trip deemed necessary at the news of Thomas's return.

'Yes, please, if you're not too busy.'

He lifted the two remaining bags from the car and followed her into the cottage, dropping the bags on to the kitchen counter.

'Having a party?' he asked, taking in the amount of food she'd purchased.

'Thomas is due back later.' She was smiling as she said it, genuinely looking forward to seeing her boy. 'Coffee?'

'No, thanks. I'd better get back. I'm due on a conference call in...' he slid his sleeve along his wrist and checked his watch, 'four minutes.'

'Oh. Well, you'd better get a move on then. Join us for dinner later?' It was an impulsive invitation and she hoped Thomas wouldn't object to an unexpected guest.

'If you're sure? I don't want to intrude.'

'Don't be silly. You're more than welcome. Seven thirty?'

'Okay, thanks. See you later.'

She began to put the shopping away, still wearing her padded coat. It was bitterly cold, the gusty wind only adding to the biting temperatures. She looked up at the wall clock. Thomas's train was due in Ayr at 14:20. She'd promised to pick him up and she didn't want to be late.

She checked her phone for messages, expecting a progress report from Thomas. Crawford's was the last name she expected to see. She'd missed a call from him last night but he hadn't left a message and he hadn't called back. Assuming it was unimportant or that he'd called her by mistake, she'd soon forgotten about it. She opened his message now and frowned at the content.

Hi. Hope you're ok. Just wondered when you'd be home x

She was so taken aback, she had to sit down. Perching on the sofa, she read the message again. Someone else must have sent it, she concluded. Crawford never put a kiss at the end of his messages. In fact, he very rarely sent messages. The last one he'd sent simply said, **Where are you**, without so much as a question mark. A dozen possible scenarios played out in her head. His physio friend had sent it, wanting to know how much longer she'd got him to herself. He was changing the locks in the house. He was leaving her and moving out. He'd found out about her affair ten years ago and was divorcing her. If she didn't already know Thomas was on his way back, she'd think Crawford was plotting to kill him and was setting her up for his murder.

'For God's sake, Florentina, get a grip!' She instantly regretted her outburst, concerned that Rupert may have heard her through the wall, then realising that the walls were so thick you wouldn't hear if an aircraft landed next door. She looked at the message again. Maybe it was genuine. Maybe she'd imagined his rantings through the door of his study, she hadn't exactly been coherent at the time. One thing was for sure, there was nothing to be gained by worrying about it.

She looked up at the clock once more and decided to leave for Ayr. She'd be very early, but there was no point sitting around the cottage tormenting herself with conspiracy theories. There was probably a perfectly innocent explanation behind Crawford's text message. She just wished she knew what it was.

Thomas emerged from the station and ran towards the silver Lexus, his hold-all bouncing heavily on his back. He snatched open the passenger door and hauled his bag onto the back seat. The rain had left dark spots on his denim jacket and he smelt of public transport, grimy and stale. Nevertheless, his mother hugged him for longer than was necessary. He broke away and smiled. 'Hello, stranger.'

'Hello, yourself,' she answered, starting the engine. 'It's good to see you.' She pulled out of the station car park and joined the queue of traffic snaking alongside the taxi rank. 'How was your journey?'

'Uncomfortable, compared to yours,' he answered, already appreciating the plush leather interior of his mother's car and the benefit of the heated seat. He'd travelled standard class again, still unwilling to pay the inflated cost of a first-class ticket. His seat had a dip in it the size of a wok and his smartphone earPods had failed to drown out the constant chatter that surrounded him in the carriage, regardless how loud he set the volume.

'You look well,' said his mother, 'if a little tired.'

'Yeah, it'll be good to get home.' He was conscious of his mention of 'home' but if his mother noticed, she chose not to comment.

'Did you see your father?'

'Yeah. Can we talk about it later though? It's been a long day.'

'Of course we can, darling. Although...' Thomas glanced at his mother, waiting for her to continue. 'We have company for dinner. I invited Rupert to join us.'

Thomas couldn't suppress his surprise. 'Really? How come?'

'He's been very good to me while you've been away. Showed me around, made sure I had everything I needed. We went to Portpatrick on Sunday.'

'Wow. And here was me picturing you cooped up in the cottage all by yourself, watching *Strictly* and eating pork scratchings.'

Florentina laughed out loud. 'I don't know anybody in this world who eats pork scratchings,' she shivered dramatically at the thought, 'other than you, of course, so your stash remains intact. I will admit to watching *Strictly* though. That rugby player is a bit of all right, don't you think?'

Now it was his turn to laugh. Did his mother just encourage him to comment on another man's sex appeal? This was a conversation he could never have imagined having with his mother. It felt good, if a little surreal.

They left the town of Ayr behind, the spires and chimney pots replaced by the lush, green Carrick Hills, fields dotted with hungry sheep, and magnificent views of the Isle of Arran. They left the rain behind too. The clouds had lifted and the contours of Arran were clearly visible. Some days there was no sign of the island at all, as though the clouds had swallowed it whole leaving not so much as a crumb. Not today, though. The sky was now a brilliant blue.

Thomas felt himself unwind, his body and mind relaxing with every mile. 'He seems a nice guy. Rupert, I mean. I don't know him well, but he's always pleasant enough.'

'He's a widower. Did you know? Lost his wife to MND three years ago.'

They turned a corner, heading inland.

'MND?'

'Motor neurone disease.'

'No, I didn't know. I just presumed he was divorced.' Thomas thought it was sad that his mother had discovered more about his neighbour in six days, than he'd managed to ascertain in two months. He really must make more of an effort; although, he wasn't exactly feeling sociable when he'd first arrived in town. 'Is that what Stephen Hawking had?'

'Yes, I think so. Sad, isn't it? She was only fifty-one.'

'It certainly puts our own problems into perspective, doesn't it?'

They were following a tractor now, their progress slow and their view somewhat curtailed.

'Have you managed to resolve any of your problems?' she asked. 'I know you don't want to talk about your father, but was it worth it, your trip back to London?'

He sighed and turned to watch a kestrel hovering above the hedgerow. He lost sight of it as it swooped. Thomas felt sorry for its prey.

'Let's just say we cleared the air,' he said, turning back to his mother. 'I'm not sure our relationship's any better for it, but at least I don't have to pretend anymore.'

An opportunity to overtake presented itself and he felt the increase in speed as she accelerated past the tractor, the scenic view restored.

'I was worried about you,' she said, reducing her speed. 'I didn't like to think of you down there, alone with your father. He's been acting strange.'

'What do you mean, strange?'

'I'm not sure exactly, just strange.'

Thomas realised he probably knew the reason for his father's strange behaviour, but he had neither the energy nor the inclination to explain. 'He said he's trying to change.'

'Change how?'

'I dunno. Be a better person I guess.'

'Ha! I'll believe it when I see it. Although, that might explain the text message he sent me.'

'What text message?'

'Oh, it's nothing. Let's just say it was out of character.'

She indicated, slowed, and turned into the castle grounds, then followed the road down to the cottage. Thomas climbed out, dragged his bag from the back seat and fished around for his keys. His mother beat him to it and opened the door. The warmth embraced them, welcoming them like a faithful Labrador. It smelt different, Thomas noticed. The familiar smell of paint remained but it was diluted by his mother's perfume, strong and sweet. His favourite wood-burning smell was also missing, an obvious absence in the circumstances.

He shook off his jacket and laid it over the back of the sofa.

'Any beers in the fridge?' he asked.

'You're in luck,' she smiled. 'I went shopping earlier.' She handed him a chilled bottle of Budweiser and he removed the lid with the magnetic bottle opener from the fridge door.

'What time is Rupert coming round?' he asked, before swallowing the top half of his beer.

'Seven thirty.'

'And what are you cooking?'

She looked at him as though he'd just asked her to strip naked.

'Me?'

'Yes, Mother, you. You're the one who invited him.'

'But... but I can't cook!'

He laughed then, unable to keep up the pretence. He'd known as soon as she'd mentioned it that he'd be the one to cook dinner. His mother could barely boil an egg let alone cook for a guest.

'Don't worry, I'll make something,' he said. 'What's in the fridge?'

He opened the door to scan the contents, smiling as he heard his mother's footsteps disappearing up the stairs.

'I think you should just forget about it, Abi. He's said he's sorry. He's sent you flowers. What more do you want?'

Abi was perched in the window seat in Sasha's bedroom, her legs stretched out in front of her, a contented Eiffel snoring loudly on her lap. Sasha was sitting at her desk trying, unsuccessfully it would seem, to complete an assignment for uni.

'I want a proper relationship,' she said sulkily. 'We never go anywhere. We never do anything.'

'I don't think that's strictly true,' said Sasha, grinning. 'Not from what you've told me, anyway.'

Abi didn't rise to the humour. 'You know what I mean. He's still insisting we don't tell anybody.'

'Well, there is your dad to think about. He's probably worried he'll lose his place in the team if your dad finds out.'

'I'm seventeen, Sash, not seven. I can see whoever I like.'

'I don't suppose your dad sees it like that.' She put her pen down and leant back in her chair. 'You're still his little girl. And let's face it, Cory does have a bit of a reputation, even I know that.'

Abi's eyes shot an arrow in Sasha's direction and her friend held her hands up in surrender.

'I'm sorry. I'm just saying it how it is. I'd love to be able to give you a first-hand opinion but as you know, I've never even met the guy. And before you saying anything, a glimpse across the room at the launch party doesn't count.'

It was a sore point between the girls. Sasha was clearly put out that she'd never been introduced to Cory, but Abi didn't get to see him that often. When she did, she wanted him all to herself.

'How am I supposed to introduce you if we never go anywhere?' Abi was a party girl; she took after her mother in that respect. She thrived on attention and craved recognition. And as much as she loved playing happy families in Cory's house, she was beginning to tire of their cosy nights in. In fact, she thought his playboy reputation was a bit of joke. He didn't even drink!

'So, tell him. Tell him you want to go public. Just make sure you're prepared for the consequences. Or the rejection.'

Finally giving up on her assignment, Sasha swapped her chair for the bed. She was immediately joined by Eiffel, who jumped up and rested his head on her thighs. Abi, grateful the weight had lifted from her legs, was now missing the warmth of the dog's little body. She pulled her knees under her chin and hugged them tight.

'What do you think my dad will say?' she asked.

Sasha thought about it for a second. 'I honestly don't know, Abs. What happened when Thomas came back? Has your dad mentioned it?'

'I haven't seen him, to be honest. Thomas said they'd talked but I haven't seen Dad since. Thomas told me something else as well.' Abi wasn't sure if she should tell Sasha about Justin, but there didn't seem much point keeping it a secret now. Sasha already knew he was gay, so it wasn't as though she would be upset by the news.

'He's seeing Jock the Doc.'

Sasha's eyes widened in surprise. 'No way! Really?'

'Yeah. Apparently Justin went up to Scotland to see him and then they got together again when Thomas came back.'

'I still can't believe it,' Sasha said, running a hand over Eiffel's back. 'How did I not know he was gay?'

'I didn't spot it either,' admitted Abi, 'but anyway, they have a bit of a thing going on.'

'I take it your dad doesn't know about that either?'

'I have no idea. Presumably not.'

'What about your mum?'

'What about her?' Abi felt her heckles rise at the mention of her mother.

'Does she know?'

Abi shrugged. 'Dunno. Rumour has it she's coming back at the weekend, so we'll soon find out.'

'And what are you doing at the weekend?' Sasha asked. 'Is your dad home or away?'

'Away. They're playing Leicester.'

'So you won't be seeing Cory?'

'Doubt it. It will do him good to stew for a bit longer anyway.' She turned to stare out of the window, her attention caught by two pigeons mating on the boundary wall.

'Don't let him stew for too long, will you? Someone else might come along and gobble him up.'

This time Abi did manage a smile, albeit brief. She was aware of the risk she was taking by playing games with Cory. The line of girls waiting to take her place was longer than the Boxing Day queue at Harrods. Maybe she'd let him stew long enough. Leave it any longer, he might just slip through her fingers.

'What about you?' she asked, keenly aware she'd spent all day talking about herself and conscious of the promise she'd made to be less selfish.

'What about me?'

'Any talent at uni?'

Sasha pulled a face. 'You must be joking! Anyway, I want a man not a boy. The lads at uni are sooo immature.'

'You know what you need, don't you?' said Abi, releasing her legs and leaning against the window. 'A good night out!'

Sasha rolled onto her side and propped herself up on an elbow. Eiffel immediately curled himself into her tummy.

'I can't, Abi, I've got so much to do. It's not just the night out itself, it's the day after. Last time we went out I couldn't move for two days.' She let her head drop, as though re-enacting the zombie-like state their night out had induced.

Abi sighed in frustration, then smiled at a genius idea. *I wonder what Ursla's doing this weekend...*

While his wife and son were enjoying an intimate meal with Thomas's neighbour, and his daughter was having dinner with the Templeton-Howes, Crawford was still trying to find out the whereabouts of a certain Vince Savage. Without the list of telephone numbers that Thomas had presumably taken from his study, it was proving rather difficult. The bundle of mail he'd intercepted hadn't included anything useful and he was starting to wonder if he should just forget about the whole sorry saga. And let's face it, turning over a new leaf definitely didn't include chasing around London looking for a bloke who'd conned him out of two thousand quid. But it wasn't about the money – that was neither here nor there – it was about pride. He could cope with Spurs beating them four-nil. Results like that happened in football. If your pride couldn't handle a bad result like that, you were in the wrong job. This was different.

Vince Savage had got one over on him and he didn't like it one little bit. And to make matters worse, he had no one to blame but himself.

He eyed the bottle of Scotch at the side of his desk but resisted the temptation. He'd promised himself he wouldn't drink, not at home anyway. The steps he was taking towards 'the new Crawford Kelly' weren't just small, they were minuscule. But they were steps all the same. He'd ended his affair with Simone, he'd apologised to his son, he'd reached out to his wife (if you could all one text message reaching out), and he'd cut down on the drink. If it was physically possible, he would have given himself a pat on the back.

The bottom drawer of his desk remained open, the stack of newspapers taunting him from inside. Bile formed at the back of his throat, but he reached down all the same, spreading the top one across his desk and thumbing to the appropriate page. He flinched at the now familiar image of his son and stifled a sob, pressing a fist against his lips.

'No!' His fist crashed onto the desk, the resulting vibrations disturbing the dust on the bookshelves. Stunned by his own outburst, he took a moment to compose himself then reached for the phone in his jacket pocket. There were still people he could call. People who knew people. It might cost him more money, but if it produced the result he wanted, then all well and good. He listened for the ring tone whilst lifting the paperweight from his desk with his free hand. Consciously aware of the weight and density in his palm, he studied its shape and size, a whole new thought process running through his mind.

Chapter 32

As far as he could tell, all hotel rooms were the same. He was sick to death of their depressing décor, lumpy pillows and oppressive heating systems. They'd travelled up to Leicester yesterday, checking into their hotel just in time for dinner at six thirty. Crawford had retired to his room immediately after, anxious to avoid the increasing number of fans waiting in the bar; not to mention Simone, who was still as bristly as a dog groomer's hairbrush. He played with the switches beside his bed, blinding himself with a poorly positioned spotlight, before giving up and opening the curtains. He checked his phone for messages (none), filled and switched on the kettle, and turned on the TV. The eight o'clock news had just started and he listened to the headlines. A sixteen-year-old boy had been stabbed to death in North London, a flu epidemic was expected to hit the UK, and online retailers were predicting record sales for Christmas. Crawford cursed at the mention of Christmas. Christmas, for him, meant back-to-back games, the results of which would probably determine whether or not he kept his job. He emptied a sachet of cheap coffee into a mug and added boiling water, breathing in the strong, bitter smell. That was another thing about hotel rooms, the coffee was always rank. He winced at the first sip and abandoned his mug, hoping a shower would liven him up instead.

Thirty minutes later he was enjoying a proper cup of coffee, courtesy of room service. Casually dressed in jeans and a club sweater, he sat at the desk-cum-dressing table and began reading the bundle of newspapers he'd requested when he'd checked in. Unsurprisingly, there was much speculation about today's result after last week's defeat to Spurs. He'd learned a long time ago not to take it personally when sports journalists were less than complimentary about his managerial skills, but still, it hurt. He couldn't afford another loss today and hoped to God Cory Flemming had his shooting boots on. He looked up, as though offering a silent prayer, but only succeeded in catching the eye of Richard III. He vaguely remembered reading that the king's remains had been unearthed somewhere in Leicester. Consequently, the city was now cashing in on the discovery and his picture could be found in virtually every hotel with an LE post code. Personally, he thought Jamie Vardy had done more for Leicester than King Dick ever had, but what did he know?

His mobile phone announced the arrival of a text message and he opened it up, glad of the distraction. Max.

Good luck today.

'I need it, mate,' he said aloud. 'I need it.'

Putting the last of her belongings in the boot of her Lexus, Florentina felt a pang of sadness at having to leave. Undeniably, the trip had done her good. Her pills remained untouched in the bottom of her handbag, she'd barely touched alcohol, other than a glass of wine or two with dinner, and she'd made a new friend in Rupert. Not only that, she'd spent more time with Thomas than she had in years. He'd told her about the conversation with his father and his reasons for fleeing to Scotland. And she'd opened up about her insecurities, including her jealousy of Abi. It felt good to talk about it, she realised, without being judged. She'd also talked about her parents, something she hadn't done for a very long time. Thomas was a good listener; a genuine, sensitive human being. She'd felt her heart tear in two when he'd talked about his sadness as a child, how lonely he'd been and how desperate for love. They'd cried together, their silent tears of sorrow and regret, an unspoken promise of love and support.

'Time to leave?'

She turned at the sound of Rupert's voice. He was standing in his cottage doorway, bright red socks sticking out from beneath his black jeans, the sleeves of his grey V-neck sweater pushed up from his forearms.

'I'm afraid so. All good things must come to an end.' She smiled and walked towards him, dodging a muddy puddle. 'Thank you for your company. It wouldn't have been the same without you.'

'There's no need for thanks. Just take care of yourself. And have a think about my invitation. You'd be most welcome.'

He'd surprised her by inviting her to his daughter's wedding, assuring her that a formal invitation would follow. 'I will, thank you.'

They shared a hug and she breathed in his unfamiliar scent, natural not perfumed. His body shape, so different to Crawford's, felt alien but comforting in her arms.

'Drive safe,' he said.

'I will. And look after Thomas for me.'

'I don't need looking after, Mother.' Thomas appeared beside her, his reprimanding words softened with a smile.

She ruffled his hair and winked at Rupert. 'I know you don't, darling.'

'Let me know when you get back,' Thomas said as he closed the driver's door behind her.

She started the engine and the window slid down. Pharrell Williams blasted from the radio. 'Sorry,' she said, reducing the volume. 'I'm glad we talked,' she whispered, aware that Rupert was still standing in his doorway. 'And whatever you decide is fine by me. Just do what makes you happy.'

Thomas nodded. He looked emotional, as though sorry to see her leave.

'Bye!' She watched them both in her rear-view mirror until they'd disappeared, then blinked away the tears that had blurred her vision. She turned the radio back up and tapped her fingers on the steering wheel, singing along to the words. Feeling as happy as the song intended, she took Pharrell's advice, clapping and singing until she reached the main road when reluctantly, concentration was restored.

Thomas stripped the bed in the spare room and stuffed the sheets in the washing machine along with the clothes he'd bought back from London. He'd enjoyed having a house guest and resolved to do it more often. He'd enjoyed Rupert's company too. Their evening together had been full of laughter and chatter. The seafood dish he'd rustled up had gone down well, the courgette ribbons proving the perfect substitute for spaghetti, the splash of Tabasco sauce adding just the right amount of fire. Rupert had bought three slices of lemon cheesecake, purchased from the local farm shop, and Thomas had been amazed when his mother had devoured her slice. He shook his head at the memory, a smile of disbelief lifting his lips.

He knelt to light the fire, watching as the tiny flickers of flame danced around the logs. In just a few seconds, his face was glowing with warmth and the familiar smell of burning wood filled the cottage. He opened the door of the dining room-cum-studio, inviting the heat inside. His mother may have favoured the central heating, but Thomas rarely switched it on and had turned it off the moment she left. Sliding an old paint-stained apron over his jumper, he studied his work in progress. He'd missed the therapeutic strokes of his brushes, the smell of his paints, the feel of the canvas. He perched on the round wooden stool, found in the tiny attic when he'd moved in, and assessed his latest painting of Dunure Castle. Rupert had marvelled over it on Thursday evening, but Thomas felt it was lacking a certain something. He thought about riding his bike to Dunure, standing once more in the castle ruins and feeling its mood, connecting to its history. One look to the window changed his mind. Heavy raindrops fell like bullets, the gunmetal sky turning slowly black. He wouldn't get any painting done today. He removed his apron and returned to the lounge, aiming the remote control at the TV. He scanned the schedule for the rest of the day, his eyes lighting up at the Rugby 7s, live from Dubai. He'd invite Rupert round to watch it, he decided. That was another reason to like his neighbour. Not only did his mother like him enough to eat his cheesecake, he didn't like football. 'I'm more of a rugby man,' he'd said when the unavoidable conversation of football was raised. His apologetic shrug was endearing and Thomas had found his take-me-as-you-find-me attitude a refreshing change from the eager to please hangers-on he usually encountered.

The washing machine began to spin and he felt the floor vibrate beneath his feet. The fire was hissing and spitting and the rain was playing the drums on the window ledge. He sat down on the sofa, plumping up a cushion behind him, his legs stretched out and crossed at the ankles. He thought about his conversation with his mother and her parting words as she left. *Just do what makes you happy.* He was happy now, he thought to himself. He loved his little cottage, at one with nature, surrounded by history. He was no longer hiding, but the isolated position of the cottage suited him perfectly. He'd never been one for socialising.

He knew his mother would prefer it if he moved back to London, but the thought of giving up the cottage was not a thought he wanted to contemplate. And even if he did, eventually, make peace with his father, moving back into the family home was not an option. The fractious atmosphere at Hollywood Road was ingrained in the furniture. It clung to the walls, festered in the carpets and seeped through the ceilings. He took a deep breath, deliberately breathing in the light, uncomplicated air of the cottage. This was his home now. *Do what makes you happy.*

The coach journey back to London had been swift, the jovial atmosphere and unusually quiet M1 ensuring an easy, stress-free ride. The players' cheery banter and occasional burst into song had entertained him for most of the journey until, one by one, they'd succumbed to their mobile phones or their giant, cushioned headphones and lapsed into silence. He was still replaying their ninetieth minute winner in his head – an audacious back-heeled shot from Flemming – when they pulled into the car park at their home ground. He patted each of his players on the back as they stepped from the coach, each digging out the keys to their chosen supercar. He grimaced as they revved engines and screeched tyres.

'Sounds like a Formula 1 pit lane,' Crawford said to the coach driver, who shook his head having seen it all before. The old Crawford would have downed a few pints, maybe a Scotch or two, and then fell into bed with Simone, or some other piece of skirt silly enough to bat her eyelids at him. The new Crawford, however, decided to call it a night. There was a lot be said for waking up with a clear head and if he got a move on, he'd be home in time for *Match of the Day.*

The sight of Florentina's Lexus in the drive caught him by surprise. So too did his reaction to it. So used was he to putting up defensive barriers at the very sight of his wife (or her car), his lack of aggression amazed him. He clambered out of the taxi and was about to put his key in the lock when the door opened from inside.

'Congratulations,' said Florentina.

Still slightly stunned by her unexpected return, his key poised mid-air, he was momentarily stuck for words.

'You won today, right? One-nil?'

Suddenly finding his tongue he stammered an answer. 'Err, aye. Aye, one-nil.'

'So are you coming in or are you going to stand there all night?'

He stepped inside and heard the door latch behind him. Whatever he was expecting from Florentina, it wasn't this. Thomas must have told her what he'd done, so why wasn't she scratching his eyes out with her fingernails? Or pounding his chest with her fists? For the second time in less than a week, Crawford was nervous. Maybe she had a knife behind her back or a gun in her handbag.

'I wasn't expecting you back yet. When did you leave?' She hadn't replied to his text message and he hadn't seen Abi for days, assuming his daughter even knew of her mother's plans.

'I left this morning, just after nine. Have you eaten?'

He watched her walk into the kitchen, a pair of red and black pompoms bobbing on her feet. He could feel himself frowning. Her carefree behaviour was more than a little unsettling.

'Are you okay?' he asked.

'I'm fine,' she answered without looking at him. 'Have you eaten or not?'

Maybe she intended to poison him. 'Err, aye. I mean no. I'm not hungry.' He watched her as she busied herself in the kitchen, putting things in drawers, rearranging things in cupboards, wiping down the taps.

'What's going on?'

'What do you mean?' she asked, still looking anywhere but at him.

'You're in a strange mood.'

'I'm perfectly fine,' she said, a little too breezily, in his opinion. 'I wasn't expecting you back yet either. No celebratory drinks?'

'Err, no. Not tonight. I'm trying to cut down.'

She looked at him then, as though about to say something but deciding against it.

'I think I'll take a shower,' he said, backing out of the kitchen.

She didn't answer, but followed him out, her familiar Prada perfume confirming that this was indeed his wife and not some alien imposter. Unable to resist for a moment longer, he finally asked the question that had been forming on his lips since he arrived.

'Florentina? What are you wearing on your feet?'

219

She looked down at the offending footwear, the look of delight clear on her face.

'Slippers,' she said, as proud as a victorious child on sports day. 'Cute, aren't they?'

He watched her saunter into the lounge, the spring in her step undeniable. For once, he was lost for words.

Chapter 33

The courier had arrived late yesterday afternoon and his studio was now crammed with easels, canvases, frames and everything else he was unable to carry on the train. They'd also delivered a suitcase of clothes which he'd hung in the spare wardrobe upstairs.

He looked once more at the unfinished London landscapes and reconsidered his decision to dispose of them. His paintings were selling well in the castle gift shop but they weren't commanding anywhere near the price of his London art. They were smaller for a start but also, they didn't have the audience that his work in the capital could attract. Buyers up here were mainly tourists, many constricted by airline baggage restrictions or the confines of their mobile homes. Others just wanted a little something to remind them of their visit to the castle. His mother had already proved what his paintings could command if shown to the right audience; he'd be a fool not to follow it up. He thought back to what Max had said all those weeks ago in his office. *It didn't do George Michael any harm, did it?* As much as he shied away from the spotlight, he knew if he wanted to make a name for himself in the art world, he'd have to put himself out there. Besides, thanks to his father, the whole world now knew he was gay, so what did he have to lose?

Before he could change his mind, he grabbed his mobile phone and rang his mother, the words tumbling out faster than children at the school gates.

'Slow down, Thomas,' she laughed. 'What are you so excited about?'

'Would you organise an exhibition for me? At the studio? Justin told me what a great job you did for the party and it's silly paying someone else to do it. I could have it at the gallery in Islington, but then I'd have to pay them commission on any sales. What do you think? Could you do it?'

His mother was still laughing. It was a rare and pleasant sound.

'Are you asking me because my services are free or because you think I'll do a good job?'

'Both,' he admitted, then felt guilty at his assumption. 'Sorry. I shouldn't take advantage of you, of course I'll pay you.'

'Don't be silly, Thomas, I don't want your money. And of course I'll do it, I think it's a fabulous idea.'

'Really?' Great! I was thinking maybe towards the end of January. I wish I'd thought of it before, we could've done it before Christmas.'

'The end of January will be fine, darling. It will give people something to look forward to. January's always such a dull month. I'll start putting a guest list together. Have a think about the date and let me know.'

'Thanks, Mum.'

'It's my pleasure. And Thomas? Leave the price tags to me.'

Time alone with her father was a rare treat these days. Her mother was over at the Templeton-Howes and Abi was flicking through the latest issue of *Cosmopolitan,* her feet resting on her father's lap. The Manchester derby was due to kick-off in half an hour, and although she knew his attention would be on the TV rather than on her, she was still content to be in his company, relaxing on the sofa and soaking up his praise.

'If you stare at the page any longer, you'll go cross-eyed.'

Her father had correctly predicted that she had paused at page twelve where her own face stared back at her with a glorious sultry pout. The photoshoot for Max Factor had been one of the toughest yet – the photographer insisting they continued well beyond the timescale allotted – but she had to admit, the results were amazing.

'Have you seen it?' she asked, holding up the page in front of him, knowing very well that he'd seen it at least a dozen times already.

'Aye, I've seen it,' he laughed, the pride in his eyes unmistakable. 'You look stunning, my angel.'

She laid the magazine over her legs, unable to drag her eyes away from the page. 'I saw it on the side of a bus the other day! Can you imagine? I nearly ran into a cyclist when I saw it. And there's a huge one by the slip road on the M1. I saw it when I drove to Milton Keynes yesterday.'

'Milton Keynes?'

'Yeah, I went to meet Ursla. She's a new model. We went shopping.'

'In Milton Keynes?'

'I know,' she laughed, 'It's not the best, is it? We had a nice afternoon though. And we had dinner after, talked about the agency and stuff. She's nice. I really like her. Hang on, I'll show you a picture.' She lifted her phone from the arm of the sofa and pressed the Instagram icon, pointing the screen at her father.

'She's certainly striking,' he said, taking in the blue eyes and sharp, shadowed cheekbones. 'Not as striking as you though, princess.'

His praise was predictable but appreciated nonetheless. 'You would say that,' she smiled, checking the number of likes her picture had attracted, before killing the screen.

'What does Cory think of your new friend?'

'Sorry?' If he hadn't been sitting right next to her, she would've thought she'd misheard him.

He turned his head towards her and repeated the question. 'I said, what does Cory think of your new friend?'

Abi was frozen by his stare, her tongue heavier than the makeup on her Max Factor photoshoot.

'I know you're seeing him, Abi, so don't bother denying it.'

'Actually, I'm not,' she finally managed to say.

He continued to stare at her.

'We broke up.'

'When?'

'A few days ago. It was something and nothing. He apologised.'

'Did he hurt you?'

His calm demeanour was unnerving. She would have expected raised voices, stamping feet and clenched fists. This version of her father was disarming, to say the least.

'No, it was nothing like that. Honest. We just had a bit of a fall out.' She raised her eyes to meet his but immediately dropped them again. 'How did you find out?'

'What you fail to realise, Abi, is that I know most things that go on this house. I may not be here very often, but I have a nose for certain things. Not forgetting, he's one of my players. Did you honestly expect me not to find out?'

'I guess not. Does Cory know that you know?' She had a sudden vision of Cory lying face down in his pool, only this time it wasn't a joke.

'No.'

'What are you going to do?'

'I'm going to watch the football,' he said, reaching for the remote. 'And you, my darling daughter, are going to leave me in peace for ninety minutes.'

Abi was more confused than ever. His behaviour was bizarre. She didn't need telling twice, though. She grabbed her phone, threw the magazine on the coffee table and ran upstairs to her room. But not before she'd seen the sly smile spread across her father's face.

A one-one draw was better than he could have hoped for. He didn't particular want either Manchester team clocking up another three points so he was more than happy with the result. He switched off the TV, unwilling to listen to Graeme Souness spouting a loud of old nonsense, and wandered through to the kitchen. His stomach growled, objecting to the lack of food since breakfast and he rummaged around in the fridge for something to eat. It was surprisingly well stocked. Florentina must have been shopping yesterday. He was deliberating between salmon fishcakes and a chicken stir-fry when he heard the front door open and close, followed by the familiar sound of his wife's spiky footsteps. He was still baffled by her impervious behaviour the night before, but had accepted that if she was going to finish him off, she would have done it by now.

'What are you making?' she asked, assuming correctly he was looking for something to eat.

'Fish cakes?' He slid the packet from beneath a tub of cottage cheese and held it up, surprising himself with his inviting gesture.

'Yes, great.' She hung her handbag over the back of a dining chair and sat down at the table, kicking off her boots. 'I think it might snow,' she said, glancing at the sky through the French doors. 'It feels weird out there and the sky's a strange colour.'

Crawford always kept one eye on the weather forecast, although it was rare for matches to be called off these days. Under-soil heating ensured most Premiership fixtures went ahead, regardless of the weather. It was different when he first played. Snow was more common than sunshine in Scotland so as long as the lines were cleared, the games went ahead. He shivered at the thought. He'd suffered the effects of more than one frozen pitch in his time.

'It's coming from Russia, apparently,' he said now, randomly opening and closing cabinet doors. 'It should miss us with a bit of luck.'

'Bottom drawer, to the left of the oven,' said Florentina, realising he was looking for a baking tray. 'I hope it's not as bad as the last time. The whole country came to a standstill.'

He slid the fish cakes into the oven and tore open two packets of microwaveable rice. 'I doubt it'll even settle,' he said, more in hope than expectation. 'Are you back in the office tomorrow?'

'Yes. Although, Lydia did a wonderful job in my absence. She's just been telling me about her little protégé.'

Crawford raised an inquisitive eyebrow. 'Who's that?'

'Ursla Enderby. Lydia spotted her at Marylebone station. She's quite something.'

He was about to say that he'd seen a picture of Ursla, but Florentina was on a roll.

'She's already secured two major contracts, Berry Cosmetics and Dior. And Lydia thinks Danny Venus will be next. We've been inundated with enquiries. We were lucky to sign him, he's the next big thing, I'm sure of it.'

'Danny Venus? Is that his real name?'

Florentina nodded, rubbing the ball of her feet at the same time.

Crawford smiled. 'Danny Venus. Sounds like something out of a Disney film. A love interest for Pocahontas, maybe?'

Florentina snorted with laughter. 'What do you know about Pocahontas?'

'Absolutely nothing,' he admitted. 'And despite being married to the original supermodel, I know absolutely nothing about modelling either, other than the fact that you and Lydia seem to be doing a great job with the agency.'

He couldn't remember the last time he'd complimented his wife on anything and he'd surprised himself with his honesty. Florentina, it seemed, was equally surprised. She abandoned her foot massage and leant back in her chair, squinting at him through suspicious eyes.

'Don't for one minute think you can charm me with flattery, Crawford. I don't actually care what you think, one way or the other.'

He was used to their bickering, but her reply stung. It was the second time he'd been rebuffed for telling the truth. He was starting to think it was easier to lie. He turned his attention to the oven, feigning interest in two deep-filled fish cakes.

'Did you see Abi's picture in *Cosmopolitan*?' It was a low punch, he knew. But he was still unnerved by her cool response. If anything could rile her, it was mention of their daughter.

'Of course I saw it.'

He was watching her reflection in the oven door, expecting an evil stare, at the very least. But she simply switched her attention back to her feet. He saw one last opportunity to goad her and turned around, prepared for whatever reaction would follow.

'Did you know she was seeing Cory Flemming?'

He saw her take a deep breath before sitting upright in her chair. Her hands were folded neatly in her lap, her bare feet flat on the floor. 'Yes.'

Crawford was stunned. He was also more than a little indignant. There was no way Abi would have confided in her mother so how the hell did she know? He'd only found out himself after the wisecrack in the dressing room, followed by a few discreet enquiries and more than one oiled palm. He wasn't sure what irritated him the most, Florentina knowing before he did or her simple, one-word reply.

'Is that all you can say? Are you not bothered?'

'She's seventeen, Crawford. She can, and will, see whomever she likes.'

'Does that apply to Thomas as well?' He couldn't help himself. One way or another, he *had* to get a reaction.

'Thomas is happier than he's ever been, no thanks to you.' Her tone was light but her hands, he noticed, were now clenched. 'And who he sees is none of our business. He's twenty-four-years old. We were married at that age.'

Again, not the reaction he'd anticipated. This version of his wife was proving very difficult to read. She *looked* different too. Her hair wasn't quite so stiff, her makeup not as heavy. She looked softer, somehow.

'He's holding an exhibition, by the way, at his studio. I shall expect you to contribute to the guest list. And to be there, in person.'

'I can't promise, Florentina. I'll need to check the fixtures.'

She stared at him, the disappointment clear on her face. He couldn't help but wonder if that was the face *he* used when he looked at his son. He suspected it was and an unfamiliar sadness squeezed his heart.

'If you can work it around the fixtures, I'll be there,' he conceded.

'Good,' she said, a victorious smile lighting up her face. 'I'm off to get changed before dinner.'

He watched her leave the kitchen then tried, unsuccessfully, to turn on the microwave. He seemed to be pressing all the wrong buttons tonight.

Chapter 34

Thomas had worked flat out for the last two weeks. He'd finished the London landscapes, working solely from the photographs he'd taken back in September, and had added two slightly smaller paintings: one of the Shard, its distorted reflection shaded yellow in the Thames, and one of Tower Bridge, entirely black and white but for a smudge of red depicting the embers of a sunset. The exhibition had been arranged for the last Friday in January. That gave him only six weeks to get ready. Ideally, he needed twelve paintings, preferably more. He could use three from his Ayrshire collection: Troon Yacht Haven, Maidens harbour and Turnberry beach. People seemed to appreciate pictures of boats and water regardless of where in the world they originated. He also intended to paint a picture of the football ground. His mother had invited a number of guests from the club (with his father's blessing, apparently), so he'd have a captive audience. A number of the players had also been invited which, assuming they turned up, was exactly what he needed. People with money to burn.

A knock on the door startled him and he jumped up from his stool, wiping his hands on his apron.

'Rupert, hi.'

'Sorry to bother you, Thomas. I was just on my way to the café, wondered if you'd like to join me? Don't know about you, but I'm fed up of looking at the same four walls.'

He was about to decline, the exhibition deadline never far from his mind, but changed his mind. 'Thanks, Rupert. That sounds like an excellent idea. Come in, just let me get cleaned up. Have a seat.'

Thomas closed the door behind them, untying his apron as he did so, then slipping it over his head. Rupert sat beside the fire, rubbing his hands in front of the flames.

'How's it going?' he asked. 'Making progress?'

'Yeah, slowly but surely,' he answered, washing his hands in the kitchen sink. 'I finished another one this morning so I'm on track.' He peered through the window at a young couple heading towards to the castle. 'I take it it's cold?' he asked, noting their woolly hats, sheepskin mittens and pink noses.

'Well, I've only walked two steps from my door to yours, but it was enough to feel the chill.'

'Right. Big coat it is!' He fastened up his new, bright red, padded anorak (a purchase deemed necessary by the Scottish winter temperatures), pulled a hat over his ears and grabbed his keys. 'Ready when you are.'

'Let's go,' said Rupert, tearing himself away from the fire.

It took them less than five minutes to walk to the bustling café in the castle courtyard. Thomas urged Rupert to find a seat while he waited in the queue to order their coffees. After the silence of the cottage the noise was a shock to his system. The clatter of crockery, hiss of the coffee machine and squeals of at least one overexcited child, were enough to send him scurrying back to the sanctuary of his studio. The sight of his neighbour, patiently waiting for his coffee, stopped him from doing just that.

'I bought a fruit scone as well,' he said, placing a laden tray on the table, the proffered scone the size of a house brick. 'Thought we could share it.'

Thomas shrugged off his coat, his hat already stuffed in the pocket, and lay it on top of Rupert's on a spare chair.

'Business is certainly booming,' said Rupert, observing the constant stream of people coming in from the cold.

'It's the usual pre-Christmas madness I suspect. They'll no doubt be taking a fortune in the gift shop as well as the café.' He sipped his decaf Americano, his fingers cupping the mug for warmth.

'That's good news for you, isn't it? You should sell more of your paintings.' Rupert cut the scone in half, offering the plate to Thomas.

'It would be if I had any to sell,' he said, taking a bite from his half. 'They sold the last one a couple of weeks ago and I haven't been able to give them any more. I need them all for the exhibition.'

'Have you thought about prints?' Rupert emptied a sachet of sugar into his cappuccino and stirred, careful not to slosh it over the top of the cup.

'What do you mean?'

'Seems to me you can't keep up with demand. I'm guessing painting is both labour intensive and time consuming, hence the asking price for the finished article.' He took a bite of his scone and swallowed before continuing. 'So why don't you make limited edition prints? That way your work would reach a larger market, the price and size would be smaller, therefore appealing to more buyers.'

Thomas leant forward, resting his elbows on the table. Rupert had a point. It wasn't a perfect scenario – he was all for original art, not cheap imitations – but if he did it right, it could work.

'That's not a bad idea,' he said, after a while. 'I'll give it some thought.' His mind was already working overtime but, as usual, he needed time to weigh up the pros and cons.

'I could put you in touch with a decent printer. There's a guy in Glasgow I sometimes use. High quality stuff.'

'Great, thanks.' He finished off his scone and winced as a baby began to cry at a nearby table. 'So what are your plans for Christmas?' Thomas asked. 'Heading to Warwick?'

'Actually, Izzie and Will are coming up here, staying with me for a few days.'

Thomas didn't need to ask how he felt about the impending visit, his smile said it all.

'Why don't you join us? For dinner, I mean?'

Once he'd made the decision to stay in Scotland, he'd actually intended to treat the day as any other. He'd take a walk in the morning, do a bit of painting, make himself some dinner (nothing fancy), then watch the Queen's speech. There was bound to be a decent film on in the evening so he'd curl up in front of the fire with a packet of pork scratchings and before he knew it, Christmas would be over.

'One extra seat at the table is no big deal, Thomas. Please, I'd feel awful knowing you were sitting next door on your own.'

'Well, if you're sure.' He could try and convince himself he'd be happy on his own, but why bother?

'Of course I'm sure. You'd be most welcome. It'll be fun.'

'Thanks. Although I'm not sure Mum will ever forgive me for not going home.'

'Actually, I think your mother will forgive you anything. She just wants you to be happy.'

Thomas ran a thumb up and down his coffee mug, her parting words coming back to him once more. 'I know.'

'How's she doing, anyway? Is she still enjoying the agency?'

'As far as I know. You probably talk to her more than I do.' He laughed but was serious nonetheless.

Rupert smiled in response. 'Only because you youngsters insist on texting instead of talking. A phone call means so much more than a text message, regardless of who sends it.'

He thought of his sporadic communication with Justin.

'Yeah, you're right. Did she mention her parents' graves to you?' The subject had been festering in the back of his mind since his mother's visit last month, and as much as he didn't want to betray her confidence, he felt he could trust Rupert with the secret. If indeed, it was a secret.

'She told me she'd visited the cemetery and that someone had left flowers.'

So she'd already confided in Rupert. He wasn't entirely surprised. 'She's been tying herself in knots trying to think who left them. I think I might go myself, see if there's any more. You never know, there might be a note this time.' He drank the last of his coffee and pushed his mug to one side.

'There could be any number of explanations,' said Rupert. 'Sometimes people leave flowers if they think a grave looks neglected. Or maybe kids were messing about, swapping them around. It happens sometimes.'

'Yeah. I still might go, though.'

'I'll drive you, if you like? I need to go to Glasgow before Christmas, to see the printer I mentioned. It'll save you messing around with trains and buses.' He popped the last of his scone in his mouth and washed it down with the dregs of his cappuccino.

'Really? That would be fab, thanks. Let me know what day would be best.'

'Sure. Now, shall we get out of here? Let someone else have our seats?'

They tugged their coats back on and exited the café, their breath forming clouds in the cold air.

'You not bothering with a Christmas tree this year?' Rupert asked, eyeing the festive decorations in the window of the gift shop.

'Hardly,' he laughed. 'I haven't got so much as a bauble. What about you, will you get one?'

'I doubt it. I haven't got the room. I might put some lights round the window, maybe a wreath on the door.'

'Ha! You'll have a stocking on the fireplace before you know it.'

'Those days are long gone, I'm afraid, more's the pity.'

'Are you sure I look all right?'

'Sasha, for the hundredth time, you look amazing! Will you stop worrying?'

'That's easy for you to say, you're one of *them*.'

The two girls were heading to the KTH Christmas party, and Sasha was daunted by the prospect of being surrounded by professional models. Despite having spent two hours in the hair salon, two hours in the nail bar and another hour applying her makeup, she still claimed to feel like one of Cinderella's ugly sisters. The only thing she was happy with, as far as Abi could tell, was her dress. The metallic silver creation was nothing more than a long blazer, its hem barely covering her backside, the neckline plunging deeper than a Tom Daley dive. At least she had a cleavage, which was more than could be said for most of the models on the KTH books. Abi looked down at her own revealing outfit and allowed herself a smug smile. No one could accuse *her* of being flat-chested.

The taxi pulled up outside the wine bar where KTH had hired the private party room, and Abi slipped a twenty-pound note to the driver. The cold air hit her as she opened the cab door, and the flash of a camera lit up the sky like lightning. She linked Sasha's arm and hurried inside, grateful for the blast of hot air that greeted them. The doorman welcomed them with a well-rehearsed smile.

'Evening, ladies,' he said, his teeth whiter than the pristine shirt under his black, corporate suit.

They both smiled a silent response before following the noise to the private room at the far end of the bar. Their mothers were posing for a photograph with Jenna Constance, one of the models. Jenna was gamine in appearance, with dark, elf-like hair and wide, brown eyes. She was shorter than the rest of the models at KTH but no less popular, with clients or followers.

'Sasha! Abi! Come on, let's have a photo.' Lydia Templeton-Howe gestured them over and they slotted in between their mothers, Jenna graciously moving aside. The flash from the camera left Abi blinking wildly, trying to bat away the spots that blurred her vision.

'You both look beautiful,' said Lydia. 'Help yourselves to a drink, there's Prosecco, red wine, white wine and some kind of punch. I've no idea what's in it but it tastes wonderful.'

'Thanks, we will,' said Sasha. 'It looks amazing in here, Mrs Kelly. You should have been a party planner.'

'Thank you, Sasha. Although, it didn't take much planning. And your mother helped.'

'You're being modest, Florentina,' said Lydia. 'I barely lifted a finger, so the credit is all yours.'

'It's just a shame it's on a Sunday,' said Abi, unable to resist a minor dig in her mother's direction.

'It's the quietest day of the week,' Lydia said, apparently switched on to Abi's intended snipe. 'Which meant we got the venue we wanted and more people were able to attend. It was a win-win.'

'Talking of which,' said Max, appearing at their side, 'I see the Blues secured another win yesterday.'

At the mention of football, Abi grabbed Sasha by the arm and went off in search of a drink.

'Your mum looks good tonight,' said Sasha, sipping her Prosecco.

Abi rolled her eyes to the vaulted ceiling. She'd rather talk about football than talk about her mother. That said, she had to agree with Sasha. Her mother did, indeed, look good. Her midnight-blue body-con dress was long-sleeved and high-necked, the hemline just skimming her knees. Her usually coiffed hair was perfectly straight, the ends curling just above her shoulders. And her makeup was less obvious. She looked younger, Abi realised. Not that she'd share any of her thoughts out loud. Thankfully, the arrival of Danny Venus diverted Sasha's attention.

'Wow!' said Sasha. 'Who. Is. That?'

Abi laughed. 'Put your tongue back in, Sasha, you look like a thirsty dog. It's Danny Venus. The new model. I told you about him.'

'Yes, you told me about him. But you didn't tell me he looked like that.' She was speaking through gritted teeth, trying to maintain the perfect smile currently pointing in Danny's direction.

'He's ginger!' protested Abi.

'I don't care what colour he is. You *have* to introduce me.'

'Since when have you been into redheads?'

'Since about two minutes ago when that divine creature walked in.'

'I thought you wanted a man, not a boy. He's only nineteen.'

'Abi, I don't care how old he is, what colour he is, or how he likes his eggs in the morning. With regard to the latter, however, I do intend to find out.'

Abi laughed again and they both watched as he made his way around the room, stopping at each group to shake a hand, kiss a cheek or pat a back. He oozed self-confidence and, it had to be said, a certain amount of charm, unusual for someone so young. Even Abi had to admit he looked good. His copper hair was loose, falling just below his shoulders in chaotic waves, his perfectly shaped eyebrows framed his blue eyes, drawing attention from both male and female admirers, and his lips, the colour of a Louboutin sole, were almost shocking against his smooth, pale skin.

'He's coming over!' hissed Sasha. 'Act natural.'

Abi was highly entertained by her friend's obvious flustered state, but prepared herself for the introductions.

'Hi, Abi, you look stunning, as always.' She accepted a kiss on either cheek before turning to Sasha.

'This is my friend, Sasha. Sasha, this is Danny.'

'Delighted,' he said, repeating the kisses. 'Are you a model too?'

Sasha laughed, a little too loudly. 'No. I'm at uni. I'm studying sports therapy.'

'Sasha is Lydia's daughter,' Abi interjected.

'Oh, I didn't realise. I'd better stay in your good books then, hadn't I? Can I get you both a drink?'

'Thanks, we already have one,' answered Sasha, holding up her half-empty glass of Prosecco.

'Congratulations on the BooHoo contract, by the way,' said Abi. 'Not a bad way to kick-start your career.' She was genuinely pleased for him and impressed by his bashful smile and discreet nod of thanks. Although, she was still smirking at his use of the word 'delighted'. Very *Downton Abbey.*

'Oh, there's Ursla,' she said, grateful for the excuse to leave the two love-birds alone. 'I promised I'd look out for her, so I'll go and say hi. I'll see you guys later.' She winked at Sasha then rescued Ursla from the doorman.

Social media accounts were already brimming with pictures from the KTH party. Selfies were posted, shared, liked and commented upon in their thousands. Thanks to a quiet word in Patrick's ear, they could also be sure of a picture or two in tomorrow's papers. Not only was there a posse of paparazzi outside, there was also an official photographer taking pictures at the party itself. And not one of them would show Florentina holding a drink. She was smugly proud of her self-control, but also acutely aware of the image she wanted to portray, and it wasn't that of a washed-up model with a drink problem. She'd deliberately toned down her brash appearance and was delighted with the number of compliments. Her stiff, peroxide hair was well out of date anyway and, as much as she hated to admit it, her knees and elbows had exceeded their shelf life by a good few years. Even Crawford had looked twice when she'd emerged from her bedroom earlier. She had to admit, it felt good. Things were definitely looking up in Florentina's world, and she had a feeling next year would be even better.

Chapter 35

There were indeed an impressive number of photographs in the papers. Admittedly, most of them were of Abi, but even Florentina had to admit it could only be good for the agency. She expected to see more tomorrow. The offerings from this morning's tabloids were limited to those taken early in the evening, including one of Abi climbing out of a taxi, her hemline and neckline both revealing more than intended. Florentina allowed herself a spiteful smile. She might be turning over a new leaf, but she wasn't quite perfect yet.

She made herself an espresso and carried it to the table with the papers. Thankfully, the promised snow had failed to materialize, but a thick frost had transformed the garden from a suburban sanctuary to an Arctic plain. She half expected a penguin to come waddling along the patio. She shivered and took a sip of coffee, appreciating both the smell and taste of the rich, Brazilian bean.

Various pictures caught her attention as she continued to scan the papers. There was a particularly striking image of Danny Venus looking like a modern-day Heathcliff, plus one of Ursla alongside Sadie Torch, the youngster easily outshining her better-known counterpart. Once satisfied she'd seen all the pictures of interest, she turned to the headlines on the front page of her least favourite tabloid. This particular broadsheet rarely included celebrity gossip, but it printed unbiased reports on the news in general. She cringed at reports of the wild fires in California, horrified at the thought of being forced out of her home by rampant flames, only to see it burn to the ground. The story of a suicide in a local tower block was equally disturbing, the victim jumping twenty-four stories to his death. She'd certainly had her troubles but she could never imagine being desperate enough to throw herself to the ground from a great height. Her buoyant mood was in danger of being swept away in a tidal wave of depressing news stories so she cast the papers aside and drained the last of her coffee. She resisted the temptation to study the sport pages, unwilling to succumb to the regret that Cory Flemming's picture was likely to rouse. She paused at the window, appreciating the icy scene once more before preparing to leave. Another good thing about not drinking last night was waking up with a clear head. She suspected her daughter had yet to wake up at all.

Abi was lying face down in bed with a bowl on the floor beside her. Thankfully, she hadn't actually been sick, but if she moved her head, she suspected she might be. She groaned into the pillow, the smell of her breath foul and sour. What on earth had possessed her to drink tequila? The sound of an incoming text message roused her and she stretched out an arm, feeling around on the bedside table for her phone and knocking over a glass of water. 'Shit!' She sat up a little too quickly, regretting it immediately, and pressed the palm of her hand against her forehead. Another groan escaped her lips as she leant over the side of the bed to assess the damage. The water had already soaked into the carpet so she abandoned any thoughts of mopping it up and just rescued the glass instead. Retrieving her phone from beside the empty bowl, she read the message from Sasha.

Feel like shit!

The message was accompanied by a green-faced emoji, a fair representation of what Abi suspected she looked like. She took tentative steps to her en suite, dodging the wet patch on the carpet, and leant on the wash basin for support. Her reflection swayed in front of her, the very sight of her bloodshot eyes enough to make her heave. She was usually so disciplined when it came to drinking alcohol. What the hell had she been thinking?

She felt marginally better after a shower, the hot, pummelling jets going some way to restoring her status as a functioning human being.

Her father was sitting at the breakfast bar reading the newspapers when she shuffled into the kitchen, her oversized jumper pulled down over her hands, her hastily dried hair piled on top of her head in an unruly bun.

'Good morning.'

'Is it?' She slid on to an adjacent stool and leant forward on the marble counter, her head resting sideways on her folded arms.

'Good night?'

'I think so,' she muttered, her words lost somewhere in the crook of her elbow.

She heard movement but remained tucked up with her eyes closed.

'Here.' The word was accompanied by the sound of a cup being slid across the counter. She felt a hot sensation through the sleeve of her jumper and the smell of coffee somehow made it to her nostrils. She lifted her head and reached gratefully for the mug.

'Thanks.'

'It's not like you to over-do it, princess. What happened?'

She took a sip before answering, wincing as the scolding liquid hit her tongue. 'Tequila.'

She winced again, this time at the volume of her father's laughter.

'Tequila? No wonder you look like shit.'

'Thanks a lot,' she said, unused to hearing anything other than compliments from her father.

'Sorry, my angel, but it's true! You look greener than a Brussels sprout.'

'I just wanted to enjoy myself,' she said. 'It's been ages since I had a good night out. Guess I overdid it.'

'I'll say.'

She caught his wry smile and was reminded of their conversation about Cory. It hadn't been mentioned since, her father seeming to accept that it was indeed over. She'd warned Cory that their secret was out and had asked, hopeful of a kiss and make up reunion, if they could get together. But thanks to his training schedule and her modelling commitments, she'd been unable to arrange a reconciliation. It was almost three weeks since the 'pool incident' and although they'd communicated by text, they hadn't actually spoken. Abi was unsure whether Cory thought they were still an item or not, or in fact, if they ever were. She thought once more of the slap on her face and subconsciously lifted her hand to her cheek.

She took another sip of coffee and slid one of the newspapers from the pile. It didn't take her long to find the photo of her arriving at the wine bar. It went without saying that not every picture printed would be a good one, but this one was particularly bad. 'Oh my God, I look about fifty! Why did they have to print that one?'

Her father, clearly still amused, laughed once more. 'Why worry about one bad picture when there are ten good ones? You're just like your mother.'

Abi discarded the offending paper and reached for another. 'Where is she anyway?'

'At the office. She left before eight.'

Florentina's new image seemed to have gone beyond a new hair style. Not only had she made subtle, but flattering, changes to her appearance, she'd also stopped drinking, if not altogether, then certainly in large quantities. Abi hadn't seen her take any pills lately either, which, considering she used to eat them like Smarties, was another surprise.

'I need to be on my way too,' said Crawford, taking strides to the hallway, 'my taxi will be here shortly. Do you need anything before I go?'

'No, thanks. I think I'll go back to bed.' She watched her father gather his phone, keys and coat then waited a couple of minutes for the front door to slam. Spending an entire morning in bed was a rare luxury and, despite feeling like her head was about to explode, she was determined to make the most of it. Bundling up the newspapers she retraced her steps to her bedroom and closed the door quietly behind her.

It was quiet for a Monday morning. The phone had only rung twice, once to confirm an order for more stationery, and once to invite Florentina and Lydia to the opening of a new fashion boutique in January.

'Of course we'll be there, darling,' Florentina had purred, 'we wouldn't miss it for the world.'

Unsurprisingly, it was all quiet on the model front too. Abi hadn't been the only one to over indulge last night.

'How's Sasha this morning?' she asked, making a beeline for the espresso machine.

'No idea,' said Lydia. 'She was still in bed when I left. Feeling less than great I would imagine. Still, it was nice to see her enjoying herself, she's been working so hard at uni.'

'She seemed very taken by Danny.'

'Yes, she did, didn't she?' They both turned to look at the image of Danny Venus staring down at them from the gallery of portraits. The absence of Cory's picture hadn't gone unnoticed, and Florentina was grateful for her friend's uncanny ability to read between the lines, as well as her subsequent unspoken words of accusation or acknowledgment. She was unsure whether he was still dating Abi or not, but was far too proud to ask. Besides, although her relationship with Rupert was both platonic and long-distance, she was happy with the distraction and the pleasure that came from his friendship. She'd told Lydia about Rupert, expecting a word of warning or, at the very least, a raised eyebrow. What she actually got was a guffaw.

'Rupert? You're not seriously dating a man called Rupert? Oh, Florentina, that's hilarious.'

Florentina was baffled by her friend's amusement and was none the wiser when she'd asked, 'Does he wear checked trousers?' Eventually, once Lydia had stopped laughing, she'd shown Florentina a picture of Rupert the Bear on the internet. Having spent her childhood in Italy and been disinterested in her own children's adolescent heroes, she was unfamiliar with the white bear with the bright yellow checked trousers and was bewildered by the mirth associated with the name.

'I'm not dating him,' she'd said. 'He's just a friend.'

When she'd switched on her computer the next morning, she'd been greeted with a Rupert the Bear screensaver and a mischievous smile from Lydia. She hadn't bothered to delete it.

Back at her desk, she was distracted by an incoming email. She clicked on the envelope icon at the bottom of her screen. 'That's another acceptance for Thomas's exhibition,' she said. 'That makes sixty-two already. I must say, Crawford has excelled himself. There's some pretty impressive names on the guest list.'

'It's the talk of the town already, Florentina. Everyone's talking about it. This could be the start of something very big for that son of yours.' Lydia was filing a broken nail but sounded no less enthusiastic because of it.

Florentina was well aware of the importance of the event but her confidence in her son outweighed any sliver of doubt that might exist. Between the Kellys and the Templeton-Howes, a lot of wealthy people would be viewing Thomas's work. And she had to hand it to Crawford, he'd certainly come up trumps when it came to his contacts at the club. Even the chairman had accepted his invitation.

'It's the least he deserves,' she said, taking a sip of her espresso. 'And if Crawford does anything to spoil it for him, I'll rip his evil tongue out of his filthy mouth with my very own bare hands.'

Clearly startled by the venom in her voice, Lydia looked up from her nail-filing duties. By the look on her face, she couldn't quite work out if Florentina was serious or not.

Chapter 36

It took Thomas over thirty minutes to find his grandparents' grave. Rupert had dropped him at the gates to the cemetery and he'd walked around the maze of paths until his nose was numb from the cold. There was a small posy of flowers beside the gravestone. He had no idea what kind of flowers they were, the frost having strangled the life out of them long before he arrived. He felt surprisingly melancholy. Regretful at never having met them, disturbed by the circumstances surrounding their death, but gratified that they were, at least, together. He traced his fingers over their names, as though connecting with his past, then placed his own floral tribute on the ground. The white roses combined with dark green holly leaves and red berries were a popular seasonal choice, the florist had told him. Personally, he thought the berries looked like drops of blood but what did he know? He stood again, his knees objecting to the crouched position, and tried to picture his mother standing at this exact same spot. He couldn't imagine ever having to stand at his own parents' graves, although he knew, unless anything unforeseen happened to him, one day he would have to. He thought back to the last time he saw his father, when he'd told him about his 'arrangement' with Vince. He felt a physical pain when he thought about it, as though someone was prodding his heart with the tip of a knife. But how would he feel if something happened to his father? If he had to stand at his graveside knowing he could have put things right? He looked at the endless rows of headstones and tried to imagine how many loved ones were still full of regret. Remorseful over something that was said or, more likely, something that was not.

A flash of movement forced his eyes to the right. The priest was walking briskly towards him, his black cassock swelling around his feet. Thomas always felt guilty at the sight of a priest, like walking through the 'nothing to declare' aisle in an airport. He always imagined a priest could see through to your soul, the same as a customs officer could see straight through your suitcase. He knew it was nonsense, but it made him nervous, all the same.

'Hello, Father.' He nodded a greeting as the priest approached. He was tall, at least six-foot, with dark, wiry eyebrows and hair to match. Wire rimmed glasses were perched on a bulbous nose and Saint Bernard-like jowls hung over his collar.

'Good afternoon. It's another chilly one.'

Thomas couldn't quite place his accent. Lancashire maybe, or Yorkshire? Certainly not Scottish.

'It is indeed,' he answered, rubbing his hands together. 'Not the day to be standing outside.' He leant down to pick up the dead flowers and looked around for a waste bin.

'There's a bin over by the church,' the priest told him. 'No doubt she'll be back later with more. It's usually a Tuesday when she visits.'

Thomas stared at him, astonished by the information. It hadn't even occurred to him to ask.

'Were they relatives of yours?'

'What?' Oh, yes. Grandparents.' Thomas was still reeling at the prospect of finding out who the mystery woman was. 'I don't suppose you know what time she usually arrives do you? The lady with the flowers?'

'I do as it happens,' said the priest, looking more than a little pleased with himself. 'It's usually about four o'clock. Doesn't stay long this time of year mind, scared of the dark. As most people are when it comes to graveyards.'

'Quite,' said Thomas, unable to join the priest in a hearty chuckle.

'Well, I must get on. And you must get out of the cold, young man. You're turning a very peculiar shade of blue.'

This time, Thomas did manage a smile. He could hardly feel his toes and his nose would rival that of everyone's favourite reindeer. His odd skin tone, however, was probably down to the realisation that he was about to unravel the mystery of the phantom grave visitor.

'I will,' he said. 'Merry Christmas, Father.'

The priest was already striding away towards the church but waved a hand in response. Thomas checked his watch. Three fifteen. Rupert was due to collect him at three thirty. He sent him a brief text message.

I have news. Can you bring coffee?

He waited in the church. The unmistakable smell of incense greeted him like an old friend. He slid into the rear pew, the hard-wooden seat both cold and comforting to the touch. His nan used to take him to the Catholic Church in Ayr. He remembered feeling dwarfed by the sheer size of the space and mesmerized by the sun shining through the stained-glass windows. The sun was absent today, but the colourful glass was just as impressive. There was no sign of the priest, but he could hear the faint echo of footsteps and the opening and closing of doors. He closed his eyes and took a long, deep breath, savouring the smell of history and the sense of peace that a church could always instil. They'd passed at least two derelict churches on their way to Glasgow today. It pained him to see the boards at the windows, the graffiti and decay. He felt his phone vibrate in his pocket and he shuffled along the pew, back outside into the cold.

Rupert was waiting for him in the car park, two cups of coffee releasing steam through the tiny holes in the lids. He sank gratefully into the warm seat and informed Rupert of his conversation with the priest.

'If you don't mind waiting, I'd like to hang around, see if she turns up.'

'Of course. Do you want me to come with you? To talk to her?'

'I'm not sure how she'll feel being approached by a strange man in a graveyard. Two of us might frighten her off.'

'Good point,' said Rupert. 'I'll wait in the car.'

'No offence.'

'None taken.'

Thomas kept his eyes on the entrance. His heart was beating a little too fast. He was nervous, he realised. He had no idea who his woman was, how she knew his grandparents, or why she was leaving flowers on their grave. He did, however, intend to find out.

At ten minutes past four, they watched as a middle-aged woman, a head full of curly, dark hair, a long, red coat with a black fur collar, and high, black patent boots walked into the cemetery. She was carrying a small posy of red flowers in one hand and a black, Chanel handbag in the other.

'If that's her, she's certainly got money,' said Rupert.

Thomas was thinking the same thing. Sometimes you could sense someone's wealth just by looking at them and this woman's wealth was written all over her. She may as well have hung a sign around her neck saying, 'I'm rich'.

Convinced this was the woman he'd been waiting for, he opened the door, stuffed his empty coffee cup in the door pocket and zipped up his jacket.

'Good luck,' said Rupert, his eyes still on the mystery woman.

'Thanks.' The door closed with the reassuring clunk of quality so typically associated with German automobile engineering.

He entered the cemetery, pausing occasionally to study a headstone or replace a fallen flower arrangement, one eye following her progress. She slowed as she approached the grave. Thomas noticed her frown of confusion followed by a quick look over her shoulder. She crouched, her coat forming a circle around her feet, and picked up the roses. Finding no card, she put them back, her own posy now lying beside them. Thomas moved a little closer. It was getting dark and the silence was unnerving. He looked towards Rupert, but a streetlight was casting a yellow glow on his car windscreen, so he was unable to see inside. He was hoping for a nod of encouragement. The sound of hurried footsteps broke the silence and he looked back to see her walking briskly towards him. *It's now or never,* he thought.

'Excuse me.'

She jumped at his voice and stopped. 'Yes?'

She looked impatient, irritated even by the interruption. Despite the frown, she was beautiful. She had the air of someone in their mid-forties, maybe older, but her face was smooth and unlined and her wide eyes were bright and crease free. Thomas could smell her perfume. That too, was rich.

'I hope you don't mind me asking, but I was curious how you knew my grandparents. Nicolo and Viola Vanzetti? I saw you leave flowers on their grave.'

She stared at him, seemingly lost for words. 'I... I... You are Florentina's son.'

It wasn't a question. She knew who he was.

245

'Yes. Thomas.' He waited for her to say more but she covered her mouth with a gloved hand.

'Do you know her? My mother?'

She slid her hand into her coat pocket and sighed. 'Yes.'

She glanced around. Thomas hoped she wasn't about to run off.

'Is there somewhere we can talk?' she asked. 'The church, perhaps?'

He began to notice an accent. Italian. It was barely there when his mother spoke, but every so often she would say something with a hint of her native tongue. This was the same, but stronger.

'My friend's waiting in the car. What should I tell him?'

She looked towards the car park, at the silhouette in the BMW. 'It won't take long,' she said. 'Just tell him to wait.' She turned then, already walking towards the church.

Thomas stood for a second, unwilling to let her out of his sight but equally reluctant to leave Rupert wondering. He ran back to the car and quickly told Rupert what was happening. 'Sorry,' he said, his arm stretched along the top of the car door. 'She said it wouldn't take long.'

'Don't worry. Do what you have to do. There's a decent John Grisham in the glove box. That should keep me entertained.'

Thomas didn't move.

'Go!' Rupert urged. 'Stand there much longer we'll both freeze to death.'

Inside the church, she was sitting in the exact same spot that Thomas himself had occupied earlier. She'd removed her gloves, her hands now clasped on her lap. A diamond the size of an eyeball winked on her finger. Her posture was elegant, he noticed, although he conceded that any position other than upright was practically impossible in a church pew. Even so, her shoulders were back, her knees and feet together, her head up. She didn't look at him when he slid in the pew beside her but kept her head and her eyes forward. Thomas did the same. The silence eventually became intolerable.

'So, how do you know my mother?'

'We were friends,' she said, 'in Italy. I have not seen her since we were twelve years old. We lost touch.'

'Does she know you're in Scotland? Have you spoken to her?' Thomas was excited on his mother's behalf. He had a head full of questions but something about her demeanour stopped him from asking.

'No. She does not know. I did not tell her.'

'How long have you been leaving flowers for her parents?'

'Almost ten years.'

Thomas's head swung round so fast his neck almost snapped. 'Ten years? You've been leaving flowers on her parents' grave for ten years? Every week?'

She still hadn't moved, still hadn't looked at him.

'But why?' he asked.

'I cannot tell you. It is something I must tell to your mother. Only to her.'

Thomas ran a hand over his beard, unable to comprehend the enormity of his discovery. 'Were you ever going to tell her? Before I came along?'

'No.'

Her simple, one-word answer caused him to shiver involuntarily. Clearly, she was hiding something and, as beautiful as she was, he didn't think it was something good.

'What happens now?' she asked, finally turning to face him. 'You will tell her?'

'I have to,' he answered. 'I can't keep this from her. She was here herself. She saw your flowers.'

Her eyes widened and her hand, once more, shot to her mouth. 'She was here? When?'

'A few weeks ago. Three weeks, maybe?'

'She left flowers.' Again, not a question, but a statement.

'Yes.'

She bowed her head, her hands now clutching the edge of the seat. 'When will you tell her?'

'I don't know. She's in London. I won't see her until the end of January. But I have to call her. I must.'

'I understand.' She opened the side pocket of her handbag and handed Thomas a card. 'Here, this is my number. Call me when you have spoken to her.'

She stood to leave and Thomas backed out of the pew to allow her to pass. The click of her heels echoed around the church until she stopped at the door.

'And tell her I am sorry,' she said, before disappearing through the heavy oak door.

He stood for a moment, breathing in the lingering trace of her scent. Then he looked down at the card she had given him. *Pia De Santis.*

The card lay on the table between them. They'd stopped at a pub in Ayr on the way home, the Racecourse Road destination strangely, nowhere near the racecourse. As well as being hungry, Thomas was too agitated to go straight home. His head wasn't just swimming it was drowning with possible scenarios, all of them, he decided, equally ridiculous.

'You need to speak to your mother,' said Rupert, fast becoming the Kelly family's independent voice of reason. 'There's no point guessing, you'll tie yourself up in knots.'

'I know. You're right. I just don't want to see Mum upset. And I have a feeling that whatever it is this Pia has to be sorry about, it's not going to be good.' He took a sip of his beer, licking the froth from his top lip.

'Has your mother ever mentioned her?'

'Not that I can recall. But she doesn't talk about her childhood much. She says she was happy, until her parents died, obviously, but she rarely mentions Italy. And I've certainly never heard the name Pia.'

The arrival of their food interrupted their conversation. Thomas's mac and cheese had barely touched the table before he was forking the creamy pasta tubes into his mouth. Rupert meanwhile, had lifted the flaky pastry lid from his steak and ale pie and was liberally dousing the contents with salt.

A group of four women, all glitter and giggles, arrived at a neighbouring table. They performed a 'who wants to sit where?' dance around the four chairs, before landing on their chosen seats with a clang of bangles. Rupert appeared oblivious, but Thomas was entertained by, and also a little jealous of, their festive spirit.

'Maybe they had a falling out,' Rupert said in between mouthfuls of gravy covered steak. 'I can't imagine it could be much worse than that, not at twelve years old.'

'You wouldn't think so, would you? But it didn't sound like she was talking about a childhood tiff.' He stirred the contents of his bowl with his fork, releasing spirals of steam from beneath the cheesy pasta. 'And why not get in touch before? Let's face it, it's not exactly difficult to get hold of someone these days is it? Particularly someone in the public eye, like Mum.'

'True.' Rupert balanced his knife on the side of his plate and picked up the card. 'It doesn't give much away, does it? Just a name and telephone number. No address, no business details. You should Google her.'

The idea had already occurred to Thomas, but he had no intention of doing so over dinner. The four glamour girls were a perfect example of why he hated the use of mobile phones in company. Having confirmed their order to the young, smartly dressed waitress, all four of them had now lapsed into silence, heads bent, screens scrolling. Thomas shook his head. Abi was the same. She was obsessed with how many followers she had, how many likes she could attract and what the so-called influencers were saying about her. Thomas couldn't see the point of virtual friends. He'd rather have a handful of genuine friends than a million fake ones. He certainly wouldn't forsake the company of real people in favour of a cyber experience.

'I'll do it when I get home,' he said. 'Don't want to end up like that.' He gestured towards the four girls, perplexed at their apparent oblivion.

Rupert laughed. 'Sign of the times, I'm afraid. Although it's unfair to place all youngsters in the same media-obsessed category; otherwise you'd fall in it yourself.'

'I'm flattered to still be considered a youngster,' he said, stabbing the last tube of macaroni with his fork. 'But trust me, you will never see me glued to my phone like that.'

'I don't doubt it. But let me know what you find out about the mysterious Pia.' He pushed his plate to the side, the untouched pastry lid indicative of the size of the portions rather than the quality of the food.

'I will. Room for dessert?'

'Absolutely not! The pie was amazing but I can't eat another thing. I don't even think I have room for coffee.'

Thomas waited until the waitress had served the last main course to the four girls and then asked for the bill. 'My treat,' he said. 'A thank you for driving me to Glasgow and back.'

'It was no trouble,' said Rupert, rising from his seat and gathering his coat from the back of the chair. 'I was going anyway. Oh, by the way, the printer I went to see, he gave me the name of someone who specialises in art prints. I'll text you the number when we get home.'

'Great, thanks.' He looked over his shoulder as they made their way to the door. 'Taking pictures of their food now. Does anyone really care what they had for their dinner?'

Rupert smiled. 'I'm sure the chef's delighted. It's his work of art, after all.'

'There you go again, the voice of reason.'

Chapter 37

She was just admiring her new navy Max Mara trouser suit in the free-standing bedroom mirror when her phone rang. She tutted, pausing to appreciate the pearl silk blouse she'd teamed with it, before silencing the ring.

'Thomas?' She looked back to the mirror, her new toned-down look still taking her by surprise.

'Hi, Mum. Are you in the office?'

'No, darling, I'm still at home. We're starting late for the rest of the week, ten o'clock. Making the most of the pre-Christmas lull.' She reached for her perfume with her free hand and sprayed a generous mist of Prada La Femme on her neck.

'Good. I need to talk to you about something.'

She caught the edge in his voice and sat down on the end of the bed. 'Are you okay?' she asked.

'Yes, Mum, I'm fine. But I have something to tell you. I found out who's been leaving the flowers.'

She felt her heart stammer and lay a hand on her chest. 'You've been to the grave?'

'Yes. Do you know someone call Pia?'

She looked up at her reflection and saw a nervous smile shape her lips. 'Pia?' she whispered. 'It was Pia?'

'Yes. Who is she, Mum? She said to say she was sorry.'

'You saw her?' Florentina had imagined that he'd found a card at the graveside. She stood at the unexpected news that Thomas had actually seen her; spoken to her.

'Yes. What is she sorry about, Mum?'

'I have no idea. I haven't seen her since I left Italy. We lost touch.' She was pacing now, her bare feet sinking in the lush carpet with each and every step.

'That's what she said. But get this,' he paused for effect. 'She's been leaving flowers at the grave for the last ten years.'

She stopped pacing, her body as still as a mannequin. 'What?' The snippets of information were making no sense. When did Pia leave Italy? What was she doing in Glasgow? How did she find out about her parents' deaths? And, more to the point, why was she visiting their grave?

'It makes no sense,' she said. 'Why hasn't she contacted me?'

'I don't know. She seemed a bit shell-shocked to be honest. Anyway, she gave me her card so you can call her. I was going to Google her but if you know her, there's no point.'

Florentina sat back down on the bed. 'I can't believe it,' she said. 'Pia. After all this time.'

'Did I do the right thing, Mum? Telling you about her?'

'Of course you did, darling. I'm just a bit surprised that's all. Send me her number, I'll call her.'

Four games in just twelve days would stretch his squad to the limit. He'd received a curt email from Simone earlier to say that Josh Franklin was doubtful for the first of those games against Brighton. Gone were the days when she was grateful of the excuse to visit his office. These days she was frostier than the proverbial snowman. He had to admit, Franklin's injury was a worry. It meant he was completely reliant upon Flemming and every manager with an ounce of gumption knew one striker was never enough. Not unless you had Messi or Ronaldo in your team which, much to his regret, he had not. He studied the names on the proposed team sheet in front of him, his eyes resting on Flemming once more. He'd done some digging after finding out about his little romance with Abi. Turns out he's not much of a party boy after all. He likes a night out, as do most of the players, but he only ever drinks water and never stays out late. His housewarming party was apparently an ice-breaker; a chance to impress the other players and to prove himself 'one of the lads'. Abi had been at that party, allegedly. He didn't like it when people got the better of him, not one little bit. When it came to his daughter, however, he could forgive most things. He could even forgive Cory Flemming. As long as he'd treated Abi properly, and from what he'd been told he had no reason to think otherwise, he had no beef with the young American. Vincent Savage, however, was a different matter. He'd got one over on Crawford and there was no way he was going to let him get away with it. The rental property in Fulham was a dead end. According to his sources he hadn't been seen there for weeks. So too was the bundle of post he'd intercepted from the postman. Nothing there other than the address and phone number he already had. He'd considered returning to the car park in Ealing to see if he turned up there, but not being able to drive had put paid to that idea.

He thought back to their initial meeting. Vince's cheap leather jacket, his grubby jeans and the faint whiff of BO. He scrunched his nose, the very thought of the encounter enough to conjure the offensive odour.

He was starting to give up hope of ever finding the bastard when he'd received a promising text message. Crawford knew better than most people that money talked (he'd received his fair share of brown envelopes in the past) and that certainly seemed true in this case. The right money had now been slipped into the right pockets and the wild goose chase was finally coming to an end. Crawford smiled at the analogy. This particular goose was about to get well and truly stuffed.

Chapter 38

Christmas in the Kelly household had never been festive, despite the giant Norway Spruce that turned up every year. Abi had soon learned that the delicate decorations were not intended for her clumsy hands and that the crystal snowflakes, elaborate wreath and perfectly positioned fairy lights were for the benefit of her mother's friends rather than the enjoyment of her children.

Quite often, it was only the three of them, her father insisting it was 'just another day' before travelling to whichever city was hosting his team for the much-anticipated Boxing Day fixture. This year was no different, the Blues' away match at Newcastle ensuring he was absent, once again, on December twenty-fifth.

Thankfully, the Templeton-Howes had invited Abi and her mother to join in their Christmas celebrations, sparing them both the agony of pretence that had always accompanied their own disastrous turkey dinner. Justin had been invited too, and Abi had enjoyed getting to know her brother's partner, his insistence that they all wore their paper hats, somehow adding to his appeal.

But although the day had been full of fun and laughter, Abi couldn't help but feel sorry for herself; her emotions serving up a Christmas cocktail of sad memories, bitter rejection and, she had to admit, a generous dose of envy. She'd been jealous when Sasha had proudly displayed the earrings that Danny had bought for her, the smile on her face as bright as the star on top of the tree. It wasn't the earrings themselves (she'd never been a fan of Pandora), it was the suggestion of seduction that came with them. In the week since the party, Sasha and Danny had met twice, once for a pizza and once for a coffee. Both times Sasha had inundated Abi with text messages to say what a dreamboat *he* was and how smitten *she* was. For Abi, it rubbed salt into her very raw Cory Flemming wound which, sadly, appeared to be getting deeper. Cory was not answering Abi's calls and was responding to her text messages with one-word replies. She'd well and truly shot herself in the foot with her stunt in the swimming pool and was beginning to wish she'd just accepted his apology instead of sulking like a petulant school girl. The two of them together could have been the next Posh 'n Becks. Still, even Abi knew better than to hassle him over Christmas. If her father's mood was anything to go by after the loss against Brighton on Saturday, she'd leave Cory Flemming well and truly alone.

Sharing Christmas Day with Max and Lydia had also caused childhood memories to resurface for Florentina. She recalled things she hadn't thought about for years. The felt stocking, handmade by her mother, carefully attached to the fireplace before bedtime on Christmas Eve. The basket of chestnuts, tempting her taste buds long before they were roasted by her father. And the celebration of Santo Stefano on December twenty-sixth, when she and Pia would dress up in their favourite dresses and their shiny shoes and chatter until the sky grew dark and their eyelids closed.

She still hadn't called Pia. Thomas had sent her the number, as promised, but she just couldn't bring herself to call her old friend. But, once released, the memories from her childhood had tumbled, unchecked, from their dormancy. Running to school, hand in hand, pulling up socks as they ran. Playing hopscotch in the garden; muddy knees and gappy smiles. Collecting wild flowers for their mothers, yellow primroses as bright as the sun, sticky sap on fingers and thumbs. She'd call after Christmas, she decided. Perhaps invite her to Thomas's exhibition. She'd discussed it briefly with Rupert when they'd talked on Christmas Eve. He was deserved of the 'voice of reason' title Thomas had given him. His practical, no-nonsense attitude was exactly what she needed to put things into perspective and to stop worrying about things over which she had no control. And whatever Pia wanted to apologise for, it couldn't be that bad.

Chapter 39

After the unexpected, but very welcome, three-two win against Manchester United on New Year's Day, Crawford had been tempted to celebrate with a glass of his best Scotch. Determined, however, not to break his New Year's Resolution on the very first day, he'd avoided the lure of what lay behind the door to his study and had made himself a coffee instead. Now, three days later, he was whistling a merry tune like a window cleaner in a greenhouse.

'What are you so happy about?' Florentina asked, striding into the kitchen in a sharp Ann Klein trouser suit. Sometimes, he still had to look twice at his wife. Her new sober image was as pleasing as it was surprising. She'd taken to wearing trousers, previously non-existent in her wardrobe of very short, very tight skirts, and Crawford approved of the result.

'I'm surprised you even need to ask. But seeing as you have, I'm happy because we won three out of our four festive fixtures, we're playing non-league opposition in the FA Cup tomorrow, and we've started the new year with barely a name on the injury list.'

There was also another, equally significant reason for his chirpy mood, but he was unable to share that particular morsel of information with anybody else, least of all his wife. The prospect of revenge was becoming ever closer and, having established the whereabouts of the elusive Mr Savage, he was plotting the downfall of his tormentor with a pleasure that was bordering on psychotic.

'In that case, long may it continue,' said Florentina, clearly appreciative of his good mood. Her smile was more attractive too, Crawford noticed, no longer weighed down with heavy makeup or disguised behind mistrusting eyes. The two of them were a reflection of each other, he realised. He'd noticed similar, subtle changes in his own appearance. Being guilt-free had lifted his shoulders a little, and the vast reduction in alcohol consumption had lightened his skin, both in colour and clarity. He'd also lost a couple of pounds. His shirt buttons no longer strained across his stomach and his trousers sat a little more comfortably on his hips. The opposite was true of Florentina. She'd actually filled out, he was sure. Her face was less gaunt and her bones less pronounced. He studied her as she sipped her espresso. She was standing at the French doors, her favourite spot in the house, looking out across the vast lawn towards the summer house and the ivy-covered arbour. The light shone on her hair. It was the colour of their favourite beach, an arc of beautiful, soft sand known as Plage des Sablettes in Menton, the last French town before Italy. His memories were so vivid he could feel the sand between his toes, hear the ripple of the shallow water and smell the freshly squeezed lemons in the air. He pictured Florentina in a tiny white bikini, the admiring gaze of onlookers hiding, unsuccessfully, behind shades. *We should go back,* he thought, surprising himself with his desire to spend time with his wife.

A squirrel caught their attention, its brazen exploration of the patio taking them both by surprise. Florentina turned to watch its progress, her body now angled towards him. His eyes were drawn to the area of skin revealed by her V-neck cashmere sweater; the décolletage. He smiled. He could say it, but he doubted he'd be able to spell it. The skin was smooth, free of lines or creases, the contour of her collarbone just visible. The change was subtle, but noticeable. The bones had previously jutted out like a wire coat hanger. A finger of weak, winter sun poked through the window, settling on the diamond worn around her neck. More memories revealed themselves and an image of a young Florentina emerged. A hospital bed, a beaming smile, a bonnie baby boy. Crawford had to sit down, such was the force of the emotions stirred by the memory. He'd been so proud; a beautiful wife, a newborn son. He could smell the flowers at the side of her bed, see the happiness in her eyes, feel the tiny fist clenched around his thumb. The diamond pendant had been a gift, a thank you for giving him a son. He closed his eyes, full of regret for the twenty-four years that had followed. He still hadn't spoken to Thomas, not since his apology had been rejected almost six weeks ago. Giving up alcohol wasn't his only New Year's resolution.

Florentina lifted the sleeve of her sweater to check the time, left her position at the window, and helped herself to a handful of seedless grapes from the fridge. Crawford shut down the memories, uncomfortable with his shift in mood. He unplugged his phone from its charger and grabbed his keys from the table.

'Of course, there is another reason for my jovial mood.'

'What's that?' she asked.

'No more grubby taxis. I got my licence back.' And with that, he treated her to his best smile, threw his keys in the air and went to reintroduce himself to his Jaguar.

Florentina sat in her husband's vacated seat at the breakfast bar and thumbed through the morning papers. She heard a faint purr as he started the engine of his Jaguar, followed by the crunch of tyres on gravel. She smiled at his obvious satisfaction at being back behind the wheel and hoped he'd learned his lesson. As indeed, had she. Of course, she hadn't actually been banned from driving, but that was down to good luck rather than good behaviour. They both appeared to have turned a corner as far as alcohol was concerned. She was pretty sure his fling with the physio had ended as well. He certainly wasn't staying out as late, or as often. That said, she knew better than to get used to his amiable mood. One bad result could see him slide right back down to the fiery depths of antagonism, spite and fury.

With nothing in the papers to draw her interest, she plucked her phone from the side pocket of her handbag. She'd promised herself she would call Pia today; she'd put it off long enough. The silly thing was, she wasn't even sure why. Her heartbeat accelerated as she scrolled to Pia's number. Thirty-five years was a long time, what would she say? She sucked in her bottom lip, oblivious to the waxy taste of her Chanel Fiery Fuchsia lipstick, then glanced once more at her watch. Deciding it was too early to call, she selected the green and white message icon instead. Her thumbs hovered, typed, deleted, and typed again, until eventually, she pressed 'send'. She imagined the words floating through cyber space, twisting round and round like the funnel of a tornado, until announcing their arrival with a ping inside Pia's phone. Her heart was still beating a little too fast and she took a deep breath before re-reading her message.

Pia. It's Florentina. It's been a long time! It would be good to see you. Thomas is holding an exhibition on 25th Jan (he's an artist). Would you like to come? Let me know. I will send details. F

x

She cringed at the kiss. *Too much? Not enough?* Whatever she thought, it was too late now. The message had been sent. All she could do now was wait.

With the exhibition date creeping ever closer, Thomas was beginning to despair at the lack of daylight hours. During the summer, he was told, it didn't get properly dark until well after ten o'clock. In January, however, he was lucky to work beyond four p.m. He turned to the window, raising his eyes to the charcoal clouds slowly growing in size above the trees. He untied his apron and lifted it over his head, resigned to the fact that his brushes had painted their last strokes, for today, at least. He cleaned them methodically, then stood back to assess his work. He tilted his head to one side, mentally listing the areas to be tweaked, until his neck ached and his tummy growled.

In the kitchen, he scrubbed and stabbed an extra-large potato and put it in the oven to cook. The fire had almost died, the last of the glowing embers fading along with the daylight. Thomas felt a sudden, almost desperate need for fresh air. He'd worked non-stop every day for as long as he could remember, only leaving the house for basic provisions and, once, to watch a magnificent, if unexpected, sunset. He grabbed his coat from the hook on the back of the door, pulled a hat over his hair and set off.

The path to the castle was predictably quiet. The castle itself was closed until the end of March and any stragglers from the café would be long gone, the dark and the cold offering no incentive to loiter. He followed the path to the walled garden, the ornate Camellia House high to his right, the incurious herd of red deer to his left. He quickened his step, his footsteps disturbing the otherwise silent air. By the time he reached the swan pond, it was totally dark. He paused for a moment, resting on a cold bench, his eyes searching the sky for a peek of the moon. He found it, playing hide and seek with the clouds, its lustrous light winking on the water. He could hear birds, the rustle of leaves, and the scurry of tiny feet. And something else. A whimper? He cocked his head towards the sound. An injured animal of some kind? A fox perhaps? He took his phone from his pocket and turned on the torch, an arc of light scanning the area around him. Two big, dark eyes blinked back at him. Long, floppy ears, a white nose, tiny paws. He put his phone away and walked slowly towards what appeared to be a lost and frightened puppy.

'Hello, little fella. What are you doing out here?' He crouched down, rubbing his fingers and thumb together and making the universal clicking sound with his tongue, used with animals worldwide. He stroked the top of its head and felt it tremble. 'Are you lost? And hungry too, I'll bet.' He continued to stroke the animal before curling his hand under its belly and lifting it from the floor. He held it against him, the violent trembling causing he himself to shiver. He unzipped his coat and the pup instinctively nestled inside. There was no collar and he could hear no one shouting, nobody desperately searching for their lost pet. Thomas assumed it had been dumped and wondered if there was more than one. He retrieved his phone with his free hand and scanned the area once more, his eyes searching beneath bushes, beside trees and among dead, dry leaves. Satisfied it was just one, lone puppy, he slipped his phone back in his pocket and hurried home. He wasn't the only one who needed some dinner.

Back at the cottage he pulled the throw from the sofa and bunched it on the floor to form a nest. He lay the puppy at the centre then piled more logs on the fire, the spark of the freshly struck match briefly masking the smell of his now over-baked potato. At least the oven had kept the cottage relatively warm in his absence. He filled a saucer with water, placed it on the floor, then searched the fridge for something suitable for a dog. Nothing. He took a packet of pork scratchings from the cupboard but put them back again. If *he* struggled to chew them, this little fella would have no chance. Unwilling to leave his new friend, even for a minute, he knelt beside the pup and called his neighbour.

'Sorry to bother you, Rupert. I don't suppose you have anything in your fridge suitable for a puppy, do you?'

Predictably, his request was met with a moment of confused silence.

'I found a pup down by the duck pond, but I haven't any food.'

'Oh. Just a minute. Let me check.'

He heard the opening of a fridge, bottles clinking in the door, the rustling of wrappers, cheese perhaps? Rupert's pondering hum to let him know he was still there.

'I've some cooked chicken. That should be okay. Do you want me to pop it round?'

'Would you? Thanks, Rupert, I don't really want to leave him.'

Thomas opened the door in preparation for his visitor, then returned to his position on the floor.

A tap on the door followed a couple of minutes later.

'Come in, Rupert. Thanks for this, I appreciate it. I hope we haven't just stolen your dinner.'

Noticing the partially hidden bundle of fur, Rupert joined Thomas in front of the fire, a waft of cold air accompanying him.

'Not at all, I've eaten already. Which is more than can be said for this little guy.' He ran a finger along the furry white nose. The pup raised its head and licked Rupert's fingers. Thomas melted at the cuteness overload.

'He can probably smell the chicken,' said Rupert. 'Here you go, mate.' He removed a saucer of finely chopped chicken from a plastic bag and held it under the pup's nose. 'You like that, don't you?'

They watched its little pink tongue dart back and forth across the saucer.

'You really think he was dumped?' Rupert asked.

'I think so. How else would it have got there? There are no houses nearby and it didn't have a collar on. I could put a sign up in the café, but I doubt anyone would claim it. And how would I know if was really theirs with no name or anything?'

'Maybe it's got one of those chip things. You should take it to a vet.'

'Yeah. I'll take it anyway, get it checked over.' He watched it lick the saucer clean, then sniff Rupert's hands, looking for more.

'It's worrying that you found it by the pond,' Rupert said, his face a picture of concern.

'What do you mean?'

'I wonder if their intention was to drown it.'

The thought had never even occurred to Thomas. His hands shot to his mouth and for a second he stopped breathing. 'What if there *were* more? There might've been a whole litter! Oh my God, that's terrible.' He shifted from his knees, his legs now tucked to the side. 'I'll go back in the morning and have another look around.'

The pup was now looking up at Thomas, the flames from the fire reflected in its huge, brown eyes. 'How could anyone do that?' he asked, the very thought, inconceivable

'It happens, unfortunately. Lucky for this little guy, you came along at the right time.'

'Didn't I just?' Thomas smiled down at the puppy, now curled up like a comma.

'You're going to keep him, aren't you?'

Thomas didn't answer straight away, despite knowing the answer. He ran a finger over its velvety head, watched the little body rise and fall with each contented breath, pictured long walks along the beach, throwing sticks and balls and splashing in the waves. 'Yes,' he said eventually, 'I think I am.'

'What are you going to call him? I assume it is a he?'

Thomas smiled. 'Yes, it's most definitely a he. I'm not sure. What do you think he is? A spaniel of some kind?'

'Possibly. It's difficult to tell. Ask at the vet.'

Rupert clambered up off his knees. 'I'll leave you two to it. Might be a good idea to put some newspaper on the floor.'

'Good thinking. And thanks for the chicken, you're a life saver. Looks like I'm going shopping tomorrow, doesn't it, little guy?' The pup was now oblivious, sleeping soundly on its fleecy bed.

'Give me a knock in the morning if you're going back to the pond. I'll help you have a scout around.'

'Brilliant. Thanks, Rupert.'

Another blast of cold air filled the room as Rupert closed the door behind him. Suddenly remembering his own hunger, he rescued his shrivelled, hard potato from the oven. 'Cheese on toast it is then,' he said, throwing the potato in the bin.

Chapter 40

'Turns out he had a girlfriend the whole time.'

Abi and Sasha were enjoying a rare night out in Notting Hill. Abi wasn't entirely convinced by the audaciously named Paradise venue, but Sasha had persuaded her to take the twenty-minute taxi ride to the quirky night spot. They were perched on two bar stools pretending not to notice the admiring glances from most of the males in the room.

'You're kidding me!' said Sasha, sipping her bright blue cocktail delicately through a straw.

'It's true. Thought he'd string me along until she flew over from America to join him.' She pretended not to care, but her blasé attitude was pointless. Sasha knew her well enough to know she was pretty pissed off.

'So, what did he say? "Sorry, Abi, you're dumped, my proper girlfriend's moving in."'

'Something like that. I thought we were gonna get back together. He asked me over to his house so I was expecting him to give me my key back. I put my best underwear on and everything.' She took a sip of her Chardonnay, wincing at its warmth. She gestured to the barman. 'Can I get some ice please?'

'So, what happened?' asked Sasha.

'Well, I thought it was a bit strange that he didn't kiss me or anything. Then he just sat at the kitchen table. He didn't even offer me a drink. And I'm sitting there wondering what's going on and he just slid his phone across the table.'

'With her picture on it?'

'Yeah, the two of them. All lovey-dovey and stuff. And he just said, "She's my girlfriend." I mean, fuck's sake, what was I supposed to say to that?'

A miniature ice bucket appeared beside her and she paused to tip a mound of ice-cubes into her glass. 'I presumed he'd just met her. I mean,

I hadn't seen him for over a month, and I was silently kicking myself for leaving it so long. And then he said, "She's coming over from America next week."'

'What a cheek!'

'I know. So then he said, "Sorry, I know I should've said something before, but I wasn't sure if she was gonna come to England or not."'

'So, if she hadn't come over, he would've carried on seeing you?' Sasha asked, her face a picture of disgust.

Abi shrugged, then took another sip of wine. 'Spose so. He should've told me though, either way. At least it explains why he never wanted to go out. Bastard. Anyway, she's welcome to him. The guy has no sense of humour.' That wasn't strictly true, but the image of his furious face when she'd dumped him into the swimming pool was still fresh in her mind. As was the slap she'd received during the previous pool drama. She was starting to think she'd had a lucky escape.

'Just forget about him, Abs. You're too good for him anyway.' She was stirring the straw around in her cocktail, the blue liquid swirling around like juice in a blender. 'Is Thomas looking forward to his exhibition?'

'I think so. Oh, did I tell you he's got a puppy?' She plucked her phone from her handbag and scrolled to the picture of her brother's new dog, its brown and white face looking up at them with big, sad eyes.

'Aww, it's gorgeous.' Sasha put her drink down and took the phone from Abi. 'You didn't tell me he was getting a dog.'

'I didn't know,' said Abi. 'Neither did Thomas. He found it.'

Sasha looked up at her in horror. 'He found it? What, you mean it was lost?'

'Dumped.'

'No! Oh, the poor thing.' Sasha was trying to stroke the dog through the screen, her forefinger making tiny movements, up and down. 'What's its name?'

'Jerry.'

'Jerry?' The frown was back. 'Why Jerry?'

'It's a Springer Spaniel. Jerry Springer.'

'Oh, that's awful,' she laughed. 'And not very original. I bet half the Springer Spaniels in the world are called Jerry.'

'Says the girl with a French Bulldog called Eiffel.'

Sasha had the decency to look embarrassed. 'Fair point,' she said, 'I take it back. Is he bringing it with him when he comes down for the exhibition?' She handed the phone back to Abi and retrieved her drink from the bar.

'I'm not sure. I guess so. Anyway, to answer your original question, I think he's looking forward to it. He's worked really hard. I hope he sells lots of paintings.'

'Is he still seeing Jock the Doc?'

'We need to stop calling him that,' she said, rubbing a thumb along the condensation on the outside of her glass. 'I nearly said it to his face on Christmas Day! And he's not even a doctor. Anyway, I'm not sure what their relationship is, to be honest. They obviously don't see much of each other; they live at opposite ends of the country.'

'He's coming to the exhibition though, right?'

'I think so. It's gonna be great. Even Dad says he'll be there. Although I'll believe it when I see it.'

'Are they still getting on better? Your mum and dad, I mean?'

Abi had told Sasha about the somewhat surreal atmosphere that seemed to have settled in at the Kelly house.

'Yeah. It's weird. They both seem really different. Like, mellow, you know?'

'Another drink, ladies?'

They both looked at their ever-decreasing drinks and nodded at the barman.

'Maybe they've reached a truce. It must've been tiring, all that arguing.'

'I think it's got something to do with the agency. It gave Mum a new lease of life, you know? I think she was bored and she resented the rest of us for having something to do.'

Abi made no secret of her antagonistic relationship with her mother, particularly where Sasha was concerned. Her friend had been present for many a mother-daughter spat, as well as witnessing her father's unpredictable mood swings. No doubt Max and Lydia also had tales to tell when it came to the hostile Kelly household.

'Anyway, let's hope the truce continues until after the exhibition,' Abi continued. 'Thomas will never forgive them if they spoil his big night. Cheers.'

The clink of glasses was barely audible above the sound of Calvin Harris, thanks to the recent arrival of the club DJ. The lights dimmed, the floor filled and their conversation, for the time being, was over. Abi took a selfie, instantly posting the picture on her Instagram account with the words: Back on the scene. *Stick that up your American flag pole, Cory Flemming!*

Chapter 41

Thomas felt sick. But it wasn't the motion of the high-speed train from Glasgow to Euston that was making him feel queasy. Nor was it the limp prawn sandwich served to him in the first-class carriage just over an hour ago. It was the thought of his precious artwork rumbling down the M6 in the back of a courier van. It was the prospect of him hosting his first ever exhibition and not selling a single painting. It was the knowledge that in just a few short hours, he'd be in the same room as his father.

He wished he'd brought Jerry with him. The comfort gleaned from rubbing his soft, papery ears, seeing his wagging tail and feeling his warm, wet tongue had taken him completely by surprise. He and Rupert had returned to the swan pond the following morning and conducted a thorough search, but there had been no sign of any other puppies. He didn't know whether to be sad or glad. It was later in the day, when he'd taken his new furry friend to the vet, that he'd learned it was a Springer Spaniel of around twelve weeks old. The vet suspected it had been abandoned rather than lost, perhaps by the family of a young child who had quickly bored of the novelty of a new pup, or grown resentful of the attention its age and vulnerability would inevitably demand.

In the three weeks since Thomas had found him, the two of them had bonded like two mice in a cattery. For the first time in his life, Thomas knew what it felt like to be truly loved. To know that his company was appreciated rather than tolerated. To come home to a happy face and to spend time with someone who didn't judge, criticise or complain. The fact that that someone was a dog didn't matter to Thomas. He was overwhelmed with the love he felt for Jerry and by the unconditional love he received in return. It had broken his heart to leave him with Rupert when he'd left this morning. He looked around the carriage and told himself, not for the first time, he'd done the right thing. Jerry would be much more comfortable in Rupert's BMW than he would on the floor of a train and they'd be reunited tomorrow. Rupert was driving down to

London for the exhibition before visiting Izzie in Warwick over the weekend. And Justin was giving Thomas (and Jerry) a lift back up to Scotland later in the week. Everything was planned to perfection. If only he could stop his stomach from doing somersaults.

Still feeling nauseous, he alighted the train at Euston and fought his way through the crowds of shoppers, tourists, office workers and beggars. A damp drizzle greeted him outside and he jumped gratefully into a waiting taxi. The faint trace of cigar smoke added to his nausea and he opened the window a fraction to dilute the fetid smell. 'Fulham, please, mate. Byam Road.'

He clipped his seatbelt around him then sat back and marvelled at the sights of this once, so familiar city. It would have been cheaper, and quicker, to get the tube, but the thought of standing in those cramped carriages, his nose only inches from someone else's armpit, or breathing in someone else's breath, was enough to make him puke in his own rucksack. He'd already splashed out on a first-class train ticket; he could stretch to an eight-mile cab ride.

The rain was heavier now and umbrellas began to shoot up, the flimsy Union Jacks purchased hastily from street vendors jostling for space with their professional, black equivalents. Thomas pressed the button to close the cab window. Progress along Marylebone Road was slow and he considered reading his book, the latest novel from James Patterson, to pass the time. He decided against it, opting instead to focus his attention on preparations for tomorrow's exhibition. The knot in his stomach immediately tightened as anxiety crept in. *What if nobody turns up? What if I don't sell anything? What if...?*

The rubber wipers squealed an objection across the damp windscreen of the taxi and the inside of the windows began to steam up. He took a deep breath, letting it out in one long exhalation. The cabbie eyed him in the rear-view mirror, mistakenly thinking he was sighing in frustration. 'Sorry, guv, traffic's always bad this time of day.'

He rubbed the window with the sleeve of his coat and peered through the clear circle of glass. He and Abi used to play a game when they were younger, guessing where people were going. He watched a young woman hurrying along the pavement, a bright red umbrella keeping her blonde, shoulder length hair dry. She was wearing a black business suit with a plain white collared shirt. Her skirt was clinging to her tights and her bright, white trainers looked too big for her feet. *Late for a business meeting*, he concluded, imagining a pair of black, patent court shoes in her drawstring bag. He saw a young man sitting in a doorway, a scruffy hood pulled over his head, dirty fingers curled round a paper cup, begging. Their eyes met briefly until the taxi lurched forward, but not before Thomas saw the look of complete hopelessness on his face. He couldn't begin to imagine where that young man was going. Nowhere probably. Thomas caught sight of the red digits on the meter and felt instantly guilty at his frivolous spending. Abi would no doubt say it was the guy's own fault he was sleeping in a doorway. Thomas was less convinced. He believed no one would sleep rough unless they were absolutely desperate. It's like those refugees piling into overcrowded boats. They wouldn't risk their lives, and the lives of their children, unless the prospect of staying in their own war-torn country was worse than the risk of drowning at sea. Abi just thought they were stupid. She didn't get it.

He spotted a faded poster in a bus shelter, advertising a Christmas pantomime. It would probably still be there next Christmas, he mused, the faintest of chuckles escaping his lips. He thought back to his own festivities and the wonderful day he'd spent with Rupert, Izzie and Will. The four of them had eaten too much, drank too much and laughed incessantly which, from Thomas's point of view, had resulted in the best Christmas ever. Thanks to his father's absences and his mother's permanent diet (and lack of culinary skills), Christmas Day had always resulted in a miserable day much the same as any other. Growing up, he and Abi had been compensated with a ridiculous number of gifts, designed to make up for the lack of quality, family fun. He tried to imagine what Christmas would have been like for the homeless guy in the doorway and shook his head at the gross injustice of life.

The stop-start traffic continued along Marylebone Road, eased a little on Westway, then clogged up again in Kensington High Street before thinning out in North End Road. It was almost dark when he arrived at the studio. He counted out the required notes for the taxi driver then let himself in the main door. It smelt different, he realised. No candles. He peered through the tiny pane of glass in the downstairs door.

Empty. He felt sad. He didn't see his candle-making neighbours very often, but it was nice to know they were there, and their heavily accented greetings always made him smile. He wondered who might take their place but didn't dwell on the thought. Lugging his rucksack up the stairs, he unlocked the door, pushed it open with his hip and flicked the light switch with his thumb.

'I don't believe it.'

His rucksack dropped to the floor with a thud and he stood, open-mouthed, in the doorway. He didn't notice the red carpet running through the centre of the room, the once dusty, paint-splattered floor swept and scrubbed until it shone. Nor did he notice the chunky, chrome freestanding spotlights waiting to light up his twelve chosen paintings on the walls. The rows of polished champagne flutes also went unnoticed, as did his own black and white photograph looking down at him from the wall. Thomas was oblivious to everything other than the newly erected stage with its huge rainbow backdrop. He was well aware of the significance of the rainbow. It was a symbol of lesbian, gay, bisexual and transgender pride. He cringed at the sight of it, fearful of the reaction its presence would provoke. He wanted to jump up and tear it down, hide beyond the anonymity that he'd relied upon for so many years. Free of the initial shock that had rooted him to the floor, he swung open the cupboard door, searched the kitchen units and threw back the starched, white cloths placed neatly over tables. It was a fruitless exercise; he'd removed all of his paints during his last visit to London. But his desire to erase the rainbow, taunting him from its superior position above the stage, was primal. Suddenly exhausted, the long journey south and subsequent emotional torment proving too much, he collapsed to the floor and cried, the blood-red carpet thirstily drinking his tears.

He awoke an hour later, his neck stiff and his bones cold. He unfolded himself from the floor, averting his eyes from the stage. Only then did he notice the miraculous transformation from shabby studio to edgy gallery. He imagined his paintings on the wall, lit up for all to see. An admiring audience full of praise and respect. A pile of receipts and a string of glowing reviews. He pictured a room full of famous faces. His mother with a beaming smile. His sister, as always, turning heads. His father… He lifted his rucksack from the floor and rubbed the life back into his legs. Then, without looking back, he switched off the light, locked the door and left the rainbow behind. He was in serious need of a pint. And some company.

He'd already finished a pint of Old Peculiar and a bag of pork scratchings by the time Justin arrived in The Half Moon. It was busy for a Thursday evening, a combination of smartly dressed office workers yet to make it home, empty wine bottles and mobile phones decorating their tables, and students, hugging each pint as if it were their last, holey jeans and fingerless gloves indicative of their status. Thomas's mood lifted at the sight of Justin, those auroral green eyes instantly easing the tight, nervous knot in his stomach.

'Thanks for the text. I didn't expect to see you until tomorrow,' said Justin, two new pints now sitting on the table in front of them. 'How are you feeling about it? All set?'

Thomas sipped his pint, unsure how to express his feelings. 'I was. Until I went to the studio earlier. Mum's really gone to town on the décor.' An ironic laugh accompanied his words prompting a frown from Justin.

'That's good, isn't it? She did a brilliant job for their launch party.'

He took a deep breath. 'She's erected a giant gay pride flag.'

Justin laughed, the foam from the top of his pint spraying across the table and all over Thomas's jumper. His startled, silent reaction seemed to amuse Justin even more and his raucous laughter continued. Thomas desperately tried to remain indignant but felt the corners of his mouth lift involuntarily. He wiped the spots of froth from his jumper, trying to stifle the giggle that was threatening to erupt. Justin was still laughing, along with numerous other customers clearly entertained by the exchange. Eventually, Thomas joined in. Not with the discreet chuckle that usually accompanied his humour, but a hearty guffaw that felt so good it hurt.

'You've got froth on your chin,' Justin managed to say between giggles, his finger demonstrating the spot on his own chin where the offending spray had landed. Thomas wiped it away with his hand, the smile still evident on his face.

'As I was saying,' he said, trying to restore some order to their conversation, 'Mum has seen fit to display a huge rainbow flag in preparation for my exhibition tomorrow night.'

Justin wiped his eyes and cleared his throat, struggling to contain himself after the unexpected burst of laughter.

'Well, "Pride" *is* the title of your exhibition. I think it's a great idea. And isn't it good to know you have your family's full support?'

Thomas grunted. 'I may have my mother's support, and Abi's, but my father is a different matter.'

'From what Max has told me they all intend to be there tomorrow night, so what are you worried about? He knows you're gay, Thomas. Everyone does. Why are you still hiding?'

This time his indignation showed. 'I'm not hiding!'

'You are. Why are you so upset about a gay pride flag? The clue's in the name. Be proud.'

'Be proud.' Thomas repeated the words. Justin was right. What was he worried about? He was an independent adult about to host his very first art exhibition. He had cut the strings that previously tied him to his parents. He could, even if he didn't sell any paintings tomorrow, stand on his own two feet. He was finally happy with who he was and *what* he was. And, most importantly of all, he had just laughed until he'd cried.

'You're right,' he said, the realisation as clear as his empty pint glass. 'I am proud. The flag stays. Another beer?'

Chapter 42

Thomas had been to the studio twice in advance of the exhibition, once when he'd first arrived back in London and had reacted badly to the gay pride flag, and again the following afternoon to meet the courier. He'd arranged his paintings in the appropriate order, displayed the title of each one and stood back to appraise the finished result, rainbow flag and all. Nothing, however, had prepared him for the magical scene that greeted him on his third visit. Dressed in his evening suit, the starched white collar uncomfortable on his neck, his black bow-tie not quite straight, he stood at the doorway in awe. Now that darkness had settled, the room had lost its cold, industrial air and taken on a softer, serene semblance. The smell of fresh flowers filled the room and delicate fairy lights shone like stars. The tripod spotlights were expertly placed, drawing attention to each of his paintings, whilst at the same time, eliminating the need for the harsh, overhead bulbs. On the stage, an elegant harp stood tall and expectant, its vertical strings temporarily still.

'There you are, darling. I didn't hear you come in.' Florentina emerged from the kitchen, its existence concealed by the makeshift stage. She walked across the red carpet and straightened his tie before kissing him on both cheeks.

'You look fabulous, Mum. And so does this.' He extended his arm, like a compere announcing his next act. 'I can't believe how different it looks.'

'I'm glad you like it. But it doesn't matter what the room looks like, Thomas. Tonight is all about your paintings. Shall we do the prices?' She was smiling at him as if she knew they were about to disagree.

'You go ahead, Mum. I trust you.'

Her smile widened and he watched as she retrieved a bundle of white cards from her handbag. The new modest image suited her. Without the stiff, bleached hair, thick, dark makeup and tight, almost obscene clothes, she looked ten years younger. She was wearing a shimmering gold, wraparound dress with a matching belt, tied at the side. Its fluted sleeves covered her elbows and the hemline just skimmed her knees. The V-shaped neckline was more flattering than revealing, and her straightened hair, curled under slightly at the ends, framed her simple diamond pendant. She looked radiant.

'What time is Dad getting here?' He hadn't yet seen his father and the impending reunion was doing nothing to ease his nerves. Thomas could only hope that the Blues' run of good results would ensure a jovial mood and, therefore, a drama-free evening.

'He's bringing Max and Lydia. They should be here about seven.'

'He's driving? Is that a good idea?'

His mother stopped what she was doing and looked at him. 'He won't drink if that's what you're worried about. Rarely touches a drop these days. Makes him much easier to live with I must admit.' She continued to study his painting of Troon Yacht Haven, apparently considering what figure to write on the price tag.

Thomas, meanwhile, was still trying to process the fact that his father was on the wagon. The idea of one reformed parent was hard enough to fathom, let alone two.

A tap on the door indicated the arrival of the caterers. Thomas made a point of acknowledging them all individually before retreating to the bathroom. He was that nervous he could pee for England.

Abi and Sasha were first to arrive, accompanied by a young guy far too handsome for his own good. Actually, handsome wasn't the right word, Thomas decided. He was… arresting. He was dressed casually in black skinny jeans and a sky-blue shirt, open at the neck. His long, bronze hair was tied back loosely in a band and he stood a good few inches taller than anyone else.

'You must be Danny?' Thomas said, extending his hand.

Danny shook it, his grip firm. 'Pleased to meet you.'

'Likewise.'

'I've told Danny all about you,' said Sasha, hugging Thomas warmly and kissing his cheek. 'And I showed him your painting of Eiffel. Oh! Talking of which, where's Jerry?' Sasha looked to the ground, as though expecting the little spaniel to be bounding around their feet. 'I can't wait to meet him.'

'He'll be here later,' laughed Thomas. 'You both look stunning, by the way.' Abi and Sasha grinned at him, their beaming faces entirely different but equally beautiful. 'Help yourselves to a drink.' He gestured to a waiter, a tray full of bubbling champagne glasses balanced on one hand. 'And feel free to buy a painting or two!' He left them to it as more guests began to arrive, the hypnotic sound of the harp accompanying their arrival.

Florentina was bursting with pride, the jagged edges of her heart softening at the sight of her son. The feeling was unfamiliar, but welcome. She watched him now, smart as an officer in his pristine suit, his facial hair neatly manicured, his smile as warm as his heart. He greeted each guest with genuine enthusiasm, his response to their praise both modest and endearing. He'd never been one for the limelight, always shied away from attention. Pia had been the same. *Pia*. She hadn't replied to her text message. She'd been both disappointed and relieved but resolved to call her after the exhibition. Preparation for this event had taken up so much of her time she'd barely had a minute to think about anything else. Her dealings with the cleaners, the caterers, the harpist, the florist, the stage erector and the electrical contractor had turned into a full-time job, not to mention the guests themselves. She could, of course, have handed the entire event over to a professional event management company, but where was the fun in that? And she belied anyone to do a better job than she herself had done. As for the rainbow, that was inspired! Thomas hadn't said much about it, but he hadn't objected to it either. Quite what Crawford would think was another matter entirely.

By the time Crawford arrived, there was already an impressive number of supercars lined up outside. He slotted his Jaguar in a prominent position – grateful, for once, for his personal plate – and followed Max and Lydia up the stairs. He was ashamed to admit he'd never been to his son's studio. Such was his refusal to accept his choice of career, he'd deliberately avoided the arty warehouse and anything to do with the goings on inside. He was here now though, and that's all that mattered. He'd assured Thomas he would become a better person and was determined to prove that he had. Since their heated exchange in his office he'd hardly had a drink, he'd been completely celibate (the longest he'd ever gone without sex in his adult life) and he'd remembered to thank Ivy every time she'd made him a coffee. He'd also managed to be polite and respectful to Florentina. Although, he had to admit, her new sultry look had made that particular task very easy indeed.

As they reached the top of the stairs, Crawford could hear the faint, mellow tune of a harp combined with the rumble of conversation. He could also hear his own heartbeat, its rhythm a beat too fast. The presence of cameras could be seen as well as heard, their constant clicks accompanied by flashes of light illuminating the dim staircase. Once inside, he was bombarded with images he found almost impossible to process. A giant rainbow banner, a display of quite brilliant paintings, the owner of his football club, his wife in a beautiful gold dress, at least four players from his football team, the Queen's granddaughter, a pop star... and Thomas, holding court with a group of influential, prospective buyers admiring a painting of the Shard. He looked at his son, handsome in his dinner suit, confident in his stance, and felt a sudden urge to hold him tight, to apologise for a lifetime of hurt, and to tell him he loved him. *Later,* he told himself. *I'll do it later.*

The arrival of Cory Flemming, accompanied by a tall, attractive brunette, caused heads to turn from all directions. Crawford noticed Abi's look of indifference and was reassured that the striker's relationship with his daughter was indeed over. The thought cheered him but his satisfaction was curtailed by Simone's unexpected arrival with Grayson Delaney. The pair looked particularly pleased with themselves as they swanned into the room looking like two school kids emerging from behind the bike sheds. Crawford gritted his teeth, his clenched jaw belying the passive expression he so badly wanted to portray. In truth, he was glad to be rid of her. Her tenacious tendencies had the makings to become troublesome. As for Grayson, with six days until the transfer window closed, he might just find himself the subject of a last-minute transfer deal. He allowed himself a sly smile at the thought, and the fact that he had another two witnesses to his presence tonight.

Justin's arrival allowed Thomas the opportunity to extract himself from a Russian couple who had monopolised him for the last twenty-five minutes. He'd been conversing with them for so long he was beginning to speak with a Russian accent.

'How's it going?' Justin asked. 'I see your father made it then.'

Thomas hadn't even noticed his father come in. Although, he had spotted Max's bald head among the crowd, so it followed that his father was here somewhere.

'It's going great,' said Thomas, unwilling to be sidetracked by the imminent father-son reunion. 'I've sold four so far, all Scottish, funny enough.'

'Paintings or buyers?'

Thomas laughed at his accidental ambiguity. 'Paintings.'

'Well, I'm sure they'll all be sold before the night's out.' Justin stepped towards the black and white painting of Tower Bridge. 'This is amazing. Has Max seen this?'

'I'm not sure. I guess so. Why?'

'He's got an old print of Tower Bridge in his office. It's an original, limited edition, but it's not a patch on this. He should replace it, buy this one.'

'I'm perfectly capable of deciding what goes on my office wall thank you, Mr McKenzie.'

Max's sudden arrival caught them both by surprise and Justin blushed with embarrassment. 'Sorry, Max.'

'But you're absolutely right. I do need to replace that old print and this...' He stepped closer, his face just inches from the painting, '... is exactly what I'm looking for.'

'Don't feel obliged, Max. You shouldn't feel bullied into it.'

'I never let anyone bully me into anything, Thomas. To be truthful, I've been inching my way towards this ever since I got here. Kept getting waylaid. Had a horrible feeling someone was going to beat me to it.'

'You'd be entitled to a discount,' said Thomas, embarrassed by the price tag displayed underneath.

'Absolutely not! I wouldn't hear of it. Besides, it's worth every penny. Now get a "sold" sticker on it before someone outbids me.'

A little after eight thirty, Rupert arrived. 'Sorry I'm late, Thomas. I was late leaving this morning and the drive took longer than expected.'

'Don't worry. You got here, that's the main thing. Have you eaten? There's still some nibbles knocking around if you're hungry. They won't exactly fill you up, but they'll take the edge off.'

Thomas raised his hand to attract the attention of a passing waiter, his tray full of exquisite hors d'oeuvres; slivers of smoked salmon on tiny squares of toasted ciabatta, crescents of avocado, topped with soft goat's cheese and dusted with paprika, garlic sautéed mushrooms atop puff pastry circles, sprinkled with parsley and parmesan shavings. Rupert helped himself to a miniature treat and Thomas, unable to resist the temptation, did the same. The avocado melted in his mouth. He looked around for a drink, the burn of paprika unexpectedly hot on his tongue.

'While I remember,' said Rupert, 'Take my car keys. Jerry's on the back seat. He's curled up in his blanket. Pop down when you get five minutes.'

Thomas took the keys, sliding them inside his trouser pocket. 'Were they okay at the hotel? No problems?'

'None at all. They made a big fuss of him. Even gave him a biscuit.'

Thomas smiled at the image conjured by the tale. 'Thanks again for looking after him. Are you sure you don't mind dropping him off in the morning? I can collect him from your hotel if it's easier.'

'Of course I don't mind. Text me your postcode so I can use satnav. Now, let's have a look at these paintings. I've only ever seen them stacked up in your dining room.'

'Who's that with Thomas?'

Florentina followed Lydia's appreciative gaze. 'Oh! That's Rupert. I didn't see him come in. Come on, I'll introduce you.'

'That's Rupert? You didn't tell me he was the next James Bond.'

Florentina laughed and led her friend through the crowd towards Rupert. It was good to see him again, she realised, as she made the introductions. It was a pleasure to see his genuine smile. A smile that revealed a perfect set of neat, white teeth, fine lines beside each eye and a sparkle in his toffee-brown eyes. Features that hadn't gone unnoticed to Lydia, if her speechless trance was anything to go by.

It was a warm, brief exchange, the conversation swinging from Jerry the Springer Spaniel to Izzie's upcoming wedding at Warwick Castle and, perhaps somewhat predictably, to Rupert's praise for his neighbour's extraordinary talent. Lydia appeared to shake off her reverie at the mention of Thomas's paintings and agreed that they were, indeed, stunning.

'Max has already bought one,' she told them. 'I'm actually rather jealous. In fact, I'm thinking of buying one of my own.'

'Well, you'll have to be quick,' Florentina said. 'They're selling faster than an *X-Factor* single at Christmas.'

Crawford made a conscious effort to edge towards the door. He'd had made a point of talking to as many people as possible and was satisfied that a short absence would go largely unnoticed. He checked the time on his Omega watch and looked back at the throng. He then made his way through the door, down the stairs and out to his car. It was time.

Thomas had felt like an impatient child ever since Rupert had arrived. He was desperate to go and see Jerry, to hold his little body against him and see the wag of his happy tail. Unable to deprive himself any longer, he made his excuses to the two models currently massaging his ego and slipped downstairs to Rupert's car. It took him a moment to find it, slotted between a white Porsche Cayenne and a soft-top Range Rover Evoque. He was just about to press the button to unlock the doors when the lights of another vehicle flashed on and off. He was surprised to see his father walking away from his Jaguar, tucking something inside his jacket as he did so. But instead of walking back towards the exhibition, Crawford walked away from the warehouse towards Eel Brook Common. Thomas watched him disappear into the darkness, a string of emotions pulling tight in his chest. His initial reaction was one of relief, the inevitable confrontation delayed once more. This was followed, however, by an overwhelming sense of unease. A muffled yap interrupted his thoughts and he opened the car. A furry tail beat a tune like a drum and a frantic tongue danced along. Thomas didn't think anyone had ever been so happy to see him in his entire life and lifting Jerry to his chest, all thoughts of his father were, for the time being, forgotten.

By ten o'clock people were beginning to leave. The harpist had packed away her harp (a performance even more meticulous than the one on the stage), the food had long since disappeared and, more importantly, every single painting had sold. Thomas was beside himself with joy. He'd written a very short thank you speech which he'd delivered with acute embarrassment and was now lapping up the pats on his back, kisses on his cheeks and warm words of congratulations. Thanks to his mother, there really was a pot of gold at the end of the rainbow and he hugged her now with genuine thanks and appreciation.

'If only you had as much faith in yourself as I have in you, darling, you'd be conquering the world.'

He smiled at her words and looked around at the few remaining guests. Sasha was still arm in arm with Danny, their limbs linked like a rope through a padlock. Max and Lydia were deep in conversation with Justin. Abi was chatting happily with Rupert. And a handful of football players were gathered around his painting of their football ground. It was then he noticed his father. He was standing among the huddle of footballers, his hair slightly damp, a trace of mud on his shoes.

Oblivious to her son's distraction, Florentina continued to talk to him about the evening, casting an eye over the sales invoices as she did so.

'Who would've thought?' she said, smiling at the improbable situation she found herself in. 'In the space of a few short months I'm not only representing my daughter in her modelling career, I'm also acting as an agent for my son at his first art exhibition. It's incredible, isn't it?'

Receiving no response, she looked up from the paperwork and frowned at Thomas's troubled expression. 'Thomas?'

He remained silent and she tutted in frustration. She slotted the invoices back inside her handbag and then tugged his jacket sleeve. 'Thomas? Are you all right?'

'What? Oh, yeah, sorry. I was just thinking. Actually, I need a glass of water.'

She watched him stride along the red carpet and disappear behind the stage. She felt momentarily uncomfortable. It was the first time she'd been alone all evening and automatically looked around for Lydia. A flash of red caught her eye and she turned towards the door. She didn't recognise her straight away, although there was something familiar about the curly, dark hair and big, round eyes. *Pia?* She wanted to run to her old friend, throw her arms around her and hug her till they were breathless, but her legs wouldn't move. She knew she was staring, but she couldn't help it. The room was still, tongues temporarily silenced as though sensing a scandal.

'Hello, Florentina.'

The sound of her name with its native Italian lilt was almost too much. The childhood memories formed a whirlpool in her mind and she swayed with the power of its current. Eventually, she forced her legs forward and closed the gap between herself and her long-lost friend. Their embrace was brief and awkward, like that between in-laws at a wedding. Thomas came to the rescue.

'Hello, Pia,' he said. 'Nice to see you again. Shall I take your coat? I think there's some champagne left. Would you like a glass?'

Florentina watched as Pia unfastened the buttons on her red coat and handed it to Thomas. 'Yes, that would be lovely. Thank you. I am so sorry I am late. Was your exhibition a success?'

'It was a great success, wasn't it, Thomas?' Florentina jumped on the opportunity to boast about her son's talent. 'He sold all of his paintings.'

'You can still see them though,' he said, 'if you'd like to. They won't be delivered to their new owners until next week.'

'I would like that very much. Thank you.'

Thomas hung the coat on the temporary rail, the spare wire hangers clanging together in protest. He then handed a glass of champagne to Pia. Florentina felt herself being led towards the back of the room. She followed Thomas like an obedient puppy.

'I'll leave you to it,' he said, once the two of them were seated.

'You should've told me you were coming,' Florentina said to Pia. They were perched on two chrome and leather bar stools, a mirror image of each other: backs straight, shoulders back, legs crossed. Two glasses of champagne stood on the table between them, slowly losing their fizz.

'I am sorry I did not reply to your message. I kept putting it off, trying to decide whether to come or not. I found the details on the internet. I wanted so badly to see you, but I was scared.'

'Scared? Scared of what?'

'I have things to tell you, Florentina. Things you will not want to hear.'

'What things?' She wrapped her fingers around the stem of her glass, twisting it round and round.

'About your parents.'

Florentina stared at her, her heart hammering hard.

'What about my parents? Thomas told me you'd been visiting their grave.'

'Yes. For many years. It was tragic, how they died.'

She took a long sip of her champagne, her first of the night. 'How did you know?'

'I heard my father talking about it. He and his brother were in my father's study. I heard him mention your parents' names. It was him, Florentina. My father killed your parents.'

She felt as though she'd been slapped. The blood in her veins turned icy cold and she looked at Pia through wide, disbelieving eyes.

'They ran from the Mafia,' Pia said. 'They ran, but they could not hide.'

Florentina remembered her parents waking her in the middle of the night, urging her to get dressed, struggling with bulging suitcases. 'Your family was the Mafia?'

Pia nodded, unable to meet her eye. 'I did not know, Florentina, I promise you.'

She felt sick; swallowed the mouthful of champagne for a second time.

'It was only when my mother died that I learned the truth. She gave me an envelope, before she died. Made me promise not to open it until she had gone.'

Florentina was saddened at the news of Maria De Santis' death. She was like a second mother to her young self. Always ready with a warm smile, a hot dinner or a comforting hug. The very thought of her conjured the smell of rich, Bolognese sauce, the sound of traditional Italian endearments (*Patatino*, 'my little potato') and the feel of her soft, floury hands.

'And the letter told you? About your father?'

'Yes. She had protected me from the truth for her entire life. She told me to be careful, to keep my distance from my father and his family.'

'But your father loved you.' She could still picture Mr De Santis. A giant of a man with big hands and thick, grey hair. He would tickle his daughter until she begged him to stop, hide sweets under her pillow and come home from abroad laden with gifts. Sometimes he would have one for Florentina. A snow globe from Austria or chocolate from Switzerland.

'Yes. He did. But he was a bad man. He hurt many people.'

'Did you stay? After your mother died?'

'Of course. Where else would I go? I was barely eighteen.'

Florentina realised she was swinging her leg back and forth and forced it to stop.

'How did he find them? My parents?'

'After I heard them talking, in his study, I went through his desk.' She looked at Florentina now, the first time since they'd sat down. 'I found the letters you sent to me.'

She let out a small gasp, as though suddenly learning the world was round. 'You didn't get them?'

'No.'

She closed her eyes, remembering the days, weeks and months she'd spent waiting for a reply, praying that the postman would deliver a letter from her best friend, Pia, with the rabbit-like eyes and curly-wurly hair. Those letters, full of innocent words and childish tales, had led a killer to her parents' door. She buried her head in her hands at the realisation.

'It is not your fault, Florentina. Neither is it mine. We were children. We cannot be held responsible for the actions of our parents, no more than your children can be held responsible for yours.'

'I still don't understand. Why did you come to Glasgow? And why didn't you get in touch with me before?'

'After I found your letters, I promised myself I would find you. But my father would never allow it.'

'You asked him?'

'No. But I knew my father. He loved me but he also controlled me. He dictated where I went, who I went with.'

'You never married?'

'No. There was someone, many years ago. But my father disapproved. I suspect he refused to join my father's payroll so I was forbidden from seeing him. He disappeared.'

'Disappeared? You mean killed?' Florentina was horrified.

'Perhaps.' She shrugged her shoulders. 'Killed or paid off.'

'How can you be so matter-of-fact?' Her voice was rising, her fingers clenched tightly around the stem of her glass.

'I have had longer to get used to the idea than you have, Florentina. I knew my father would die sooner or later. He was unhealthy. He smoked and he drank too much. He was always coughing. The colour of his skin was wrong. If he did not die from a disease, he would be murdered. His brother was shot in the head and thrown from the side of his boat. I knew my father would not make it to old age.'

She could hear her heartbeat pulsing in her ears, feel a trickle of sweat running down her spine.

'I looked you up on the internet after he died. You were not difficult to find.' She smiled, as though proud of what she'd found. 'I was happy for you. You had a family. You were famous. You did not need me to spoil it for you. But I wanted to apologise to your parents. To pay my respects.'

'And you stayed? In Glasgow?'

'Yes. There was nothing in Italy for me. I felt free for the first time in years. I enjoyed feeling the rain on my face, hearing the funny accent and just being Pia. I was never Pia in Italy. I was Aldo De Santis' daughter.'

Despite the revelations about her parents' deaths, Florentina felt sorry for Pia. She had grown into a beautiful woman, but she was obviously lonely. That said, her family had murdered the two people she loved most in the world. Pia could wear as many diamond rings as she liked, but ultimately, there was blood on her hands.

Chapter 43

The reviews from the exhibition were all positive. Thomas scrolled through his iPad reading the countless tweets, news stories and critiques. His smile was so wide he could barely chew his muesli. One particular camera had caught him talking to the owner of his father's club. They were both studying his painting of the football ground, the rainbow backdrop blurry but evident. The photograph appeared to be the clear favourite as far as the newspapers were concerned, their online additions all choosing it as their feature shot. Thomas didn't mind. He could hardly complain that football was, once again, overshadowing his art when he'd invited half of the Premier League to his exhibition. He'd yet to find out who had bought that particular painting.

Most of the articles, he noticed, made passing reference to the LGBT aspect, but one writer had used the gay pride angle as the focus of his story. It was well written and unbiased and, despite the writer openly admitting he knew absolutely nothing about art, was full of praise for Thomas's work. However, being a football writer, he went on to discuss the lack of openly gay players in the football league. It was something Thomas had never even considered. He'd naively believed that gay men just didn't play football. What a ridiculous notion! Of course there were gay footballers, plenty of them. But like him, they were too scared to 'come out'. Scared of what people would think and how it might affect their career. He was unsure whether the writer himself was gay, but he was certainly promoting the LGBT community and encouraging sportsmen and women to open up about their sexuality.

'Well, if it isn't Liberace himself.' Abi breezed into the kitchen, a vision of pink loveliness in a short, satin wraparound robe. 'How are you feeling, big brother? Other than rich?'

She dropped a kiss on his forehead before jumping onto the stool beside him, her bare feet dangling like a child in a highchair.

Thomas laughed. 'Hardly rich. But feeling great, thank you very much. And for your information, Liberace was a pianist not an artist.'

'Was he? Oh, well. Anyway, forget about him. You're the man of the moment now. I'm proud of you.'

Their eyes met for a brief, heartfelt second before she turned her attention to the pile of newspapers on the counter.

'Any good pictures?'

'Only a couple, from early in the evening. You know how it is, evening events rarely get covered the next day.'

She flicked through the pages anyway, barely pausing when a picture of her mother tried to force her to stop. She pretended not to see it and carried on.

'Have you spoken to Dad yet?'

'Other than patting me on the back as he left last night, I've had no contact with him whatsoever. Anyone would think he was avoiding me.' He laughed at the irony. 'The tables have finally turned.' He thought back to his father's suspicious behaviour and the laughter abruptly stopped.

'Who are they playing today?' Abi asked.

'They're not playing until tomorrow. And if you keep leafing through the paper at that speed you'll find out yourself soon enough.' He chased the last bit of muesli around the bottom of his bowl and spooned it into his mouth.

'Away to Wolves,' said Abi, proving his point. 'Where's that?'

Thomas almost spat out his breakfast. 'Where's that? Are you serious?' He rolled his eyes in exasperation. 'Wolverhampton. It's in the Midlands. Near Birmingham. You really should get a map of the UK, Abi. How do you ever know where you're going?'

'Satnav,' she said, as though it was the most obvious thing in the world.

'Anyway,' he said, stacking his bowl in the dishwasher. 'What did you make of Mum's friend turning up like that?'

'I dunno. Didn't really pay much attention. Mum was acting a bit funny afterwards though. A bit spaced out, you know?'

'Yeah. I think it was a bit of a shock. She hadn't seen her for thirty-five years! Can you imagine?'

'No. Not really.'

He should have known better than to try and talk to Abi about their mother. Her boredom of the chosen subject was clearly evident in her tone of voice. He didn't think she'd be too impressed with his next question either, but he asked it anyway.

'So, I take it you and Cory are definitely over then?'

'It would appear so.' She pushed the newspaper to one side and thumbed through another.

'His loss. Anyway,' she added cheerfully, 'your neighbour is lovely. He asked me for a signed photo for his son-in-law. Or should that be son-in-law-to-be? They're not married yet, right? Are you going to wedding? They're having it at a real-life castle. It's got towers and a dungeon, even a peacock garden!'

He smiled at her enthusiasm and respected her attempt to change the subject.

'Yeah, they invited me at Christmas. I'm looking forward to it. Talking of Rupert, he should be here soon. He's dropping Jerry off on his way back to Warwick.'

'Yay!' She abandoned the newspapers and jumped off the stool. 'I'd better get changed. Don't want to frighten the little guy!'

Thomas couldn't imagine Abi ever frightening anybody. Not with her looks anyway. Her tongue, however, was a different matter.

Florentina was still in her bedroom. She'd been awake for hours; what little sleep she'd had disturbed by dreams of fierce flames, choking smoke and a young Pia, blood dripping from her fingers. She studied her reflection in the mirror, the dark smudges under her eyes evidence of a restless night. She squeezed a dot of concealer onto her fingertip and smeared it on the delicate skin, rubbing gently below each eye. She felt an inexplicable need to talk to Crawford. It was so unexpected she laughed, the sound in complete contrast to her mood. It was her friendship with Rupert that had shifted her perspective. She enjoyed having someone to talk to, someone who understood and sympathised, someone she could laugh with, have fun with. That someone used to be Crawford. She couldn't blame him entirely for their troubles. He wasn't blameless, but then, neither was she. After the shoot with Per Jorgensen and her subsequent blacklisting, she'd been appalled. Disgusted with herself and ashamed of her body. So ashamed, she didn't want anyone to see it. Not even Crawford. It was no wonder he'd sought gratification elsewhere. She'd pushed him away, offered him on a plate to the queue of young hopefuls eager to take her place. She was lucky he was still around. He might be obnoxious, arrogant and chauvinistic, but he was still her husband. She could even forgive his treatment of Thomas. She'd done nothing to stop it, after all, just stood by and watched it escalate. And if her near-mistake with Cory Flemming had taught her anything, it was that she didn't want an affair. Not with Cory, not with Rupert, not with anyone. She'd had dalliances in the past and she knew they didn't solve anything. They made you feel better for a couple of hours (if you were lucky) but the euphoria soon wore off. She didn't want a temporary fix. She wanted Crawford. She wanted to be happy, like Max and Lydia. She wanted to smile when he walked in the room, feel his arm around her waist, wake up beside him in the morning. But most importantly of all, she wanted to talk to him, *needed* to talk to him

Her eyes settled on the unmade bed in the mirror and visions of last night's rare moment of tenderness returned. A small smile lifted her lips as she dared to hope that from the seeds of sadness, happiness may bloom.

The high-pitched yap of a dog disturbed her wishful thinking. Realising Rupert was downstairs with Thomas's spaniel, she left her position at the mirror, smoothed down her Chloé tie-waist trousers and slipped her feet into her pom-pom slippers.

Chapter 44

Unusually, all four members of the Kelly family were at home on Monday evening (five, if you counted Jerry). The predicted fiery confrontation with his father hadn't materialised. Instead, they'd exchanged a courteous acknowledgement, both nodding a greeting before lapsing into trivial conversation. The match at Molineux yesterday had resulted in a two-two draw, not ideal but enough for his father to be amiable, particularly as they were losing until the ninety-second minute, when Aran Hennessy had scored a text-book free kick from twenty-five yards. In fact, Thomas noticed, the atmosphere around the table was almost jovial. They'd feasted on a home cooked meal of chicken in a white wine and mushroom sauce, served on a bed of rice (well, Florentina had cooked the chicken breasts in the oven, opened a jar of sauce, and prepared four boil-in-the-bag packets of rice), and were now chatting enthusiastically about the reviews in the morning's papers. As predicted, the papers were full of glowing reports about Thomas's debut "Pride" exhibition. It was cited as the 'event of the year so far' – not much of an accolade bearing in mind it was only January, but still – and predicted a 'bright, successful future' for the 'young, openly gay talent'. So used was he to hiding behind a heterosexual façade, his stomach dropped to the floor when he read that particular sentence. Then remembering Justin's words, *be proud*, he sat up tall, lifted his head and soaked up the praise.

'Your mother and I are very proud of you, Thomas.'

He stared at his father as though he'd just admitted to being a porn star. He'd waited his entire life to hear those words, yet his father had just dropped them into the conversation as if he said them every day. Even Abi stopped scrolling through her phone.

'Your father's right, Thomas,' his mother added. 'You have exceptional talent. Although you certainly didn't get it from me, I can hardly draw a stick man.'

A titter of laughter followed, but Thomas didn't join in. He wanted to pause, rewind and replay those long-awaited words from his father. He was so happy he could cry. Relief ran through his blood, filling his heart till it could burst.

'Where *did* you get your artistic genes from, Thomas?' asked Abi. 'I certainly didn't get any. I was crap at art at school.'

At the mention of genes, his thoughts immediately returned to the possibility that Crawford was not his father. He'd pushed the nagging doubt to the back of his mind, but his sister's throwaway comment brought it straight back to the front, like a racing car on pole position.

'My mother used to paint,' said Florentina, surprising them all, 'when she was younger. She gave up when she married my father. Sacrificed her talent to raise her family and help with the business. I remember some of her paintings were on the kitchen wall. Lemons in a bowl, flowers in a vase, that sort of thing.'

'You never said.' The news was all the confirmation Thomas needed to steer the doubt over his parentage back to the pit lane, regardless of how tenuous the reassurance was.

'It's hard for me to talk about my childhood. It wasn't as blessed as yours. Things were very different.'

'Your mother certainly wouldn't have been allowed to use a mobile phone at the dinner table,' said Crawford, his eyebrows raised at Abi, who was tapping the screen of her smartphone.

She missed her cue completely and just laughed at his apparent gaff. 'That's because there weren't any mobile phones in those days, stupid.'

Thomas winced, half expecting a snide retort from their mother or a sarcastic response from their father. For a moment, the only sound in the room was Jerry sniffing around their feet and the faint tapping of rain on the windows. The equilibrium had shifted. It was strange enough that they were all sitting at the table at the same time, but the lack of insults, frosty stares and temper tantrums was making Thomas nervous. He was afraid to open his mouth in case he burst the buoyant bubble. He could ask his mother about Pia, but something about her manner, both at the exhibition and since, told him it was a subject best avoided. He could ask Abi about Sasha's relationship with Danny, but realised his timing, bearing in mind her recent split with Cory, was probably not great. And he could ask his father where he was going when he saw him walking away from the studio on Friday night. He'd been puzzling over it all weekend and could only assume he'd gone to meet another woman. A clandestine meeting in a dark alley was right up his father's street.

'Did you find out who bought the painting of the football ground, Thomas?'

It was Abi who broke the silence, clearly uncomfortable with the stilted atmosphere that had temporarily joined them at the table like an uninvited guest.

'They wish to remain anonymous,' said Florentina, answering on his behalf. 'The purchase was dealt with by a third party agent, so we have no way of knowing who it was.'

'Oh, how annoying,' said Abi. 'Why would they do that? What's the big secret?'

'Maybe it was an Arsenal fan,' said Thomas, jumping on the opportunity to renew the banter. The smiles returned and he felt his shoulders relax once more. 'Shall I make the coffee?' He rose from his seat. Jerry followed him across the kitchen, his soft paws tapping on the tiles.

'Only if you're making proper coffee,' his mother said. 'Don't even think about giving me that instant stuff.'

The light-hearted chatter continued around the table, Thomas chipping in occasionally from his position by the coffee machine. He thumbed through a local paper, waiting for the machine to work its magic, still floating on the cloud of happiness formed by his father's words. There wasn't much in the paper to snag his attention, just the depressing news of drug possession and house repossession, computer hacks and acid attacks. But then something *did* catch his eye. News of a dead body found in the early hours of Saturday morning. Thomas felt the air leave his lungs, the blood drain from his face, and the hairs on his arms stand up en masse. Jerry looked up at him from his position on the floor, as though sensing the sudden change in his master's mood.

The body of a man was found on Eel Brook Common in the early hours of Saturday morning.

Police were called just after one a.m. when a body was found with apparent head injuries.

292

Officers say they are trying to establish the circumstances surrounding the death which is being treated as suspicious. The man has been named as Vincent Savage, a 49-year-old from Ealing, West London. Next of kin have been informed.

Thomas looked across at his father, in no doubt whatsoever of his involvement. He rested his weight on a stool and tried to swallow the knot that had formed in his throat. He was struggling to breathe. Just when he thought they'd turned a corner, when he'd finally earned the respect he'd been looking for his entire life, the poison had returned. But it wasn't London that stole the breath from his lungs. It wasn't the city that squeezed the very soul from his being. It was his father.

Chapter 45

In the days that followed, Thomas read every report he could get his hands on about the death of Vincent Savage. The police had confirmed it was a murder investigation and that no suspect had either been arrested or charged. He lived in fear of a knock on the door. Surely he would be questioned. Someone must know it was Vince that had exposed him, a motive for murder if ever there was one. And what would he say when they finally turned up? *It wasn't me, Officer, but you might want to have a word with my father?*

He'd avoided his father since learning of Vince's demise, not trusting himself to keep his thoughts and suspicions to himself. As much as he'd tried to convince himself his father had nothing to do with it, he knew, deep down, he was involved. Today, though, his father was driving them all to the football club. The Blues had a midweek game against Southampton and his father was presenting a cheque to a representative from Great Ormond Street Hospital before kick-off. The club had close ties with the hospital. The players sometimes visited the sick children, gave them signed shirts, injected happiness through the wards like an intravenous drip. Thomas had agreed to donate five percent of his sales from his exhibition and, coupled with the money raised from a charity dinner at the club before Christmas, the amount to be donated was an impressive five figure sum. As a result of the family's efforts with the fundraising, his father had insisted they all come along to the club and take part in the presentation. Thomas had happily agreed but was now regretting his decision.

Despite the continued truce between his mother and father, the atmosphere in the car was strained. His father was always tense before a match and, knowing better than to annoy him with trivial conversation, the rest of them remained silent. He stared at his father's profile from his position in the back seat. Tiny grey hairs were curling over the top of his shirt collar, creases gathered around his eyes, moisture clung to his pores.

He didn't look like a murderer. He looked like a middle-aged man in a smart suit, taking his family out for dinner. He studied the hands on the steering wheel, tried to imagine them taking someone's life. Squeezing a fragile neck or plunging a knife into soft, tender flesh. But Vince had died of head injuries. A brick then, or a hammer, smashing into a delicate skull. The nausea returned. He'd been unable to shake it since Monday. He looked out of the window. Business suits merged with football shirts. Briefcases blended with shopping bags. He looked at the swarm of faces. Happy, contemplative, hopeful. If only they knew, he thought. If only they knew this man was a killer.

Crawford disappeared as soon as they arrived at the stadium. 'Wait in my office,' he said. 'Someone will come and get you when we're ready. Help yourself to drinks.'

The first thing Thomas noticed when he walked in was the painting. His painting of the football ground dominated the room, its position behind the desk demanding attention from all four corners. Thomas tried to remember what hung there before but couldn't recall.

'It was Dad? Dad bought it?' His incredulity was obvious.

'I didn't know,' said his mother, the surprise on her face matching that of her son's. 'It was dealt with by a third party and collected by a courier. I had no idea.'

'Why would he keep it a secret?' asked Abi, removing her long, blue French Connection coat and making herself comfortable on the sofa.

'He must have wanted it to be a surprise,' his mother said, sitting down on the chair beside Abi. 'Who knows what your father's motives are? It looks good though, doesn't it? It's the perfect spot for it.'

Thomas couldn't agree more. It was, indeed, the perfect wall. But his joy at seeing one of his paintings in his father's office was soured by the suspicions surrounding Vince's death. He hated his father at that moment. Hated him for stealing the perfect, sweet moment of pride that he'd waited so long for.

'Who wants a drink?' He walked over to where the crystal whisky decanter glistened in the artificial light and opened the cabinet beneath. The smell of alcohol was overpowering and he coughed a little, the fumes almost tangible.

'Mum? There's a bit of everything in here.'

'No thanks, darling. Don't want to be sitting with my legs crossed for ninety minutes.'

'Abi?'

His sister was tapping the screen of her smartphone and answered without looking up. 'Any Malibu?'

He stifled a laugh. 'No. I'm not sure Premiership managers, or their friends, are that into Malibu.'

He took her lack of response as a rejection of any other spirit and closed the cabinet door. The TV burst into life and he noticed his mother studying the remote control. Gary Neville and Jamie Carragher were sharing their usual pre-match predictions on the huge, flat screen, until they were silenced by the Emmerdale theme tune. With his mother and sister both pre-occupied, he began to study the various trophies, medals and photographs that cluttered every surface. There was no denying it was an impressive collection. His father had certainly enjoyed plenty of success over the years. And his career wasn't over yet.

With his suspicions still swinging from niggling doubt to absolutely certainly, he sat in his father's chair behind his desk, as though trying to conjure his guilt or innocence from the fabric of the seat. The surface of the desk was tidy compared to elsewhere and he ran his hand across the top of the smooth, mahogany wood. It was cold to the touch and undoubtedly expensive. As with his desk at home, a lamp stood upright in the corner next to a slim, black telephone, its spiral cord disappearing through a cleverly concealed hole. The paperweight was there too. Thomas was about to pick it up, remembering the comforting feel of its smooth, round shape as he transferred it from one hand to another. It was the same paperweight, he was sure. But why was it here and not at home? He cocked his head to the side, studying the black and white glass from different angles, his eyes squinting as he did so. It didn't look as polished as before. He could see the smudge of a fingerprint and something else. Something red, like dried paint. No. Not paint. Blood. Using the handkerchief in his coat pocket he picked up the paperweight and dropped it, like a stone, into his pocket.

Chapter 46

After the shock of Pia's unexpected arrival and subsequent revelations, Florentina was coming to terms with the details surrounding her parents' deaths. She couldn't hold Pia responsible for anything her father had done, and as much as she wanted someone to pay, there was nothing to be gained by dragging up the whole sorry mess. At least now she knew exactly what had happened. She no longer needed to torture herself with visions of melting flesh and smoke-filled rooms. She would no longer wake from a fitful sleep, convinced she was choking, her hands clawing at an imaginary ligature. Tempted as she'd been to reach for her tablets after hearing Pia's confession, and washing them down with a bottle of gin, she'd sought solace from Crawford instead. She'd waited for Thomas and Abi to retire to bed and then told her husband all about Pia's father, her letters in his office drawer, Pia's sad and lonely life in Italy. Crawford was the only one who knew about Florentina's past. The only one who would understand. It was less than a year after her parents' deaths when she'd met the handsome young footballer. She had signed with Melody Models, their Glasgow office only a few hundred yards from the flat she'd rented in Ingram Street. Her role as a promotional model at a glitzy charity event in the city had been much the same as any other, aside from the number of famous faces milling around the room. She'd been instantly smitten at the sight of Crawford Kelly. And the feeling, it seemed, was mutual.

She thought back now to his perfect smile, his athletic physique and his kind, attentive nature. Glimpses of that nature had reappeared when she'd told him about Pia. He'd stroked her hand as she talked, sympathised as she cried, and held her tight when she lay, exhausted, on the bed.

'Don't go,' she'd whispered. And he didn't. He lay beside her all night, the sound of his breathing accompanying her fitful sleep.

It had been a turning point for both of them. They appeared to reach a silent understanding, one of mutual trust and respect. Florentina had high hopes for their marriage now that so many demons had been laid to rest. All she needed to do now was talk to Pia. Her understanding and forgiveness would seal their friendship, she was sure. Yes, things were definitely looking up for the Kelly family.

The scenery was much the same through the window of Justin's Audi as it was through that of an Avanti train. A little clearer perhaps, without the smear of a child's grubby hand or the lingering moisture of a stranger's breath, but similar nonetheless. They'd chatted amiably since leaving London and played along to Pop Master on Radio Two (Justin's music knowledge proving marginally better than his own), but had now lapsed into a comfortable silence. Jerry was curled up on a blanket on the back seat, comfortable and content. Thomas envied him his simple, carefree existence.

They overtook an old VW camper van, its driver tapping his fingers on the steering wheel, his passenger engrossed in a book. Tatty suitcases were strapped to the roof, their waterproof cover flapping in the wind. Thomas wondered where they were going. Up to the Highlands maybe? Or eloping to Gretna Green? His study of their fellow travellers continued. The business man in a Mazda 6, jacket hung up behind his seat, collar and tie pristine. The young girl in a Fiat 500, chatting to an invisible friend, sunglasses perched on her head. And the old man in a Ford Fiesta, eyes forward, hands gripping the steering wheel, refusing to budge from the middle lane.

'Do you want to stop at the next services or carry on?' Justin turned briefly to look at him before turning his attention back to the road.

'Let's carry on.'

Thomas was looking forward to returning to the cottage. He longed for the smell of burning wood, the cosy, confined space and the uncomplicated, peaceful life. The success of the exhibition, coupled with his modest lifestyle, meant he was financially secure for the foreseeable future and could take his time pondering his next move. He wouldn't return to London, of that he was sure. Regardless of his relationship with Justin, he had no intention of returning to the so-called swinging city.

The elation he'd experienced from his father's acceptance of his homosexuality and his chosen career was so short-lived it was as though he'd imagined it. The smile had been wiped from his face quicker than a speck of dust in a new car showroom. Thomas felt as though he was back where he'd started. His toxic relationship with his father may have turned a corner, but it had already reached another dead end. The irony of it was, he no longer cared what his father thought. He couldn't care less if his father was ashamed or proud. He couldn't care less that one of his paintings was hanging above the desk in his father's office. What he *did* care about was that his father had burdened him with a secret he could never share. At twenty-four years of age, he'd finally formed lasting, meaningful friendships with people he could trust. People he could talk to without fear of judgment or ridicule. People who cared about him. His friendships with Justin and Rupert meant the world to him. They'd restored his faith in human nature and filled a void so deep it had nearly swallowed him whole. But thanks to his father, he was still tormented by secrets. He couldn't be open and honest with the people he loved and cared for the most. He may have shed the shackles guarding his own guilty secrets, but he was still unable to walk free. He was now chained to the guilt of someone else's secrets and he didn't like it one little bit.

Florentina had arranged to meet Pia at her hotel. The public venue would, she hoped, help to keep her emotions in check. The two women sat opposite each other in the foyer, their postures elegantly synchronised. A polished silver coffee pot shone on the circular table between them alongside a dish of crystallised sugar cubes and miniature silver tongs. Florentina took a sip from her china cup, the coffee a little too weak for her taste. She set it back on its saucer and placed it on the table, eager for their conversation to begin.

'I cried when you left,' Pia said, surprising Florentina with her honesty. 'I could not believe you left without saying goodbye.'

Her soft Italian accent was almost hypnotic. Florentina felt sure if she closed her eyes, she would be lulled to sleep by the warm, gentle tone.

'We left in the middle of the night. I had no idea what was happening. I explained everything in my letters but…'

They exchanged a sad smile. There was no need for further explanations. Their friendship had been torn apart by the actions of their parents. As a result, both girls had felt rejected, betrayed and very lonely.

She watched Pia take a sip of coffee, the delicate cup dwarfed by the ever-present diamond on her finger. She'd aged well, Florentina noticed. Her skin was free of lines, her neck firm and smooth. A graceful butterfly decorated her Sophia Webster ankle boots and her rust-coloured trouser suit, she suspected, was handmade. Presumably, she'd inherited her father's entire estate and Florentina could only guess at the extent of her wealth. But that was a conversation for another day. They had the rest of their lives to catch up.

'I'd like to see more of you,' Florentina said, determined not to dwell on the past. She'd had time to digest the news about her parents' deaths and also to regret her friend's thirty-five-year absence. They'd missed out on so much of each other's lives through no fault of their own and Florentina wanted nothing more than to rekindle their friendship. The reason she was never able to talk about her childhood was not just because of the tragic loss of her parents, but the painful loss of her best friend and the desperate loneliness that followed. It was like a permanent ache in her heart. Later, she'd assumed the dull, persistent pain was the result of the abrupt ending of her glamorous career, the slow deterioration of her marriage, or the intense jealously of her daughter. She'd sought relief from pills and alcohol but the pain remained. Only now did she realise its true cause. Only now, decades later, was the pain finally beginning to subside.

'I would like that,' said Pia. 'Although Glasgow is so far away from London. Perhaps I should stay here for a while. Rent an apartment, perhaps. What do you think?'

'I think that's a fabulous idea,' she replied, blinking rapidly to stave off the threat of tears. 'We have a lot of catching up to do.'

'Yes, we do. And I would like to get to know your family. We barely exchanged a word at the exhibition. Crawford is very handsome. And your daughter, Abi? She is beautiful. Like you.'

Florentina smiled at the compliment. But it wasn't a selfish smile spawned from the welcome praise of her own, timeless beauty. It was pride. Pride in her daughter. Florentina was so shocked she could barely breathe. A faint sound escaped her lips, neither a laugh nor a cry but something in between. She coughed to disguise her emotions and shifted in her seat.

'And Thomas,' Pia continued, seemingly oblivious to her friend's life changing realisation, 'he is very talented. His art is extraordinary.'

'Yes. I am very proud of them both,' Florentina managed to say, the smile on her face more genuine than it had been in years.

Chapter 47

Crawford was sweating. He ran a finger along the inside of his shirt collar and cursed his own stupidity. So elated was he at the apparent ease of his crime, he'd neglected to conceal the one thing that could link him to the victim. He'd been astute enough to take the phone from Vince's coat pocket and dump it in a random wheelie bin on the way back to the warehouse. He'd also paid someone to remove all relevant messages and calls from his own mobile phone, blaming a spurned lover for the inconvenience. But the paperweight, the thing he'd actually used to smash a hole in the scumbag's skull, the prize that sat proudly on his desk like a trophy, was missing. Despite using it to commit murder, he never intended to dispose of it. As risky as it was, he wanted to keep it. It was a reminder of the action he'd taken to protect the honour of his son. It was a declaration of love and an expression of power. It screamed a silent 'do not mess with me' message and without it, he felt weak. Not to mention vulnerable. *Where the fuck was it?*

He retraced his steps in his mind, thinking back to the night of the exhibition when he'd returned from his little absence. He'd wrapped the paperweight in a couple of tissues and stashed it in the glove compartment of his car. Early the next morning, he'd retrieved it, wiped it down and hidden it in the grass collection box of his ride-on lawn mower in the garage, along with the clothes he'd worn to the exhibition. On Monday morning, keen to remove the evidence from the house, he'd wiped down the paperweight once more, slipped it in his coat pocket and put it on the desk in his office. His clothes, clean to the naked eye, were in the recycling bin in the car park of the local supermarket. Someone would be glad of them, he was sure. But now the paperweight was gone. He felt his jaw clench. For a man of reasonable intelligence, he could be bloody stupid sometimes.

He stood to look out of the window, the dreary February weather doing nothing to lift his mood. He should be concentrating on his team selection, not worrying about a stupid paperweight. He'd managed to rid himself of Grayson Delaney, convincing the chairman he was past his best and surplus to requirements, but he hadn't managed to secure a replacement. As for Cory Flemming, seems he wasn't as gentlemanly as Crawford had been led to believe. He may be stuck with him until the summer, but as far as Crawford was concerned, Cory's days with the Blues were well and truly numbered.

He squeezed his eyes shut and pinched the top of his nose. He was starting to get a headache. Try as he might to picture the weekend's team formation in his mind, all he could see was a football-shaped paperweight. He'd wiped it clean, of that he was sure, but was that enough? Could they identify the weapon by the shape and weight of it in relation to the wound? He'd seen enough TV police and courtroom dramas to know how crimes were solved these days so should he be worried? He caught sight of his faint reflection in the window and cursed once more. 'You stupid bastard,' he said aloud.

Thomas looked at the round object currently sitting in the centre of his coffee table. To the unsuspecting eye, it looked, to all intents and purposes, just like a paperweight. To Thomas, however, it represented a life sentence. The object had forced him to keep a lifelong secret. His father had, without doubt, committed murder and, whatever his feelings towards his father might be, he had no intention of sharing that fact with anyone else. His father, however, didn't know that. If Thomas kept the object, he would have the upper hand for the rest of his life. He could threaten his father with exposure and make his life a misery. He could torment him, bribe him and blackmail him for the sheer hell of it. It might even go some way to make up for the years of hell he'd suffered at his father's hands, or rather, his father's tongue. The thought of it made him laugh and Jerry jumped up from his new basket, startled by the sound.

'Sorry, little fella,' he said, patting his thighs for Jerry to jump up. 'I was just laughing at a ridiculous notion. As if I could ever torment or bribe anybody.'

Jerry circled on Thomas's lap before curling up with a contended sigh. Thomas stroked the soft fur on his back and continued the one-way conversation.

'I could no sooner blackmail my father than I could throw you in the duck pond, could I?' His casual comment spawned an idea and he resumed the dissection of his dilemma. The object didn't just implicate his father, it implicated himself. He thought back to the day in his father's study when he'd picked up the paperweight and passed it from one hand to another, enjoying the feel of its smooth, round shape. He may not have touched it since, but his fingerprints were still on it. And if he wiped it clean, he wouldn't just remove his own fingerprints, he'd erase those of his father, as well as the speck of blood that was still clearly evident.

'What should I do, Jerry?' he said, staring at the paperweight. 'I'm damned if I do and damned if I don't.'

The dog barely cocked an ear and Thomas sighed at his predicament. If he left it untouched, he would have something on his father but it would also implicate himself. If he wiped it clean, it would destroy the evidence linking his father to Vince's death meaning a killer would probably walk free. And either of those options meant that Thomas was still concealing a murder weapon. To his mind, he had three choices; keep it, hand it in, or dispose of it.

'Up you get, Jerry,' he said, disturbing the dog once more. 'We're going for a walk.'

Chapter 48

Florentina's mouth was watering at the aroma escaping from Pia's kitchen. Pia had wasted no time arranging a short-term rental in Chelsea Harbour and had already demonstrated her culinary skills to Florentina on more than one occasion. The two of them had talked, laughed and cried endlessly since their reunion and had now reached a comfortable truce eliminating the need for further blame or apology.

Topping up her wine glass from a chilled bottle of Chablis, she gazed outside at the obvious display of decadence. Gleaming white yachts lined up in the harbour, boats of all shapes and sizes vying for attention. It reminded her of the old harbour in Menton, 'Vieux Port'. Nicknamed 'Pearl of France', Menton was one of her favourite holiday spots. It represented a joyful, carefree time of her life. A time she and Crawford were at their happiest. She pictured them strolling along the harbour, hands entwined, skin bronzed. They would take turns to pick out a boat, rename it and choose a destination. Their imaginations knew no bounds. They were unrestricted by distance, capability or climate. She chose a twenty-one-foot Sunseeker yacht and named it *Flawless*. They were to set sail to French Guiana in the Caribbean and speak nothing but French. Crawford selected a thirty-nine-foot speedboat, naming it *Striker*. They would speed off at forty knots and keep going until the fuel ran dry. Then they would drink champagne, make love and wait to be rescued like James Bond. She laughed at the thought of their foolish wishful thinking.

'Something is amusing you?' Pia emerged from the kitchen and placed two steaming bowls of pasta on the dining table.

'I was just reminiscing,' said Florentina, reluctant to cut short her blissful memories of Menton. They should go back there, she thought; revisit the harbour as well as their feelings. She could take her camera. Practise her photography and capture new memories. Suddenly hungry, she rose to join Pia at the table. 'That smells and looks delicious,' she said, appreciating the smell of onion, garlic and lemon that filled the air.

'It is crab linguine,' said Pia, 'and it is so easy, even you could make it.'

They shared a wry smile, both knowing Florentina had neither the desire nor the intention to do so.

'I'll leave it the expert,' she said, winding a string of pasta around her fork.

'So, are we still going to the football match tomorrow?' asked Pia.

Florentina nodded, the glorious flavours of crab, lemon, chili and garlic combining on her tongue. She took a sip of wine before answering.

'If you're sure? I still can't believe you want to go.'

Florentina had been dumbfounded when Pia had first suggested they go to watch the Blues. 'What on earth for?' she'd asked. 'Wouldn't you rather go shopping?'

But Pia had insisted. 'You need to understand what makes your husband tick. How can you possibly sympathise or empathise when you know nothing about his career?'

Florentina had been about to object, what did Pia know about marriage, after all? But something about her comments rang true. And, it had to be said, Crawford had been delighted when she'd asked him for two tickets. Gone was the permanent frown of the last few weeks, replaced by a genuine smile and a glint in his eye.

'Of course I am sure,' said Pia now. 'I have been looking forward to it. The FA Cup is very important, no?'

Florentina smiled at her friend's excitement. She may as well join in with the enthusiasm. Why bother fighting it? And an FA Cup tie against Arsenal was, it seemed, something to get excited about.

'Yes,' she conceded, 'it's very important.'

'And we are still going to the fashion show next week?'

Florentina may have been reluctant to attend a football match on a cold, February afternoon, but she had no intention of missing Abi's debut at London Fashion Week. Her new acceptance of Abi's career had taken her completely by surprise but, encouraged by Pia and Lydia, she was now enjoying the unexpected pride that accompanied every one of her daughter's assignments. So what if it was fame by association? She'd never denied her need for recognition but now, at least, it wasn't soured by an unhealthy dose of jealousy. She was genuinely proud of Abi's achievements and felt so much better for it.

'Absolutely,' she said, winding the last of her pasta around her fork. 'It's the highlight of the fashion calendar and we have six models appearing, including two novices. It's going to be amazing!'

She watched the smile spread across Pia's face, a smile that mirrored her own, and realised how much their lives had changed in just a few short weeks. Pia was no longer a lonely woman full of regret. She had unburdened herself of the secret she had carried for over thirty years and, in doing so, had gained not just a friend, but a family. Crawford and Abi had welcomed Pia with unbridled enthusiasm and the Templeton-Howes too, had taken to her instantly. Florentina wondered if Pia might move to London permanently, but it was early days, life-changing decisions of that magnitude could wait. From her own point of view, she'd love it if Pia moved from Glasgow. London suited her friend. She looked at her now, a picture of health and wealth and couldn't imagine a more suitable city for her to live. Glasgow was dull in comparison. And cold. But regardless of where Pia chose to live, Florentina's life was richer for her friendship. Pia had returned to lick Florentina's wounds, to heal her mental scars and to lead her to a brighter future. Despite being surrounded by family and friends, Florentina had been just as lonely as Pia. She'd rejected any offer of love and support, choosing instead to live a life of bitterness and spite. What a sad, tragic waste. But no more. She now glowed with pride at the mention of her daughter. She was fiercely protective and immensely proud of her son. And, perhaps most surprisingly of all, she still loved Crawford. In fact, she realised, she had never stopped.

Chapter 49

In the two weeks since returning to Scotland, Thomas had pondered, debated and concluded four very important decisions. Jerry was the perfect confidant. He listened intently without interrupting, occasionally twitching his ears to confirm his interest or sighing heavily to indicate his boredom. Thomas had been tempted to confide in Rupert in relation to one of his dilemmas but, in the end, decided against it. He needed to come to his own conclusions and, eventually, had done just that.

The first decision, and the most important, had actually been the easiest. He'd walked Jerry to the duck pond at dusk, the sky rapidly changing from dove grey, to charcoal, to black. He'd perched on the low perimeter wall, the cold bricks penetrating his jeans and biting the backs of his thighs. Jerry whined at his feet, objecting to the forced interruption to his walk, or perhaps remembering his first traumatic visit to the pond, all those weeks ago. Thomas sat for a while and surmised once more. Presumably the police had not connected Vince Savage to the Kelly family. Vince had made such a good job of keeping his identity a secret, there was no evidence linking him to the 'outing' of Crawford Kelly's gay son. Thomas suspected Vince hadn't even sold the pictures to the tabloids, but merely sent them as a final act of spite; a punishment for not paying the ransom. Vince's anonymity had, it seemed, worked against him.

Eventually, convinced he was alone, Thomas removed the paperweight from his pocket. Standing up, he stretched his arm out behind him and threw the paperweight, as far as he could, into the pond. After a few seconds, he heard a heavy, satisfying splash.

He'd felt lighter walking back to the cottage. But it wasn't just the weight of the paperweight that was missing. It was the weight from his shoulders.

The second decision related to Justin. He had stayed with Thomas for a few days after their long drive from London. Thomas had jumped in with both feet and told Justin exactly how he felt. Life was too short. You had to grasp every opportunity and make the most of what life had to offer. Thankfully, Justin had agreed. They'd talked at length about the complications and difficulties of a long-distance relationship, but with Justin's family still living in Glasgow and Thomas's family, and studio, in London, there was already ample reason for respective journeys north or south.

'We can make it work, if we both want it badly enough,' Justin had said.

Thomas had almost melted at the words. It wouldn't be easy, living so far away from Justin, but with Rupert next door and Jerry by his side, he'd manage. And with Abi's appearance at London Fashion Week looming, he already had reason to return to London.

The third decision was, perhaps, the easiest. He'd been undecided whether to stay on at the cottage or return to London full time. His conversation with Justin had helped and he was thankful for his lover's support.

'You're at your happiest up here,' he'd said. 'Why move back to London? Don't do it for me, Thomas, you'll only end up resenting me. Stay on at the cottage. We'll manage just fine.'

He knew Justin was right. But he also knew London was the best place to sell his art. In the end, he'd made the decision to stay on at the cottage but also to keep his studio. He'd divide his time between England and Scotland and, in doing so, would enjoy the best of both worlds. His prints would sell in the castle gift shop and he could still paint and hold exhibitions in his studio. It was, he hoped, the perfect solution.

'Come on then, Jerry,' he said now, reaching for the lead hanging on the back of the door. 'I think a run along the beach is in order.'

The dog jumped up from his position by the fire, his tail wagging excitedly. Thomas pulled on his coat and hat and peered out of the window. Rupert's BMW was parked in its usual spot, its sleek design at odds with the quaint surroundings. It reminded Thomas of a predatory tiger, just waiting for an opportunity to spring into action. His mind began to whir once more. He'd promised his mother he would pay regular visits to his grandparents' grave. He could hardly expect Rupert to take him and the journey by bus and train was far from ideal.

'That's decision number four made, Jerry,' he said, opening the door to a gust of cold air. 'I'm going to buy myself a car.'

At the sound of the final whistle, Crawford ran on to the pitch in a rare display of emotion, his arms held aloft in a victory salute. They'd beaten Arsenal one-nil to secure a place in the quarter-final of the FA Cup. The fact that the win had come from an own goal was neither here nor there. It was still a win, regardless of who scored. He could feel his face stretching with the size of his smile and, after breaking away from the team huddle in the middle of the pitch, he sought out Florentina in the crowd. She wasn't difficult to spot, but this time it was thanks to Pia's red coat (a football faux pas if ever there was one) rather than his wife's inappropriate outfit choice. He waved enthusiastically, the smile never leaving his face, and saw them both wave back. He liked having her there, he realised. Once she had shed the mutton-dressed-as-lamb look and toned down her bleached hair and heavy makeup, he'd started to see her as the woman she once was. The woman he'd fallen in love with. Her support was important to him. He beamed at the realisation.

'Do you always run onto the pitch like that?' Pia asked afterwards.

Crawford smiled at the memory. He was still buzzing from the win. 'I was running from your red coat, Pia. It had nothing to do with the result. Who, in their right mind, wears a coat in the opposition's colours?'

'I had no idea!' she objected. 'Why did you not tell me, Florentina? I could have bought a blue one.'

'I didn't think,' Florentina said, clearly enjoying the ongoing banter. 'Besides, it's a lovely coat.'

'Apart from the fact that it's red,' said Crawford, his face still aching from the permanent smile he'd worn since the final whistle. He'd given countless interviews, enjoyed a celebratory drink with the chairman, shared a euphoric sing-song with the players and still, the smile remained. But it wasn't just the result that accounted for his grin. The prospect of an evening with his two favourite ladies (excluding his daughter, obviously) was, surprisingly, filling him with joy. He'd promised them, if the Blues won, he'd take them to The Ledbury for dinner. He had, until recently, gone out of his way to avoid a public dinner with his wife. For one thing, it was a complete waste of money, the amount of food she ate was barely worth the chef's time and effort, let alone the money spent on the bill. But watching her push her food around her plate was, from Crawford's point of view, almost painful. These days, however, she seemed to really enjoy her food. Admittedly, she'd put on a little weight, but she looked all the better for it. He'd heard her telling Pia that her new black coat was a size ten – the first time she'd bought a size ten in her life – but she didn't sound horrified or regretful. Strangely, she sounded rather proud.

'It is a shame Abi could not join us tonight,' Pia said as they left the football ground. 'You would have been in your element, Crawford, no? Surrounded by three beautiful women?'

Her smile was a mischievous one and he responded with a wink. 'I'm already in my element, Pia,' he answered, holding open the rear door of his Jaguar as she climbed inside. He exchanged a glance with Florentina, holding her gaze in what he hoped was a moment of understanding. They had crossed a bridge, he was sure. And not just a footbridge. This was a bridge of mammoth proportions.

Arriving at the restaurant, Crawford felt the inside pocket of his coat. He had a surprise for his wife, one that he hoped would be met with genuine pleasure rather than suspicion or doubt. He'd thought long and hard before booking the trip to Menton. It was a risk that could backfire spectacularly but, in the end, he had decided it was a risk worth taking. Their relationship was still recovering, but a break in the French resort would speed along that recovery, he was sure, particularly as Simone had handed in her notice and would be leaving the club at the end of the season. He had a feeling the envelope in his pocket was the key to their future, the start of happier times. If only he knew what had happened to that damned paperweight.

Chapter 50

Thomas had never known an atmosphere like this one. Everywhere he looked he saw a famous face. There were fashion designers, film stars, football players, TV presenters and pop stars. This was clearly the place to be seen. The chatter was almost deafening, rows of expectant ticket holders eagerly waiting for the show to begin. He looked to his left where his mother and father were seated alongside Max, Lydia and Sasha Templeton-Howe. He'd been shocked by the new version of his parents, their togetherness as unexpected as it was gratifying. According to Abi, they were even going on holiday together once the football season was over. His eyes fell to their clasped hands and he shook his head in wonder. *Miracles do happen,* he thought.

Pia was seated to his immediate left, her perfume a poignant reminder of their first encounter at the cemetery. His mother had eventually filled him in with the details of Pia's so-called apology. He'd been horrified by the tale, astounded by the atrocity and angered that his grandparents' murderer had gone unpunished. It had taken him a while to recognise his own hypocrisy. Besides, it was hardly Pia's fault. He turned to look at her and was rewarded with an enigmatic smile. She really was a beautiful woman. *She would get on well with Rupert,* he thought, unable to curtail the matchmaking efforts he so loathed from anyone else. Apparently his mother was taking Pia to Izzie's wedding as her 'plus one' so who knew what might develop? And he and Justin would be there to help things along, if need be.

He felt a hand on his right thigh and looked up into those familiar green eyes. Still unused to public displays of affection, the heat from Justin's hand felt as though it was burning a hole through Thomas's trousers. Not to mention the blush he could feel rising from his neck. He swallowed the panic and forced his eyes to remain on Justin's. *Be proud.* He repeated it over and over in his head until the panic subsided. *Be proud.* Forcing a smile to his lips, he put his own hand on top of Justin's and squeezed it tight. *Be proud.* It wasn't easy, but he was learning.

Eventually, the room plunged into darkness and the audience fell silent. Every pair of eyes was focused on the runway, one single spotlight forming a circle of anticipation. A sudden blast of music boomed through the room, coloured lights danced to the beat and a single figure emerged from behind the curtain. Thomas felt a lump in his throat the size of a golf ball as he watched Abi strut along the runway like a hungry lioness. *That's my sister!* He blinked away emotional tears and tried to focus on the show.

'She's incredible!' said Justin in his right ear.

Thomas could only nod in response. Unable to take his eyes off Abi, he watched as she glided back down the runway, a vision of beauty, confidence and vigour. He waited until she'd disappeared from sight before he stole a look towards his parents. His father was, predictably, smug with pride, but for once, Thomas didn't resent his obvious delight. His mother's reaction, however, was a little trickier to fathom. So used was he to seeing hatred and jealousy painted on her face, he was somewhat taken aback by the softness of her features. She looked genuinely happy. He knew the relationship between his mother and sister had thawed but he'd expected a few stubborn icicles to remain. His mother's smile was no longer glacial, nor was it lukewarm. It was smouldering. For the second time in just a few minutes the thought returned. *Miracles do happen.*

Thomas was the first to congratulate Abi after the show, although, he doubted she even heard his words of praise over her own frenzied squeals of excitement. Abi wasn't just sitting on cloud nine, she was jumping up and down on cloud ninety-nine. Thomas suspected there was more to her elation than the obvious joy of a successful runway debut.

Somewhere between arriving for rehearsals this morning and closing the show this evening, she'd managed to snare the best-looking male model at the show. She introduced him to everyone as Dominic. Thomas looked around the group and smiled at their individual reactions. His mother raised an amused eyebrow at Abi, as though approving of her choice. Pia's smile appeared to be one of regret, perhaps thinking of what could have been in her own loveless life. Crawford hid his feelings well, but Thomas knew him well enough to know he wouldn't trust anyone as far as his daughter was concerned, least of all a young, black model with a body as fit as any footballer. Sasha didn't hang around long enough to comment. No sooner had she shouted, 'Abs, you were amazing!' she was off in search of Danny to congratulate him on his own outstanding performance. Equally, Max Templeton-Howe didn't react to the young stallion on Abi's arm but commented instead on his wife's tongue-tied status.

'Are you okay, Lydia?' Max teased. 'You look a little flushed.'

'It's all these virile young bodies,' she said, fanning herself exaggeratedly with a hastily grabbed promotional leaflet. 'I'm feeling a little overwhelmed.'

Her eyes were fixed on Dominic's smooth, toned abs, brazenly displayed beneath his unbuttoned shirt. Clearly used to the attention, he made no attempt to conceal his impressive torso. Instead, he made them all laugh with a shameless wink.

Still grinning, Thomas watched his sister basking in her new-found glory. She was buzzing with excitement, her skin glowing, her smile beaming. This was just the beginning for Abi, he realised. She was sensational on the runway, and with his mother and Lydia on her side, was assured of a long, successful career. He looked at her now, a star in the making, her radiant face reminding him of the portrait he'd painted. He would auction it, he decided. Abi would have enough pictures of herself without the need for his painting and, if he timed it right, it could raise a lot of money for charity. In a rare moment of confidence, he allowed himself to think that his own name as an artist could add just as much value to the painting as the model herself. The two combined could secure an eye-watering sum for any charity.

'Everything all right, son? You look miles away.'

Thomas looked up at his father, their previous heated conversation never far from his mind. His father had promised to become a better person. He certainly seemed to be heading in the right direction, although, he'd taken an unfortunate detour on the way. No point dwelling, Thomas decided. That was in the past. It was the future that mattered. He silently debated whether to tell him about the paperweight.

Should he put him out of his misery or leave him forever wondering? He reached for Justin's hand, noticing his father's darkened eyes and clenched jaw as he did so. Decision made.

'Everything's fine, Dad,' he said. 'Absolutely fine.'